He who has health…has hope.

In the not so distant future, cancers called the Cluster rage through the populace. The government sells expensive Cluster fighting drugs in the name of improved health but the people lack a true cure or the will to find one. When a child is born that could potentially lead to this cure, his father seeks to hide him from those that vow to do him harm.

In a post-modern world balanced on the precipice of extinction, the father and his son embark on separate journeys in separate worlds, to save their family. With the help of April Wolfe, a fiercely independent young woman who is determined to save her own family, the three face horrors manifested from the mystical realm that is the Interzone.

Pursuing them and leaving destruction in his wake is Roosevelt Cleveland. A power neither our world nor the Interzone can contain. The journey leads them all to a final showdown in the desert of Texas, fighting for the very survival of humanity itself.

Variant X

Patrick Pearce

Amethyst Press

Sherman, Texas

ISBN-13: 978-0692849903

ISBN-10: 0692849904

Variant X. Copyright © 2017 by Michael Westbrook. Manufactured in the United States of America. All rights reserved. No part of this book may be used or reproduced in any manner whatsoever without written permission, except in the case of brief quotations embodied in critical articles and reviews. Published by Amethyst-Press, P.O. Box 1393, Sherman, Texas 75091. Phone (903) 814-2916. First Edition.

For information, address Amethyst-Press. Visit Amethyst-Press on the World Wide Web at www.amethyst-press.com

Printed in the United States of America

Cover Designs by Cory Hicks

This is a work of fiction. Any similarities to persons living or dead is purely coincidental.

First Edition

16 15 14 13 12 11 10 / 10 9 8 7 6 5 4 3 2 1

Library of Congress Control Number: 2017903087
Amethyst-Press, Sherman, TX

PREFACE

There was no beginning. There was just a day when everyone knew life would never be the same again. That was fifteen years ago. Before the Variant.

Before the Variant, cities burned and the cancers raged. They called the cancers the Cluster. The question was no longer *if* you were going to get cancer, but when. Would you make it to thirty-five? Forty? The searing heat of the world triggered something cataclysmic in the human body, igniting cancers that devoured its host within weeks, sometimes days. Not everyone was dying but nearly everyone was sick. Except the Variant. The Variant was a small boy born in the mountains of Colorado. The Grey Suits knew immediately that this boy was special. That he could be the answer.

On the twelfth night after his birth, his father disappeared across the mountains with the boy. The Grey Suits chased.

CHAPTER 1

Sometime in 2106

I'm cold.

You're not cold. Go back to sleep.

I know. I saw my breath, so I thought you might be cold.

I'm fine.

Will there be Lessons today?

Not likely. Mechs roaming the south this morning. Close. So no fire. Sounded like they dropped in by drones. Couldn't be sure though. Won't be until I go out and have a look. In any event, we may have to leave for Summer Cabin.

There's too much snow, Dad. It's still too deep.

We need more coverage. We're too exposed here. If the Mechs are south, then someone knows we're here. Or they suspect someone's here. Either way, we may need to move.

Last time they left. They couldn't find us.

Last time was nearly a year ago, Son. Might be the Grey Suits worked out the problems with the last models. They're back and I don't want us taking chances. Last time was too close. You're bigger now. We can move in the snow.

Will we take the solar skis?

No. We move on foot if we must go. I'll do a perimeter sweep. You eat some of that jerky. I'll be back in an hour.

The boy looked at his father in the still dim light of morning. He swallowed the question he wanted to ask. His father did not like dealing with hypotheticals. They would deal with the situation as it arose. The boy knew the answer anyway. If he didn't return, the boy would load up and head north by himself. And he'd avoid the Grey Suits at all costs.

The father grabbed his rifle, two pistols and strapped on his snow shoes. As he slipped the straps through the bindings, he felt the now too often burst of pain in his stomach. He straightened up and let the pain pass, as it was prone to do, and then went back to buckling the snow shoes into place. After all this time, these relics of the past still provided more security than any machine ever had for him. He longed for the days before the world burned. At least here, the cold leveled the playing field somewhat.

The father held the door for a moment and turned to say something to the boy but thought better of it. Best to leave some things unsaid. The boy knew what to do. They'd practiced it a million times before and after Lessons. The boy could survive on his own. He knew the way to Summer Cabin. Knew the things to look for. He wanted to tell the boy he loved him but saying those words seemed so final. As if he might not make it back. He preferred to keep the boy strong.

He simply said, always, and shut the door.

The boy turned toward the door but didn't get to respond before the man shut the door behind him.

He got out of bed and went into the waste room. He lifted the lid to the toilet and smelled what his father had left behind. They couldn't incinerate if the Mechs were close. They'd pick up on the heat signature. So no fire. No incineration.

The boy placed his hands into the cold water of the sink. For most, the water would be ice cold. For the boy it was merely an annoyance. The cold was just an indistinct sensation on his skin. He knew it to be cold from when he was a child. But now, now it was different. Every day it was something different. Some new sensation. Or lack thereof.

He went into the galley, as his father called it, and pulled down the jar of jerky. Bear jerky was not his favorite, but he knew it to be nourishing. He ate only a sliver, knowing it might be some time before they had meat again if the sounds his father heard had really been Mechs.

The galley was simply laid out. The boy stood before a long counter with a sink in the middle. A picture window rested just above the sink. Not too big, but big enough to see much of the back of the cabin. The boy pulled the slender handle on the faucet and poured himself a glass of water. The water was fresh and flowed from a stream that never froze. The boy did not understand fully how it worked because there were times the surface of the river would definitely be frozen. But the water would still flow. His father had told him when he was older he would explain just how he got it to do that. A Lesson soon to come, the boy hoped.

He sipped the water and peered outside. He could not see his father in this light. It was still too dim. He believed it to be five hours since midnight. But he was never as sure of the time as his father was. It was still too dark to make out shapes. The trees swayed ever so slightly against the backdrop of the night.

That's when he saw the light. Blue at first, then a glistening white. He felt the light hit his face directly and he instinctively dropped to the floor. His mind raced and he thought of his own rifle near the bed. He reached under the counter and pulled the .45 from beneath it. Just like he'd been taught. He ejected the magazine and reloaded it, pushed the safety off and took a moment to breathe.

His mind scrambled to make sense of the light. It definitely hadn't been his father. He wouldn't be so careless. He didn't know if it was a Mech. They typically shot first. They wouldn't spotlight something to give their position away. So he thought and he struggled to recall his Lessons. What to do first if he was spotted. So he sat beneath the counter on the floor and he took deep breaths. As he took those breaths, his father's words, recited over and over and through the years flooded his brain. Begin to pack. Think only of

those things you will need to live a few days. Your weapons. To
protect yourself. Your knife. To construct those items you can't carry.
Your fire. Levin. Your emergency rations. Jerky. Your warmth.
The flesh coat. Sunglasses. Always sunglasses because the white of
the snow could blind you, he would say in his calm, reassuring voice.
And your pack, to carry it all.

The boy crawled to the living quarters. He rose slowly,
remembering those things he needed. And he remembered, perhaps
too late, to lower the blast shades. In the darkness he felt for the panel
on the wall and found it. The cabin went pitch black. They'd
rehearsed this so many times he could do it with no light. He found
his pack. His Levin was in the base of it. He went to the gun locker
and took out the Colt and the cartridges his father had created. The
rifle was there and he pulled it toward him. His boots sat next to the
locker and he pulled them on. He thought of his inventory. He
needed his knife. It wasn't in the locker. He felt for it on the shelf
but it wasn't there. Where had he left it? Why hadn't he returned it?
Life and death, his father preached. These things will keep you alive.
You mustn't grow complacent. You mustn't forget. The knife will
build your shelter. Slaughter your meat. Protect you at close range.
When the guns have failed. And they will fail. They always do.
Especially in the cold.

He felt on the side of the pack and he remembered he sewed a
new sheath there just for the knife. Father had been proud that day.
Forethought he said. One less thing to think about should you need to
scatter.

Relieved at finding the knife, he walked to the door and pulled
it toward him.

His father was on the other side panting.
Dad?
I'm fine. Get back inside.

The boy shuffled back in.

You shut the blast shades. What happened?

I saw a light. Blue then white as snow.

Mechs were blasting something. Looks like they got weapons upgrades as well. They were damn near silent out there. Until they started shooting.

Were they shooting at you?

No. Probably a bear or moose. I couldn't tell. It was too dark. It'll be light soon. Maybe we can scavenge some of the meat if they didn't vaporize it.

The boy looked at his father. He sounded angry.

I can't stand the waste. And the bear and moose are in such short supply now.

You don't think it was a person they shot, do you?

Not likely. I haven't seen any signs of humans around here in quite awhile. Too remote. Too many things could go wrong to someone on their way out here. We're in the middle of 300,000 acres of forest surrounded by about another 300,000 acres of ice. Only Mechs are getting out here. But, where there are Mechs, there are Grey Suits on the other side watching through them. There'll be Grey Suits here soon enough if we're spotted.

Should we just stay here then? Hope they go? Like last time?

It's time to move, boy. I feared this would happen. I got a message last night from the Lighthouse. They said the Mechs were on the move.

April? Mom?

That's why I didn't bring it up last night. Don't get your hopes up Son. They don't know. There's still no word from my contact about either.

But they know they're alive?

I told you, don't start thinking of things we simply can't know. I don't know. The information I get is several days old. Sometimes weeks. It goes through several layers to get to us. If I knew for sure, I'd tell you. But I simply don't know. Worrying about them will make us prone to mistakes. We'll never make it if we sit around here and worry if they're okay.

Or alive.

The father eyed the boy and could see that look the boy got when he thought of April. He wanted to push him but he feared pushing him too far. He wasn't afraid of the boy. But he was afraid the boy didn't understand his own power.

The man said, right. Or if they're even alive. What we do know is that you and I are alive and well. And I intend to stay that way.

We could travel again. To the Lighthouse.

You were just a small boy when we were there.

I know. But just to see.

See what?

What if they're both fine and looking for us?

If either of them is looking for us, they won't be at the Lighthouse. They'll find us. Trust me. Both of them knew the stakes just as well as I did when we left. We can't all be found together. That would seal our fate.

What fate? Why don't you just tell me?

In time.

But if they're dead and not looking, then it's just us.

Son, there are things happening that I can't begin to describe to you. Mostly because I can't wrap my brain around them. In time, I will share them with you. But for now, I can't afford to have you worried about things that don't exist.

Hypotheticals are pointless. I got it. Okay.

Your pack ready?

Yessir.

You ready?

You know the snow doesn't bother me, Dad. Are *you* ready?

The father smiled and pulled the boy to him. You'll catch me if I fall. I know that.

I will try.

He opened the door and they set off north toward Summer Cabin.

Variant

CHAPTER 2

It's insane, you know that right, she said as she smiled at him through the glint of sunlight piercing through the partially closed shade. The light illuminated her face and he thought of angels and then he thought of escaping with her.

What's insane?

Going to Alaska.

It's part of my family. That land's been in the family for over a hundred years. Maybe more.

Not another story of your frontier family, please. She laughed.

No, baby, it's not that. You know. It seems like the last place on earth that's still alive. We could escape all this. I mean, they're telling us now that we must have a child. I know we *want* to have a child and I know we've been trying, but when the government tells you that you *must* have a child, well, that's a whole other situation.

I know you're right, she started and then paused, but maybe it will happen naturally and then all the things they've said we get in return will make it better.

Why do you think they're bribing us with promises of larger salaries and nicer housing? Think about it. They want our kid so they can use him or her like a lab rat. Two Heteroclites have a child and you think the government isn't going to be all in on finding out what that does to a person?

You always see the negative. I wish you'd look at it from the positive.

Please, tell me what's positive about all this?

All this isn't that bad. Besides, what will you do for work if we run off to Alaska? You'll need something to do to provide for our child, won't you? And they aren't making Mechs in Alaska.

Well, not yet. But they need me. It's my design. I know all the secrets.

Those secrets belong to the Grey Suits.

That's the point. It all belongs to them. My ideas and even my body. Every day I watch as they destroy more and more all in the name of water and land. They've had me arm these things with some of the most deadly weaponry ever known to man. They claim it's to protect their precious water supplies. But these Mechs could be an awfully effective army. We'd have little hope of defeating that army given that they're robots and bulletproof and we're human with really crappy armor.

I don't want to think about those things. Not now. I'm tired. I'd like to take a nap. Tell me frontier stories. Those always put me to sleep. She winked at him and her beauty washed over him and made him long for the days before Grey Suits was all they talked about.

Dad?

Yes Son?

Were you thinking of her?

No. I was just thinking.

Are you scared?

No, we'll be fine. There's been no signs of Mechs for days now.

The snow is so heavy, though. It just keeps coming. It hasn't stopped for days. It's to your hips.

Well, you know this is our wet season. That's why we stay south normally. I'm feeling fine. Better than fine actually.

The treatments have helped?

I think so. I'm cold, but not as cold as I would've been without the treatments.

You need to record those results in your journal then. It could help others.

You don't worry about my journal. I'll handle documenting our results. We just need to make it to Summer Cabin and then I'll sit down and make some notes. We haven't made it yet.

If you die, I'll make it, right?

He wanted to hold the boy and reassure him that he wasn't going to die. But he was pleased that the boy was thinking ahead.

You will be fine Son. Of that, I have no doubt.

Maybe with the treatments, you will be fine too.

We will see.

How long do we need to stay out here? We seem so exposed.

We'll head out in a few hours. Sleep some, if you can. I know the shelter is primitive, but it's keeping us warm and out of the elements.

I like sleeping in our snow cabin. It's like that story you used to tell me. He had an ice castle right? Was it the Escapist?

The father smiled and said, Superman. He had the ice castle. The Escapist had the golden key.

He hadn't read him stories about Superman since the boy was teething. The Escapist came later.

Those were different times, Son.

I know, sure, but tonight, tonight we're just like Superman. Safe in our ice castle.

I'm going to put out the light.

Ok Dad. I've got my pack right here. Just in case. I'm ready. I'm –

His voice trailed off as he fell asleep. The father pulled his journal from his jacket pocket. He swept away a small area for it and pulled the stylus from its side. It blinked on and he started to write. *January, third or fourth day since full moon, 200 hours.*

The boy and I rest beneath a hastily assembled snow shelter. He, of course, was instrumental in the digging and construction. My strength in walking has improved, as has my endurance. We walked a good fifteen miles, give or take, in a blinding snowstorm. No adverse effects discovered yet. The cold did not bother me as much as I thought it would. My tolerance to the cold was almost as good as when I was a kid visiting Gerald. The treatments may, in fact, be working. But I cannot rule out the placebo effect. However, I am not a good enough scientist to trust that the treatments aren't working so I will not cease the treatments until I have the boy safe. My priority remains getting him to the safety of Summer Cabin, then going back for her. Perhaps at Summer Cabin I will alter the treatment schedule and see if there are any adverse effects. Should I cease the treatments and continue to feel as I do, I will modify my schedule and attempt further study on myself to determine if the treatments are changing my physiology as I suspect they have done. I have not shared these results with the boy and I do not plan on doing so at this time. There is still so much to tell him about his own abilities and even still more for me to learn about them. They seem to change daily. He recalled a story I used to tell him as an infant just to pass the time when I'd hold him until he slept. How he could remember such a fact is beyond me. Perhaps I mentioned it again. I cannot be sure. So his mind grows for sure, but also his strength.

Although the stronger he gets, the more pronounced his delay in aging becomes. I've lost track of the years, but I feel fairly certain that the boy should be fourteen or fifteen by now. Yet, he still appears to be a boy of no more than eight or nine. Of those numbers I cannot be sure. I am only guessing. But it's either the boy or the world that's slowed down and I can't be sure of which might be causing the gap. Maybe it's both.

Also of note, I still have not told the boy everything I received through the Lighthouse. I cannot be sure if I should trust the information, but I will not share it with the boy. It would only get his hopes up about his mother and April and I cannot do that to the boy. He must stay strong. If he knew of my plans, I am not sure he would remain vigilant against capture. I shall continue to monitor the transmissions and make a determination of my next move once we reach Summer Cabin. I know what I want to do. I know the boy is ready.

The only concern I have is the boy's dreams and his talk of a man at a train station. I just need –

The father paused writing and closed his journal. It winked shut and he placed it in his pack. The sound of metal scraping glass echoed across the valley. The man froze, closed his eyes and tried to pinpoint the direction of the reverberation.

A Hex? Definitely not a Mech. Mechs would crunch the snow. This sound was more automated. A power-driven piece of machinery dragging itself across the vast ice fields. Maybe a Hex Bot. But he destroyed the only Hex Bots he knew of the day he escaped with the boy in Colorado. He knew of no others.

The man crawled from his sack. He was careful not to disturb the boy as he pulled himself through the tunnel and toward the metal blocking his escape. He gave a slight push and the metal fell to the side. He stopped and listened again. Hoping it was his imagination or maybe a downed tree. But then he heard it again. This time it was closer and sounded like sheet metal being stamped in a factory. He strained his eyes against the snow and darkness to no avail. The snow swarmed his face like mosquitoes. Then the sound was much closer. His eyes swam into focus as though someone had turned on night vision around him.

The creature stood at least ten feet tall and walked on six legs. Its color was indecipherable in the blue-green of his hazy vision. A small cargo container made up the body with three legs attached to each side. A half-sphere protruded from each side of the body like eyes and a searing blue light shone from small rectangular slits on each. The light surveyed left and right, side to side. Then blinked out. The machine was on a direct path toward the snow cave they had dug. He wasn't sure how heavy this robotic organism was, but he was sure if it continued on its path, they would be crushed inside. The machine stood silent and he held his breath. The temperature reading he had taken before bedding down indicated it was well below the threshold for most machines he knew of to operate. That's why he'd decided to head out to Summer Cabin. The cold was supposed to hide him and the boy. He didn't know what the capacity of this machine was in this frigid cold.

Two yellow lights blinked into awareness at the top of the body. He could see two antennas illuminated in the light. The yellow lights started to grow brighter and the man could hear a hum. As the hum grew more intense, so did the light. Suddenly the antennas moved toward one another and the yellow lights sparked between them. The hum grew to a piercing whine and the yellow light shot toward the man at fantastic speed. He had no time to react. As the yellow light slammed into the cave, he felt a jolt and was slammed backward into the cave. He came to rest at the back end of it. He looked for the boy, but he was gone.

The man felt his own body for damage but could find nothing. He scurried to the door once again but this time it was blocked with snow and ice. Two bare feet stuck out from the snow. He yanked on them and pulled the boy from the cave-in. His chest was red hot and glowing. He grimaced.

Are you okay, Dad?

Me? Are you okay? How did you get out there that fast? How did you –

A minute, Dad. Please. That thing knocked the wind out of me.

Your chest –

The boy opened his eyes and looked down at his chest and stomach. The blast radius filled the boy's chest down to his waist. His neck glowed white hot as though coals burned on his skin. It pulsed with the boy's breaths.

A second, he said holding up a finger. He laid his head back on the ground. He felt for the ice above him and grabbed several handfuls and rubbed them on his neck and chest. The ice boiled, melting. The machine outside made a whirring noise and suddenly sounded like it was back to life and they both heard it begin to move. With each step, the ground shook and the valley echoed with the sounds of metallic stamping.

Can you move? We have to get out of here. I don't know what that thing is but we have to move.

I'm fine, the boy said. The blast ring was fading.

The man dug upwards and through the ice enveloping them. The roof of the shelter caved in.

The machine approached slowly. It moved deliberately, but slowly. The yellow blast lights were out but the red eyes were scanning. They grabbed their packs and trudged through the snow toward the forest. The boy followed his father, still barefoot. As they disappeared into the forest, the machine spoke.

Mech Unit One, this is Hex 12. Area clear. No signs of life. And then it went silent. Hex Bots, he thought. They had upgraded.

Once they reached the forest, they continued on for several hours. At times, the snow blinded them but more often than not, the man found that he was seeing better than he had in years. The greens of the trees were crisper and more alive. The white of the snow washed over him in a calming therapeutic way. The machine had long since passed them, unable to navigate the hardy evergreens. It tried to enter but lacked familiarity with the trees. As it clumsily bumped its large body against the unforgiving trees, it gave up and continued on, toward the edge of the ice and then toward the sea.

They quickly set up camp and the man realized the boy was without his boots.

Your boots?

I didn't have time to grab them. I did not have them near the pack. I am sorry Dad.

It's okay. Are you – the man ran his hands over the boy's feet and toes. There was no sign of frostbite or any issues.

The cold does not affect me the way it does you. My skin is tough. Tough as metal I think.

That blast should have killed you. It shot you three feet into the ground. But you survived. Unreal.

That's what I do right, Dad? I survive.

Yes. That you do, my boy.

You were about to fall. I caught you, he said.

You did. I thank you for that. But you could have gotten yourself killed. You didn't know what that thing was going to do.

But I did, Dad. I could see it in my mind.

What do you mean? You could see what?

I could see the big robot blowing you up. I saw you on fire and bleeding from so many spots on your body. I saw myself, watching you. I was going to be fine. You weren't. You were going to die. I just reacted.

You saw it shooting me?

In my mind I did, yes.

Was it a dream?

I don't know Dad. It came to me like a memory. Like something I'd already experienced. But, of course, I couldn't have since it just happened.

The man surveyed the boy unsure of the ramifications of what he just said. He wanted more information but thought it best to wait for a better time. As was his custom, the man redirected the conversation.

You did well but our goal is to keep you safe. You know that. I am expendable.

Expendable, Dad?

I'm not as important as you, my Son. The world needs you. Me? Not as much. At least not as much as you.

Do you think April found her yet?

I don't know. She'll be back as soon as she does. I know that.

How much longer till we're at Summer Cabin?

The snow is coming down hard. I'm not sure. A few days. A week at most. We will travel in the forest. That Hex unit, or whatever it called itself, couldn't follow us in. I don't think it can traverse through the trees. We'll be safer in here and, barring any Mechs visiting us, we should be at Summer Cabin in just a few days.

The cold is worse here, though. Are you going to be okay?

We have the flesh coats. I'll be fine.

Is the treatment making you stronger?

I'm fine, boy.

Will April know where to find us if she returns?

She knows. We have to move.

They walked for hours. The man lost count just how long. The boy showed no signs of slowing down and as long as the man could walk, he was going to do so. The man remembered these woods. He'd explored them with Gerald when he was just a boy not much older than his son. They'd spend hours chasing one another and even more tracking game. In those days, the game was plentiful. Moose, caribou, and bear of many sorts. He preferred the taste of the black bear but his grandfather always knew the best ways to prepare whatever it was they hunted. There were always fresh vegetables and fruits. Even in the winter, Gerald knew the secrets to growing fresh food. When the Earth grew too hot, he could even grow them in the darkness of Summer Cabin. He would spend hours teaching his grandson the specifics of growing your own food, even without the sun. Or in spite of it. He always called those times Lessons and the man recalled them fondly.

After the Great Surge, Gerald's health failed. He watched from afar as his grandfather died. Something was eating him from inside. At least, to his ten-year-old brain, that's what it sounded like. His mother and father went next and much too soon. They were barely in their thirties but the cancers killed them too. By then he was nearly fifteen.

He wanted to return to Gerald's then, but the Grey Suits got to him first. He spent the next four years in training but not a day went by when he didn't think of Summer Cabin and all the Lessons Gerald had shared with him. He vowed if he could ever be rid of the Grey Suits, he was coming back to this place.

He knew of a cabin that once belonged to an old trapper in the days the e-history texts called the gold rush. It had fallen into severe disrepair in the 1960s but his great-great-grandfather and several others resurrected it. They worked on it and protected it from further damage. He hoped it was still standing. It lacked the security of Summer Cabin and the winter home he shared with the boy, but what it lacked in modern security it made up for in isolation and invisibility. He hoped to make it there so that they could rest for a few days. Maybe find some meat. Relax and recuperate for the final leg of the trip to Summer Cabin. The snow was relentless though, and the cold, as his grandfather always said, was as frigid as Death's breath. He hoped they could find that little trapper's cabin.

Dad? The boy called to the father in the drone of the wind and snow.

He turned and the boy was pointing.

Is that it?

The man looked to his right but saw nothing but trees and snow. Any further and his eyesight failed him.

You see the cabin?

I see a cabin, the boy shouted.

That must be the trapper's cabin. Can you lead the way?

The boy paused for a moment. His father never let him lead. It was always determined to be too dangerous. He was suddenly warm with pride.

I can.

The boy trudged past his father and walked toward the cabin he could see despite the blinding snow and darkening skies. The wind howled in his face like an oncoming train. He wondered if this was part of his Lessons for the day. Lead the hike. Take control. Be ready for anything. At that moment he remembered a Lesson from long ago. While leading the team, have your rifle at hand. Load a round in the chamber. Be ready for warfare. The boy beamed. He was ready. He pulled the rifle from his shoulder and loaded a round.

They walked through waist-deep snow. The boy easily cleared each post hole. The man was winded and could feel the day's hiking wearing on him. His lower back ached and he was thirsty. He still could not see the cabin but trusted the boy. The man wished it was a Lesson but it was really just out of necessity.

The snow picked up in intensity. The flakes grew heavier with moisture and pellets of ice assaulted the man's face. The boy continued on, oblivious to the change in conditions. Despite the palm sized flakes falling, the cabin came into view. It was just as he remembered. And it was a welcome sight.

They approached with the boy still in the lead.

Son, the man called.

The boy turned before walking up the steps to the door.

Use caution. The flooring in front has nails pointing up, to keep out the bear.

The boy marveled that bear had been so prevalent once that someone would try to keep them away from the cabin. Now you'd want the easy shot of killing the bear on your front stoop. He wished he lived in those days.

They walked carefully toward the door and as the man suspected, the front stoop was littered with hundreds of nails filed razor sharp and waiting for an unsuspecting paw to make contact.

How do we get in, the boy asked? He assessed the walk and found no way to get past the nails.

It's just a wooden piece placed on top of the real floor. There's pieces.

The boy saw a small gap between two boards.

Here?

That's it, the man said and bent down and helped the boy move the piece of wood aside. Once clear, the man advanced to the door. Three large rectangular pieces of wood were nailed into the door. He slid the pack from his back and removed a metal ax from its side. He began removing each piece of wood. Within minutes, they were inside.

They were enveloped in the darkness of the cabin. The man's eyes took a moment to acclimate, as the dark was as black as oil. The air had a thickness about it that smelled of rotted wood and decaying flesh. He saw the outline of a table to his right and placed his pack on it. Ahead, he saw a small pinhole where the window covering was. He couldn't tell how big the window might be but knew it was best to keep it covered. An old stove hid in the corner.

The boy was already there with his fire. He cut off a small piece of the Levin stick and placed it in the stove. As he sparked his fire maker, his father grabbed him by the arm and shoved him aside.

No! What the hell are you thinking? Check that chimney. Could be full of god knows what and we'll smoke ourselves out or burn this place to the ground. You know better!

The boy glared at his father. He wanted to continue to lead the party and thought if he could warm the cabin, his father would be pleased. He hadn't considered the chimney. That was a mistake. One which could have proven costly.

Sorry, Dad. I was just trying –

No, no excuses. That shit will get you killed graveyard dead. You must be smarter than that. You *are* smarter than that!

Dad–

He took a deep breath and said, always check a chimney in a place you're not familiar with. Always.

The boy stepped back some. His father did not usually get so angry. He usually used these moments for Lessons. But not this time. The boy tried to recall this particular Lesson but could not. He thought it best to remain quiet though. This did not appear to be the time to confront his father about it.

In the future, Father, I will make sure that I've checked the chimney before I light a fire.

The man pulled at the pipe leading from the stove to the ceiling. Debris and dust scattered to the floor from the end the man had just released from the stove.

Can you see anything up it?

The boy crouched down on the ground, near the floor and looked up. He was about to announce that he couldn't see well enough up the pipe, but then he felt the snow start to hit his face as it floated down.

I see snow. Other than that, it looks clear.

The man reattached the pipe to the stove and held his hand out to the boy. Light the Levin. The boy did as he was told. Soon, the Levin glowed a piercing blue. The heat was immediate and the light was bright as the sun.

We're not worried about the smoke out this far, Dad?

Not this far out. They can't get close enough to get a proper measurement. The trees are too thick. We'll just look like game out here. The smoke will dissipate before they can get a reading on it.

The man closed the grate and surveyed the small cabin that now sat bathed in a golden glow. Two beds were to his left, resting against the wooden walls. They were made from steel but lacked bedding of any sort. Strong, coiled springs laced across the bodies of the beds. Legs were anchored into the floor and from the looks of the bolts, they had been installed in the not-too-distant past. They were smaller than the man but the boy would fit just fine. They would do for a few nights.

There was the table and several chairs. They appeared old and dilapidated but would make for good kindling when the Levin died out. There was no kitchen save for a large piece of granite which sat against the wall with the window. The granite had been bored into from the top and the side, perhaps for waste. The man peered down the hole that had been bored into it and saw that it was empty.

We'll need some water. And something to eat.

The boy nodded his head. Can I come?

No. You stay here. I'll head out and survey the area a bit. See what there is to see. You watch the fire. Break up some of those chairs if need be and feed it. Levin won't burn forever.

The man grabbed his pack and his rifle and headed out. He paused at the door.

The boy called to him first, always. The man nodded his head and pulled the door behind him.

He counted his steps from the cabin and began to trace out a circle. Trees blocked his path at every step. Brush was overgrown and compressed with the weight of the snow. He saw the moose before the beast had a chance to escape. He pulled his rifle and fired. It was a perfect shot. And just what he and the boy needed.

They sat before the fire, still glowing and throwing massive heat at them, eating rare moose steaks. It was a welcome respite from the challenges they had faced getting this far. Neither spoke while they butchered the moose. The boy watched his father expertly slice up the animal. He hoped that in time he too would be expert enough to so deftly fell an animal and render it edible.

As they finished their steaks, the man turned to the boy.

You still doing okay?

I'm fine, Dad.

Your chest?

Like it never happened. It did hurt some at first. But now it's like nothing.

Good to hear.

Do you still think we are only a few days away from Summer Cabin?

I think so. We made good time finding this place.

Did you come here with Gerald?

I did. As a boy. About your age.

He showed you how to slaughter moose?

He showed me how to slaughter a great many things. Game was much more plentiful in those days.

Why is that, Dad?

The man shook his head. He didn't want to get into too much. He never did. And the boy usually left those things alone.

You won't tell me? I'm older now. I think I can handle it.

The man thought on it for a moment. He sighed heavily. The time had come to tell him what he knew.

There is so much to tell. I don't even know all the whys of what happened. But I know people started getting sick when the planet began to warm. At first, it was ignored. There was no connection between the heat and the people dying. But in time, the scientists found a connection. They called it the Cluster. What was the connection between the heat and the cancers ravaging people? I don't know. But as the Earth warmed, people died. Soon, it was widespread. All over the Earth. Hundreds a day. Then thousands. They searched for a cure but there was no cure. Doctors working on it died. World governments couldn't keep up because they had ignored it for so long, they were too late. Some of the best minds were eaten up by the disease. And suddenly survival was more important than a cure.

Then, by accident, a team of scientists from halfway across the world identified a gene. A defect really. In the old days, if you had this gene, you would have died from a great many things. But after the warm-up, the gene splintered – I guess that's how I would describe it. Remember, I'm a mechanic, not a scientist. I don't really understand why the gene did what it did, but it began to eat the disease. It feasted on it. The heat turned that gene on. And those people with the gene survived. Scientists identified fifteen people with the gene. Fifteen people on a planet with nine billion. Needle in a haystack, as Gerald used to say. The government called those with the defect Heteroclites.

Basically, it means we were identified as irregular or abnormal. Fortunately, for us, being abnormal meant we weren't going to die as fast as everyone else. The Heteroclites were hard to find. But since the government had our Codes cataloged, they ran those Codes until they identified the people that matched. I was a match. The Grey Suits pulled me from a classroom when I was about sixteen. This was right before my mom and dad died. I was stuck with needles and probed. I was studied. They did things to me that I won't ever talk about. But suffice it to say, they thought they had the answer after several years of testing us. Some of those answers they discovered worked, but only for a short time. For those short-term solutions, pills were made and the government made millions. People clamored for them.

The mutations grew as the Earth continued to warm. But human DNA also continued to change. Even as people continued to die, there were reports human DNA adapted in the face of the changing environment. The government slowed the dying down and continued to make money, but they couldn't keep up. They trained your mother to be a scientist so that she could continue to study the disease. I was working for the Grey Suits, building their Mechs and making their war machines. Our government stole water from countries near and far with those things. And when I couldn't take it anymore, your mother and I decided to escape. But, there was a problem. She was pregnant with you.

We opted to continue in our jobs. Travel in her condition, we figured out, was just not possible. She was sick daily. We didn't know why. There was pregnancy sickness and then there was her sickness. It was like her body was trying to get you out of there as fast as possible and we didn't think you'd make it full term. And you didn't. While most babies take nine months to grow, you took less than five.

You were born on a Grey Suit base in Colorado. It was deep within a vast mountain. We didn't see the outside world that whole time. When you were delivered, they immediately took you from us and your mother and I didn't know if we'd ever see you again. We didn't understand what or why they were doing what they were doing. That first night they took your blood and sampled your DNA. Your mother was practically tortured during that time. They would bring you into the room to feed and then immediately take you away. My anger grew. But the more I protested, the more they retaliated. Again, they did things to me during that time especially that I care not to recall. But those times hardened me. Made me truly believe that taking you from that place and hiding you was the best possible solution.

As we sat in the darkness of her hospital room one night, the tenth after you were born, we decided we had to leave. And we had to get you out of there. It was on that night, during your feeding, that they got sloppy. They left a med-tablet behind and your mother and I tried to download it. Unfortunately, it required a higher security clearance than I had to access it. The crazy thing was, I thought I had the highest clearance there was since I was working on their Mechs. But not even I could access those files. I gave up trying and your mother tried using her security codes. She was able to access it through some backdoor code. We studied those files and we couldn't believe what we were reading. You were free of the disease and your Code was clear. You would be the first. Or at least the first we knew of.

At this point, everyone was getting Coded. The government basically wanted to know how long people had to live. They would identify those who had longer to live and focus their marketing efforts for the Cluster drugs toward them. Everyone was required by law to wear their Code bracelets and register them with their local hospitals. The color Codes corresponded to how long you had to live. Red meant you only had a few weeks left. Maybe a month or two at the extreme limits of a Red Code. Orange was a year, yellow two, green five, blue ten. A White Code meant you had to be re-evaluated in ten years. In the early stages of the Cluster, most children were White Codes. And Black Codes, well, black was the color of the Heteroclite. Our Codes couldn't be catalogued with the equipment they had in place. The assumption was that we were immune. But as they continued to study us, they found that we carried the Cluster, we just didn't get sick as quickly as everyone else. It was a big discovery but not nearly as big as when you were born.

Your results were unlike anything anyone had ever seen. We decided that night that we would get you out of there and try to hide you from the Grey Suits. They didn't care about you the person. You would become an experiment. And you were expendable.

Not important, right, Dad?

Right. So, the following night, the nurse brought you in and while I am not proud of what I did, I got you off that base.

How?

Not tonight. Maybe not ever. I don't like to think of the things I did. Many people died that night. And I left your mother behind.

But you both agreed that you would leave with me, right? You both couldn't be caught with me.

The man considered this lie that he had told the boy for years. But instead of correcting him, he simply nodded and continued.

We fled Colorado and headed north. If I could get you to Alaska, we stood a chance of camouflaging ourselves in the snow and forests. Plus, I had places to hide up there. And I knew that they knew nothing of my connections to this land. So we spent those first few years migrating up here.

Is that when we met April?

We met April pretty early on. She was with us from the beginning almost.

But not mom?

No, not mom. During that time, I didn't have any contact with your mother.

It was about four years before we came into contact with the Lighthouse. We were traveling with April. We met George. He's the one that told us the ice was changing the further north you went. That it grew thicker. Stronger. The snows were heavier. Unfortunately, the disease was still ravaging the world. The heat had grown too intense.

The disease continued its warpath. Death was everywhere. Then the Grey Suits isolated a gene or something and developed a temporary cure for those they deemed worthy and could pay. But like I said, it was only temporary. Eventually, even with this temporary cure, people still died.

When we met George and the others at the Lighthouse, I didn't trust them. But I learned that the information your mother gave to the Rising put you in certain danger. They had your DNA profiled, but they lacked enough DNA to reproduce it. I knew at that point you could never fall into their hands. If you did, you would spend whatever life you had in a lab.

Do they know about me?

Well, of course.

No, not me as a person but me and my abilities?

I don't know. And I don't want them to.

But couldn't I beat them?

One day maybe. But you're still young.

Dad, I have a question and I know you don't like speaking on hypotheticals.

Then I'll stop you right there –

No, I have had this question to ask you for too long.

Okay.

It's been years. I have counted them. We have moved between Summer Cabin and the ocean more than twenty times. Maybe more. Shouldn't I be older? Taller?

The man pondered the question. He felt the need to lie. But he didn't

Yes. I believe so. But I think whatever it is within you is taking its time getting you to adulthood. At first you grew so fast and now…now I just don't know.

The serum you developed from my blood, it has helped you, right?

It has. But it might be temporary. It might be a cure. I don't know enough to be able to tell you. And drawing your blood now is so difficult. You know that. You've become resistant to the needles.

My fingernails can still draw the blood out.

But last time we did that, you nearly bled to death. I can't risk that again.

That was before I was shot with a laser and survived.

True. We will work on that. Get some sleep. The next leg of this trip to Summer Cabin will likely be the hardest.

The boy rolled over and pretended to sleep. He listened for his father to begin his journal writing for the night. Instead, the man stoked the fire one last time and fell to sleep almost immediately. The boy wondered what his father wasn't telling him. He could feel the man holding back. But it wasn't his place to question his father so he kept those thoughts to himself. He sensed that things were not right between his father and mother. He had said something earlier about her sharing something with the Rising which put them at risk. The accusatory tone of that statement made the boy think that perhaps more was at stake between the two of them than he first realized. For all the boy knew though, his mother may be dead. Even if he had that tickle in the back of his head that kept telling him that she was still alive. If only barely.

The boy thought hard on his mother but he could not recall her face. When he remembered her, hairs of various hues washed over him and sometimes she was a redhead, sometimes blonde. Usually though, she was somewhere in the middle. She was always tall. At least to him. She was probably not as tall as his father, but then again, he was well over six feet tall. Her eyes were a fusion of blues and greens. Sometimes, in his dreams, she stared at him with eyes the color of the sea. He would imagine the three of them at Kotz Butte Bay on the Bering Sea. They'd gorge themselves on banana fish and sea mussels. She would laugh so hard sometimes she'd cry. And father would wipe the tears of happiness away with a finger. She would slap at him playfully and, for a moment, all the world was right.

But when he thought of her, she would inevitably disappear like smoke on the wind. The beach scene would dissolve and he wouldn't be able to see her face. She'd lose her shape, shimmering in his mind. She would reach for him and he her, but then she'd be gone.

The boy awoke in the darkness. It took his eyes a moment to adjust but then he could make out shapes. The fire smoldered in the stove, winking at the boy. He thought of putting more wood on the fire because he knew his father would be getting cold but he heard something that stopped him in his tracks. Voices. Men. And they sounded like they were right outside the door.

Dad, he whispered.

Sleep boy.

Dad, he whispered again, can you hear them?

The man lay still and didn't even breathe. His own dream still churned in his brain like a hurricane.....

CHAPTER 3

.....The dream started with the man standing at the train platform with his grandfather. In the dream, he was just a child. His grandfather was dressed unlike he'd ever seen. He wore pants that looked like burlap, stained black and cuffed at the bottom and sitting like an accordion over black boots. He wore spurs and occasionally, when he shifted his weight or moved his feet, they rattled over the wood platform like a steel wind chime.

The man could see a pearl-handled revolver poking through the long black duster Gerald wore as well. It was facing butt backward but something told him he was still pretty fast on the draw. A silver belt buckle with the words "Fide et Fiducia" held Gerald's pants up over his black shirt. Royal Army Pay Corps buttons lined the outside of the duster. They each had a lion sitting atop a crown over a scroll on them. The same Latin phrase was on the scrolls as was on his belt buckle. He had a large bushy moustache tucked under his nose and tickling his lips. His eyes were the same grey color as his handlebar moustache.

He pointed to the tracks and reminded him that they were dangerous. Not a place for a child to play. The man nodded his understanding as to the dangers of train tracks but not as to why he was standing on this platform with his long-dead grandfather. In the distance, a train whistle thundered.

Ah, that's her my boy, Gerald said, placing a stern but loving hand on the boy's shoulder. He glanced off into the distance although there was nothing to see.

That must be her stopping in Dry Gulch. You can hear the echo, can't you, Son?

The man nodded. How much longer?

Probably thirty minutes, why don't you run in and get yerself something to eat. Here's a three cent gold. Get whatever you want.

The man started in and noticed the wooden sign, freshly painted with crimson paint that said Mount Enterprise, nailed to the wall. He walked in and found an empty station house. There were five rows of pews that could hold five or six people each lined up in the center of the station. A window to the right had bars crossing it and a shade pulled down. A small white sign said, Next Window Please, but there was no other window. A black potbellied stove sat in the corner, near the window, a quiet fire burning within it. He suddenly noticed how warm it was in the lobby.

Taking a train ride today, sonny, a voice behind him said. The man jumped at the sound of his voice, surprised that anyone was in the station house. The man turned and faced a gentleman with a pencil-thin moustache dressed similarly to his grandfather. He looked like every Old West sheriff he'd ever read about. A name wafted across his mind like a subtle fragrance and he thought of Gary Cooper. The name elicited no other recall for him and he wondered who that was. The sheriff-looking man lit a hand-rolled cigarette with a match that he struck across the bottom of his boot.

I'm a grown man, sir. I've had plenty of train rides. I'm not sure what I'm doing here.

If I had a nickel for every time someone said that to me, I'd be a rich man, the sheriff replied. Here for a reason. Of that, I'm sure.

I haven't seen my grandfather in years, the man said. But I've never seen him like this.

This isn't just any place, sonny.

I'm not a kid–

Right, sorry. This is very unusual. Before me, I see a boy. That's odd.

Why is that odd?

I usually see people pretty accurately. If you're a man, I see a man. If you're a boy, I see a boy. But, in your case, I'm seeing you as a child. I do have to say, you look a lot like your son.

You've seen my son?

Indeed I have. But I've never spoken to him. Not like this.

What is *this* place?

A train station.

I know that. I mean, why am I here, in this train station?

I don't know. I'm just supposed to make sure people are where they're supposed to be.

Then, where am I supposed to be?

You left where you're supposed to be. Destroyed much of what you were supposed to protect.

What are you talking about?

The destruction of the base in Colorado, the sheriff said.

I had to get my son out of there.

Ok, but that wasn't your job. That wasn't where you were supposed to be.

I wasn't supposed to protect my son?

I'm sorry to say, but no. Your job has always been your creations. The Mechs. You created them. They are a part of you. Your blood courses through them, doesn't it?

That was just symbolic. I was being stupid when I did that. It didn't mean anything.

Didn't it? Why would you take the time to inject your own DNA into the coolant solution for a mechanized robot? Weren't you hoping for something?

It was stupid. It didn't work.

It didn't? Didn't they protect you when you escaped? Didn't they fight when you terminated them?

No. They're robots. I terminated them. They're just metal and computer commands. Nothing more, nothing less.

And yet, here you are. Your grandfather and I see you as a child. You're telling me you're not a child. That you're much more. Yet, all I see is a child.

They're not sentient.

Maybe not yet. But you were close. Maybe closer than you knew. Your purpose. It's always been the Mechs. Without them, the Variant cannot succeed. The Children of the Infinite could perish.

I don't understand anything you're saying. What's this got to do with Mattie? What are the Children of the Infinite?

Who is more appropriate. And I cannot tell you. You must find these on your own.

My son is involved? Is it my son? He's different. I know that.

Like I said, I cannot tell you. The Variant. The Children of the Infinite. All will become clear. The train is coming. You do have a choice to make. Coming up. That choice will dictate your path. As it so often does in life.

Son, the voice called from the platform. The elderly cowboy approached the door and pushed his way in, turning the burnished gold knob and slipping into the station waiting room.

Who's this, he said to the boy.

The boy looked between the two men. McBride removed his hat. He held out a grizzled hand, calloused and split by time.

Eugene McBride, he said, waiting for the stranger to take his hand.

I know who you are, the man said, not removing his hat or offering his hand.

Remember kid, the Mechs are key. Jump on that train. Get out of here. Make good decisions.

44

He's not going anywhere, Gerald said, without me.

The boy struggled to follow what was happening.

Gerald pulled his duster back, showing his pearl handled revolver.

McBride slowly pulled his white coat apart. His two revolvers faced butts out.

A train whistle blustered behind them.

Get on the train, boy, McBride said.

Don't move, Gerald said.

The whistle blew again and suddenly the station was filled with bullets and explosions. The dream held on for a few seconds. But then his son was waking him…..

Variant

CHAPTER 4

.....The train station faded into the darkness. He could hear men's voices. And they were close. He glanced up in the dim light of the cabin and surveyed the room. Now, the door was bolted. The boy's rifle was next to the boy's bedding. The man's pistol was still on his hip. The butt faced out. His rifle was within reach. The smoke would have drawn anyone in that might have been out in the forests. But who the hell was out in the forests in sub-zero temps and no shelter? Unless –

He heard the click of the lock on the door and the grunting of the man as he tried to push it in.

Harder, one said to the other.

Another push and then they both heard the snap of something metallic. Another metallic clunk and a whine whirred into existence.

Dad, move!

He did as his son said and they rushed to the back of the cabin. Within seconds, the whine stopped and the door to the cabin exploded into thousands of wooden chips.

Two men stomped through the door wearing nothing more than white pants and white pullovers. They raised weapons neither the boy nor the man had ever seen. Polished steel blasters that buzzed when they pulled the triggers. White hot, yellow lasers shot from them and blew holes in the cabin above the man's head and the boy's.

We are here for Lt. Colonel James Cathey. Identify yourself.

The man sat silent as did the boy. His heart raced. He wanted to tackle the men and engage them. But his father's silence told him to stay put.

One of the men walked toward the boy.

You, your name?

The boy looked to his father and then back to the man.

I don't really have a name. As the boy spoke, he began to stand.

Sit down, boy, the man said. He swung the stock of the blaster at the boys knees but the boy reacted instantly and slid to his right, just out of the man's reach.

I said sit down.

I prefer to stand.

Boy, his father screamed through clinched teeth. Get down!

The boy glanced at his father and as he did so, the soldier in front of him glanced as well. The boy could see the soldier's attention drawn to his father. Before he could think again, he summoned every ounce of strength he had and smashed the man in front of him with his right elbow. The man went down but was up without a moment's hesitation. Both soldiers moved in and the one the boy hit fired his weapons.

You'll kill him, you fool! The other shouted.

They grabbed the boy by his upper arms. As they did so, his father moved in and engaged the man to the boy's left. He struggled to get his arm around the man's neck. He took that one to the ground and they grappled. The father pulled at the man's neck with all his strength.

The boy immediately swung his body into the man still clutching his arm. He took that man's arm and whipped it around his back. They crashed into the wall and the boy thought this man to be a fierce competitor. He was not backing down and the boy was struggling against his strength. The man pushed the two of them away from the wall but the boy took him to the ground. As they crashed to the ground, the boy pulled at the man's head and slammed it to the ground.

The father continued to struggle to cut off the air of the man he was fighting. But the harder he pulled, the harder the man fought.

48

The man drove powerful elbows into the father's right side. Each successive blow caused excruciating pain and shattered his ribs. Finally, he crushed the side of the father and he let out a whimper as a splinter of a rib sliced through his lung. The man swung around, on top of the father and began to beat the man in the head. Each punch took flesh from the back of the man's head.

The boy saw this and became enraged. He slammed the man's head down over and over again with such brutality that the boy wondered how this man was still alive. He smashed the man's head into the flooring so hard that eventually the floor splintered and the boy was shoving the man's head through the floor, into the cellar. He lifted the man's head again and this time caught a glimpse of the man's face he was trying to destroy. The skin had pulled from bone and hung in flaps like strips of jerky. His eyes were driven back into his head and his nose was nothing more than a black hole that gushed blood. Blood jetted from the man's head yet he kept coming. The boy scurried for the soldier's blaster and pulled the trigger. The soldier's head exploded like an overripe melon, gone in a shower of blood, brain and bone.

The other man sat atop his father and continued to pound at his father's head. The boy swung the blaster around, fired and hit the man in the chest. He fell backward and the boy was on him in a black rage. He dropped the blaster and began to drop his fists over and over into the man's face. The man struggled for a moment but then went cold. The boy kept at him, covering himself in the man's gore, but he beat and beat and beat until his own hands hurt and bled.

His father lay motionless on the ground.

Dad, the boy said as he crouched to feel his father's breath against his cheek. He could feel shallow puffs of air coming from the man, but he lay still, saying nothing. The boy leaned up and surveyed the damage to his father's head. He could see it was curved unnaturally in. It oozed blood and a putrid-smelling whitish liquid seeped out. He thought of his father dying and suddenly he couldn't imagine being alone out here. He would not survive here. He may not survive anywhere, the boy thought, but certainly not in this drafty cabin that was now shot full of holes and held two dead men.

There may be more coming.

The boy heard his father's voice clearly. But the father still lay motionless on the ground.

Get moving. Where's the two, there's twenty more.

The boy gathered the gear together, collecting the two blasters as well. He couldn't carry the gear, though, and the man at the same time. He needed some way to transport the man. Then he remembered a Lesson.

They'd been high in the mountains when the father told the boy to fetch some firewood. The boy had been confused because they were miles from the cabin and any wood he collected out here would never be enough to heat the cabin for any great length of time.

I can't collect enough here. I'm strong but not strong enough to carry much more than a few pieces back to the cabin.

Although the boy thought the Lessons for the day were over, his father simply smiled and told him he'd have to build a sled.

Like I used to ride when I was little?

Similar, the man said. He pulled his ax from his belt and went into the forest and came out with several branches. He spent some time paring them down and the boy watched as his father put together a sled from nothing more than what the forest gave him. After an hour, father and son trekked back through the rough terrain. The boy pulled a sled behind him with enough wood for two nights.

He thought of this Lesson as he removed part of the floor of the cabin. Within hours, he had enough wood cut to put together a sled good enough to pull his father through the snow. He rolled the man onto the sled, covered him and hoped he remembered the way to Summer Cabin from here.

He pulled his father through the waist-deep snow and after several hours even he was tired. His chest burned and his heart beat violently in his chest. He was winded, but he continued on.

For three more days, he pulled his father through the snow. He rested only when his heart felt like it was going to explode. He did not sleep. On the fourth day, in a blinding snowstorm, the boy saw Summer Cabin.

His father lay on the sled. Halting, shallow breaths were his only movements, followed by the stillness of the dead. He left the sled and walked toward a small clearing in the forest. Much of it was overgrown but the boy could sense the energy that flowed from a tree that didn't belong in this forest. He touched the razor-sharp bark of the Madlik Tree. A panel slowly appeared as the bark retreated. A series of symbols, letters and numbers glowed before him. They had practiced the codes repeatedly and the boy entered the ten digit code.

The forest floor slowly opened and the snow that had been resting there cascaded down the tunnel that was revealed by the opening. They had finally made it to Summer Cabin.

Variant

CHAPTER 5

He pulled the man down the tunnel. The opening closed behind them and the spot where the door had been quickly filled with snow. The forest shook as the winds picked up. The snow blanketed the spot where they had just been, nature correcting for the interference of man.

The boy pulled the man down the long corridor. Solar lights weakly lit the rounded walls of the hallway and glowed weakly in spots. There was just enough room for the boy to drag his father to the next portal. As they approached, he realized he wouldn't be able to take the sled any further. The boy would have to shoulder his father and walk down the twenty flights of stairs. They arrived at the door to the stairs. Another panel blocked the passage and the boy expertly entered the code and the door rose into the recess of the hallway roof. Ten steps at a time, followed by a turn, then ten more steps. The boy lifted his father who was only barely breathing now and began the descent. His weight was cumbersome, but not wholly unbearable. The boy felt strong. Stronger than he had in years.

It took the boy nearly an hour to make the trip down. He stopped occasionally to rest but he made it. Two blast doors awaited him at the bottom. To the left were the sleeping quarters and living areas. To the right were the gardens and food storage. The deep freeze the man had designed was just before him.

The blast doors and quarters were built in the 1960s to withstand an explosive force of over 500 megatons. Meant to house high ranking government officials in the event of a nuclear war, Gerald's great grandparents had purchased the facility sight unseen to prepare for what they saw coming.

The boy entered the code to the living quarter's section and faced another long hallway. The lights flickered to life, dimly lighting the area and the boy walked to a bed and gently placed his father on it. The man made no sounds. Shallow breaths came, but only rarely. The boy feared his father would die. His fear was replaced by his wish that his blood could save his father. He longed to understand more about the process but his father had never shared that information. If he even knew.

He went to the kitchen and brought out a knife. Within his father's backpack he took out a syringe, elastic tubing and a vial. He tested the knife across the kitchen counter and found it slashed through the countertop with relative ease. It made a deep groove and he thought the knife could handle opening up his vein for the procedure. He pushed the knife against his skin where the vein rose from the crease in his arm to the bicep. At first, he applied moderate pressure to ensure a sufficient cut, but he found his skin impervious to the steel. It was the first time he'd been unable to pierce his skin for bloodletting.

He thought for a few minutes, pushing on the skin to his bicep and manipulating the vein under his fingers. As he rubbed his arm, the overly long fingernail on his middle finger accidently swiped too closely to his skin. It nicked him, drawing a thin scratch of blood across its path. He pushed the tip of his middle finger into the tip of his thumb for support. Then he swiped the nail across the skin covering the vein. The boy fought against his skin with the nail and, after some trying, found the vein. It bled, but much more slowly than the last time his father had tried to draw his blood. He filled the vial with his blood.

He filled the syringe full and went to his father. He found the man's vein in his hand quickly and injected the blood into him. Then the boy collapsed, exhausted, and waited.

Sometime during the night (or what the boy thought of as night), the man stirred and spoke nonsense.

He is a Distorter, the man said faintly. You cannot trust him. The boy put his ear to the man's lips but he couldn't discern what the man was saying. The man drifted back off to sleep. The boy didn't know if this was a positive sign or not. He curled up next to his father and slept as well.

Before he knew it, the lights of the sleeping quarters flickered to life. The codes, when correctly entered, would have activated the generators. Right on cue, these lights signaled it was eight in the morning. They were not as bright as he remembered but they provided enough light to wake the boy.

He examined his father. The man rested on his back with his eyes still closed. There was too much blood on the bedding. The boy didn't know what to do to stem the flow of blood from the man's head. He knew if he didn't stop it, the man would die. Whether he had blood from the boy or not.

The boy partially turned his father and examined his head. There was significant damage to the back of the man's head. The boy could see the area where the attacker's fist slammed into the man's head, crushing his skull. The boy wept. He didn't have the skills to fix such a horrific wound. He held the man, closing his eyes, wishing that the man was stronger.

These types of events would occur, the boy remembered his father saying. Hydration was important. Equally important was sustenance. The boy left his father's side and headed to the galley.

He prepared a bone soup his father had taught him during Lessons. A hip bone from a moose killed late several years ago boiled with the hoofs produced a nutrient rich, fatty concoction. The boy added frozen vegetables for himself. As it cooked, the boy reviewed Lessons from his father's tablet. The man had discussed transfusions. He read about the procedure and decided he would try this once the man had eaten.

The boy brought in a tray with the bone soup and placed it next to his father. The man stirred and the boy went to him. He applied a cold rag to the man's forehead, which was burning up, and he waited. Somewhere deep within him, the man implored his eyes to open. But they refused. He could smell the soup but could not will his body to life. His breaths were too shallow, his body too weak. The pain in his head was unbearable. All of these things fought against the man.

The boy lifted a spoon to the man's lips. A small teaspoon of the liquid found its way in but the man gurgled it back out. He let out three severe coughs and the boy feared he would drown the man in the soup. On instinct, the boy grabbed the rubber tubing and forced the man's mouth open. He moistened the tubing with the soup and forced it down the man's throat. It bent and refused the path the boy sought but after a struggle, he found the tubing sliding down the man's throat. He thought if he could get the soup into the tubing, it would find its way into the man's stomach.

He dribbled a few drops of the liquid down the tubing. The man did not stir nor did he choke. Feeding the man this way would take hours and the boy decided to rig a system of feeding the man with a controlled dispenser.

He searched for a container for the soup and found a zippered bag they used for the deep freezer. It was rugged and would withstand abuse. He inserted the other end of the tubing into the bottom of the bag. He secured it with a putty the man produced to deal with leaks of all sorts around Summer Cabin. After a test with water, the boy was satisfied the soup would not leak. The boy measured a cup of soup and placed it in the bag. He hung the bag over the bed and held the tubing. He released his grip and let a small amount of the liquid descend down the tubing. Again, the man did not stir. The boy felt as though the man was getting nourishment. But he couldn't be sure.

Soon enough, the bag was empty. As time progressed, the boy would design a clip that allowed the soup to drip slowly and feed the man without the need for the boy to manually hold the tubing. He did this for many days, four times a day and the man lived. He cleaned the man as he extinguished the nourishment. It was nasty work, but with practice he was able to handle the duties without much hesitation. He bathed the man daily and ensured he was not in the same position for too many hours. His sheets were changed daily. Time went by and the boy wondered if the man would ever wake.

During this time, the boy provided his blood to the man three times a day via the transfusion system he developed. For an hour, the boy would lay next to the man and allow his life-giving blood to flow through the man. During these times, the boy would recite his Lessons out loud. It passed the hours. Still, the boy wondered if his blood was doing any good. The blood had stopped seeping from the man's head after a few weeks. He was satisfied that his blood was having some beneficial effect. He cleaned the wound as well and in time, the man's skull healed.

The boy was also going through his own metamorphosis. His body was changing and he experienced exponential growth. During this time, the boy grew nearly eight inches. His muscle mass increased as he worked his body against resistance when he wasn't caring for his father.

It had been several months since they arrived at Summer Cabin. The boy had been out nearly four times a week, hunting for game. He replenished the deep freeze with a black bear he stumbled across and a moose that got too close to the cabin. He had seen little Mech activity and what he had seen was usually just remote patrols that did not appear to notice him or engage him in any way. He had not seen any more men. Of this, he was thankful. They had been powerful adversaries. He didn't know if he could handle more than two on his own.

Then there was a day when he returned from a daily survey of the area and he found the man sitting up in bed.

My gods, he said when the boy entered the room. The boy sat his pack down and placed the rifle next to it.

Dad?

How long was I out?

A long time, Dad. Many months. So many that I stopped counting. I could not rely on the snow fall to tell me the season. It just keeps coming. I thought it might be because of the Great Surge. Too difficult to tell.

You've grown.

I have. The changes are amazing. Do you think it's because of my blood?

Maybe. Let's not worry about it right now. Please, come here and tell me how you nursed me back to life.

The boy drew a chair, turned on the tablet and began to tell his father what transpired since he was last awake.

CHAPTER 6

The boy talked for hours and the man soaked in the boy's ingenuity. He had changed not only physically but intellectually as well. He had designed transfusion systems, feeding systems and had literally nursed the man back from death. He had few memories from his coma but he felt the boy willing him to life. The passage of time had changed the man's plans. Without contact with the Lighthouse and the Rising for so long, he assumed they would have moved on with alternate plans, if they were even still in existence.

He also realized that he should have been more vigilant in teaching the boy everything he could before it was too late. Despite his size, he still thought of the young man before him as a boy but he was nearly a man now. The boy showed he could survive on his own, so perhaps he had all the knowledge now that he needed. Keeping a dying man alive was no small accomplishment.

He watched the boy handle daily chores. As the man's strength grew, so did the boy's. The man no longer protested when the boy went out for daily patrols. Soon, the man was strong enough to accompany him. He marveled at what the boy learned while the man was comatose. The fears he had about the boy's ability to survive were assuaged by his actions. The boy was no longer careless in his footing. Each step he took was precise and deliberate. Several times, the boy saw game in the distance that the man was blind to until he saw them through his glass. The boy had no such needs. He was agile and shrewd. Things the man could never teach him. These were things that were learned. And he'd learned them on his own.

You've learned much, Mattie, he said as they stooped to cross under a Madlik tree.

The boy paused and turned to his father. The stern look that spread across his brow told his father that he still couldn't utter those words.

Sorry, Son, he said. It just came out naturally. It was the first time he'd called the boy by his name since April left.

Until we find her, please don't call me that. I'm not trying to be disrespectful. It's just painful.

I know, I'm sorry. His father had forgotten somewhere deep within him that calling him Mattie only reminded him of April. It worried him. Forgetting such an important fact.

Changing the subject, the boy said, those needles on the Madlik tree make a very nice tea. I tried it one day after some testing and it's very soothing. You had some while you were asleep.

Medicinal qualities?

I don't know. I only had you and me to experiment on. There was a rat, but he died. I killed him with too much food I think. So I cut yours back. But the tea, you seemed to enjoy. And it's plentiful.

We should have a cup tonight when we get back.

Are you gonna leave now? Now that you're feeling better?

So abrupt. What happened to that kid I left behind?

I'm not a child anymore, Dad.

No, you certainly are not a child. You've grown into a fine young man. But-

But?

You read my entries?

There wasn't much else to do, Dad. I had to know if you had any information or advice contained in the tablet that I didn't know already.

In case I was holding something back?

Something like that. I understand why you didn't share some things with me. I was just a boy.

I didn't know what you could or could not handle, Son.

And now?

Now I feel differently. You've shown you're capable of so much more than I ever expected.

So?

Will I leave?

Mattie nodded his head. They stopped walking and the man faced his son.

I will have to go soon. I made her a promise. And I've got a job to do. We can't sit up here and wait for them to come for us. We have to know what is waiting out there for us.

What if there is nothing? What if everyone is gone but us?

Then there is nothing to fear. I'll do my job, get the Mechs back under control and we go on living.

We will die.

We're going to die anyway. You're safe up here. Obviously you're adept enough to survive here on your own. You did it while I was out. So, I have less fear leaving you now.

But, you wrote that you were just going to leave me here before. You weren't going to tell me. That hurt me.

I'm sorry, Son. Truly. I should have known that you would be capable of handling things. I just didn't trust myself. To turn my back on you and leave you here would have been tough enough. To do it to your face would have been unbearable.

Forgive me for saying this, Dad, but I've thought on it long enough. That is very cowardly.

The man recoiled from the comment. His cheeks flushed with anger. But he knew the boy was right. He had his reasons for lying to his son, but maybe they were just excuses. The truth was he didn't know how to tell his boy that he had to finish what he started in Colorado. If he didn't, neither one of them would ever rest peacefully.

You're right, Son. It *was* cowardly.

You were just going to leave me? Really?

Son, understand, I had my reasons. Luckily it didn't transpire the way I had planned.

But you're still leaving.

What can I say? You are self-sufficient. You can survive up here. Depending on what this crazy weather does up here, you should be able to survive until I return.

And if you don't?

Then you're no worse off. You're safe.

Am I?

You've managed to survive without me. I would think so.

Well, I didn't exactly tell you everything either, Dad.

The man eyed the boy gravely. He motioned the boy forward, toward Summer Cabin. Let's get inside. You can tell me *every*thing over a pot of bear stew.

And maybe a pint of ale.

Ale?

I had a lot of time on my hands, Dad. What was it you used to say about an idle mind being the devil's playground?

Ok, he said and laughed. And we'll try your ale.

CHAPTER 7

The young man went to work on the stew, chopping vegetables and tossing them into a deep pot. The gas whined on and lit immediately. The man returned from the deep freeze with several cuts of bear meat. He slid the drawer of the graphene lined magnetic oven open. He placed the steaks in and within seconds they were defrosted. He never trusted the oven for much longer. There was something comforting about letting a meal cook over a fire rather than being zapped by electromagnets. He seasoned the meat and waited for the young man to give him the okay to toss them in.

Where's this ale you concocted?

It's in cold storage. First batch spoiled too quickly. Now we've got about fifty gallons resting nicely in the old barrel we used to collect Piney fruit. You can taste the fruit in it. It's nice. But potent. Just a little goes a long way. I thought about calling it Devil's Ale.

Once dinner was over, the father and his son sat in the living quarters of the Summer Cabin. A gas fireplace crackled with imitation log sound effects.

So, tell me what's happened. He took a sip from the Devil's Ale. It was sweet and dark brown. He couldn't smell the alcohol in it, but he could feel it in his head almost immediately. He poured a second glass while his son sipped his first.

Those two men that attacked us…they weren't the only ones that came, Mattie said.

How many?

There have been dozens. And they're all dead. They know we are here, I'm sure of it.

You killed them all?

Yessir. Every last one of them. You were right when you said where there were two there would be twenty. The first patrol unit showed up about three days after our encounter. The vid-monitors outside were only working sporadically but I saw the drop ship in them. They fanned out after landing and set up a camp not far from here. It was quite a spectacle. A self-inflating structure that was as big as our work shed back at Winter Cabin. Twenty men climbed in and started searching for us.

It took me a few days to figure out how they knew where we were but I had confiscated the blasters from the first two and was holding them to use later. It wasn't until I took one of them outside to take a look around that I realized they must have had some type of tracking device implanted in them. They were almost immediately upon me when I went outside. I shot the first two straightaway. The blaster is clumsy but eventually it'll find its target if you hold the trigger down and spray the weapon toward your intended victim. They were blown into pieces too small for even the tiniest field mouse to enjoy.

Then there were five of them. I led them away from Summer Cabin. I had a pretty good idea that they didn't know exactly where the signal from the blaster was coming from but once I was out in the open, they were on me and they were relentless. I abandoned the blaster about a mile from the cabin in Settlers Stream. It was flowing and the blaster sank quickly. I lost sight of it almost immediately. I think the water carried it down pretty far because they immediately dispersed, down river. I unshouldered my rifle and picked them off like a herd of buffalo.

The remaining Grey Suits took refuge in their inflated structure. I got back to Summer Cabin through one of the venting shafts.

You crawled through a venting shaft? That's got to be five miles from the cabin.

It took most of the night. I got you fed and bathed-

God, Son, the man said and hung his head.

It's fine, Dad. I got you cleaned up and then I set back out to finish the rest of them off. I couldn't afford to have them out there plotting their next move.

I was in my flesh coat and approached the structure. I could hear them in there discussing who or what was out there taking the others out. They thought we had an army out here and they spoke of reinforcements.....

.....*Get her back on the broadcast line, a gravelly voice shouted.*

Sir, a female voice responded.

This information that you gave us is failing by the minute. There is no cabin here. There's snow, ice and something else out there but there's no goddamn cabin.

You won't see it. I told you. The information we have on it says it's an underground bunker.

There's twenty feet of snow out here. No way anyone made it under this with bare hands.

I have only a general idea of where it is, the woman said.

The tracker stopped down river about thirty clicks from here. If they had the blaster, they got rid of it. I don't see how anyone can survive out here without shelter.

He's there. Those Lighthouse prisoners assured me that he was headed that way. Before they lost contact with him. Please tell me your men didn't kill him. If he's dead, then we can stop with this idea that we're going to find the boy.

Hell, we don't even know if your boy is still alive. Someone killed my two men. Someone with an insane amount of strength. Those men were genetically engineered to be warriors.

Up there, strength is relative. He's not stupid.

Neither am I, he roared. He survived, but god only knows how.

The boy withdrew his knife and tried cutting a slit in the fabric at the base of the frame. Nothing happened. The fabric was too tough. He bent down, gathered a small portion between his fingers and drug his index finger fingernail across the fabric. A small tear emerged and warm stale air began to escape. The structure began to deflate and the men began scrambling through the opening to the tent.

What the hell is going on here, the gravelly voiced man yelled to no one in particular. The stumbled out like clowns in a clown car.

They stood outside, struggling to zip up their parkas. The snow was falling in sheets and the thirteen men left huddled together.

I don't care how it happened. These structures have housed the Martian colony for decades. It's not just supposed to deflate. These damn things can take meteor strikes and keep inflated. Something did this!

They scanned the horizon around them. The boy crouched behind a large bristlecone tree. He raised his rifle and sighted in the men. Four shots later, they lay next to their deflated, not-so-impervious shelter. The boy piled the bodies on top of one another atop the shelter. He set the evidence on fire and returned to Summer Cabin.

His dad sat staring at the floor. The ale warmed his body and his head swam from the intoxicants. The boy sat quietly and waited for his dad to say something.

The man put his face in his hands and reached out for the boy. I'm so sorry to put you through that, Son. Have there been anymore?

I found a unit stationed down by Settlers Stream but they haven't made it this close. Occasionally a sentry will pass by the grove of bristlecones but they don't stay long. I thought the longer I stayed out of sight the more likely it would be they would think you - or whoever they suspect might be out here – was gone. I spent a lot of time indoors.

They won't give up until they kill someone out here. I'm sure they're dug in for the duration. Until they capture us or confirm we're dead.

They don't know I'm still alive. How could they, Mattie said.

April?

She wouldn't have said. She would've died before telling them anything.

I'm sure she wouldn't have wanted to say anything. But if they tortured her, they may have convinced her.

If they did, so help me –

In time, Son. In time.

Dad, you keep saying that. In time we'll find mom. In time we'll find April. We've wasted years. The time is now. We have to get them and finish this.

Finish what?

What you started when you left Colorado.

You don't know anything about that.

I know I was just a boy, but I understood what you men were talking about at the Lighthouse. I couldn't wait to get old enough to fight for the Rising. Staying out here is just a waste of both of our talents.

Where is this defiance coming from?

I just feel like we've wasted so much time. All to keep me hidden. You were so scared they were going to do me harm, but you know not much can hurt me.

They did horrible things to me, Son.

You keep saying that, like it's supposed to appease me. All it does is make me wonder what the hell they did to you and then how we can punish them for it.

He thought about it for a moment and then began, I was in my early twenties, maybe twenty-one or two and I was sitting in this engineering class in Colorado. I was only half listening that day and I remembered thinking they were at the door because I was considering how I was going to escape and destroy this sorry excuse for a government. I actually believed they were reading my thoughts. I should have known they weren't that smart.

There were four or five of them at the door. They were all dressed in those drab grey suits with green ties.

Ties for soldiers?

It was a long time ago. This was before they went full soldier mode. Back then, they still held out hope that there could be a separation between the military and government. In any event, they stood there, looking official and one of them walked in. He interrupted Dr. Burton then handed him a yellow slip of paper. Burton read it then glanced up at me as if to say sorry. He nodded his head, handed the paper back to the Greys and the five of them started walking up toward me. They asked for me to come down. There were only fifteen or sixteen people in class. At that point, the Greys limited education to those who weren't going to die within the next ten years or so. No sense wasting education on an Orange or Yellow Code. They made sure only Blues and Whites were given any education and even then, that they would do something that advanced the goals of survival for the Greys. They controlled so much at that point and we just let them take it all over.

I sat stoically in my seat. They scanned the faces in the classroom. I shifted in my seat and that's when they saw the Black code bracelet. I tried to hide it, but it was too late. They pointed at me and I reluctantly gathered my things and walked down to the front of the room. In the days before the Cluster, those halls were crowded with kids eager to learn. Now, we learned what they wanted us to learn. For their purposes. We were just vessels.

As I approached the five men, one grabbed my backpack and another deftly moved in and slipped cuffs around my wrists. I tried to fight against it, but these cuffs were unlike anything I'd ever heard of before or experienced. The cuffs delivered a vicious, biting shock of electricity each time I tried to fight against them. As I struggled out of the classroom, I felt a needle pierce my neck and everything went black.

I awoke in a dimly lit room that smelled of bleach and bristlecones. That piney, nutty, buttery scent wafted over me and I thought of the room I slept in when I visited my grandparents in Kotz Butte Bay. It always smelled of bristlecones. I realized I was strapped to a bed and I couldn't move more than an inch or two. Both my hands and feet were constrained and my mind reeled thinking of what they would do to me. I struggled against a restraint across my brow as well. My head was stuck against the bed and I couldn't lift it to see where I was or what was going on around me.

Mr. Cathey, a voice called, walking into the room and grabbing the chart from the front of the bed. How're we feeling?

I tried to say something but my mouth wouldn't cooperate. I realized there was an IV needle pierced into my wrist and whatever they were delivering into my blood was making speech nearly impossible. My thoughts were hazy, my vision dull.

He's close, the same voice that called my name said. I could feel him checking my pulse at my neck. Then he shined a brilliant OLED light into both of my pupils. Despite the intensity of the light,

I couldn't shut my eyes to avoid it. Whatever they were giving me made movement impossible.

They brought in a long, slender metal tube wrapped in plastic. I remembered the plastic because it had been so long since I'd seen any after it was banned in the late 2020s. They unwrapped the tube and laid it beside me on the bed. I could feel tugging at my neck and then my body began to feel tight, like my skin was being stretched across my torso. The pain medication they gave me was working but the feeling of being torn apart made my mind scream. Suddenly, the tugging at my neck got more severe, tighter and the metal tube began to disappear from beside me. There were people behind me holding me and I realized that they were sliding that tube down the base of my spine. My skin continued to grow taut and then I felt a liquid hitting me just above my hips. Another nurse came in, adjusted the IV and then I went dark.

I awoke, I don't know how much later, but the feeling that my skin was about to burst from my body was intense. I could hardly breathe through my oxygen mask. As much as I wanted to escape, my body wouldn't cooperate. The tubing remained inserted in my back and I could hear liquid sounds coming from it.

After an unknown length of time, I woke up in another room. It was brightly lit and several vases of flowers sat on the table near the door. I was no longer strapped to my bed but my body ached all over. As I tried to move, I found the pain so unbearable that I dared not try that again for quite some time.

The door opened and a doctor entered. His name tag said Dr. Walsh and he shined the penlight in my eyes again, wrote something down on his tablet and then he stood back and asked me how I was feeling.

Shitty, I said.

It is to be expected, he said. After a lumbar puncture, some people experience varying degrees of pain.

Lumbar puncture, Mattie asked.

His father replied, that was the story they were feeding me. But it was much more than that.

What was it?

He took a deep breath and said, I can't say for a fact and I've never shared this with anyone, not even your mom or April, but I think they removed something from me to clone me.

To clone you?

Yeah, I know how it sounds. Back then, human cloning was in its infancy. But it was around. And I wouldn't put anything past the Grey Suits.

You weren't just hallucinating or something?

I've considered so many different scenarios since it happened. That's what I believed happened. Maybe they were just drilling for some spinal fluid to make sure I really wasn't sick with anything. But I'll tell you this, on the day I could first stand on my own and walk to the bathroom, the door was ajar. It was late, probably eleven thirty or twelve. I stuck my head out my door and the nurses' station directly across from my room was vacant. A lone light shone on the desk but the hallway lights to the left and right were all off. The darkness was overwhelming but down the hall to the left, another light was on. I took a look right and, not seeing anyone, shuffled down to the light. There were four large glass windows separating the hall from the room where the lights were on. They were bright and streaming from the ceiling. I wondered for a minute or two what kind of room this was and then it hit me that this was an old maternity ward. There were no babies to speak of in it but on a long table that lined the wall in the back, several large jars rested with tubes coming in and out of them. Fluid flowed freely between the tubes and jars. There were probably about twenty jars lined up. The fluid in the jars was an opaque pink color. I couldn't tell what was in the jars but then one of them had movement. I felt a sting at the base of my skull, turned and saw a nurse with a hypodermic needle standing next to me. As I collapsed, I saw that jar move again and then I saw eyes and a tiny body. It was an embryo. As I spun around, I saw three women lying on stretchers in the corner of the room. Two of them were very pregnant.

I woke up several days later. Again, my door was open and the place looked deserted. I had to see if what I saw was real or a dream. When I got down to the end of the hall, the room was empty save for a few chairs and hospital beds.

So, you believe it was clones?

I don't have any other explanation for it.

But you never saw them?

Clones?

Yeah, Mattie said.

I never did run into myself at the base, if that's what you're asking. I don't know what it was but that was just the tip of the iceberg of the things they put us through at that base. I couldn't have you subjected to that.

But I'm different, Dad.

So, you just want to waltz down to some Grey Suit bases and fight them all?

I haven't decided how I'm going to do it. But you know I'm no safer here than I would be with you on the road. Eventually they'll find the vents. Once they do, it's just a matter of time until they find Summer Cabin.

Unless they start digging up the vents, there's no way, at least not to my way of thinking, that they'll find you. The shafts are too narrow. I doubt you'd even fit in them now. And this ground's been frozen for eons. They won't be digging anything up. And that's assuming they find the vents. They've had time to find them and they're still miles away. If I give myself up, they may leave, the father said and gauged his son's reaction to the news.

The boy thought on this plan. If you give yourself up, you could die.

They need me. At least I think they do. They did when I escaped with you. At least with me, they can run their experiments.

Who's to say they haven't figured out a cure by now?

The last I heard from George, there was still no cure.

I don't think there is a Lighthouse anymore, Dad. I tried for months to get someone on the comm when we got here, but every channel was nothing but static.

The man still had not looked up. He patted his son on the leg and rose. I need rest, Son. We'll discuss these things in the morning. Sleep will do us both some good.

Sometime during the night, the man disappeared. He left a note that simply said, *Thank you for all that you have done. Stay put. I'll be back shortly. One day you'll understand why I had to do this.*

The boy stared at the note as he cooked his breakfast. He wasn't angry. He knew his father was going to leave. He just didn't know it would be so soon. But maybe something the boy said had gotten to his father. He stirred a second bowl of food and a sliver of a smile slid across his face. He had not been exactly truthful with his father either. The numbers he killed didn't match up and he didn't know if his father suspected that the numbers had been much more. He also didn't mention that the voice on the other end of the comm had been a female.

He picked up the second bowl and made his way through the living quarters, pulling the blast door behind him. He continued on through the passageway to the storage and deep freeze. Beyond the freeze was a storage locker. The boy pressed his thumb to the electric panel. The door opened sluggishly, fighting against itself. An ancient bulb flickered to life and struck a yellowish white light on a hooded figure chained to a mattress. He approached, placed the bowl down and pulled the IV from the figure's arm, blood spraying from the end until he crimped it shut. He reached for a bandage from the night stand and applied it to the vein. He forcibly lifted the hood from the figure's head.

He's gone, he said. Here's your breakfast, Mom. Eat up. We gotta figure out what to do next.

The sarcasm in his voice was thick.

CHAPTER 8

Sometime in 2108

He sat at the derelict bar and nursed an extraordinarily cold beer. It wasn't nearly as good as the ale the boy had made, but sitting in this place, he felt like a beer.

You got gold for that mister, the bartender asked as he cleaned a glass. His face was a tattooed chart mapping the location of some long ago forgotten treasure. Several silver bolts burst through the cartilage of each of his ears like the rungs of a ladder. His ear lobes hung below them like tire swings. Yet another bolt was driven through the high point of his nose, between his eyes. The man had not seen anything like the person he was now talking to.

If I didn't, the man asked in reply and took a slow sip.

The bartender bent his head to the left a bit and directed the man's attention to the hulking figure sitting in the corner. He sat under a single light, smoke wafting from a hand-rolled cigarette over his equally metalized face. He sat stoically reading a tattered paperback novel, *Blood Meridian*. His arms bulged like a Roman gladiator's and he looked to be about four feet wide. The man recognized him immediately. Lennon Stipe. He hoped that what he had done to Lennon so long ago had worked. He prayed Lennon would not recognize him.

Good thing I have gold, the man said turning his attention back to the bartender, that's a big sonofabitch. He withdrew a thumb-sized bar of gold from inside his coat. Will this work, he asked.

The bartender examined the bar and turned toward the empty shelves. From under the counter he withdrew a scale and a six-inch-long implement that glowed blue when the bartender pushed the black button on the side. As it settled upon the scale, the bartender waved

the wand over the bar of gold. Two small beeps chirped from the
object and then the blue light blinked twice and came to a green color.

Looks good, he said as he turned back toward the man.

How much will that buy me?

Depends.

On?

On how much trouble you'll be the more you drink.

I don't plan on staying long. I've got a long way to go.

Headed north or south?

South.

How far?

Lower forty-eight.

The bartender laughed and wiped the counter in front of the
man.

Something funny?

You just said you were headed south like it was nothing.

What? It's cold. So what?

So what? Well, if you can make it through the Yupik Front,
there's rumors of discord on the Canadian border.

What the hell is the Yupik Front?

Well, I do lack formal education, see, in the ways of
meteorology. So don't quote me on this. But my understanding is
that this front is some sort of anomaly created when the screws in
charge decided to try and blow this planet up during the Great Surge.
For whatever reason, the extreme heat from the south and extreme
cold from the north meet somewhere about the sixtieth parallel, give
or take. Violent storms, heavy rains, even snow and ice are reported
daily along the line. The two fronts battle for position so there's no
stability. The front may move a few miles north or south but for the
most part, it's stationary. And a real bitch to get through. Especially
if you haven't already done it a few times.

So, rain and snow? I've dealt with snow like you wouldn't believe the last several years. That don't scare me.

This isn't like anything on Earth man. Trust me, I'm here because I couldn't get through. Most folks here are in the same boat. We tried escaping the cold as it inched down from the pole, but that front is like something out of an old sci-fi film. So we just sorta landed here and gave up. But be my guest. Give it a shot. What do you have to lose? Right? You're probably a foot in the grave anyway. Most of us are. That's the shit of it.

You sick?

Dunno man. I left before they could round me up and stick all their probes in me. They Coded me once, but hell, that was years ago. But everyone I know that's old and I mean like forty or older is dying. If they ain't already dead. They screwed us man. Screwed this planet and then screwed us.

I don't have too many options left. I gotta get down south.

If you've got gold burning through yer pockets, I can point you to someone that's done the trip a couple dozen times. But he's a sonofabitch. Mean. And he just might kill ya on the way down.

How's he get through?

He's got a train of sorts.

The rails are still operational?

Nah, man. It's all souped up and modified. Goes through the snow and then the rain. I think the damn thing can float on open water and then course through a desert. He's one of the few that can get you through. But it ain't cheap.

He around?

He's probably passing back through here in a week or two. Could tell him you're looking for him.

Not interested then. I need something now.

Suit yourself. Another drink?

77

The man nodded his head.

Something stronger than the beer, the bartender asked.

The man nodded his head again.

The bartender pulled a nondescript bottle from beneath the bar. It was caramel-colored and smelled of coffee and vanilla.

The man took a sip and the burn spread across his lips and leapt down his throat like a wildfire.

Gotta drink that one down straightaway. Otherwise, it burns like a bitch.

The man finished the shot off and tapped his glass. The bartender refilled it and the man shot it fast.

Another?

Thanks, but I'm probably good.

You need a room?

What's that going to involve?

A little gold.

How little?

You're all paid up. That bar will get you two day's rest. Right above this bar. Couple of rooms still left.

The man thought of his other options. Sleeping in the cold with little heat versus a bed and some warmth. But with that came the possibility of Grey Suits.

You ever have any problems with guests?

Not usually. Len over there can take most comers.

What about with - he paused and looked around, Grey Suits?

You got problems with them?

No, no. Just like to lay low, you know? Just curious.

The bartender eyed the man cautiously and said, it's gonna be another bar of gold for you mister. No offense, but I don't need anyone coming in here and giving the place any more atmosphere than it already has. Know what I'm saying? Another gold and your secret's safe with me.

The man thought about it and withdrew another gold piece for the bartender. He slid it across the bar. I just want a little peace and quiet for a few days. That's all.

The bartender winked at him and turned to the empty shelves. With the swipe of his thumb print across a small slit in the base of the shelving, an access panel opened and several silver cards hung on rusted pins nailed to an ancient board behind it. The bartender grabbed one with what looked like handwriting on it. It was marked three. He pulled a card reader from beneath the bar and slid the silver card into it. In a second, the reader spit the card out and the bartender slid the card across to Cathey.

Put your thumbprint on the card and we'll get you all settled in.

Cathey thought about it for a moment and returned to thoughts of sleeping in the cold. He paused noticeably.

I ain't in the business of collecting thumbprints for anyone if that's what's got ya restless. It's just for the room.

Cathey thought another few seconds and then pushed his thumb into the card. The bartender slid the card back into the reader and a green light appeared at the base of it.

Ok. You're all set. It's up the stairs to the left. First door on right. There's Levin stick in a jar. Small fireplace is in the corner. You got it for a night. Be gone before sunrise.

I thought you said two days!

Changed my mind. I don't think you're just passing through. I think you're bringing a world of shit with you and I'd prefer you just pass on through and meet whatever end you're gonna meet somewhere else. No offense.

My extra gold? He held his hand out and waited for the bartender.

That extra bar's so I don't call the Grey Suits myself right now. Something's got you itchy. I'd prefer not to find out what.

The man reached across the bar and grabbed the bartender with a crumpled fist. Before he could demand his gold back, Len was on him and the man was flung against the wall.

The bartender smiled slyly. I told you no trouble. Now you've gone and started trouble. You're dangerously close to losing the room. But I'm willing to overlook your disrespect.

The man stood up and dusted himself off. The ache in his stomach returned with a vengeance, pulsing with each breath.

Fine, the man said. Keep the gold.

Uh-uh-uh. I told you trouble costs money. I'll be needing another one of those bars before you get up those stairs.

He reached once again inside his jacket and withdrew another gold bar. He placed it on the bar. The man wondered how long it would be before they realized the gold was fake. Worthless, in fact. Comprised of nothing more than iron pyrite and a mixture of arsenides and sulfosalts. It was found by the ton on Mars. When it was discovered, people worried the price of gold would plummet as soon as Kelland Mining started mining it and bringing it back to Earth. Kelland brought it back, but once they started more rigorous testing, they discovered it was a cousin of gold. But worthless. He was lucky the bartender was still using a first-gen mineral scanner. The newer ones would've picked the man's gold out for the useless rock it was. But those were expensive. So expensive, they weren't really worth it. And out here, there wasn't much time for expensive toys that didn't serve a purpose. Most people had no idea how to beat the first-gen machines. The man had to though. The Mechs he designed had to know the difference between minerals. Their survival depended on it.

The man pulled his pack on his shoulder. He walked toward the stairs and headed up to his room. In the corner of the bar, Len watched the man walk up the stairs.

Hey, Len said, raising his voice. Come back down here.

The man turned and could see the recognition on Len's face. However, it wasn't instant recall. It was more that look you see when someone might recognize someone, but can't quite place where they knew that person from or what that someone's name might be.

I think I know you.

The man stopped midway up the stairs and Len approached. He towered over the man and that was a rare occurrence.

You ever in the Army?

Me? No, the man laughed. Got a bad ticker, he said and pumped his fist at his chest.

No, not the fightin' side. The Mech side. Engineering. You look a whole lot like this Mech builder I knew back in the old days.

I have one of those faces, I'll admit. People are always saying I remind them of someone or look like someone they know.

Cathey was his name. Or his wife's name.

Well, that solves it. I haven't been married. Not to a Cathey or anyone else.

No. For some reason your face says Cathey to me. What was his name? He had this serpent or dragon tattoo on his left forearm. From the crease of his arm down to his wrist. Monster of a tattoo. Fierce colors. Always looked like it was moving. I remember asking him about it more than once.

Sorry friend, the man said lifting the sleeve to his left arm, nothing here. Len looked over the man's arm and it was tattoo-free. If that's everything, I'm beat.

The man turned to walk back up the stairs and Len reached for him. He turned the man around.

It's been a long time. Maybe it was the right arm. You don't mind if I have a look at that one d'ya?

You're really interested in this Cathey guy, aren't you?

You would be too. Been a bounty on his head since he went AWOL nearly fifteen years ago. Kidnapped a baby and killed the baby's mother. Then sliced up a bunch of soldiers and killed them too. Blew up an army base, killing thousands of innocent women and children. He was a real piece of work. And fifteen years ago, the bounty was about a million dollars. No telling how much he'd be worth today.

Well, like I said, I'm not him. And it's a good thing. You're a very intimidating man. The man slowly put his backpack down on the step ahead of him. He rolled his sleeve up and exposed his right arm. It was wrapped in scar tissue from his bicep to the base of his thumb.

Len surveyed the damage and flipped the man's arm over and back again.

That don't prove you're not him. You coulda had that tattoo burned off. Knowing we'd be looking for that.

True. But my arm's been a mess like this since I was twelve. Damned near burned it off repairing a solar ski. It's all part of my medical recs. But I stopped carrying those with me. I think most people did.

Len rubbed a finger over the scar tissue. He was no doctor, but it felt real.

He nodded his head toward the man.

The man rolled his sleeve down and picked up his coat and pack. To your health, he said.

He who has health, has hope, the bartender said.

Sleep well, Len said.

Thanks guys. I will. He turned and walked stridently up the stairs.

The bartender turned the gold pieces over in his hand and handed them to Len. He'd only seen gold like this once before and it was the last time a Grey Suit stopped in.

Something about him, eh?

Len turned the bars over in his hands. He took one and put it between his teeth and bit down. Seems legit, he said. But yeah, he was off. I swear he looked just like Cathey.

What do you want to do?

I'd like to call up some old army buddies and have them look at his thumb print. Just to make sure we're not letting a couple million dollars walk out of here tomorrow. He reminds me of that dude, I'm telling you.

We got lots of issues with Grey Suits if they come walking in. The alcohol doesn't have tax stamps. The rooms aren't to code. I ain't paid taxes in ten years.

Lock everything up. They'll look the other way if they're capturing the dude at the top of their most wanted list.

That dude was that bad?

Yeah, and then some.

Variant

CHAPTER 9

.....Lennon Stipe arrived at Fort Carson in 2105, three years before Cathey would set about to destroy the base and escape with his son. Assigned to the Mech Operational Units in the early days, he managed to get in good with the engineers and enjoyed his mundane job as a result. Cathey wasn't the engineer for any of his units, but he saw him around. He kept to himself. Seemed like he was pissed all the time and that he hated his job. But there were those types around in those days.

Lennon and Cathey were stationed beneath a fourteen thousand foot mountain. Buried and hidden deep within it, only the highest security clearances were allowed through to the production area. The engineers designed state-of-the-art Mechs, and men like Lennon were the grunts tasked with making sure they kept running. In the beginning, there were all sorts of problems with them.

After a few years, the men noticed a female doctor coming through more often. After a while, it was obvious she was pregnant and it appeared that she was married to Cathey or they were together somehow.

He didn't talk much. Kept to himself. The mechanic assigned to him, Jorie, said he would leave notes about repairs, but rarely even spoke to him.

There was some sort of issue that popped up between them and when Jorie pressed Cathey on it, he snapped. Beat Jorie into the ground, breaking his nose and shattering his orbital bone. Lennon helped Jorie to the medical unit and he said he didn't even know what had set him off. But he said he saw rage in Cathey's eyes like a cornered dog.

Next morning, Jorie went in to talk to his superiors beneath a couple layers of bandages. The next day, Jorie was gone. So the men got the hint and left Cathey alone.

Cathey spent most of his time in the infirmary with the female doctor. As a result, the men didn't see much of him until Lennon got called one night, maybe a month after the Jorie situation. His CO, Lucas Cabell, ordered the mechanics down to the production depot. Once they arrived, there were Mech blasters lined up on a table. Campbell hastily told them to grab one and kill anyone that tried to get out from the infirmary. The men knew they were holding Cathey and his wife in there for whatever reason.

The men, five in all, sat there for two days with no further orders. The engineers were eventually moved to another area of the base, leaving just the infirmary and production depot soldiers. And, of course, Cathey. On the third day, the mechanics heard shouting and the sound of rapid-fire gun shots. The shooting lasted for a while. And then silence. The mechanics waited, guns drawn.

Two or three nurses came scrambling out at some point. They were covered in blood and the mechanics weren't sure whose blood it was. They ran toward the doors and one of the mechanics, Goldie, opened fire on them. Three short bursts and the nurses were down.

What the hell man, Compos, another mechanic, screamed at the shooter. He puts his hand on the blaster stock and forces it down.

Captain said to take out anyone trying to escape, Goldie screamed.

He meant Cathey.

That's not what he freaking said. He said anyone. And with that, he jerked the blaster back up and pointed it squarely at the two remaining nurses that sat huddled beneath the security panel.

Not them idiot, Compos said and hit Goldie in the forehead with the butt of his blaster. The shock sent Goldie reeling back, blood trickling down his forehead.

In an instant, Goldie's finger was on the trigger again and he pelted Compos with five rounds. Two of them hit Compos in the face and the other three pierced his neck and chest. He slid down in front of the table. The blood spilled from his wounds and pooled about him.

It's not supposed to be this way man, another mechanic, Wayne, said. Shooting each other. This is seriously deranged.

The door to the infirmary opened again and Cathey appeared, wearing a large backpack and carrying a blaster in one hand and a traditional assault weapon in the other. A large clip hung below the assault rifle. He had modified it and he aimed it at the group of mechanics.

I'm not here to hurt any of you. The last thing I want is to kill anyone else. All I want, the only thing I want right now is to get out of this building and get my little boy safe. If you knew what they were planning to do with him, you'd do the same. Cathey surveyed the mechanics and swiped his guns from side to side. No one has to die.

As he walked toward the mechanics, Dr. Clara Cathey emerged from the doorway. No one knew her but she had the most golden of blonde hair and piercing blue eyes. Like the ocean and the sky merged into one. She was so beautiful, she was impossible not to stare at. She wore hospital scrubs and walked with a severe limp. Blood trickled from a gash just beneath her rib cage.

Cathey and Clara took several steps into the depot and faced the remaining four mechanics. Compos shifted, turning his weapon on Clara. He fired quickly and purposefully, hitting her several times in the chest. She wobbled as each bullet tore through her. She lost her footing and collapsed near the door.

Cathey trained both his weapons on Compos. He fired repeatedly and Compos finally went down. There were three mechanics left.

I can leave you alive or kill you where you stand. Your choice. Put your guns down and let me walk out of here.

Lennon thought about his options but didn't know what to do. The orders were to shoot anyone trying to leave and Lennon was a man of principle. Clara sat near the door, gasping for air. Cathey stepped back and said something to her. She tried to get to her feet but collapsed as he reached for her.

Jones, the new mechanic working with Cathey stood and fired toward the woman. He missed widely and Cathey returned fire, dropping him with two head shots.

Two of you left. I'm walking out of here –

Before he could finish, three shots came from the direction of the door with the security panel. One of the bullets tore through Cathey's left knee, buckling him.

The nurse with a pistol bigger than her hand fumbled with its weight and tried to fire again but not before Cathey killed her and the other nurse with a volley of automatic shots. He struggled to stand. And that's when the two remaining mechanics heard the child and saw the blood trickling out from the backpack.

Can you stand, he asked the woman.

She shook her head, no.

I can't feel my legs. I think they may have severed my spine. I don't know but the pain is unbearable.

You go. Take him. Do as we planned.

I'm not leaving without you. He glanced up at the video monitor.

Yes. You are. For his sake you must. They will destroy him. I'll catch up. Promise.

I can't leave you. They'll-

They'll do what they'll do. You must get him to safety. And you will.

A group of Grey Suits entered the hallway and began shooting, cutting Clara off. The child screamed from the violence of the rounds striking all around his father. The woman sank to the floor. Blood dotted her body. Breaths came much too quickly. Cathey turned and fired repeatedly, hitting several of them.

The last two mechanics stood and fired at Cathey as he was engaged with the soldiers. Their shots were errant, missing widely. Cathey managed to turn and fire at Len, dropping him with a shot to his thigh. The other one tried to turn and run but not before Cathey clipped his ankle with a shot. Cathey quickly fired again, hitting the man between his eyes. The force of the impact destroyed the front of his skull and sent the mechanic reeling against the wall. The soldiers approached and Cathey kicked the door shut, separating them. He fired two rounds into the security panel and the soldiers were trapped behind the doors. Cathey, Clara, the child and Len remained on the outside. The soldiers fired several times at the doors but the area was secure. Their bullets ricocheted about them, killing another three of them. The remaining soldiers turned and started their way toward the old mine shaft. The only remaining exit in the base.

Cathey walked toward Len. He aimed his weapons at him. Please don't make me kill you. She needs help and I've got to get my son out of here. They'll both die if I stay.

Why? What do they want from you?

It's a long complicated story. I don't have time to explain it all. I've got to go. Can you walk?

Barely. I've been hit in the back and thigh. I'm losing a lot of blood.

He turned to Clara and her breathing was ragged.

I don't know what to do, Cathey said.

They're going to kill you. Whether it's now or sometime down the road, they'll get you. That's what they do. You know that. You can't escape.

Well, I've got to try. For my son's sake. What's your name?

Len. Lennie.

Cathey lowered the back pack to the ground. His son squirmed inside, covered in blood.

Is he okay?

He's in a backpack full of sacks of blood. His mother's and mine. They shot them up. The boy is fine. My experiments will have to wait. Besides, he said, pointing at Clara, she was the scientist in the family.

Cathey withdrew a series of cables from his bag connected to two round sensors on either end.

Do you know what this is?

Len looked the cables over and nodded.

You ever had this done to you?

A mind wipe, Len asked.

Yeah, a mind wipe.

No. I heard it's horrible.

Cathey smiled. The old ones were but not mine. These are a walk on the beach compared to the old ones. Give me your arm.

Len reached out for Cathey and he saw the dragon tattoo on Cathey's right arm. It could've been the loss of blood or the exhaustion but as Cathey put the sensors on his arm, he swore that dragon was moving in swirls up and down Cathey's arm.

Couple of things. Before I start this. My name's not Cathey. Repeat that.

Your name's not Cathey.

You don't know me.

I don't know you.

She is very important and must live.
She is very important and must live.
The child is dead.
Len paused and looked at Cathey.
Repeat it. Now!
The child is dead, Len said.
Now again, all together.

Your name's not Cathey, I do not know you, she is very important and must live, the child is dead. He exhaled deeply.

Again.

As he began to speak again, Cathey touched the sensor that he had placed on Len's hand. It glowed a brilliant red and sparked up the cords attaching it to the sensor on the man's temple. Sparks flew and Cathey backed away. He hoped it wouldn't kill him. This was, after all, Cathey's own design of a mind wipe. Len shook.

As the sparks flew, he bent over the woman that looked so like his love. She took shallow breaths and opened her eyes. He knelt before her and she spoke in his ear, how'd I do?

He put his lips to her ear, I couldn't have asked for more. Neither could Clara.

They will come, you know. I can't keep them away forever.
We all know that.

They'll figure it out. Sooner or later.

Maybe not. Their top scientist is hopefully at the end of that mineshaft back there. In ten minutes, she'll be out and in an hour, she'll be back in town. Just another dead person walking. Waiting for the Cluster to take her.

He pulled back from her and kissed her forehead.

Wasting time aren't you, she asked with eyes closed and the scent of butterscotch on her breath. The damndest thing about clones. Their breath always smells like butterscotch.

I've got to do this last thing. Like we talked about.

I know.

I'm sorry. But-

Don't be such a pussy and do it. I'll be fine. I just got shot like ten times and I'm still here. What's a little mind mushing going to do that these bullets haven't?

He pulled the second set of wires from the backpack and attached the sensors to her hand and temple.

You are not his mother, repeat it.

I am not his mother.

There is no James Cathey.

There is no James Cathey.

Your boy is dead.

She grimaced as she prepared to say the words.

He looked at her and a single tear dropped from her left eye. The blue swimming in a haze of tears. Just say the words. She was doing fantastically. Anyone watching this over the video feed would see nothing but the tragic parting of two lovers forced to take extraordinary steps to save their child. He'd find her, he promised.

My boy is dead, she said.

And with that, James Cathey tore his identity from her mind.

He stood as she shook from the jolt of the mind wipe. Len was convulsing and he felt his neck for a pulse. He was still alive. Cathey pulled a black panel box out of the backpack. He approached the door where the two nurses lost their lives. He shoved them out of the way with his boot and ripped the panel from the wall. As he did this, a conduit of electricity snaked out of the wall and clutched his right arm. It shot him full of electricity and lit his arm on fire. The electricity forced his hand to contract around the source and he couldn't let go.

Reflexively, he gripped the panel tighter. It dug into his hand, splitting the skin and spilling more of his blood. His arm was on fire and his skin boiled beneath it. He tried to brush it away with his other hand, but the fire raged. He clenched his teeth as the electricity filled his body and the skin bubbled. The pain jolted his brain and he felt himself swimming away from where he was tethered. Forcing himself to stay focused, he turned his attention to the wires feeding the electricity. He fought through the pain and the wave of unconsciousness that threatened to bring him down. He cut the wires to the live panel. Once the electricity stopped, his hand released its grip and the panel dropped to the floor. He gently smothered the fire with his other arm and he was left with blackened, barbecued skin hanging from his right arm.

He spun the split wires into his new panel and punched in a code and the door opened with a swoosh of cold air spilling out. He pulled the backpack on and turned one last time. He saw her and Len both breathing, with gentle spasms coursing through their bodies. At least they weren't smoking. That was a plus.

He pulled his frayed sleeves over his scorched arm. The pain of pulling that fabric from his wounds later would bring him to his knees. But for the moment, he was free.

Limping through the doorway, he turned and disarmed the panel on this side of the hall. The door drew shut and then he heard the lock. He ripped the panel from the wall again, ensuring no one would make it through this spot for a while.

He made his way down the hall when his son began to cry. He took the pack off and brought the child out.

He rocked him and made soft shushing noises toward the child. The baby was instantly quiet and he thought the child was smiling. The boy was covered in blood and Cathey made an attempt to clear the blood away from his mouth and eyes. He did a good job of smearing the blood across the boy's face but failed to clean him up much. The boy resembled a deranged clown with too much rouge all over his face. But the boy was happy and continued smiling.

The man tilted the pack and spilled the remaining blood bags onto the floor. He wiped it out as best he could and rearranged the blankets the boy's mother had assembled for the journey. She had also stuffed steel bottles within the multiple pockets of the pack. She had told him to heat the bottles for a minute or two but he had no way to do this. He cradled the boy and offered him the cold bottle. At first, the boy spit out the nipple from the bottle, but after some coaxing, he was able to get the boy to eat. Once the bottle was empty, he rocked the boy and soon he was asleep. He put the boy back into the pack and gently slid it on his back.

The hallway was quiet, as he had hoped it would be even with the events that transpired. This particular hallway, he learned, led to what was once a storage unit for warheads. It was immense. As he walked down the hall, it grew from a height of seven feet to soaring ceilings lost in the darkness more than fifty feet high. It was as long as a soccer field across. The warheads had long since vanished, used to jump-start the cooling of the Earth during the Great Surge and never replaced because this facility's purpose changed after that. That's when they started making Mechs. Now, lining the walls were hundreds, if not thousands, of Mechs ready for dispersal. A hangar of Mechs. His Mechs.

Making his way down the vast corridor, he silently counted the rows of stored Mechs. Once he made it to row one hundred, he guessed there were another two hundred rows. Each row contained twenty Mechs. This was just on the left side of the hangar. The right side was a mirror image of the left, just with different models of Mechs. He designed most of the units lined up and knew their strengths and weaknesses. Toward the front, those Mechs that made up the first twenty or so rows, were Mech Bots or Mechanical Robots.

They were machines capable of standing on two legs, carrying shoulder mortar launchers on each side of their heads, multiple blasters in their arms and equipped with over fifty explosive tip projectiles housed within each leg. The machines stood approximately eight feet high and four feet across and had complete three-hundred-and-sixty-degree vision, day or night. They were nearly indestructible unless pierced between the housing unit of the head, which contains the CPU for the machine, and the body portion of the unit. The space is incredibly small, but if one was up close, a knife swipe could sever the CPU from the power supply, thus terminating the unit. He had tried several options to house the CPU but found this current configuration to be the most sustainable. The Grey Suits wanted CPU survival if the unit was compromised with a direct strike to the body portion of the machine. However, in over ten thousand simulations, he was never once able to compromise the unit. Thus, they were greenlit for production.

The most glaring weakness, at least in Cathey's eyes, was that the Grey Suits also insisted on a centralized control system for the entire fleet of Mechs. Cathey fought against it for a few days, but realized if there was no outside override for the Mechs, then destroying them would be as simple as destroying the unit housing the Mech CPU. On the other hand, taking control of the centralized control system meant you would have control of the entire fleet of Mechs. Assuming you had passwords.

Cathey wasn't about to leave his creations that vulnerable to destruction or take-over. Unbeknownst to the Grey Suits, Cathey created a Cargo Radio Maintenance (CRM) failsafe and hid a viral program deep within the software design of the Mechs' memory. Activating the CRM and then executing a series of commands would place the Mechs in the control of whoever had access to the failsafe codes. Any attempt to recall the Mechs from that point forward would result in a total block of all transmissions other than those preceded by the CRM codes. The CRM code allowed the keeper of the codes to operate the units via radio frequency or computer. Cathey believed that if the Mechs needed to be recalled in such a manner, computers might have failed or the grid operating the computers was compromised.

Radio frequency operation was central to recalling the Mechs. The code Cathey imbedded deep within the entire fleet was CRM-114. It was criminally simple but infinitely impossible to access. The difficulty arose once the CRM was set to receive transmissions. The only way to recall the Mechs at that point would be to enter a lengthy RSA code. An RSA code was simply a recall code for the Mechs. The code, based on semi-prime numerology, required the code-breaker to come up with a natural number that was the product of two prime numbers. Cathey's code was over two-hundred and thirty-two decimal digits.

To his right, the hall was lined with the much larger Hex Bots. Those units would hunt him and his boy later in life. This version of the six-legged walkers was much smaller than the later ones. These early units were good for mass destruction but little else. They were cumbersome and prone to tripping. In later years, the middle legs would be equipped with balance tiers which would keep the unit upright. If, on the off-chance it fell, the middle legs would stabilize the unit and bring it back up within seconds. At this point, Cathey didn't care that they might fall over themselves. They would still be capable of extensive damage if loaded correctly. He counted nearly seventy of these units.

As he counted, he was surprised to see several units of the only machine housed here that he didn't create. These were the

Autonomous Robotic Explorers or ARex, designed by Dr. Britney Schneider at Georgia State Technical University, in the early days of the Martian Colonies. He had improved on the solar batteries, the CPU power and added a more ferocious drill bit, but otherwise, they were the same today as they were when Stone Aerospace launched them in the early 2030s.

These units were designed to explore the Martian subsurface, drilling several hundred feet at a time. The ARex was roughly four meters long and two and a half meters wide. It possessed sonars for navigation, a super computer to process information, eight thrusters with twin battery stacks, a suite of accelerometers, and velocity loggers. The machines also contained a full array of observational instruments, including liquid and core samplers, as well as an autonomous onboard microscope which sought evidence of life.

The ARex communicated with a positional Kelland mother craft using Wi-Fi. In order to keep the one and half ton machine boring into the Earth, the ARex employed two variable-resistant engines that sensed temperature, soil composition, and salinity of the soil around it. The massive machine was capable of reaching depths exceeding two thousand meters.

The most impressive feature of the ARex was its self-guided navigation. An array of sonars located objects within a four-hundred-meter radius to map the machine's surroundings while the onboard accelerometers, velocity loggers and guidance instruments helped to inform the ARex about its position within the space. The specialized sonar array also generated 3D maps in real time. The technique, known as 3D Simultaneous Localization and Mapping (3D-SLAM), allowed the robot to navigate for itself.

He approached the units and rested his hand on one of its drill bits. The machine resembled the extinct rhinoceros, albeit on a much larger scale. It sat on four massive legs with the formidable drill in the center of its head acting as its horn. These machines would be widely useful to him. They could be set to bore into the surface hundreds of miles from here and map the surface from amazing depths. He'd at least know where they were for a time until they discovered how to turn them off. As he surveyed the hangar, they'd also be invaluable in boring into the surrounding mountain that encased them. He'd tunnel his way out of this bitch if he had to.

The Grey Suits would be on their way down into the mountain and he had to get these units up and running. He made his way back to the computer terminals that operated the Mechs. Mounted above them, the wrist gauntlets hung silently. He pulled one down, untethered the connecting cable and hoped it would charge in time. It was black in color and covered the man's full lower arm, up to his elbow. Within the wrist gauntlet were several technologically advanced features including Sat-Com, self-destruct and cloaking. The most important feature currently would be the ability to control the Mechs remotely. He flipped the graphene cover that hid the CPU and held the power button. It flashed twice but then nothing. He had to get the computers up to charge the unit.

He swiped the card Clara had given him before they separated and as he suspected, the screen stayed black. He carefully opened the back pack and his son was sleeping soundly. He was tiny, but his color was good and he seemed content, even given the shit they'd just been through.

He took out the master card reader and plugged it into the side of the centralized control computer terminal. After a few seconds, he tried to power the computers back up. This time, they blinked to life and the home screen emerged from its sleep. He swiped her card again and waited. After several seconds, the machine started to roll through numbers.

Activity to his right distracted him and he glanced up from the table. The Grey Suits were assembling in the room he'd sealed off. Several Grey Suits approached the doors wearing K-Gloves and full combat uniforms. The K-Gloves were relics from the Space Station days when astronauts needed more force in their mechanical abilities to repair and build the space station. After some modifications, the K-Gloves these soldiers wore gave them about three hundred foot pounds of pressure to apply to most any situation. They began to pull on the door but the man had little fear that they would break through. The doors were designed to withstand multiple hits by neutron bombs. They weren't opening without a code, he hoped.

Behind them, several other Grey Suits put Len and Clara on stretchers. He didn't know if they were alive or dead. And he had no time to worry about that now. His singular focus was getting the boy off the base and to safety.

Finally, the card reader chirped and the computer system blinked on. At the same time, the wrist gauntlet began to pulse red. It was charging. He began typing and it was obvious that no one in operations had bothered to change his codes to the units. He pulled up the diagnostics for the hangar and one by one each row came to life.

As the Mechs lowered to the ground, Cathey saw the AU soldiers fire up a photon cutting blade. Another relic of NASA, this blade was a thousand times more powerful than a diamond bit and could cut through rugged Martian minerals. This blast door would only be a minimal impediment to the Greys getting in and allowing the whole base access to the hangar.

He quickly set up the Mech Bots and assembled them to protect the door. They began their slow, deliberate walk aiming their dual blasters directly at the door. He had twenty rows of ten Mech Bots across protecting him from the door.

The photon blade began to spew sparks on the other side. Once it got through, he would have only minutes to get out.

He sent the ARex units, six in all, to the back of the hangar. He could hear them lumbering toward their designated spot. He had each one programmed to drill into the walls of the hangar and into the mountain. From there, their paths would snake out until the unit reached the outside world. He'd follow unit 9. It was boring into the section of the mountain that contained the old Aerospace Defense Command. From there, he could take various routes to escape. The old Aerospace compound had not been used in nearly seventy years. It would take the Grey Suits hours to figure out where he went.

The Hex Bots would guard the back of the hangar and protect the boring holes of the ARex units. He went through the code once again to make sure he hadn't missed anything and set the units in motion. Then he transferred the command control to the wrist gauntlet.

A message appeared on the computer screen

Cathey, you will not escape this, you have to know that. Give yourself up. Save your son. Save yourself.

He thought about doing the right thing for a moment. He wanted to simply power the computer off and send the Mechs out to do his bidding. But that wasn't him. Not anymore.

I am saving myself and my son. Who is this?

Serafino. Let's stop this nonsense. We can talk.

What's to talk about? You want my boy. It was right there in the notes. And I can't figure out if you mean to kill him or just keep him alive long enough to find a cure.

We don't have any such plans, Cathey. If we needed him for a cure, we've got more than enough stem cells collected through his umbilical cord. You know that.

I'm not a scientist. I don't know what you need.

No, your scientist is back here with us. She's in critical condition. We don't have any illusions that she's going to make it. I don't know how you and the boy will make it without her.

We'll figure it out.

We're nearly through the door. This is your last chance. Call the Mechs off.

Why don't you turn them off? You're in the system.

You know we can't do that.

Guess you should've listened to me when I told you not to centralize command of the killer robots.

Lots of firepower in there with you, Cathey.

You've got an army behind you. My firepower dwarfs yours. You'll be fine, Serafino.

My guys bleed. Yours don't.

Then I guess you better give up. Let me walk out of here. Save your men.

He could see the flash of sparks finally appearing on his side of the door. They began to slice upwards, shearing the door.

If I have them stand down, you'll turn the Mechs off?

Tell your men to stand down.

With that, the sparks from the photon blade stopped and he could see the Greys lower their weapons. They stood before the door, shoulder to shoulder. His finger hovered over the keyboard. He pondered shutting the Mechs down. They would operate on his instructions until the batteries needed recharging. He had them capable of full operation for ten days without a recharge. Once they found their way out into the sun, the solar cells they carried with them would continuously recharge them until they were either destroyed or someone was able to communicate with them.

He pulled up the cameras on the ARex units. Several were hundreds of feet into the mountain. Unit 9 was within the walls of the Aerospace compound. It was slowly rolling toward the armory.

Cathey?

I'm coming in. Tell your men to clear out. I don't like dealing with them and all their attachments. I'm only dealing with you.

That can be arranged but I'm not in the hangar. It's going to take me a little while to get there. I've got an entire base to navigate and currently everything is locked down. Once I know you're in the infirmary, I'll get there. You have my word.

Is she okay?

She's alive. Barely.

Cathey switched the cameras to view the outside surroundings. Hundreds of soldiers were lining up. Several battalions were moving into position. Tanks and armored vehicles were converging on the mountain. All over a child. She had been right. They had to get him out of here. No matter the means.

I'm disappointed.

Me too, Cathey.

You're doing what you should be doing. Moving your men outside into position.

You didn't say anything about them. We agreed on the men in the infirmary standing down.

And if I ask for you to recall your men outside?

You haven't budged. I'm not making any more deals.

Smart. Invincibility lies in the defense; the possibility of victory in the attack.

Sun Tzu?

Something like that.

He typed in a few more commands, moving the remaining Mech Bots into position. Then he unplugged the wrist gauntlet and pulled it on. He flipped the graphene cover and the control panel glowed red. Making his way toward the back of the hangar, he turned and saw the Mechs systematically marching toward the blast doors.

A digital countdown clock appeared on the wrist gauntlet and Serafino's computer screen. Serafino tried to type but his cursor merely blinked and then froze. The screen locked, taken over by the countdown clock. He watched it tick down from thirty. At ten, a cacophonous airhorn siren began to blare through the infirmary and the base. Each number down resulted in another blast from the airhorn. Nine – *blaaaaaattt,* eight – *blaaaaaattt.* Serafino stared helplessly at his screen and then glanced at the closed circuit. The Mech Bots were assembling in front of the door and for as far back as he could see. He tried to recall his men but the communications were jammed. Nothing was getting through. His men fired up the proton blade again and started cutting. As the numbers clicked down, 7, 6, 5, 4, 3, 2, 1, he knew it was too late.

The Mechs on the front line moved in as Greys continued to cut through the doors of the hangar.

Goddamit, he screamed into the microphone. Stop cutting! You're making it easier on them and they don't need any help.

The Greys continued cutting unknowingly violating a direct order from Serafino. He could only watch in horror as they ignored him. They never heard him. Cathey made sure of that.

The Mech Bots shuffled closer to the door, dual blasters raised. They came to rest before the door and an audible double click echoed across the hangar as the blasters were armed. The Bots raised their heads and a glowing blue light escaped from behind their ocular panels flooding the hangar with a piercing cerulean ocean of light.

The Greys looked up at that point and saw the hangar awash with blue. Swimming in the light was the burnished black of the Mech Bots' armor. Before the Grey Suits had a chance to question their next move, the Bots opened fire, spraying the wall with their .950 caliber rounds. The boundary between the infirmary and the hangar dissolved under the assault. Ceiling tiles crashed to the ground and the Mech Bots inched their way forward. The Greys fired a few rounds but were overwhelmed by the force and numbers of shells the Mechs discharged. They were hit so many times they were dead before the Mechs crossed the threshold into the infirmary.

Cathey and his boy made their way through the labyrinth of Mech and Hex Bots to where the ARexs were boring into the walls. He chose the path of Number Nine and slipped into the tunnel. It was just large enough for Cathey to run through with only a slight hunching of his shoulders. He turned once and saw the vibrant blue of the Mechs behind him. As he continued down the tunnel, the temperatures dropped and he worried about his boy.

He stopped and took the backpack off and opened it. The boy was sleeping soundly, wrapped in a thin blanket. He felt the boy's forehead and he felt neither hot nor cold. He pulled another blanket up around him and then re-positioned the backpack on his back and started again.

This would be one of many times that he would worry about his son's comfort, not knowing that he needn't worry. The infant was, in fact, quite comfortable, despite the jostling and thunderous explosions going off behind them.

The tunnel continued on for quite some time. The ARex made good time and the man thought perhaps the mountain's mineral composition wasn't nearly as unbreakable as they had thought. Maybe it was just the sheer power of the ARex that was making short thrift of the rock. Either way, the man ran for several miles before meeting the ARex again.

Once he caught up with the ARex, it stood ready for additional instructions. He typed a series of commands and initiated the unit.

This one paused for only a moment and was then on the move through the armory of the Aerospace Defense Command center. Despite having allegedly not been in use for nearly seventy years, he noticed quite a bit of materials strewn about with the Kelland Mining Company name and logo on it. There were jackets, helmets, shirts, binders, and jump suits all emblazoned with the familiar KMC yellow letters on the black oval. In white, beneath the KMC, were the words, Digging New Worlds. He always thought it was an ambitious slogan, given the only other world they were digging on besides Earth was Mars. But at least they were forward-thinking.

Whit'urr ye daein' 'ere, a voice bellowed from beyond a series of doors. He spoke with a thick Scottish accent.

The voice belonged to a grizzled man at least sixty years old. Emerging from the office hidden behind the doors, he aimed an ancient Colt .45 squarely at Cathey. Despite his backcountry appearance, his clothing appeared almost new. He wore the KMC jumpsuit with a yellow bandana tied to the top of his head. It too bore the KMC logo. A reddish beard peppered with gray that resembled a feral cat clung to the man's face.

It took him a moment and then he realized there was a massive bore hole behind the man he currently held a gun on. He looked past Cathey, down the tunnel.

Whit th' hell is gaun oan?

Cathey pondered his next move. The Mechs would be on the move and most likely had the infirmary under control. The other units should have moved out from there and on to the base. The likelihood soldiers from the base would be here any time soon was remote.

I didn't realize the old Aerospace Command Center was being used, Cathey said.

Fur tis tap secret, genius. Who're ya?

Probably best we not get too acquainted.

Tha's ripe. Ye dinnae hae much leverage in this situation. Now, who're ye?

Cathey placed his arms before him and quickly input a series of directives on the gauntlet.

What've ye git thare, the old man asked and pointed the gun toward the gauntlet.

Leverage, Cathey said. The bore hole behind him exploded in a spray of dirt, rock and twisted metal. Several Mechs tore through the hole in the wall, dual blasters raised. Cathey fell to his knees as they opened fire on the man before him. He wilted under the massive firepower and was shredded into a thousand pieces. He managed two shots on the lead Mech, but in the end, the gun dropped into the minced gore that was the Kelland Mining worker.

Cathey turned and typed in new commands for the Mechs. They began to walk forward, toward the newly dug bore hole. All except the one Mech that had been hit. Cathey peered into the two holes that had pierced the supposedly impenetrable armor of the Mech. A yellowish green fluid that looked like anti-freeze oozed out of the holes. The operating fluid was housed in a cylinder that lined the core of the unit. The bullet had to tear through a lining ten times tougher than diamond and it had done so with ease.

Before he made his way down the tunnel, he picked up the old man's Colt and opened his pack. His boy opened an eye when the light of the room hit him. Cathey thought the kid was smiling. He emptied the gun of its bullets before sliding it into a pocket near the boy.

The Mech with the pierced armor made a series of hisses as the operating fluid hit hot machine parts. It was now dripping through the Mech and pooling around the unit. Cathey walked up to the unit and pulled a knife from the side of his pack. The blue light scanned

106

rapidly left to right and then faded out as he swiped the knife across the CPU tether in the unit's neck cavity. Imperceptible to Cathey was the fact that as he pulled the knife across the line, the Mech was in the process of raising its weapons in self-defense.

He backed away from the unit and set the timer for self-destruct. In five minutes, if the unit detected any motion, there would be one hell of an explosion. He shouldered his backpack and made his way deeper into the mountain. Behind him, the Mechs were blasting through the infirmary.

Variant

CHAPTER 10

Sometime in 2093

For weeks now, he felt as though someone was following him. He'd taken every precaution and doubled back a few times but at each turn he'd come away with nothing more than the feeling of being watched. He had encountered people on the road, but like him, most kept their distance. He learned early on to steer clear of cities. Once he lost connections with the Mechs, he lost any advantage he once had. The boy was all he had left. And he still wasn't sure if they meant to kill him or use him for parts. Or both.

In the cities, the Grey Suits were everywhere now. Patrols were larger and local police forces had either been consumed by them or executed. Most fell into line. The cancer death rate was up significantly and the Grey Suits were the only ones with anything close to a treatment for the cancers. Some in the media were calling the phenomenon the Cluster because it was usually three or four different cancers that raged at the same time. Sometimes, the doctors couldn't tell which cancer was the killer. Brain cancer and pancreatic cancer would start their meals but then stomach cancer would erupt and the victim would be dead in days. The Grey Suits didn't have a cure, but they had the next best thing: drugs that managed to keep people alive for just a bit longer. The drugs gave them hope that life might get back to normal. Of course, the cost was significant. For willing members of the proletariat, ratting out a neighbor or two could buy months of Cluster-specific drugs. Thus, the Grey Suits had support despite their repulsive reputations. With that support came prying eyes.

He didn't know what type of bounty they'd put on his head, but he knew if they had, it would be substantial. All told, the bounty money and Cluster drugs could set someone up for quite a while to live as comfortable a life as possible now. For many, that was the dream.

When he could, he took vehicles until they ran out of fuel. When he couldn't find a vehicle, he'd walk. In those days, he did a lot of walking. Back then, the days were long and slow-going. His back would ache from the child and then he'd carry the boy in his arms. His arms would go numb more often than not. During those times, the feeling of being watched was overwhelming. He felt safer in the vehicles. But the vehicles drew their own attention. And they were dangerous for the boy. At least in his mind.

At an old diner that looked like something out of a movie, he sat amongst the waste and pondered his next move. He spoke to the boy who was propped up on the pack. He spoke of his desire to reach his family's cabin. How safe they'd be once they reached it. The boy listened intently but his hunger grew and the man had no food. Nothing the infant could eat. They ran out of formula after narrowly escaping the last city they passed through. The little boy whimpered and then broke out in a full cry.

He surveyed the parking lot through the broken glass of the diner and saw no one. So he wandered back to the kitchen of the diner, crunching glass beneath his feet. Two corpses lay next to one another and he paused, holding his breath. They'd been dead awhile he figured. The bodies had been picked over by whatever scavenger found its way into the All You Can Eat Café off scenic route 237.

Anything remotely related to food was gone. A rat scurried past him and out an opening in the weathered door at the back. He kicked aside pieces of trash, looking for anything that might be edible. Then he heard a thump to his right and a door flush with the wall opened. A girl of seventeen or eighteen emerged from the darkness, kicking the door wide and pulling an AR-15 from her shoulder in a fluid motion. She had it aimed at the man's right eye.

Move and I'll put every bullet in this magazine right through your skull. She was tall for her age and toned with a muscular frame. Her face was round with brilliant jade-colored eyes, set perfectly apart above a rather slender nose. Dazzling red hair spilled out from beneath the cap she wore and spiraled down her back. A lone lock dangled before her right eye and she shook her head to clear it.

The man froze, uncertain if she was capable of pulling the trigger. Just looking for something to eat, he said. He instinctively moved his right hand up to cover his eye.

She flicked the weapon up at the same second and fired four rounds at the wall behind him. The baby screamed, now hungry and scared.

I said don't move. That your kid?

Instincts, sorry. Yes, that's my boy. May I lower my hand?

No you may not. Keep it up. Get the other one up too and hold them both real high.

The man did as she demanded. She circled about him, inspecting him. She looked out into the diner toward the baby. Any weapons, she asked.

Leaning up against the counter out there, he said with a sigh. Stupid, he thought.

How're you surviving out here doing stupid shit like that? And with a baby?

Haven't been out here long.

You from the city? She continued to circle the man.

I'm from *a* city. What city are you talking about?

Sioux City. They got power, food, you name it. Just like the old days. Only people I see out this way seem to be escapees from there.

Why aren't you there now? You seem to be a little young to be out here all alone.

Who says I'm alone? Maybe I have a gang of killers out there just waiting to rip you apart.

She circled around one more time and dropped her eyes to the man's shoes. The next second she dipped the barrel of the rifle slightly. The man swiftly grabbed the barrel, slid to his right and brought the weapon up with tremendous force. The stock crashed into the girl's chin and sent her flying backward. He trained the weapon on her.

You were too close. Don't ever get that close to someone out here. Too many chances for that to happen to you again.

What do you know?

I know there's not any gang of killers out there.

Bullshit!

If there were, I would have seen them. I watched this place for about half the day before I decided to come in. You're alone.

Believe what you want old man. They'll be back any minute, she shouted.

Let 'em come. I'm not here to kill you or cause them any trouble. Like I said, I'm just looking for something the boy can eat.

Ain't nothing to eat. Hasn't been since the Grey Suits swept through about a month ago. They got all the food. Hoarding it in the cities.

Why aren't you in the city, then? This doesn't look like a place for a young lady on her own.

She rolled her eyes at him, thinking of a lie. They gave me six months to live. That was a year ago. I left when my parents both died. They didn't have money and I couldn't get any treatment. I figured I could come out here and die on my own terms. I just haven't died yet.

Aiming guns at strangers might change that.

Screw you! Aren't you sick? You look like you're fifty or something. I haven't seen many fifty-year-olds around. And where's your Code bracelet?

He thought for a moment, not wanting to give himself away. I must've lost it, he said. Yours?

Yeah, must've lost mine, too. She smirked at him as she said it and rolled her eyes. She could lie too.

He thought about his words carefully. I'm sick. I've been sick. But obviously I'm not dead yet.

You don't look sick.

How do sick people look?

I dunno, she said in disgust, her gaze leaving his and floating toward the gaping holes in the front of the diner where windows used to hang. Sick, you know? Pale. Skinny. Dying, shit. Your kid gonna shut up?

Not until he eats. He's a baby.

Hey, wait a minute. Wait a hot minute. She pointed at him and started nodding her head. You're the one they were talking about.

One what? He gripped the gun a little tighter and began to position himself to protect the boy better.

The one who blew that army base all to hell in Colorado. I saw your picture. The news in Sioux Falls has you plastered all over the vids all day and all night. You and that baby are worth years of Cluster drugs. Maybe enough to keep me alive as long as you.

Don't know what or who you're talking about, but you've got me confused with the wrong person.

If you were him, you think I'd really turn you in?

Don't know. Sounds like it. Cluster drugs and all that money. I'm tempted to turn myself in and see if I can collect.

Screw the Grey Suits. Once our money ran out, they kicked my mom and dad outta that hospital so fast we didn't have time to blink. Threw us right out on the sidewalk. With all our shit. We'd spent all our money on the drugs and nothing was happening for either of them. We lost our house cause all their money went to the drugs. Not even any left for me. I don't want their shit. I don't care who you are.

She looked at the man and her jade-colored eyes threatened to spill the tears she'd been holding back for months. If you look in my bag, there might be something in there for the boy. I think he might could eat it.

No games.

No, no games. Really. There's baby food in my bag. Carrots, peas, bananas. Some other shit. I think I still got cereal in there too. Just gotta mix it with water. Keep him alive at least.

Why do you –

Why do I have baby food? That's a long story mister. I don't want to talk about it. I won't ask you if you're that man and you don't ask me why I have baby food. Deal?

Deal, he said and bent down and opened the girl's pack. Sure enough, inside were numerous jars of baby food, wrapped in thin coats of bubble wrap.

There were small spoons at the bottom of the pack, too, coated in soft rubber. All the technological advances society had made and kids still got fed with rubber-coated spoons, the man thought. Guess you can't improve on perfection. Of course, the babies couldn't complain.

You want me to feed him? You could keep watch.

Ok, that's fair.

She went to get the baby and brought his backpack with her. She grabbed the rifle as she passed by as well and handed it to him. Can he sit up yet?

Barely. I haven't tried solid food. I don't know if he's going to like it.

He'll like it. Gotta eat, right?

She propped him up and started with the bananas which the baby loved. He gummed them and enthusiastically swallowed them, then bobbed his head for more.

He likes them, she said.

Looks like it. So, do you have a name?

Everyone has a name, she said.

You gonna tell me yours?

It's April. Like the month. My parents were really creative, she said sarcastically.

Just a hint of sarcasm in that, he said.

It's a long story. So what about you? What'd your wife call you?

See, now that might get you in trouble down the road. If I was that guy you thought I was. He had a name.

I don't remember it.

I could lie.

You could. But I'm feeding your kid. And when we're done here, you're going to ask me to come with you. You can't do this by yourself and stay alive.

Really?

Really.

My name's Cathey.

Oh my gods, that's awful. Even if you were going to make up a name, why a girl's name?

115

It's my last name. Everyone calls me Cathey. He laughed and said, a long time ago I had a normal name. I'm with you though. That was a million lives before this one. Just call me Cathey. Makes it easier.

And your son? What's his name?

Kid doesn't have a name.

You're kidding, right?

No.

He's got a name and you just don't want to tell me?

No.

You didn't name your own kid? He's nearly a year old! What kind of father are you to deprive this kid an identity?

Damn. I didn't realize I was doing him such harm.

You have no idea. It messes with your head.

Personal experience?

Something like that. You gotta call him something besides boy.

Kid?

C'mon Cathey. You're being a jerk.

You name him then, he said to her and then immediately regretted it. He didn't want to attach himself to an identity. If he did, then he would be susceptible to loss. Out here, he couldn't afford that emotion.

Who were your parents?

Cathey shook his head. Too much information.

Oh that's right. You can't share such confidential information with me because the Grey Suits may grab me and then I'll be a liability to you. Good lord.

I had a friend who died while we were in high school. It was probably the Cluster but it was in the early days. We called him

Mattie. His real name was Matthew Alanny. I always liked that name.

Ok, she said, not sure if he was lying or not. She went along with it though.

Mattie it is, she said.

When she looked down at the baby and called him Mattie, she swore he smiled. It was a good name. It fit him. But after April disappeared, he told his father to stop calling him that. It was too painful.

We probably need to figure out what we're doing about tonight. It's getting late.

Told you you'd want my help.

I couldn't leave you out here in good conscience.

So, you're a good guy?

I think the issue of good or evil depends on which side of the conflict you're on.

I guess. But you don't know which you are?

I have had to do a lot of things that I'm not proud of. But it was out of necessity. I know who I am but I also know now what I am capable of. Before all this, I didn't. But back then I'd have answered your question pretty fast and said I was a good guy. Now? Now I just do those things I need to survive.

Like raping young girls wasn't one of those things you did out of necessity was it?

Good lord! No! Gods no.

Just making sure. Not that I'd let you get close enough to get me anyway. I'd slice your balls off before you got near me.

Ok. You're tough. I get it. You could still stand to learn a few things. Slicing someone's balls might not be the most expeditious way to deter a rapist.

Alright. You show me.

I'll show you but we need to find somewhere safe to sleep. We can talk about Lessons in the morning.

Safe back here, she says, pointing behind her.

What's that?

Cooler. Or what was a cooler. I jimmied the locks, switched 'em around and now it only locks from the inside. There's also a little door in the floor. I dug it out and if things get too crazy, I can crawl outside. Might be big enough for you. Not sure. It was there before but it was tiny. Comes out outside.

What'll we do for food?

Yeah, sorry. I lied about that. There's enough canned goods in there to last us years.

Thank gods, he said and opened the door to the cooler wider and saw rows upon rows of canned goods.

Just steer clear of the potted meat. Shit went bad awhile back and it didn't get better with age. The chicken and tuna are to die for at this point though.

They secured the door and April turned on a few battery-powered lamps. They ate in silence, lost in their own thoughts. They were reviewing answers in their heads and trying to recollect the lies they told.

Cathey let his eyes wander around the cooler and he saw a piece of paper hanging from a nail on one of the shelves. He put his tuna down and pulled the sheet off the nail. He read the entries that consisted of various food products on the left side and then dollar amounts on the right.

What's this? Some sort of inventory? Doesn't look near long enough.

She half smiled at him and said, no, just keeping track.

Of what, he asked.

Of what I've taken. Someone paid good money to stock those shelves. I'm no thief. So I'm keeping track of what I took and I'll leave a note that she'll get her money just as soon as I can pay her back.

Cathey let out a chuckle. Wow, he said, flipping the paper over to the other side.

Wow what? You think this is funny?

No, it's just – he stopped himself, thinking of the right words. You're a good person. That's all.

I'm a killer.

I'm sure you are, he said, but you're also a good person. I'm not sure anyone's going to care if you took some canned goods to survive given the current state of the world.

I care. And I'm going to leave that note when I leave. And I'll pay her back.

There might not be anyone left to pay back though.

Yeah, but there might be. And like I said before, I'm no thief.

Ok, April. I understand. You're a special person, that's all I can say.

She took a few more bites of food and asked, where are you headed?

He considered his response carefully. Too much information could compromise both of them.

Let's assume we both told the truth to start things off. You're just a girl whose parents died and who came out here to do the same. I'm just a guy with a baby trying to find my way. Let's also assume some parts of our stories were not the most truthful. Hell, we don't know each other. We don't know what the other is capable of, right? So with those assumptions in place, I'll tell you I'm headed north. Where north? I'm probably not going to share that with you. At least not right now. Suffice it to say, I'm headed north, where I am originally from. If I give you more information, it might place you in danger.

If I know too much, the Grey Suits could torture me and get your plans. Right?

Something like that. But it's not just the Grey Suits you have to worry about anymore. There are bad guys all around.

I got it. Are you going to take me with you?

Let's talk about that in the morning. With him, that comes pretty early.

She didn't ask any more questions. Instead, she crawled to the back, where her bedding was and laid down. She hoped they were both there in the morning. She liked the man and the kid. The baby reminded her of Abby. She hoped Abby was still alive. Wherever they had taken her.

CHAPTER 11

Late 2093

Cathey and April stood in an old grocery store near dusk. Shards of pink sun setting light pierced through the darkness of the store. They were on the outskirts of Neville, Nebraska, a small, once-proud dairy and farming community. It now sat in darkness. The cows were sent to centralized processing centers months ago. The residents were transported to Lincoln and then on to Sioux City. Vast fields of crops lay in waste. Roads connecting the town to the main highway were destroyed. Likely by the Grey Suits.

They'd scoured the shelves of the store but nothing was left. Either the Grey Suits had been through on their patrols and had confiscated everything or the scavengers had done the job. The Grey Suits were commandeering all the food in the surrounding smaller towns to force everyone into the larger city centers. Walls were going up and freedom of movement was becoming less and less common.

The Grey Suits worked at pulling the smaller towns apart. Cutting off water. Felling cell towers and cutting electrical lines. If you weren't in a big city, it was darkness both figuratively and literally. Electronics were useless. Wi-Fi was nonexistent. The Grey Suits cut the smaller towns off and squeezed them until the only choice one had was to head to the larger cities. There was treatment available as well in those big cities. And that kept the Grey Suits fed and in power.

I thought this place was far enough away that they'd overlook it, April said.

Now they're just raiding for raiding's sake. They don't want anyone out here. They want us all in the cities they control. Easier to keep tabs on us. Quell insurrection.

Quell insurrection? What does that mean?

Keep the masses from revolting. More or less.

This is the third store we've tried. What are we going to do? We're running out of options.

They started walking toward the doors of the store. In the twilight, Cathey thought he saw figures on the highway. He put an arm out and held a finger to his lips. April scanned the horizon.

Suddenly, the wall behind Cathey and April exploded in a cascade of sheetrock. Several camo-clad soldiers rushed through the gaping hole left behind by the mortar shells they fired, their faces concealed behind black stockings. Their eyes glowed blue from illumination goggles. They had the advantage, they could see through oil if forced to. These were Grey Suit soldiers. Cathey only had a second to ponder why they were out here in this country grocery store. He glanced at April who was snapping the charges into her blaster.

The soldiers approached with their blasters raised and fired haphazardly, spraying the store with bullets. Cathey had his rifle in front of him as they advanced and returned fire, hitting two of the attackers in the chest. They dropped immediately and blood poured from their shattered backs.

Two more figures came through the shattered doors. They were hulking men and extraordinarily tall. One moved quickly toward Cathey, swinging his blaster at him. April pulled her blaster to her shoulder and squeezed five rounds into the assailant's head, destroying his skull and scattering brain and blood from the checkout counter to the sidewalk out front. Three more soldiers advanced, all aimed for Cathey. April hit one and dropped him. The remaining two continued to advance and then, before Cathey or April could fire, they dropped like marionettes with their strings suddenly slashed. Cathey and April looked around and standing before them, holding a butcher knife, was Mattie. He wiped the blood from the two men on his pants.

Mattie, Cathey started and reached out to him but April pulled his arm back and held him back.

They were going to kill you, Dad. And April, too. I couldn't let that happen. Just like you showed me with the antelope. Cut the tendon. Drop the animal. I did. Then I cut their throats.

Cathey took a deep breath and swallowed harshly. His nine-year-old son had just taken out two highly-trained assassins with little more than a kitchen knife.

Son, you can't risk yourself like that. No matter what's happening.

I know, Dad. But you would have died.

He approached his son and pulled him close to him. He kissed the top of his head as April scavenged everything she could from the men lying dead and bleeding on the cold linoleum of the Trailway's Market.

They all heard the crunch of glass as a man walked in through the blown-out doors. He had his hands raised and carried a light with him. He pushed the button and it illuminated, filling the store with light.

I'm friend, not foe.

Cathey pulled his blaster to his shoulder and said, we don't know that mister. Down on the ground. Now. Or I'll put these rounds through your skull.

The man did as he was asked. He laid down in front of the group, hands extended overhead, legs spread. He was a man who'd been arrested before or at least detained and checked for weapons. Cathey approached him and patted him down.

He's clean, he said.

May I get up?

Cathey? April said, aiming her blaster at the man. As she said his name, she immediately bit her tongue. He glared at her.

The kid could take him, I think. Yeah, you can get up.

The man stood and turned to face Cathey. My name's George Richmond, he said extending his hand. Cathey held his blaster at the man's chest. George lowered his hand.

We've been following you for a few days.

We?

My group and I.

And?

We figured a man with a young girl and a child weren't going to make it out of any firefight with Grey Suits. But here you are.

Those Greys are cocky. It's their Achilles heel.

They're effective.

And reckless. They assume everyone is sick. Some of us are still able to fight.

George coughed violently and put his hand to his mouth. He quickly pulled out a handkerchief and Cathey could see him spit a thick blackish-red gelatinous substance into the rag.

Some of us are sicker than others, George said. So I take it you're familiar with those bastards chasing you?

Somewhat. I used to be one. Just on the Mech side.

An engineer? Interesting. But a Grey Suit nonetheless.

Cathey could hear the contempt in his voice.

If that's a problem for you, turn around and walk out of here and we'll be on our way. I've got no love lost for those bastards.

No. No problem, George said, holding up his hands. None of you have your Coding bracelets on.

Waste of time, Cathey replied.

Then you haven't been in the city in some time.

No. We've managed to keep to ourselves out here.

If you find yourselves back in the city, any big city really, and you don't have one on, it can cause big trouble for you. Just so you know.

Thanks, Cathey said in a tone too sarcastic for the moment. He was actually grateful to know that information.

We've got a ranch. Food. Water. Electricity. Not far from here. You're welcome to join us.

Nah, we're good out –

April grabbed his arm, turning him toward her, Cathey, c'mon. It's been weeks since we've eaten anything remotely nutritious.

Cathey turned his attention back to George, how do you have electricity?

Solar. Whole place runs on it. We've got a wind turbine as well. For supplemental energy. Grow our own food too.

How have you avoided the Grey Suits?

The man smiled and let out a small laugh. That's a secret. But I'll share it with you if we can be friends. I'll share my whole story with you if you do the same.

Cathey nodded his head. Not because he was going to tell George his story but because April and Mattie needed to eat. He'd figure the rest out later.

Variant

CHAPTER 12

The dream starts the same nearly every night. The car rests on the shoulder of a dusty road, hood up. Steam spews from the radiator and hisses as it hits the boiling steel of the car's engine. A purple-bodied iguana with yellow streaks like lightning bolts coursing down its torso walks slowly away from the family as they gather their things, ready to hike. His bulbous eyes scan the terrain for food and he pauses. He always pauses. Is it to keep an eye on the humans abandoning their vehicle or on something more sinister behind them?

She carries a newborn baby girl wrapped tightly to her chest. The heat from the baby is almost as unbearable as the unrelenting Texas sun. Their car always dies in the dream, somewhere outside Alpine. The rectangular green sign for the city limits of Alpine always figures heavily in the dream. She may not recall every fact from the dream from night to night, but she always remembers Alpine.

The girl's mother can barely walk and its unclear if she's been shot but her clothes are splattered with a mucousy red fluid. In the dream, it's like she just left a slaughterhouse. Clotted parts of her stomach cling to her dress in red swollen masses. Each one leaks a reddish pink fluid adding to the gore of the outfit. She is not a tall woman nor is she pretty. She is average in every respect. Her once-faded black hair is now stained with the blood of her gore. The girl turns from her mother with the child in her arms as her mother reaches for her.

This girl, however, is not average. On her wrist she wears the black bracelet of the Heteroclite. Those identified by the government as Heteroclites simply couldn't be lumped in with the rest of the population for Coding purposes. They were classified as having irregular DNA sequences or abnormalities when scanned for the Cluster. They were originally thought to be immune to the Cluster. Later, such oversimplification of the DNA sequences would be identified and the Heteroclites usefulness to the government would wane.

While her parents ripped their Code bracelets off when they fled the city after their money ran out, she wore hers proudly. They each thought for a time that the Heteroclite bracelet might save them. Buy them shelter. But the truth was far different. In time, they were hunted.

In the distance, the soldiers wait. They shimmer in the heat and threaten to disappear. But more appear. Followed by Mechs. They line the horizon like a Cherokee war party. No need to give chase. Because there's nowhere to run.

The purple iguana turns to face the young girl and he speaks in a slow, methodical tone, April, you must find and protect the Variant.

She looks down at the iguana and feels like she is standing in quicksand. The air around her is thick and palpable and tastes of gravy and rust.

What is The Variant?

The Variant carries the codes for survival. The Children of the Infinite await.

What are the Children of the Infinite, she asks.

In time, the iguana begins slowly and precisely, the Children of the Infinite will become more clear. But they are essential for survival. For now, you must find and protect the Variant at the expense of all others.

If I don't?

Again, he crafts his words carefully, all mankind may fail if you fail to protect the Variant.

As the iguana speaks, she hears Mechs marching toward her, their massive armored legs pounding the highway, splitting the pavement as they approach, sounding like an eruption each time they take a step.

With the Mechs closing in and her parents dying, the dream usually faded. But this time was different. This time the Mechs were slower, less precise. They approached with their mechanized arms at their sides, not wielding their dual blasters, as if they were awaiting instructions. Their path was disjointed.

You must go, young April. The Variant awaits. Let nothing happen to the Variant.

She tried to speak again but her words lacked focus. She screamed in her head but nothing but gibberish came from her lips. She wanted to ask more questions but the Mechs approached. They drew near. As she turned, she saw that a boy led them. She looked in his eyes but didn't know if he was friend or foe. He wore no bracelet but he appeared to be reading something out loud that is printed on his arm like a tattoo. The Mechs come to attention. She screams again trying to speak –

April, Cathey said, shaking her awake. Are you okay? Are you awake?

It took her a moment to tear herself from the highway. This was the first time she'd seen someone with the Mechs that wasn't a soldier. She'd had the dream a dozen times or more, but she had never gotten that far in the dream. She wondered who he was and what he was doing. She felt guilty for forgetting her parents were dying in the dream as well. But, she figured, it was just a dream.

It took her a moment to focus and remember where they were. Someone's cabin. Outside a town she didn't know. The Cluster was spreading but this town seemed like it was dealing with it, perhaps better than most. This was a town with money. The hospitals were full daily. They were keeping the drug companies flush with cash.

I'm okay, she said, clawing at the fog that always surrounded her when she went from dream state to awake. She was sure that wasn't normal. But she never talked about it. With anyone.

Do you remember your dream this time?

She did. She always did. But she never told Cathey she did. She'd told him too much already.

No. Just weird shit. As usual.

You said something about a sister. I've never heard that. Just weird shit or shit you haven't told me?

She rubbed her wrists where the Grey Suits had bound her. Cathey had never seen the scars. She'd never told him about the night she was dragged away by the Grey Suits. The night they stole her innocence from her. The night they made her plead for her life.

Just weird shit, Cathey, you know me.

I do know you. I think. That stuff I hear from you while you're dreaming is alarming. He stood up and walked over to the bed his son slept in.

He patted the boy's chest. He's so big, he said to April but really just to himself.

He's fine. All kids are different.

How do you know?

I dunno. Instinct. But he's fine. He's just growing. Taking to the Lessons well. He wants you to test him.

In time. Once we get this structure in place for the Lighthouse.

Are you close?

Getting there. That boy just seems to be growing too fast. He seems too big. Too strong.

Maybe that's a good thing these days.

Maybe.

I need to tell you something. About what he did yesterday while you were out with the Lighthouse people.

Ok.

Look, don't be mad either. I was watching him close.

I can't be mad yet.

No, you can't be mad after I tell you what happened.

He glanced over at the boy, I don't like hypotheticals April. You know that. Just tell me what happened.

We were outside. Going over some of the Lessons you left. He started his Levin fire. I had told him to be careful near it. He goes and drops his starter in the pit of it. Without a thought, he reaches in as the Levin is blazing, and pulls it out. I immediately reached for the starter and it was like touching the surface of the sun. Look, she said and held her hand out.

Her index finger and thumb both had blisters where she had touched the fire starter.

She continued, he was fine. No blisters. No burns. No nothing. It didn't even seem to register with him that it was supposed to be hot. He acted like nothing happened.

Cathey bent down and looked at the boy's hands. They were unblemished.

Are you mad?

Cathey shook his head. No, I've noticed things too.

Cathey, you should'a told me. I was freaking out all day worried you were going to lose it when I told you.

You're right. I should've shared. I'm sorry. I'm not the best these days talking. I wrote it down in my e-journal. But he's done some things I can't explain.

Like?

We came in from that ride two or three weeks ago. He hadn't bathed in about that long. He was in the barn, stripped down and showered under that outdoor spigot.

The one that's fed from the river?

That one.

That shower's ice water practically.

Yeah, that spigot feeds from the snow melt. Cold as deep space. But he stood under it for several minutes just letting it pound his head and shoulders. You would've thought it was some hot spring-fed shower. I didn't say anything but after he left, I turned it back on and my hand was nearly frostbitten in a matter of seconds.

So he has no sensitivity to extreme hot or cold?

Not only does he have no sensitivity to it, his skin doesn't react to it like yours or mine would. At least not that I can tell. My skin was red from the cold for twenty minutes. His was just its normal color. It's like his skin is armor. For better or worse.

Do the Grey Suits know about this?

About this particular oddity? I doubt it.

But they know something, right? That's why you ran.

We ran because they couldn't even code him as a Heteroclite. The Grey Suits thought they had this whole Coding thing down until he was born. Once Clara gave birth, they realized there was something else. Maybe one who *was* immune. One who lacks the Cluster. Not even one cancer gene. Completely immune.

Is it because you and Clara were both identified as Heteroclite?

That's the only explanation.

Maybe he's got immunity from a whole host of issues we face down here?

Perhaps. But he has other things he can do. Things I've ignored but as he grows I can't ignore them anymore. We were putting away the canned goods that Sally Montgomery dropped off for the winter storage. Cases of jellies, vegetables, and smoked meats. George wanted them stored up in the loft of the barn. We both carried a case up the stairs and I started to stack. Once I was done with my case I turned around and there were about twenty cases behind me. He was jumping from the forty foot loft to the ground floor, grabbing a case and running it back up the ladder to me.

Wow. Did you say anything to him?

I told him he had to be careful. I should've told you as well. To watch him. To make sure he wasn't pushing himself to do these things around people who might not understand him. I don't know if this stuff can hurt him. I want him safe.

Yeah. I understand. I'll watch him. But he can't do these things around other people.

Agreed. We'll talk to him later tonight. Does he know we're leaving?

No. I didn't want him talking to the others about it. They've been so helpful. But -

But, you still don't trust them, Cathey said.

I trust them. To a certain extent.

But you're not telling them we're headed to Alaska.

Hell no. I was thinking of telling them we were heading out to find your aunt and uncle.

What aunt and uncle, asked April.

You never mentioned an aunt or uncle have you?

No, because there is no aunt or uncle. They died before my parents did.

Do they know this?

Oh...no. I've never mentioned it. I got you.

So, we tell them we're headed West to find them, let's say Albuquerque, and then we just talk to them as needed. When we need info or intel.

Ok. Have you come up with a backstory on my dear aunt and uncle, Mr. Shakespeare?

Let's keep it simple. We don't know anything other than you miss them and we heard they were in Sioux Falls but went back to New Mexico. They're all you have left, blah blah blah.

Clever. You never did tell them where you found me, did you?

No. That's need to know info. And they didn't need to know that.

Ok, she said and grabbed his hands. She was about say something sentimental when a young man, Marcus Brecken, burst through the door.

Cathey, George wants you down in the comm. It's urgent.

Cathey stared at Marcus who was still such a young man at seventeen. His dark eyes could read Cathey's doubt and he said, It's Clara. She's escaped.

Cathey's arms rippled with goose flesh on the mention of her name. Clara was alive, he thought. Dear lord, he said under his breath as he followed Marcus downstairs to the basement and the Comm room for the Lighthouse.

CHAPTER 13

He paused for a moment before entering the Lighthouse's Communications room. He had often thought of what he'd say to her if she tried to contact him. In the end, he had no way of knowing who was showing up calling herself Clara. Was it one of the clones? Was it her? He'd have no way of knowing until he saw her in person. Over the comm he would have no way to confirm her identity.

George Richmond, the owner of the farm that housed the Lighthouse, had been an English professor of some renown at a posh liberal arts college on the east coast at some point before there was a Cluster. He was particularly fond of Virginia Woolf and, given the nature of what he was trying to accomplish in the early days of the Cluster, he felt as though the Lighthouse was just about as good a name to give the joint as any. He tried in vain to explain it a few times. Something about apparitions and rising to the surface, but no one ever understood him. Now he just ignores the questions about why and people assume he's the beacon in the storm. He is quick to remind anyone who asks that the storm is the Grey Suits and all they encompass.

He is not old but his hair is mostly white. He dyed it black when he was younger and more vain. In those days, he thought he still had a chance with the sorority girls who passed his office or sat in his classes. He was always tall, nearly six-foot-five, and that helped. But at twenty-three he started going grey, just like his father. Memories of his father always hurt. So he dyed the hair. To forget that he was like his father. And to get laid.

George's dad sat down in the lush barn of the Lighthouse and put a shotgun barrel in his mouth one grey November day. He had spent what money he had on treatment and still, at sixty-one, he felt like he'd just thrown the money away. Once the treatment stopped, the Cluster came back with a vengeance. It plundered his bowels and emptied his lungs of their lining.

When he couldn't breathe without help, he loaded his grandfather's Winchester and splattered his brains across stall number four like a Jackson Pollack painting. He left George a note. In a shaky script it read: Nothing is True, Everything is Permitted. George folded the note and put it in his pocket and set about cleaning the stalls. He buried his dad on the hill overlooking Rhys Creek. Those six words consumed him for so long. Looking for meaning but finding none. If nothing was true, the Lighthouse was the warning light, flashing for all to see.

When George first met Cathey, he didn't trust him. Still didn't. Cathey was, after all, a Grey Suit, despite his protestations to the contrary. The fact that he had escaped and blown a bunch of them up along the way mattered little to George. The Mech codes he'd provided proved to be useless and George often wondered if he gave them bad codes because he didn't want to blow up his creations. He took Cathey at his word though. But with caution. He had the boy and the young lady with him. George couldn't turn them away. Plus, they all seemed perfectly healthy. That was huge. They could contribute to the farm. If they'd been sick, George wondered if he'd stopped that night and picked them up.

Cathey opened the door to the Comm room and George turned and immediately took his headset off. He pushed a red rectangular button and it started to flash red, then white.

Look, some of our people found her. About a hundred miles from Boulder, Colorado. In the mountains and trees. She kept rambling on about the Grey Suits and her escape from the base. They said she's rail thin and severely malnourished. We don't know what to make of it. But she asked for you.

For me directly?

Yes.

That's a problem.

Problem how?

Just a problem. I'll talk to her. But what did your men tell her about me? Did they tell her where we were?

We'll have to find that out later. I don't know. They shouldn't have.

Cathey took the headset and hit the button. It stopped flashing and just glowed bright red.

This is Cathey.

Lt. Col. James Cathey?

One and the same. What is it you need?

Just to convey a message to you.

He sat silently for a moment. She sounded cold and detached. There was no familiarity in her voice.

And who exactly are you?

My name's Clara Strong.

Strong was her maiden name. Maybe the mind wipe had worked after all.

What's the message, Ms. Strong?

He heard her say something to the two men who brought her in but it was muffled.

Are you receiving this message clearly?

Yes, you're clear. What's the message?

They heard the crackle of hyperstealth units deactivating, exposing two armed Greys. The screams of the men erupted over the airways as they were repeatedly stabbed.

Your men are dead Cathey. And we're coming for you. The line went dead.

Cathey? George paused, you okay?

I've put everyone in danger, Cathey said.

We were in danger the day we ripped those Coding bracelets off and started doing this. You aren't putting us in any more danger than we were already in.

If you knew who I was, who I really was, you might think different.

Who are we really? Are we who society says we are? Are you even that person you perceive in your mind when you see your reflection? Are we a sum of those two things? Does it even matter who we were before this world turned to shit? I don't think so. Who cares that I can recite Act III, Scene I of Henry V? Or that I can explain the nuances of Nabokov or the influence of Burroughs' aleatory technique on Kobain's lyrics? None of that shit matters anymore. I'm not sure it ever did.

I'm so much more now, since the world turned. Good and bad.

You're using old world terms though Cathey. What is bad?

Killing people. I think that's still bad.

Not if you're killing bad people. Grey Suits.

I was a Grey Suit though.

You were forced into that service. You had no choice. You were just a boy. You escaped a life of servitude. A life of nothing more than being beholden to the drug companies and the government keeping you alive with their Cluster drugs until your usefulness to them ran out. Or your money.

Cathey thought about what George said for a moment. He agreed for the most part, but, as usual, he had not told George the whole truth years ago when they promised to tell each other the gods' honest truth about their situations.

They had different reasons to keep me alive. Back then.

You singlehandedly built their army. I'm sure you would've been fine. You just didn't want your boy to grow up in that environment. That's what you said.

It's all so much deeper than that, George. I blew up an entire army base. I killed thousands of people. I destroyed families. All to save mine.

So it was more than just getting your son out of there then?

George, I am a Heteroclite. My wife was a Heteroclite. - What we created when we conceived Mattie was not something any of us expected.

You're one of the Heteroclite? George sounded incredulous.

That's what they told me. I'm forty-two years old and I'm as healthy as when I was fourteen. Most people my age –

Are like me, Cathey. Sick. And only getting sicker. As if on cue, George coughed violently, sounding as though he were tearing lung tissue away with each forced breath. Blood splattered across his handkerchief. He spit something black and vile onto it and closed it up, wiping his bloody lips with the back. George put the bloody cotton rag back in his jacket pocket and Cathey realized, for the first time, why George's lips always glistened like he'd just applied a coat of burgundy lipstick.

George? Cathey went to the man's side and patted his back. The man, who was three months younger than Cathey but looked twenty years older, held up a hand and gently brushed Cathey's hand aside.

I'm fine. As fine as I can be. Just a moment.

He took five deep breaths and had the appearance of a man struggling to swallow. With his eyes closed, he tried to take a single breath. Instead, he took several short, hard, ragged breaths. The Cluster was raging in him. Eating his lungs like a daily lunch buffet.

Snacking on his throat. The Cluster would eventually eat through both. But not today. Today, it was just torturing him.

So, he said after he got his breathing under control. You are a Heteroclite. I'm supposed to turn you in. They said there's only, what, fifteen of you on the whole planet?

Something like that.

You hold the keys to the cure. That's what they said.

They've said a bunch of stuff. Most of it bullshit lies.

Yeah, agreed. You know we'd never turn you in. I don't think they want a cure anyway. They came into power on the back of this gruesome disease. If they keep people sick, or just sick enough, they'll keep paying for the drugs to fight it. A cure? A cure does nothing for the Grey Suits. They lose. And from what I can see, they'll destroy this planet and all of us with it before they'll give up power.

I didn't think of it like that.

Doesn't serve us very well to be naïve about their intentions. Your son? He's also a Heteroclite?

Yes and no. I told you my son was why we ran. That's true. But the reasoning wasn't. George, when we had our son, they took him from us for days. They tied Clara down and drained her of her milk. Every three of four hours, they clamped her into their extraction units and when the skin tore, she screamed in pain and they drugged her. They restrained me with plasma security cable. I watched helplessly as they tortured her. After several days, they returned him to us. They didn't say anything. She buckled in pain as he gummed her breast to feed, but he was with us, finally. We began devising a way out of the unit they were housing us in. But Clara was worn down. She needed strength.

She'd been sick with this child for nearly four months. Although the baby gained weight, she was losing weight. The doctors had never seen anything like it. During the fifth month, they did a final ultrasound and found that the child was literally trying to tear its way out of the placenta. They rushed her to surgery and pulled him out. She was so weak from the weight loss and the struggle that we didn't think she was going to make it. Despite only being twenty-four weeks old, he came out at nine pounds ten ounces and twenty-seven inches long. All off the chart for most kids, not to mention one that should have been a barely-there preemie. When they pulled out the placenta, they could see where the child had scratched at it, trying to get out.

Obviously, no one knew what to do with this information. But it was the first live birth of a child where both parents were identified as carrying the Heteroclite gene. Cutting the umbilical cord, usually the job of scissors and a happy father, required a plasma torch, face shield and goggles. That baby was bound and determined to destroy his host on the way out.

When he returned, he fed voraciously, nearly every half hour. Poor Clara could barely keep up. They had her on IV fluids and proteins, but she was so weak. He, on the other hand, seemed to grow right before our eyes. He gained nearly a pound a day in the initial week. That's what we were told. My anger grew. But the more I protested, the more they retaliated. They did things to me during that time that I don't care to recall. But those times hardened me. Made me truly believe that taking the boy from that place and hiding him was the best possible solution. In the interim, Clara got stronger and we came up with an idea.

Now, what I'm about to tell you would get me killed if they knew. And it sounds like I'm crazy. But Clara was working on a top secret project during this time. Not just on a cure but on a way to facilitate getting healthier Heteroclites out into the DNA pool.

Clones?

Cathey nodded his head. Yeah. There were several made from her. She was smart. Young. Practically immune. They lost two other female Heteroclites when they implanted them with embryos and they tore their way through the placentas much too early. It killed both of them. So they cloned Clara and used those clones as vessels to bear the children.

Oh my god Cathey. How many survived?

We don't know. It was all wrapped up with our trying to escape.

How many clones of Clara?

Three that we knew of.

Did they survive?

I know one did. We had to leave her behind so Clara could escape.

So Clara is alive?

I don't know, George. I don't. But I know we sat in the darkness of her hospital room one night, the fifth after he was born, we knew we had to do something. We brought a clone in. She understood what she was and we had a good relationship with her. Once we told her our plans, she agreed to help. I knew I had to leave and get the boy out of there. Clara had to escape as well. Just not with us. We couldn't imagine a way out. So we left the clone in the room and tried to hack the med-tablet I filched one night.

By now, they were bringing the baby in for feedings. We noticed that they were getting sloppy and leaving the boy's med-tablet behind when they dropped him off for feedings. Clara and I left, leaving the clone behind and headed to my office. I had an off grid laptop from the late twenties that I used to store, well, let's just say I was storing personal things on it. Information I created for the Mechs. And other things.

Keep in mind, I had a top secret clearance. Yankee White they called it. I had undergone the most significant background check on the planet to design and build the Mech units. When I tried to download my son's medical charts, *medical charts,* George, I was denied access. Yankee Black or higher it said. I had no idea there was a higher clearance. I knew something was wrong.

Holy shit Cathey.

Yeah. Without the clearance, I wouldn't be able to download anything. I put the chart back in my pack and we decided at that point, Clara had to go. She took a pack I prepared for her and headed out. There was an old mining tunnel access door that led to the outside. It would take her less than two hours to reach the city. She left and I returned to the room.

When I got there, there were a dozen or so soldiers outside the door. Seeing soldiers in this area wasn't abnormal. But as I made my way down the hall to the room they formed a blockade. I could hear Clara's clone speaking to someone in the room and I heard the baby cry. The door opened slightly and one of the soldiers barked at the nurse, get back in there! We'll be done soon enough. The nurse closed the door and again I could hear their muffled voices.

Some sort of problem, fellas?

The med files on the boy. Where are they?

Guys I'm afraid I don't know what you're talking about. Med files?

The chart for your son. It was left in the room earlier. Those files do not belong to you.

They don't? This is still my child, right?

They paused and Cathey saw someone in a lab coat parting the sea of grey.

Mr. Cathey, the doctor began.

Let's try Lt. Col. Cathey, Doctor.

The doctor began again, Lt. Col., those files belong to the facility. You are certainly welcome to review them at the proper time. Currently the files are still subject to review and revision, thus they are not much use to you.

I wanted to tell them I knew about the clearance for the files. But that would suggest that I'd seen the files at some point and I wanted to keep that information to myself.

I wish I could help you Doctor. But I don't have your files, I said.

The doctor swiped his right hand to the left and suddenly the soldiers were on me. They grabbed my arms and pinned them behind me. They ripped the backpack from my body. One of the men started going through it, and finding nothing, dumped it upside down. A lone paper clip bounced to the floor.

I locked eyes with the doctor and in a moment, flung the man on my right into the wall. The one left holding me gripped me tighter, bringing his gun near me. I reached for it and pulled the trigger, splitting the man nearly in half. The doctor recoiled and ran back down the hall he'd come from.

The remaining soldiers aimed their weapons at me and released their safeties.

You boys ready, I asked. They aimed their blasters at my head. The first one was about to fire when the paper clip exploded with a louder than expected detonation followed by a brilliant burst of light and powerful concussion wave. The blast rocked the men backward.

I ran into Clara's room where the clone had the nurse tied to the chair. The clone stood behind her, scalpel to her neck.

She said she was taking the kid. I denied that request. You okay?

I'll make it.

Leave her?

No, not this one.

You two are dead. The nurse spoke through blood trickling from her nose. The clone had overpowered her with a crushing elbow and forearm directly to the nurse's nose. She dropped like a wet rag to the floor.

This was the one that laughed when she…I mean I…begged her for some help. Remember that, the clone asked and jerked the nurse's head backward.

You should've helped her, she said and swiped the scalpel across the nurse's neck. Blood sprayed in torrents from her neck, splattering the wall and ceiling. She buckled forward.

We made our way back into the hallway. The concussed soldiers still lay shaken, their heads scrambled from the blast. Both of us picked up a rifle and started down the hall where the doctor had run.

Voices hushed as their footsteps echoed across the hallway. They could hear doors locking and furniture being moved in front of doors.

I told her that we should go back through the hangar. Told her I could arm the Mechs and use them to escape. Of course, the plan was to leave her behind so I could buy time to get out with my son.

She played the part well. Like a Broadway star. She vowed that she wasn't leaving until she found the doctor that ripped our child from her.

We each played our part, laying the foundation for the monitors when they reviewed them. I pled with her to leave the doctor alone, she vowed to find him.

As though she was on my side, she followed me toward the hangar. We made our way down the hallway. Doors to patients' rooms were all closed save for the one from which we escaped. The soldiers were gone now. She was in full character. It was like watching a movie.....

.....Wait. The clone turned back and listened again. Cathey stopped, waiting on her.

We've got to keep moving, he said. Those soldiers are around here somewhere. I don't think they're taking prisoners this time.

No, hang on. I heard something back there, the clone said.

The doctor's not our problem.

But he knows what's inside that file. What they're saying about our son. Just give me a few minutes with him. That's all we need.

Clara.

Please. Otherwise we might not ever know.

Cathey looked down the hall toward the hangar. Four hundred feet and they'd be there. But he wanted to know what was in the file too.

We gotta hurry, he said and they sprinted down the hall.

They found him hiding in a maintenance closet. He was talking to someone on a comm link that blinked off as the light from the hallway flooded in.

Out, Cathey said, pointing to a spot with his rifle.

The doctor obeyed and instinctively put up his hands.

On your knees. Lace your fingers together and put them behind your head. To Clara he said, check my back pocket. The deep one on the left. Tie his hands with that zip I have in there.

She pulled it out of his pocket and moved quickly to secure the doctor.

Check him.

She patted him down and found a small-caliber revolver in his right front pocket.

Expecting trouble, Doctor?

146

He said nothing.

Listen, Terry, or whatever your name is, you're going to talk.

Or what? You'll kill me? You're going to kill me anyway.

What's in the file? Why is it classified?

I told you. It's subject to revision. They always classify those types of files until they're edited.

Classify it higher than top secret? What's in it?

Notes. Readings. Lab results. Medical information.

They don't send an entire unit of soldiers to retrieve a file with simple medical information in it. Why'd they want it so badly?

The doctor shook his head.

Why Doctor, Cathey shouted and struck the doctor in his forehead with the butt of the rifle. The doctor fell to the side, on top of his bound arms. A small trickle of blood started to ooze down his forehead from the split in his skull.

The doctor moaned in pain. Please, it's just medical information. But it's medical information about the first born child of Heteroclite parents. It's significant.

Why? Why is it significant?

I can't tell you. They'll execute me.

The clone turned sharply and thrust the butt of her rifle into the doctor's stomach. The intensity of the blow forced all the air out of his lungs. He struggled to regain his breath. She followed this with a kick to the man's groin.

She'll execute you. All I gotta do is give the word. I don't think she likes you.

The man continued to writhe on the ground in a fetal position. He began coughing up globules of blood.

You people don't understand, the doctor said through uneven breaths. The chart is just the start. We don't have enough information to connect the dots. The dots are all we have in the file.

Then tell us what the dots are.

He's like a Heteroclite, but even more so. Not only is his DNA a variation of the normal population's DNA like a Heteroclite, he's a variation of even the small percentage of Heteroclites we've studied.

What's that mean?

Only time is going to tell. But when we coded him, he came back as an X.

What does that mean?

The clone spoke up, it means either the sample was tainted or additional information would need to be input to get a good Code.

We added all the information we had and he continued to register as an X. I personally did two of the tests from the beginning and got an X each time.

Is there an explanation for that?

If he can't be coded, there there's the very real possibility that he's immune. If that's the case, he's the first. The ramifications of this are obviously monumental.

How do we know for sure?

Testing Lt. Col. Testing. But it doesn't look like you're going to let us do that.

No. We're not. He's a child. Not a lab rat. They did horrible things to me in the name of science and I'll be damned if they're doing it to my child.

They'll find you. Wherever it is you're going. And then they'll test him. And your protestations will be for naught. They'll put a bullet in both your brains before you can complain. It won't matter.

It might not, but I like our odds.

That's the soldier in you. Always cocky. I wish I could be there when they bring you in.

I'll mention that to them. Let's go, he said to the clone.

We're leaving him?

You heard him, they'll take care of him for us.

They turned to leave and were faced with four of the soldiers still groggy from the concussion blast. Their blasters raised, they asked the doctor what they should do.

They have the child. Let them pass. Nothing can happen to him. Let them pass. We'll find them.

Cathey and the clone made their way past the soldiers. Cathey stepped out of the hallway to the right, headed for the production area. The clone made sure Cathey was clear with the boy and then she reached for the nearest soldier's blaster. As she reached for it, he fired six quick bursts, hitting her in the right hip. She fought through the pain and knocked the blaster from the soldier. Scrambling for it, the soldier landed on top of her.

Cathey sat the backpack down and peered around the corner as the men began to attack the clone. He pulled his service pistol from his back and shot the three that stood over her in quick succession. She still grappled with the one on the ground.

Cathey, she screamed. The doctor had inched his way up and was now kicking her in the head with his free leg.

Cathey leapt down the hall and immediately shot the doctor in the head, spraying the corridor with his skull and its contents. He then turned and saw that the last remaining soldier had his blaster pointed at the clone's head. She was bleeding badly from the bullet hole in her hip.

Just let us walk out of here. Then you live to fight another day. I don't want to kill you. I just want to get out of here alive.

There's a team already assembled in the production area. They'll get you. There's an army lining up outside. They'll get you. Either way, you're not getting away.

Cathey raised the gun and pointed it just over the clone's shoulder. He had the soldier in his sights.

You know why I was selected for my job? Building the Mechs?

The soldier shook his head. His hand trembled just a bit.

I tested really well, you see, on the engineering tests. But I scored better on the range. Something about my vision. And aim.

Put the gun down, Cathey. Or I'm going to kill her right here.

I think they'll be pissed if you kill either one of us.

Put it down. I'll do it.

Cathey thought about it for a moment. So, he started again, they studied my eyes and oddly enough, the retinal sensor in the Mechs is basically a clone of my eye. I don't miss. Let her go.

Cathey saw the soldier's finger flinch on the trigger and Cathey immediately pulled his. The bullet ripped through the soldier's eye. He crumpled to the ground.

Cathey and the clone picked up the backpack and made their way to the production area.....

.....Cathey finished talking and stood waiting for George's reaction.

Jesus Cathey, I had no idea.

I eventually hacked the file. Took me a couple of days but I got in. I couldn't believe the things they'd discovered about the boy. And the questions that those discoveries prompted. Like the doctor said, he lacked any evidence of the Cluster genes. As you know at this point, the doctors could isolate the genes from birth. They knew not only what kind of Cluster you'd experience later in life, they could almost say when. Within a few months. Hence the Coding bracelets. For people our age, it seemed to be a little bit more of a guessing game. But for the infants, they were getting pretty good at pinpointing it. Our son lacked the Cluster genes all together.

He's truly immune? Not just a white?

Cathey nodded his head. To study him would give us the chance for a real cure. Not just drugs to prolong the miserable existences we now call lives.

He's a miracle, George said.

There were problems, though. He wasn't a normal child. At least not normal to them. His internal temperature was lower than ours. He was hovering around ninety-four and ninety-five degrees. His heart rate at times would slow to twenty or thirty beats a minute. Anti-coagulants had no effect on his blood. As soon as it was drawn, it would congeal. He was a living science experiment for the Grey Suits and they planned on doing tests on him when he was just a bit bigger.

George couldn't say anything. He just shook his head.

No, George, you really have no idea. That's why I've got to move him. I've got to get him as far away from the Grey Suits as possible.

It's safe here Cathey, it really is. Our defensive shield technology is state-of-the-art and puts the government's to shame.

Whoever that was calling herself Clara found the outpost. She convinced them she was someone to trust. She's like that. Now those men are dead. I know we all think this place is invisible but she's smart enough to exploit any weaknesses in the system.

Where will you go?

If I told you I didn't know, would you believe me?

No, but that's probably as good an answer as any. Will you take April with you?

I can talk to her about it.

When will you leave?

I'll let you know.

Variant

CHAPTER 14

They both sat on the floor, looking up at Cathey. He felt uncomfortable speaking down to them, so he joined them on the floor and thought about his next words carefully.

We've got to move.

No, Mattie said with exasperation and sadness in his voice. He ran his hands through his hair and then his head sank into his arms. He was finally starting to feel normal. He woke up in the same bed every morning. He was having three meals a day. He could take a bath. And he was learning.

Son, we have to. The outpost was attacked and two good men are dead because they're hunting us.

They? Don't you mean her? April glared at Cathey.

She was with the men that killed ours. But it's the entire army, of that we're sure. They're desperate to find him. He looked at his son and put an arm around him, bringing him closer.

If they got that close, it won't take them long to find us here. People are easily bought these days. A little money or the promise of Cluster treatment and they sing. There's been a steady stream of people through here. Although we've been careful, we haven't been careful enough. When that last group passed through, George routinely called me Cathey over the radio. They were on a work detail that day. So there's at least four people that know someone named Cathey is living here. It wouldn't take them long to do the math. Even if I wasn't the Cathey they were after, I might be someone of interest to speak with just to check.

Can I come, April asked.

Of course, I didn't even consider this as something we'd do without you. You're part of the family now. Seven years is a long time to be with people. But you're also not the little girl I found back

then. You're a young woman now. There's a certain stability here
that might make you more comfortable.

There's no stability here for a girl like me, Cathey. You guys
are my stability.

I'm just saying life's sorta normal here. As normal as it can
be without living with the Grey Suits. Who knows what that's like?
But there's a steadiness here. If I was twenty-four, I'd consider
staying.

April thought about what he was saying.

I mean, if everything *was* normal, you might have a point.
Every day I wake up, I'm shocked.

You shouldn't be. Your blood work has been normal.

But you can't Code me. We don't know for sure. I've got to
be Coded.

True. Look, I've given you whatever passes for my fatherly
advice. I told you what I might do.

Cathey, would you really stay?

He locked eyes with her and found it difficult, as usual, to turn
away.

Would you? She asked again. This time with more passion.
I love this kid like he's my own brother. I'm not leaving him. So if
you're leaving, I am too.

My plan all along has been to get north. I told you that. To
hide him. The Lighthouse was just a detour for awhile.

Ok. When do we leave?

Gather your stuff. We'll leave tonight.

CHAPTER 15

Before April's world changed forever in 2092, she sat on a park bench on an overcast Fall day. She was smiling so big from the text, she had to glance up from her phone to make sure no one was watching her. When she was sure she was alone, she allowed herself to laugh at the pictures Elizabeth had sent. She was going to respond to one of them but when she went to text Elizabeth, the phone died. The battery icon was blinking red in the corner. She'd had the phone resting on the charger in her bag all day. She should've had a full charge.

The park was quiet today, as it usually was since people started moving to the bigger cities for Cluster treatment. The town she lived in, Mount Enterprise, Texas, was quaint and a throwback to simpler times. The train station from the 1860s still stood and now housed the post office. The town remained a small town throughout most of its existence despite oil having been found not far from the train station in the early 1900s. Wildcatters flooded the city trying to stake their own claims, but when stories about several of the men disappearing started to spread, most of the men moved on. At least those who didn't, ended up dead, for one reason or another. There were the rumors no one mentioned in mixed company back then as well. There were stories about a winged beast that pulled men from their beds at night. Bodies were found. Drained of blood. But no one really believed those stories. They were just make believe.

An iron statue of a windmill stood like a silent sentry on the edge of the courthouse lawns. Most people had forgotten why it was there. The plaque to remind them had long since vanished.

She turned her attention across the street, to the town square. It was also completely deserted. She saw her parents turn down the main street. April sat stoically on a bench. She saw them immediately.

Her mom slowed the car and came to a stop before her. She rolled the window down.

April practically shouted, what are you doing out here? And why is Dad with you? Shouldn't he be in Dallas? In the freaking hospital? Her father slept in the backseat of the van.

We've been reassigned.

Reassigned? What does that mean?

It means they've got a spot for us in a really great city where people are seeing some real results. Some patients are living several years past their Codes.

How'd we get so lucky, April asked acerbically.

Sweetheart, we are so very lucky. Her mother stepped out of the car, breathing heavily as she did. Her lungs burned with each step. The Cluster was raging but she swore she'd bring the girl with her. She left the door open and walked toward her daughter, but that's why I'm here with your father. We need you to come with us.

Why? I'm not sick, she said, backing away from her mother. She could hear her mother's serrated breath slicing through the woman's swollen lung tissue.

I've got two months of school left and then I'm in high school. What's going to happen in the next two months that you need me now?

Her mother stopped walking toward her. She held out her hands as if to say it was all going to be alright. It's all very complicated, Sweetie. There're some people who want to, you know, see about why and how you're not sick.

You told them?

I had no choice, sweetie. The hospital administrator had me in a room all by myself asking me all sorts of questions. They wanted to know where you were and why you weren't with us. I told them that you were healthy and wanted to finish school.

That's outstanding.

Sweetie, it's for the best.

For who?

For your dad.

So that's the deal? Bring me in and Dad gets some fancy upgraded drugs?

Sweetie, we all get helped. She dropped her hands to her waist and as she did so, her shirt sleeve rose an inch or two off her wrist. April saw that her mother was wearing an orange bracelet.

What's that bracelet?

It's required now, Sweetie. It helps the hospitals and doctors keep track of the sickest amongst us.

And you believe that?

Well, whether I believe it or not, it's required. You can't get into the bigger cities without one.

Orange? What's it mean?

They've given me a year.

Geez, so it's like a reminder of when you're going to die? No thanks. I'll stay here.

Sweetie –

Stop calling me sweetie godsdamn it! I'm not your sweetie! I've never been your sweetie! You're using me. Like always. Shouldn't surprise me though, should it? Given why you had me in the first place. How'd that work out for Hannah?

Sweet – she stopped herself, Honey, please. We've been over that –

You've been over that. I'm definitely not over that. You had me for spare parts. To suck my bone marrow from me to save your precious firstborn. Your Hannah. She *still* died and here I am. You

think I'm going to help you now? I've wanted you dead since I was
five. Go to hell.

April turned to walk away and was faced with a series of Light
Combat All-Terrain Vehicles (L-ATV) moving toward the park. They
were painted grey with American flag decals on the doors.

I can't believe you, she screamed to her mother. You brought
them here!?

April immediately sprinted away from her mother and the
woman began to cry. She honestly believed that it was best for the
family if April came along. Maybe she could help them find a cure
for this malicious plague. And plague was exactly what she thought
of when she thought of the Cluster. She didn't understand how or
why the disease started or exploded the way it did. But she knew that
if April were immune or seemingly immune, then she'd do whatever
her government needed her to do to save others. Why her daughter
didn't view the world the same way was beyond her. But, then again,
her mother thought the girl had always been selfish. She'd always
thought of herself first and never others. It was always about April.
And she always brought up Hannah. No matter the severity of the
event.

Was she right? In a manner of speaking, yes. April had been
conceived because no bone marrow donors could be found for their
severely-ill oldest child. The doctors told them that this was their last
best chance to save their Hannah. She was diagnosed with Adenosine
Deaminase Deficiency Severe Combined Immunodeficiency (ADA-
SCID) at birth. She lacked cells that could fight infection and after
two years of starts and stops on her treatment, she faced a certain
death. The doctors didn't give her long unless a bone marrow donor
could be found. They waited but the doctors told them that the longer
they waited, the more dire the situation would become. They made
the decision at that point to have another child in the hope that this

second child could provide the matching bone marrow to save Hannah. At her birth on April 13 (she'd been named April because her parents didn't want to get too attached to her. April was easy and comprised no sentimentality), doctors collected her cord blood and performed the first of three transplants. Hannah responded positively to the transplant at first. Within a year, though, she was back to where she started. Infections ravaged her body. Doctors had warned this might happen. Unbeknownst to them, the Cluster was already at work in most severely ill patients. It would be five years before they identified the Cluster for what it was.

After April reached her first birthday, the doctors extracted the child's bone marrow in a second effort to save Hannah. Again, Hannah responded with remarkable results. But within two years, Hannah's fifth on this planet, she started to regress again. Infections attacked her tiny body and forced her on a ventilator.

The effects on April were profound. She cried relentlessly when she was touched or held. She preferred to be left alone. Her mother accommodated her and left her lying in her bed for hours on end. When the doctors told them they could try another transplant, April's father, Nathan, asked what effect this would have on April. The doctors confirmed that it was possible she could die. April's mother didn't hesitate in ordering another transplant.

But something strange happened in that third and final transplant. April didn't die. She didn't get weaker. She thrived. Hannah, on the other hand, died during the surgery. The doctors didn't know that at the same time her body was failing at fighting off infections, her blood was seething with cancer and her brain was hemorrhaging.

April, too young to know her big sister rested in the big box at the front of the church, knew deep inside that she was nothing more than spare parts for her big sister. But she refused to let that define her. She asked her mother when she was seven if she was adopted because there were no pictures of her anywhere in the house.

Her mother had laughed and shook her head. I wish, she said, maybe then I could send you back.

April made her way through the park, stopping when she came to First Street. Additional L-ATVs made their way around the corner, heading toward her. Grey Suit soldiers began to spill out of the L-ATVs, guns drawn, battle visors lowered. Why they sent all those soldiers just for her, she'd never know. She couldn't understand why they needed so many for one little girl.

She looked for anywhere to run but the soldiers were closing in. Her only option was ahead of her, at Franklin's Gas & Grocery. She worked there part-time, after school, for the last two years as a clerk. In the back of the store was a store room with a pull handle in the floor. Below that handle was a vast corridor with a series of tunnels that connected to several buildings in the town square. Old man Franklin told her that the store had once been a saloon in the 1800s and then a restaurant and speakeasy in the 1920s. Anyone drinking in the back of the restaurant in the twenties had an escape route when the sheriff showed up.

Most of the tunnels had either been filled in or blocked but one still remained. The tunnel to the jail was in regular operation. They transported groceries, gas and whatever else they needed between the facilities. If anyone followed behind her, the tunnels would appear to be in working order. It would only be after traveling down them that one would run into the blockade. She reasoned she had enough time to make it to the jail and then head west.

She sprinted for the back door of the store. Like everything else in town, the store looked shuttered. The solar shields were lowered in the front, making the store look like a shipping container. She barely slipped through a chain link fence. The Grey Suits gave chase, their boots echoing off the cobblestone streets of Mount Enterprise. Although she'd done it a thousand times, she still had to count the bricks from the top of the roof to the base of the door. It was the eighth row down, fourth from the door she needed. She placed her index finger in the center of the brick and the rust-colored brick lowered, revealing a control panel. She typed in the password that hadn't changed in twenty years.

The door swiped open and she rushed inside. Once inside, she closed the door as the sounds of the Grey Suits' boots grew louder. They stood outside the chain link fence and surveyed the alley to the east and west. The leader made a call on his comm link inside his helmet. The unit split into two, one east and one west. They walked past the grocery store without more than a casual glance.

She immediately armed the store again, securing the doors to both the front and back of the store. When she was finished, she realized she was starving. She felt for her backpack but remembered leaving it in the park. Her money, keys, and phone all left behind. She couldn't imagine being more stupid. They had her journal too. Even though she was hungry, she wasn't going to steal anything. Not from Mr. Franklin. She collected a few items, estimated how much it would be and wrote Mr. Franklin a note:

Mr. Franklin:
I took the following items:
knife (34.00),
flashlight (6.99),
batteries (5.99),
a small backpack (21.00),
six water bottles (3.75),
twelve flares (11.99),
a box of jerky (9.99).

That comes to $93.63. My check should be around $173.00. Please take what I owe you out of check and donate the rest to Mrs. Paulson. She needs it more than me. Sorry about just taking these things, but it was an emergency.

April

She left the note next to the cash register. Unbeknownst to April at the time, Mr. Franklin was lying on the floor of his bathroom in the throes of the Cluster. A bloody liquid heat was spilling from every opening in his body. Every time he coughed, he shit himself with burning excrement. His heart was slowing and he was choking on the bile filling his lungs.

Mrs. Paulson was faring no better. She'd been dead several days. Her two snow-white poodles, Edward and Edwina, had taken to nibbling on her extremities for sustenance. Their once white fur was now matted with shit and blood. Their muzzles were freakishly stained into bright red smiles and they looked like deranged clowns.

April loaded the backpack, tossing the packaging for her items into the storeroom trash can. She made her way to the back and the access tunnel.

CHAPTER 16

They traveled backcountry roads for two days to get to the Canadian border. It had been nearly a week since they lost April. Mattie was despondent and Cathey didn't know what to do or say to bring him out of it. Instead of saying anything, he said nothing.

When they crossed the Canadian line, a caravan of Grey Suits were headed in the opposite direction. They cruised down the highway in their L-ATVs which had gone from their usual camo patterns to fully grey. The American flag was gone as well. Replaced by a KMC logo. Neither Cathey nor Mattie understood the significance.

They moved in silence and it was during those times that Cathey's mind wandered back to when April disappeared. It was though she was there one minute, gone the next. The Grey Suits could have her now, he didn't know. His heart was heavy and he felt like dying. He wished he hadn't just let her go.

They ate whatever they could find and usually did that in silence. After one such meal, Cathey picked himself up off the dirt road and dusted off the grime from his clothing. He ran a hand through his hair to clear the debris and was startled when he lowered his hand with a large clump of his hair attached. Tossing it to the ground, he stepped back onto the highway. Mattie followed.

They walked until the sky darkened. Roads were mostly empty with only a few abandoned vehicles stopped on the shoulders. He expected to see the dead still gripping their steering wheels but every car he passed was empty. Car doors were ajar where survivors had escaped. It wasn't a highway littered with abandoned vehicles. He also wasn't walking over corpses in the streets, either. This was no *Walking Dead*. The world was just empty. Like everyone had disappeared. He wondered how many had died and how many were still left to fight.

A sprinter van sat beneath a towering oak a few meters up the road. The driver's side door was open as were the two back doors. He could see through it and it was empty. He thought the cargo hold of the van would keep them out of the elements and away from any prying eyes.

They walked toward the van, rifles drawn and entered. Mattie closed the two rear doors behind them and said nothing. After securing the driver door, Cathie sat behind the wheel and closed his eyes for a moment. His lower body ached and it was an odd pain. Not one he'd felt before. It was a liquid hot pain like someone was cramming a hot poker down his side. He spent a few minutes looking for a set of keys, flipping the visor, opening the glove compartment and center console. Unfortunately, there were no keys.

Without keys, they decided to bed down for the night. He climbed into the back and unrolled his sack next to the boy. Turning, he looked out through the front windshield and could see a few flashlights in the distance. They danced along like fireflies and buzzed down the highway stopping about three hundred yards from the sprinter van. A spark erupted from the middle of the group and a small fire sprung to life. The man watched the four figures. They spent some time with the fire, adding wood. It grew and eventually someone put a grate over it and hung what looked like meat from it. He could see the smoke billowing out as the fat splattered on the flames. He wondered who they were and where they were from. He wondered if they were sick. Although curious, he didn't dare venture out to meet them. He thought it best to keep out of sight.

He continued to watch them as they ate. They passed around a bottle of something and they seemed comfortable with one another. Not like strangers. They spoke but their voices were muted.

Occasionally, one would laugh and it would echo across the highway and ripple through the van. They didn't seem sick. But he really didn't know.

He realized too late that Mattie was next to him, breathing slowly, watching the group.

Someone's tied up to that tree just off the highway, Mattie said.

I don't see anything, Cathey responded.

It's a person. Could be April.

We don't know that, Mattie.

Don't call me that.

Son, Cathey said, reaching for him.

The boy shrugged him off and grabbed his rifle. I'll go have a look. You rest.

You'll do no such thing, Son! I can't just let you go after every group we encounter on the outside chance April is with them.

Why not? She'd do the same for us!

Because I can't risk losing you, he said, nearly allowing himself to lose control and scream. Instead, he measured his tone and quietly responded, then this would all be for nothing. I'm not discussing this with you any further. Now lay down.

He shoved the boy down. The boy slunk down, with his head in his hands.

The fire continued to burn up ahead. The laughter died down eventually. One by one each laid down before the fire and appeared to sleep. One person stood and stretched and walked over to the tree on the far side of the highway. The person carried one of the bright flashlights. Bright red hair fell from the figure's head that was tied to the tree and turned toward the van. The man could see the woman's face for a brief second and then she turned. The figure put something into the woman's mouth and then walked away from the tree. The figure returned to the fire and warmed his or her hands for some time. Eventually, even she slept.

The man silently opened the door to the van and grabbed his rifle. He let the group sleep until the moon was in descent. He figured at least several hours had passed. The fire was glowing embers as he approached. He immediately rushed to the tree but there was no one there. Maybe he imagined it. Because he wanted her to be okay. To be alive. At the base of the tree was a crumpled piece of trash but he could see writing on the inside of it. He fumbled with his flashlight and read:

Cathey, I know how it looks but they helped me escape the Greys. Please don't hurt them. They aren't sophisticated. Please let me go. I have to see if these dreams are right. Get him home safe. You are the shepherd. That's your job. I'll see you again before you know it.

April

He stood before the group as they slept encircling the fire. He grabbed three packs and hoisted them upon his shoulder. They were heavy and unwieldly. Much too heavy for any sort of long trips. Zippers clanged against the packs as he shifted them into position on his back. He froze. A man stirred in his sleep but quickly went back to a soft snore. He inched his way back, away from the fire and slowly made his way to the van. Once at the doors, he scurried inside like a rat.

As he went through the bags, he felt a twinge of guilt. They were full of cans, bottled water and various snacks. This would put them with no food. Perhaps they would be resourceful and search the van when he was gone. He removed the expired products from the bag including the repugnant potted meats. They'd just have to deal with it.

Most of the snacks he couldn't force himself to take. Twinkies, Snickers and potato chips. This shit probably caused half the cancers the Grey Suits were getting rich off of, but the hunger in his belly burned hotly and he ended up devouring a candy bar and washing it down with a bottle of Stewart's Ocean Ale. Tasted more like sea water than anything else but it filled him up. He looked back out and saw the fire barely glowing. The figures slept as the moon continued its descent.

He transferred what he could to his pack and the boy's. At the bottom of the smallest pack, he pulled out several vials. The writing on the labels was in Chinese or a script with which he wasn't familiar. There were also notes, written in English, notating where they'd found food or water. He pocketed the items and checked on the group. Under the stars, they all still slept. He roused the boy from his sleep and he quickly grabbed his pack, ready to move. They opened the doors to the van and slipped out the back. They gave their packs one final adjustment and then disappeared into the night. He never told the boy about the note.

Variant

CHAPTER 17

Sometime in 2108

They sat in silence eating bison steak and potatoes. Despite this, she still smelled of butterscotch and it was driving him crazy. He'd grown a nice crop of potatoes in the high tunnel this year and was pleased with himself as he chewed the starchy vegetable. He took a sip of tea and watched the woman, who called herself his mother, eat.

She refused to make eye contact with him choosing instead to focus on the cutting of her meat. It was the first meat she had eaten in months.

You not talking today?

She took a bite of her meat and chewed slowly.

I see. No more pleading? No more lies?

She stopped chewing and looked up at the young man.

Talking to you hasn't gotten me anywhere, so why bother? You don't believe anything I say.

When you stop telling me lies, I'll listen.

I can't convince you of the truth. So no, I'm not talking.

The truth? That's funny coming from you. He took a rumpled picture from his pocket and held it out. Who is this?

She closed her eyes and ran her blood-caked fingers through her matted hair. I've told you a thousand times, it's me and your father.

You keep saying that. You look like her. But something's missing. I can't put my finger on it. Trust me, I've tried. I've spent months trying to figure out why you look like my mother. The information father had on you matches. DNA, blood type. But my mother wouldn't have been working for the Grey Suits.

Things changed. I told you. After your father escaped with you, I had no choice. I had to find you, so I agreed to whatever they demanded. That's the only reason I was still with them when you found us. If you would've just told your father you found me, it would save him going in there and trying to rescue me. They'll kill him. And for what? He is a terrorist wanted in the murder of over two thousand men and the kidnapping of a very valuable resource.

Okay, okay, okay. Always the company line with you, isn't it?

It's the truth. I don't know what else to say to you.

I want you to tell me why you want him dead.

She wiped a tired dirty hand across her face. Her nails were splitting and bloody in the corners. She closed her eyes, exhaled deeply and said, I don't want him dead. I just wanted him to bring you back so we could –

Those things out there have been trying to kill us.

That's what he's told you. They're out there to bring you back in. That's why they sent me. Just to bring you back in.

A Mech that's, he holds up air quotes, just bringing me in, and he drops his hands a bit but then claps them together, isn't firing blast lasers at me.

Listen, I don't know what he told you, but a human being can't survive a direct impact from a blaster. It's impossible.

Fine, I'm lying. But if they're firing blasters, they're trying to kill me. Right?

She said nothing and only stared at him.

They're not just, and he holds up air quotes again, bringing me back in. He folds his arms across his chest. He lifts his shirt and exposes the fading ring from the blaster that struck him.

I don't know what that is.

It's from a Mech blaster.

You would have been vaporized. Those blasters can take out armored vehicles.

Well, that's what it was.

He's got you so sideways. I can't even talk to you. They were sent to bring you in–

You're still lying, lady. I should just kill you and be done with it. When I captured you, back when he was sick, you told me they would find us. They're all dead and we're still here. You've been telling me the Grey Suits are coming ever since that but here we are.

They're here. There's an entire command base set up here to bring you in. You just don't realize how valuable a resource you are.

Why? Why am I so valuable?

Because sooner or later I will die. You? There's something else going on within you. You know it. You just won't tell me anything.

There's nothing to tell.

Why do I bother speaking? You know all the answers. Just kill me and be done with it. Go find your April. Fight this war you want. Destroy humanity. But leave me the hell out of it.

He walked up to her with the Colt his father carried for all those years. He pressed the barrel to her head. These bullets pierce Mechs, he said, just so you know. She nodded her head.

A lone tear escaped from the blue sea of her left eye and he saw it course down her cheek.

Are you sad because I'm going to kill you or because you failed to bring me in, he asked as he pressed the barrel harder into her skull.

No. Just sad. Something I can't place.

Spare me. He cocked the gun. Goodbye, Mom. He put a finger on the other side of her head and a small spark leapt from her scalp to his hand. He immediately felt the charge.....

She felt the singe from the mind wipe wash over her again. She was both in the infirmary and sitting before the grown child she never knew. Cathey stood before her reciting the words:

You are not his mother.

There is no James Cathey.

Your boy is dead.

The charge continued between her head and the boy's hand. It threatened to drag her from the mind wipe. Pull her back to shore. She fought it. In the corner, the clone stood ready to take her place. The DNA connected them. And it threatened to rip apart the two time periods.

Kill me now, she said. I can't be in both places.

Mattie stood in place, shaking from the electricity passing between the two of them. In both places? What did she mean?

She wavered between the two realities and heard, He's fine baby. He's fine. Just say the words.

My boy is dead. She heard herself say the words. Then she was back in the present as the boy was cocking the Colt.

He felt the surge of electricity and was thrust between worlds. Bright, dazzling, crystal blue light sparked between the two of them. It danced between them like a Fourth of July sparkler, growing in intensity. The wave passed over him and now he stood in the infirmary.

The dead lay near the door where he stood and he could smell their blood pooling on the floor. His father was injured, bent over and applying something to his mother's head. He was bleeding from a gunshot wound to his left knee. Instinctively, the boy walked over to his father but it was like he floated to him. He felt ephemeral, yet a part of this reality wherever or whenever it was. His father continued to move very slowly in putting the device on his mother. She began to shake from the mind wipe. The boy attempted to touch his father, to reassure him, but passed right through him. He was not of this world.

He could see his father attaching the mind wipe to his mother. He saw the sparks fly but he couldn't hear what they were saying. Then he saw her. In the same transient light that held him, he saw his mother standing in the corner. But he knew, standing there, that the woman in the corner was merely a decoy. Clone. His father's words washed over him and made him suddenly sick. He wanted to vomit the word from his mouth. But he found no strength.

His mother opened her eyes as the mind wipe seized her mind and fired electromagnetic currents through her. For a moment, she locked eyes with her son. She reached for him but as the mind wipe continued its jarring mission through her skull, she vanished. He reached for her hand as it vaporized into the body on the floor. He dropped to his knees and felt the connection dissipating. She lay there motionless. A single tear slipped from the boy's eye but dispersed into the ether between the two worlds.

His father stood and Mattie's connection to this world threatened to collapse. He felt the pull and fought against it. He went to his mother. She reached for him, just as he slipped away. She opened her eyes for a moment and struggled to speak. Through the hum of electricity passing between them, he couldn't hear her.

He shouted to her, what?! Her eyes wavered and his connection to this world threatened to dissolve. He fought against it. She opened her blue eyes and they were radiating, pulsing blue and bathing him in a warm cerulean light. She licked her lips and focused on her son's eyes. Not me, she said.

The connection ignited into a searing grey light and he felt himself being pulled down a tunnel. Snow glittered through his mind, clouding his vision as he tried to focus.

He blinked his eyes in an effort to clear them over and over until finally, the snow was gone. She wept before him. The gun dug into her skull, imprinting a red ring just beyond her eye. His finger gripped the trigger and he cupped it. In his mind, he pulled it. But in reality, he fought himself. His finger wouldn't move.

Not me, he heard her say except it wasn't the woman before him. The woman who continued to claim she was his mother whimpered on her knees before him. He asked himself if this wasn't his mother, then where was she? Was she even still alive?

CHAPTER 18

Sometime in 2093, after the destruction of Ft. Carson

Take her away, she could prove useful to us in the future, Serafino said to Terrance Pool, a young man of twenty-five who was Coded Yellow and relished every second of it.

We've got to figure out what he wiped. Get Cleveland down here. Tell him to pull the Reckoning files.

Sir?

You heard me, Pool. Get him down here to figure out what she remembers and then fill in the holes. She's gotta know he kidnapped her child. That will be invaluable. The rage we can create in this woman. She'll be our best weapon against him.

But, sir. If he wiped her, and we have reason to believe he did based on the surveillance video, trying to restore memory so soon could lead to widespread damage within her mind. She is one of our best scientists. Damaging her –

I want Cleveland down here now. And get that meathead out of here. He's taking up space we could be using for real soldiers.

Aye, sir.

Roosevelt Cleveland was a slight, thin, yet oddly tall man. His head was an abnormally large-shaped oval, with eyes too big for his face. They were always opened fully, giving him the appearance that he lacked eyelids. Black irises floated in each but if you had the misfortune of speaking with him, he'd most likely look straight over you. Fixated on something behind you. His nose was slender and pointed. His lips tiny and sinking into his mouth, like he was mad about something. His entire face looked as though it might disappear at any moment.

His gangly appearance stretched into the sky and his arms looked like they extended to his ankles. But that was just an illusion.

His fingers were long and thin with nails that grew like a werewolf's fangs during a full moon, although his nails grew like that daily.

Wearing no Code bracelet, many thought he was a Heteroclite. Or some manner of Heteroclite. But Cleveland was no Heteroclite. He was much more peculiar. Once coded, doctors found a thousand reasons why he should be dead, including a rather voracious form of brain cancer eating away at poor Roosevelt. Yet, here he was.

Serafino found him living in a rural cabin when they were sweeping the Great Northwest looking for Mattie. Cleveland answered his door in a black shirt so glistening it looked moist. Serafino expected it to be dripping and pooling black around his feet. Instead, it gave the impression that it was his skin, lacking any form of thread or button holding it together. A bright red tie hung about his neck. It was a perfect, thick Windsor knot that rested against the black shirt. He looked past Serafino, into the forest, as Serafino spoke.

His lips moved as if he was speaking to someone behind Serafino and when Serafino turned there was nothing but the forest behind him.

Cleveland's photographic knowledge of the countryside and encyclopedic recall of the fauna was invaluable in developing working maps for their searches. In time, they learned he was a sociopath with no conscience. He'd do anything Serafino asked. Nothing was off limits for him. A beheading in the forest of Aldair on a deserter? Done. Threatening those who wanted to stay behind? Done. Killing those who didn't heed the threats? Done.

Grey Suits feared him because he had no boundaries. Men, women, children? Didn't matter. A rumor circulated among the men that he'd escaped from Bridle Veil Falls during the Great Surge. A notorious hospital for the criminally insane outside Bend, Oregon. He had a tattoo on the inside of his lip that said BVF, but no one had seen it. They were too frightened to ask. Word was he tattooed it himself and then tattooed a heart somewhere on his body for everyone he'd killed. Again, that was unconfirmed. No one wanted to ask him about that either, but his left forearm was littered with black ash prison tattoos in the shape of hearts.

Pool knocked on the door to Cleveland's office. It was so far underground that it was one of the few places that survived the Mech assault and self-destruction. Pool swallowed hard, always fearing Roosevelt.

The door creaked open, as if opening in a horror movie. Cleveland stood in darkness, just on the other side. Yes, he said.

Serafino sent for you. Down in the infirmary. Wants you to mind wipe Strong. Said to bring the Reckoning files.

He moved just into the light. A furtive smile crossed Cleveland's mysterious face. Pool thought he saw the man's teeth, but he couldn't be sure. He never had before.

The Reckoning files, he said, without the hint of a question in his shrill voice. I can't wait. It's been so long.

He rubbed his chin with slender, tentacle-like fingers. The fingernails dragged across his skin, nearly drawing blood. Tell him it will be done.

Yeah, okay.

Pool turned to leave and Cleveland called his name, Mr. Pool?

He stopped, heart pounding, wanting nothing more than to be away from this distortion. He turned, facing Cleveland. Yes, he said.

You disagree with Serafino's decision to wipe her again?

No sir. I have no opinion. I have orders. My orders were to get you down to the infirmary to wipe Strong. Those were my orders and I've performed them. The rest is up to you.

You fear she might not be the same with multiple wipes, this is true?

I have no such fear, Mr. Cleveland. I am a soldier. I have orders and I follow them. I have done so in this instance. I must get back.

You are a Yellow Code, I see.

That's right.

Two years, give or take, right?

I am hopeful for more.

He who has health, has hope, right Mr. Pool? The company line? I believe I've seen that line more than one time outside the Grey Suit hospitals, no?

I've seen it. But you shouldn't call us Grey Suits. It's offensive.

Is it? You're offended by it?

I don't want to get into it with you, Mr. Cleveland. Just please do your job.

Have I said something that bothers you Mr. Pool?

No. I just don't wish to talk to you anymore.

Hmm, then it is my prerogative to speak with you.

Please, Mr. Cleveland.

You know we were out, when the explosions happened. When the traitor tried to destroy us?

I understand that you were on an exercise.

An exercise. Right. That's what Serafino calls them, isn't it.

The Yellow bracelet you wear? Two years? But they've promised you more, for your service. Correct?

I'm getting the best anti-Cluster drugs known to man. Like I said –

Right, right, right. He who has health, has hope. Which is bullshit, but okay. You're getting whatever the government will give you for your service.

That's not true. I'm serving to save us. To save this country. We can be great again.

What happens when you're no longer of service to your government?

Mr. Cleveland, you're asking questions that are deeply offensive to the very government that allows you to prosper.

Am I?

You are.

Will you turn me in?

If this continues, I'll be forced to.

What would they do to me? If you turned me in?

I'm not sure.

Would it be worse than what we did to that insurrection village just outside Lamar the other day?

When he said the words, Pool cringed, but tried to maintain a stoic face.

I'm not sure, he said. I don't know what's going on in Lamar or what you did to them.

That's interesting. We traveled through there. Not knowing the evacuation orders had been ignored. The old grain silos were blinking on our comms like Christmas trees. A few holdouts, hiding inside. Vowing to fight to the end. The Mechs with us stood aside. Letting me have my fun. You know no one stopped me.

Cleveland stepped further outside his office. He stood above Pool and looked down on him.

Pool tried to hold his gaze. But Cleveland's unusual black eyes now glowed a preternatural orange. And they pulsed in his head. They bore into him like an eclipsed sun, burning his vision.

It would be immediate dismissal if they knew wouldn't it, Mr. Pool?

If they knew what?

If they knew you were feeding them information on movements. So that they could fool us. That's against the law, isn't it Mr. Pool?

Look, I don't know what you're suggesting –

I'm suggesting nothing. I'm telling you I entered that first silo with the Provincial Reconstruction Team and was attacked by a woman who shares your DNA. Your mother. I bit into her neck and ripped her weathered flesh with my teeth. She tasted so good. The arterial blood injecting into my mouth like a syringe. I bled her. And added her to my right arm.

He held his right arm out and in the crease between his forearm and bicep was a tattoo of a hypodermic needle with hearts in the cylinder.

You sick fuck. I know what you're doing. But it won't work.

Serafino was standing right behind me. He held your sister down and –

Pool launched himself at Cleveland. He held one slender arm out and caught him before he got close. He withdrew a machete from behind him and sliced Pool's scalp from his head. Pool slouched in his grip but struggled against the nearing death.

You think we wouldn't find them? Or connect the dots? I'm just the man for the job. Cleveland laughed as Pool continued to bleed out.

You, he said, gurgling on the blood pooling in his throat.

We'll find them all, Cleveland said and held Pool before him. Blood coursed down his arm, making the soldier slippery in his grasp. He whipped the machete across the man's throat, sending the body to the floor. Cleveland held the decapitated head before him. Pool stared back at him for a moment and his lips moved in silent agony. The body flooded the floor outside his office with deep crimson colored blood. He hoped the Cluster wasn't contagious. If it was, he was dead. But so far, so good. And then again, who really cared? He was dead anyway. He tossed Pool's head down the hall and holstered the machete in the scabbard on his back.

His phone beeped a few minutes later.

Cleveland.

Did you take care of him?

What do you think?

I need you down here. She's still alive. And I need everything recovered.

The Reckoning files? Nice touch.

I thought you'd enjoy that.

Not as much as I will breaking that sonofabitch Cathey.

In time Cleveland, in time. First things first. Come find this bitch's memory for her.

He wasted no time getting to the infirmary. Cleveland stood before her, the memory recovery cord still hanging from her temple. The PLC was warm in his hand. Her vacant stare betrayed nothing and yet he felt like she was either fighting him or she really had nothing to recall. Even with the most heinous of mind wipes, there was always something left behind. For this one? Nothing. He turned the dial on the PLC and threatened to activate it again when Serafino touched him lightly on his shoulder. He turned.

Let's give her a minute. That's a wipe and two recoveries in less than twenty-four hours. I'm not sure how bad we've fucked her up.

We care?

We need her. To draw Cathey back in. And to get our hands on that kid.

I know you're some sort of army wizard but you're insane if you think Cathey will ever bring that kid anywhere near here again. He's gonna hide him. I would if I were him.

We have his wife. He'll come for her. If she's in danger.

He left her and wiped her mind. I'm not sure he's going to care.

He will. We just have to make him. That's why I have you.

CHAPTER 19

Sometime in 2108

Len exhaled deeply trying to digest what his contact had just told him. Fifteen to twenty million. All in gold. And that information was over a year old. He said the bounty seemed to increase by a million every year. The Grey Suits were offering free life-time housing to whomever brought him in. A palace in the city. The best Cluster drugs known to man. Twenty-four-hour care, when it came to that. The lap of luxury.

Len's called his contact, Tony, who had been searching for Cathey for the last four years. He was operating with a skeleton crew. Promised them a twenty percent cut. Tony was paying the expenses. He didn't sound like he wanted to share.

You getting close to him, Len asked.

Trail's cold right now. I'm just burning through money. Lost a few guys along the way. Some by fire, some by the Cluster. My thought, they were Reds, looking for some quick money to buy some Cluster pills. Guess we weren't quick enough. You got something on him?

I might, Len said. You remember that bar I was working at?

Tony laughed, the one at the end of the world?

Yeah. He may be here. In a room above the bar.

You sure it's him?

Thumb prints were a partial match. I still gotta run a DNA test on him.

Like anyone's going to volunteer for that. Did he at least have the tattoo?

His arm was all burned up with scar tissue right where it was supposed to be. I checked that first thing.

Was it legit?

Felt real enough.

Coulda' burned it off. That was a pretty obvious clue to his identity.

Yeah. It might not be him, but I got chills when I locked eyes with him. He was the first one I thought of when I saw this guy. I'd hate to let him walk out of here tomorrow without so much as a double check on his identity.

Problem is, if it's Cathey and you've already confronted him about it, he's already gone. Trust me, I had him cornered a half dozen times only to see him slip through my fingers.

Len had no reason to doubt what Nick was telling him, but Cathey was in Alaska during those half dozen times while Tony was scattered over the Mid-West. Sightings of Cathey were about as common as Big Foot. And about as accurate.

There's only one way out of here. And it's straight through the bar.

I wouldn't try to take him on your own.

He's weak. I coulda' taken him earlier. He's not what he once was.

Said everyone who's tried taking him on. He's survived out there for all these years because he's smart. And he's strong. He was probably just playing possum with ya.

How long would it take you to get here?

I could be there by tomorrow night.

That might be too late.

Call in the Grey Suits. But if it's not him, you're going to have a world of shit to deal with when they figure it out.

I'll be in a world of shit anyway with them. I'm not exactly out here legally.

CHAPTER 20

The room was damp and smelled of piss. Piss that had been left to collect around the corners and recesses of a toilet. The kind that makes you breathe through your mouth so you don't have to smell that stench anymore.

Cathey unfolded his sleep sack and put it on top of the bed. As he bent to smooth it out, the sharp abdominal pain returned and erupted in his stomach and he doubled over. It was intense and burned from his balls to his throat. He sank down beside the bed, letting the pain subside. He could barely catch his breath. Since he stopped the transfusions, the pain in his gut was growing worse. He shut his eyes for a moment, but ended up sleeping for several hours. When he awoke, he was panicked. He hadn't intended on sleeping at all.

Cathey didn't know how much Len remembered from those days after the mind wipe. Hell, he didn't know how effective his wipe had been. He'd been in charge of putting them on the Mech units that were doing crowd control and dispersal for the administration in the early days of the Grey Suits. They seemed to be fairly effective but he was gone before the results could be fully analyzed.

He knew two things. One, Len was alive and had some recollection of him, albeit slightly disjointed. Two, one of those guys was most certainly going to try to trade him for the bounty. Of that, he had no doubt.

He put his sleep sack in the backpack. Then he went about finding what they used to call a penetration point in the room. Without widows, he'd need to find the spot where if push came to shove, no matter your size, you could squeeze yourself through to escape whatever bag of shit was about to be hurled your way. He felt

185

along the walls and found nothing. He ran his hand along the ceiling until it got too high to touch. It didn't look like there were any openings there either.

Despite the smell, he went into the toilet and inspected the ceiling. Nothing. Then he noticed a small door at the base of the sink. He opened it and saw the pipes leading to his sink and then down another floor. He yanked on the door and ripped it from the wall. A small passageway led to the floor below. After several minutes, he had the floor pulled up sufficiently so that escape would be possible if the hallway was blocked.

He lowered himself down to the floor below. There were no lights on and someone slept in the room adjacent to the bathroom. The bathroom was a carbon copy of the one he'd just escaped from. Light snoring came from the room. He felt along the wall and stepped quietly into the room. The floor gave way a bit with the step and creaked. As it did, multiple red tracer lights ignited and centered on his chest and skull. A light panel was touched and pale yellow light filled the room. Cathey was face to face with a room full of Grey Suits. The last thing he remembered was reaching for his pistol. The stock from a blaster crashed across the bridge of his nose, splattering blood across his vision. He tried to breathe through his nose but swallowed a throat full of blood instead. They hit him one more time and he collapsed. Blackness swept over him and they were on him.

CHAPTER 21

He awoke shackled to a bed. Tubes snaked out from his left arm and a monitor in the corner beeped with each beat of his heart. A Red Code bracelet hung from his emaciated wrist. The lights were low and he couldn't see past his feet. The walls were close, like a jail cell. He tried to move to no avail and he wondered if they'd taken him. Somewhere deep within his subconscious, he thought it had been a dream. But now it felt real. His mind swam beneath a haze of drugs but he couldn't identify them. During his Grey Suit training, he'd been subjected to a wide variety of street drugs to assist in the detection of the drugs and the best way to counteract such interactions. This felt like opioids. But much more sedate. He wanted to sleep but fought against it. The beeping was soothing. His eyes grew heavy.

A door opened somewhere in front of him. A sliver of light grew wide and an obscure figure entered, shutting the door behind.

Mr. Cathey, the male voice said in hushed tones.

He wanted to shout at the man but despite opening his mouth wide, no sounds reverberated from his vocal chords. Instead, he felt tremendous pain.

Your vocal chords have been temporarily paralyzed Mr. Cathey. You made much too much noise during the extraction process. We simply couldn't have you upsetting the entire unit. You are lucky we didn't simply kill you after we got what we needed. Normal function should return shortly. Please drink that tea next to you. That should alleviate the symptoms.

Cathy swallowed hard with each sip. The pain in his throat felt like the worst case of strep throat he'd ever had in his life.

You can whisper, Mr. Cathey. That's about it.

Where am I, he asked in a muted whisper.

Strategic Air Command, Sonora, Texas.

Why?

Why? Do you really have to ask that? For the boy. Based upon the extraction information we were able to pull from you, we now have teams headed further north. To what you call the Summer Cabin. They should be there within the hour.

Summer Cabin? I don't know any Summer Cabin, he murmured.

Your protestations are irrelevant. You've been gone a while. We used your technology on the mind wipes and reverse engineered those to create this extraction unit. We can pull the most deeply-imbedded memories from you. No matter how much you might lie to yourself, you can't lie to the Interface. Then it's just a matter of de-noising, translating and storing the information. We've been through thousands of raw waves of yours. Summer and Winter Cabin came through the most. Your thoughts on the boy were also most helpful. We know what we're up against in getting him out of there.

Cathey closed his eyes. He wished it was a dream but the pain in his throat reminded him that it was all too real. His temples burned from the brain computer interface sensors. The sides of his head felt like they'd been burned by a thousand tiny lasers.

He wondered if they were really that close to the boy. The fact that he was the one to lead them to him was even more upsetting. He never should've stopped at that damn bar. It was going to be all their undoing. He wondered what else they knew.

The man approached Cathey on the left. He adjusted the drip on the IV and Cathey felt his body go numb.

Fighting against the Maze isn't in your best interest, he said, tapping the drip chamber, causing more of the sedative to fall. Sleep would be best for you. I'll just keep adjusting it until I finally put you back under. The more I give you, the more likely I'll kill you. And

I'm not done extracting everything I need from you. The location of the Lighthouse is still unknown. We'd like to round those folks up while we're busy putting an end to the Rising. And April. We are still trying to figure out who she is. Unless you want to tell me.

Cathey looked at the man through muddled eyes. Did he say April was still alive? Immediately he corrected his thinking and began telling himself he didn't know who April was. He kept that at the forefront of his thought process.

Don't know any April, he said, his tongue thick and swollen blocking the whisper.

It's fine, the man said. In due time we'll have that information as well. It just takes further distillation of the information and then translation. We have our best men on it as we speak.

He could hear the man speaking, but it was like hearing him from the bottom of a pool. The man's voice, muted and fragmented, floated down to him. Cathey felt like he was a thousand feet under water. The Maze was coursing through his veins and he felt it pulling him further down. He fought the fatigue. But soon it was too much.

Sleep was temporary. A familiar scent drifted in the room and through the darkness he thought he could see her. He sensed it was her from the moment she entered the room. Sharp and sweet, like the most luxurious jasmine known. He had always been the only one who could smell it. He knew it was her. She was there, at the bed.

You okay, she asked. He remained shackled to the bed, unable to move.

He didn't know whether to shake his head no or nod. He didn't know what she needed to hear.

You remember, he asked hoarsely.

Remember what?

Everything? Us?

Most. I can't tell you how. Not now. They've paralyzed your vocal chords.

He nodded.

I pleaded with them not to, she said.

His head spun. She was in communication with them? Why, he asked.

They want information. Or confirmation of information they're pulling from you. Pulling the information is agonizing. I can't say more.

The Lighthouse? It was you?

She didn't acknowledge his question, instead she put a finger to his lips, silencing him. She paused, wanting to tell him everything but knowing they could both die if she did. They were listening, ready to enter the room at any moment.

You know I've always worked with them. You did at one point.

But in those days we –

She reached for him in the dark. She traced a heart shape over his chest. It was something he hadn't felt since the night the boy was born. And before that, she only did it when she was trying to comfort him and tell him everything was going to be okay without saying anything. In the early days, it was sometimes the best way for them to communicate.

He felt it that day they were thrust together. They sat in the room, two-way mirrors watching them, computers analyzing their interactions. Dozens of doctors taking notes. They were each covered with sensors.

Don't speak, she said. Let's just get this over with.

But I can't do it. Not this way. There's no way I can do anything with them watching.

She approached him and put her arms around his neck. She whispered in his ear, they're going to force us to do it this way or they're going to take it from you and inject it into me.

He pushed his lips up her neck and found her ear, this is not how I wanted any of this to happen. It's rape. They're raping both of us. I won't do it.

She stepped back for a moment and admired the man she'd fallen in love with. She took his hand with hers and traced a heart on his chest. I love you, James Cathey, she whispered. The tracing of the heart on his chest always calmed him. His heart rate slowed and he started to take deeper breaths.

But not like this, he whispered to her.

You're going to fight them, she asked, tracing the heart again with his hand. She took his hand from his chest and started to trace the heart on her chest. His hand rolled over her cleavage but fought what she was doing.

This is wrong, he said.

She nodded. Then we tell them to go to hell and suffer the consequences. He nodded. She traced the heart on her chest again with his hand. He looked at her but was looking through her. His heart began to race.

Honey, she said, and started tracing the heart on his chest.

This time, it didn't work. He peered over her shoulder and said, you can all come in here and take this shit from me. I'm not your dancing monkey.

She heard the click of the lock and the swoosh of the door as they poured in. I love you, she said. He opened his mouth to respond, but the Grey Suits smacked a small steel bat across his face, splitting his lip. They shoved Clara against the wall and immediately tied her down. She cried as they bound him and led him away. Twenty minutes later, they were back. She stiffened as they approached her.

191

Two men took each one of her legs and tried to fit her into the stirrups. She kicked and flayed, striking one in the cheek. They managed to get Clara's legs spread into the stirrups. The soldier she struck stumbled backward but quickly regained his footing. He lurched at the woman and reared back a fist to beat her for her insubordination. She flinched as he approached but the doctor standing behind him grabbed the soldier's cocked fist.

No more beatings. We need her strong. The next man in here that strikes this patient will answer to Serafino. He's left her health in my hands and I won't have you beating her for every perceived slight.

She was kicking us sir, one of the men responded.

Strike her and find out how much Serafino cares. It'll be the last thing you do. Of that, I assure you.

They secured her ankles to the stirrups and bound her head to the back of the chair. Her arms were immobile as well and she could do nothing more than twist slightly. She wanted to scream at them to stop but her mouth was covered and she couldn't open her mouth.

The doctor stood back and a nurse entered. She took the vial and loaded it into the replicator. Clara tried to bend her head to see what the nurse was doing but she felt it before she saw anything. She pulled with every muscle in her body, but to no avail. They confirmed later that night that she was officially pregnant.

He stopped talking as she continued tracing the heart on his chest in the dark. They were listening. And watching. He didn't know if she was manipulating him or signaling that everything was okay between them. He also didn't know if this was really Clara.

In those days, we were just kids, she said.

Naïve, he breathed.

Very, she responded.

I would've believed anything you said back then.

Then trust me now. She traced the heart on his chest again. We just need to confirm the location of our son.

Confirm the location of our son, he whispered, confused by the way she said it. What are you talking about?

Honey, it's me. I just need to know his position –

She paused and seemed to be resetting her words. When she spoke again, it was with precision. We just need to know where he is. So we can get him home safe.

He glared at her while trying to make sense of her speech patterns. She didn't sound like Clara and even in the haze of the drugs coursing through his body, that was a good thing.

Your hip. They were able to sew it all back?

She studied him and nodded. To prove it, she leaned to her side and pulled her pants down and away from her hip. There, on her left hip, was a faint scar where four bullets passed through her body. His Clara had been two cities over when the bullets started flying that day.

His face cracked the smallest smile and then he resumed his prepared speech. The one he practiced for a day such as this.

I'm sorry. I wish there was another way to say this. The boy is dead. He didn't make it past the first winter. Summer Cabin is just where I lost him. They're on a wild goose chase.

She listened for something in his voice. Something that told her he was being truthful. She couldn't tell anything.

Did you name him, she asked with a trembling voice. Tears streamed down her face. Her acting was quite good.

Would it matter if I did?

Maybe not. But when I think of him, maybe I could think of him as you did.

I doubt that. You brought me back here. Just to get at the boy. To save the Grey Suits. And this godforsaken planet. You don't care about me. I doubt you care about the boy.

I – she began and then stopped. She gripped the cold steel of the bar next to the bed and let out a silent breath. He heard the stitch in her breath. The one she'd get when she was stifling a thought or an argument. She had always been the better of the three clones.

I didn't really call him anything, he said and hung his head. This was all true. He hadn't named the boy. He simply never had the time. When he thought of what to call him, there was some new disaster to deal with and he had to turn his attention to survival. Names seemed senseless given the gravity of the situation. He was so young when he died, Cathey said, returning to the present. I tried a couple of names but none seemed to fit. I missed your input. So I just called him boy until he drew that last breath.

How did he – and she stopped again, finding real emotion, thinking of her son.

Starvation, far as I could tell. No milk. Formula was gone by then. I couldn't find any along the way. Lying now was second nature.

Intermixed with lies, there was always a hint of truth. He remembered, as he spoke to her, the day he truly thought the boy would die. The day he'd dropped to his knees on that dusty street in Wyoming, before they found April. The child did nothing but cry and he felt like it was just a matter of hours until the kid gave up. But as he rocked the baby, he could see in his eyes, even then, a determination. A stoic look that there was no giving up in him. The boy quieted down and watched his father weep on that empty street. The man thought the boy was dying. Instead, the child simply slept. Once quiet, the man surveyed the surroundings and placed the boy back in the pack.

On that street he saw Draper Drugs and he slipped through the shards of broken glass near the front door. The store had been ripped to pieces by looters. The pharmacy sacked for the opiates and other drugs. Under the counter, he found sixteen cases of baby formula. And a lone bottle of Jameson's. He figured Gerald had a hand in leading him here. Jameson's had always been his guilty pleasure. The man stacked the formula on the sled behind the baby carrier. He put the Jameson's in his coat pocket. Somehow, they survived that first winter. He smiled in the darkness. He hoped she could sense it....

Where did you bury him, she asked, drawing him back.

Somewhere in Wyoming.

Do you remember where? It's important.

Important? For who?

For all of us. You know that.

They would've used him as a lab rat. You know that. If I tell you where the body is buried even now, they'll whirl out there and dig him up in the hopes of extracting what little DNA is left in his tiny body. Kill me now, because I ain't telling you where he's buried.

There were voices outside the door and then a click as the lock opened. She stood and then Cathey heard footsteps. They paused at the bed and then the waters washed over him again. The voices muffled as he slid deep beneath the haze of drugs they turned up. She collapsed against the bar truly selling her performance. We have everything we need, they said. Take her away. If it's right, send her back to her cell. If not, if we find nothing in Alaska or Wyoming, kill her, Serafino said.

The boy awoke during the night. His head ached from a dream where he saw a towering figure standing over him with what looked like a steel bar. The man swung the bar across his face and he felt the explosion of pain as bones in his face splintered under its power. As he went down, he could see his father lying on a hospital bed. And as he hit the ground, he saw her face. His mother. She sat next to the bar. A lone tear rolled down her cheek and she clutched at a blanket. Then he rocked out of bed, sweating, despite the cold, clutching his pillow tight. The dreams were beginning to feel so real.

CHAPTER 22

Sometime in 2092

April lifted the false floor of the storeroom careful not to disturb the large rug covering it. She lit the flashlight, stuck it in her pocket and lowered herself onto the ladder. She cautiously let the floor close on top of her. The rug came to rest in place. No one would know there was tunnel access in this room.

The tunnel was damp and dark. The walls and floor made up of nothing more than two-by-fours nailed into the raw earth with nine inch spikes. In places, the earth was taking back over, splitting the wood with root and vine, threatening to bring the whole place down. Spider webs clung to the ceiling and draped down across the path like ghastly chandeliers. The beam from the flashlight bounced off each one and disappeared into the vastness of the tunnel. April took a few tentative steps along the uneven path and stopped suddenly when she heard voices.

She immediately killed the light and stood in the darkness. She dared not breathe. Somewhere ahead she heard the slow trickle of water, dripping from above and splattering onto the wood floor below. Warm air flowed past her, caressing her cheek and streaming through her hair, twirling it in the darkness. Her only explanation for the wind was that someone had entered the tunnel down field. The voices stopped and the web before her shuddered in the dark, sticking to her hair and climbing down her scalp. She swiped the web away and rubbed the tacky residue on her pants.

She was hopeful that they would give up when they found that most of the tunnels led to nothing but dead ends. Their voices carried down the corridor but she saw no light. She didn't know how close they were to the Franklin shaft, but she thought of climbing back up and hiding in the storeroom until the threat passed. The voices continued to grow in intensity and she decided to head back up and wait them out. She turned around and the disorientation from the darkness was amplified by the fact that she didn't know how far she had come. She'd turned to the right out of Franklin's but to the left was also a passage. Where it led now she didn't know. In the twenties, it led to a parlor room under the old Sullivan Hotel. She had been told they caved that parlor in as well as the tunnel leading to it. Now, as she felt along the wall of the tunnel, she was worried she'd gone too far. She didn't dare turn the light back on for fear of alerting whomever was down here to her position. She stopped and fought for sight in the darkness. She scanned the roof of the tunnel, looking for any sliver of light coming from the floor of Franklin's storeroom. Then, her left hand raked across the bottom rung of the ladder.

April pulled herself up and climbed the tarnished rungs slowly and silently. Her head gently struck the floor and she pushed up.

Get her in here and find out if this is her handwriting. There's no way she got far if it is.

She held her breath and looked from under the rug at a series of black boots and grey pants. Grey Suits, she thought to herself. In the store. She wondered if it was their voices she was hearing? She couldn't be sure.

The boots began to walk toward the front of the store and she heard voices shouting. It was too far away, probably in the street she supposed. Then the voices came back with a rush and too many people were talking at once to make any sense of it. Until she heard her mother's voice.

Yes, yes, yes, that's her writing. That's so like her to leave a note. Well, for Mr. Franklin. She'd never show me the same courtesy.

Bitch, April thought.

So we've got packaging over here and this note. Obviously, she was planning on hitting the road or something. Was she outdoorsy?

April, she asked incredulously, heavens no. She's much too, I don't know what the word is, girly, for that. She wouldn't last five minutes in the wild. Especially now. With all that's going on. And I'm not saying anything's going on, per se. I'm just saying –

Ma'am. It's fine. We just need to find her.

April shook her head and nearly laughed. Had she forgotten the time she'd spent with Elizabeth and her family? Hunting, fishing, camping and learning from Elizabeth's military father. April always assumed he was insane, talking about end times and preparing for the shutdown of the grid. Little did he know, he'd be nearly spot on only five short years later. April wondered if poor Elizabeth was down in the bunker now, hiding from the Grey Suits.

I just can't believe she's not around here. She was obviously here.

She a smart girl, ma'am?

I suppose. I haven't been around lately, given my husband's condition and all. But I guess she's smart – her mother began coughing violently. She cleared her throat and continued, she's not stupid by any means. A little selfish, but what teen isn't? Well, she's a bit more-

Ma'am, does she have friends? Like someone she might seek out to hide her?

No, she was pretty much a loner. April shook her head again at the absolute absurdity of everything her mother thought of her. She dipped her head below the floor for a moment to steady herself. Below her, beams bounced on the flooring like drunken fireflies. She glanced up and the Grey Suits were still in the store but she could scurry up and roll herself into the back of the storeroom. There were several racks of returns in the corner with which she could camouflage herself. She had no choice.

She pushed up the flooring and rolled to her right, across the floor and into the back of the storeroom. She twisted her body toward the wall and then slid her feet down the wall, propelling her to the racks. She pulled several sweat-suits around her and slid into a sitting position. Through the clothes, she could see them. She just hoped they couldn't see her.

A radio chirped twice on the shoulder of a tallish man with full Grey Suit regalia. He was extraordinarily skinny, what some would soon start to call the Cluster Diet skinny, and had eyes set too close together. They were the color of tar and seemed to be hiding atop his large forehead. His nose was flat and stretched across his face like a mask. April wondered how he breathed through the small slits in his flattened snout. He opened his mouth to respond and she was sickened to see fresh blood skimming across his teeth. This man was sick, she thought. As if on cue, he leaned his head back and coughed violently into a handkerchief he barely had time to pull from his back pocket. The brief second she saw it, it was sparkling-red with blood from deep within his lungs. He had maybe a month left.

Clarke, go.

Sir, we've been through the tunnels. Most of them are filled-in or caved-in. We found one that was intact leading to, we believe, the grocery store where you're stationed. But we didn't find anything.

Any signs she was down there? Footprints. Anything?

No sir. It's fairly shitty down here. I'm not sure a little girl could handle it. Spiders and shit.

If you're sure, Corporal.

Yessir. No sign of her.

What's your position?

We've assembled back at the jail.

Good, torch it. Torch everything on your way out of this godforsaken town. I'll take care of this end of town.

Burn everything?

Everything standing.

Sir, we haven't done a proper sweep of this area –

Corporal, are you questioning me?

No sir. We'll take care of it.

We'll rally in Dallas. I've got some people to drop off there. Let's call it by 1800 hours tomorrow.

Roger that. Teller out.

Clarke out.

Judy Wolfe smiled sheepishly at the commander. You're taking us with you?

Clarke nodded. It's not safe on the roads right now. We'll get you to Dallas safe and sound. It would be nice, however, if we could find your daughter along the way. I believe that was part of the agreement, was it not?

I just don't know where she could have gotten off to, she said. We desperately need those Cluster drugs that were promised, though. My husband doesn't have long without them.

We will uphold our end of the bargain, Mrs. Wolfe. You just keep working on yours. I'm sure it will be fine.

April took small, shallow breaths and ached for the moment these people left her store.

Watkins, Clarke said over the walkie.

Bring in the fire and let's get out of here.

Clarke ushered Judy out the door and April lost sight of them. A small Grey Suit entered with a large fuel canister and began dousing everything in jet propellant. He hit all the major areas of the store and then grabbed a road flare from the counter and lit it. He hurled into the middle of the store and then April heard the L-ATVs fire up and blow big black plumes of smoke from their exhaust. They began lumbering down the main street as Franklin's began to burn.

The smoke was already intense from the fuel and April stood up from behind the rack of clothes she was hiding in. She started to cough immediately and her only thought of escape was through the tunnels. Fire blocked the front of the store with large billowing plumes of scarlet-chasing trails of jet fuel. Thick black smoke swirled at the ceiling and painted the walls with soot. She yanked aside the rug and hastily made her way down into the tunnel.

As soon as her feet hit the wooden flooring, she thumbed the flashlight on and scanned the tunnel's passageways. To the right she knew she'd encounter the jail. To the left there was the possibility that the old parlor was still intact but she didn't know how far down that would take her. If she waited, well, if she waited the whole town might burn. She decided she didn't want to see if anyone was waiting for her at the jail, so she went left and hurried down the hallway.

After only a minute, she could see the tunnel's end. There was no indication of a parlor or a door. She scanned the walls around her and saw nothing but spiders and moldy wood. Then, in the mud behind the wood, she saw something metallic. It peeked up at her through the slits in the wood. She tried to stick her finger through the opening but it was too small. She dropped her backpack and took out the knife she bought (she liked to think of it as buying even though Franklin's was burning down on top of her). She pulled at the wood until it finally gave way a bit, then she worked on it harder. Pulling on the wood, it finally snapped, sending her flying against the wall behind her. What she saw was a small six-inch by six-inch brass rectangle in the earthen wall. Somewhere there was a click and then the brass fitting began to slide, exposing an opening....

…..Yes, the voice called to her.

She pulled herself up and dusted the muck from her clothes. She didn't know what to say so she shined her light on the opening. It immediately shut.

Oh, I'm sorry, she said. I'll put it out. She waited in the dark but to no avail. Cautiously, she approached the brass fixture and knocked on it gently.

Yes, a voice called from the other side.

I'm sorry, she said. I've put my light out.

What do you desire?

She thought about it for a moment and couldn't think of anything to say. A fragment of a dream wafted across her subconscious and she blurted out the word protection.

The brass fitting slid across, revealing an amber-colored light. An older man stared back at her. He looked to her left and then to her right.

You haven't come for your father, have you?

She didn't understand the question. What do you mean, she asked.

We don't have ladies down here. It's a no admittance policy for ladies.

I'm just a girl. I'm no lady.

Same for girls. Especially girls. Could you imagine the trouble we'd have down here if we let underage girls in? We couldn't buy the sheriff off for those types of rumors. We serve drinks down here for men. Good day.

Wait, she said, putting a hand to the fixture and stopping it from closing. I'm seeking protection. I need somewhere safe to hide.

Who sent you?

She thought for a moment. What did that iguana call himself? She tried in vain to remember a name, if he had one. Then, like a

switch going off deep within her, a name surfaced. Derek. Derek
Gill sent me. She had no recollection of this name. It simply popped
into her head and felt appropriate.

Derek Gill sent you, you say?

He has.

And he's offered you shelter down here?

He has, she said, not knowing if he had or not.

The ancient door, hidden behind decades of mud and wood
impaled upon it, with gigantic nails driven into its flesh, began to
open. She stepped back, amber light flooding the tunnel. The sweet
smell of pipe tobacco floated out the door. A jazz number pinged on
the piano and hovered just at the entrance. She stepped in.

At first, she couldn't see anyone in the parlor. It was just her
and the doorman. On a wall across from her, a painting shimmered
into focus. A swirling galaxy lit up the canvas and began to spin. A
ship was approaching the spiral. But the ship belonged on the ocean,
not space.

You like it, the doorman asked.

She did. But she didn't know why.

It's called *Here Gather the Stars*. Mickey's favorite.

Who is – she started but then her eyes adjusted and the lights
rose and a man in a purple tuxedo sat at a piano, pounding the keys,
singing about Betty and why she had to leave. He had a big cigar
under his pudgy nose and his black eyes rolled in his head as his
meaty fists pounded the keys. He wore a brown bowler hat with a
silver ribbon around the crown. It sparkled in the amber light like a
halo. Several men bantered about and wondered aloud why Derek
had sent this young lady down to them.

For satisfaction?

She's just a kid.

I used to be a kid.

Then tables came into view and men drinking scotch and bourbon started to pop into life like stars at dusk. She staggered amongst the tables and a man with a pencil-thin mustache stood to steady her.

She's here for protection, the doorman called.

Protect her we shall, the piano man yelled. He beat on the keys and sang

> *Why so woeful? Why so sad?*
> *Dry your eyes and fall in my arms*
> *You don't need to be blue*
> *Shadows lurk in my world too*
> *When the gloom wraps up on you*
> *I'll endure the pain*
> *No one can hurt you*
> *I'll stand by you*

The gentleman with the pencil-thin mustache sat her at his table and slid a drink over to her. She shook her head no but he insisted. She took a sip and then downed it. He had a slim, angular face with a too-slim nose. Black hair was parted severely to the right and pasted into place with a heavy dose of Dapper Dan. He had dark colored eyes that might have been black, but they could have been brown when he was a younger man. A scar on his right hand resembled a shamrock and April wondered how he got it.

This, he said, showing her the scar, got this as an idiot kid. Lye is nothing to play with. She was taken aback at his ability to hear her despite the fact she had not spoken.

Things are different here. I can hear your thoughts. He smiled.

I can't hear yours.

It's taken me years of practice to hone that skill. Imagine if every rummy in here could read my thoughts. That'd cause some trouble. But we can use words.

The piano man started to play something softer, making conversation in the parlor easier.

What is this place, she asked.

The man stared at her as though he didn't understand what she was saying. The amber light reflected from the bar and lit the man's face with subdued tones. He looked serious. More serious than the rest of the men down here.

This is just a way station. Don't go telling the gents that, though.

A way station? She looked at him with a puzzled look.

Forgot, you're a Topper.

Her puzzled look grew.

From up top. The real world. Down here, time's slowed to a crawl. These guys just don't know it. Or refuse to realize it. Now what were you asking me, Doll?

This place, you said it was a way station.

A stopover. A small railway station between two bigger stations.

There's a train down here?

Not today. Usually only stops on Mondays. What's today?

I don't even know, she said.

Yeah, me neither. But most of these gents are waiting on the train. Are you?

There was a fire. I came down to escape it. Mr. Franklin, the guy who owns the store up top, he said there was an old speakeasy down here.

Ah. Shh-shh-shh. It's called a juice joint. But I don't know what you're talking about, he said with a sly laugh. We don't need no Mulligans down here.

Are you waiting on something?

As a matter of fact, I am. It was you.

Me?

You, Doll Face. You are April Wolfe, no?

How'd you know?

I know a great many things Miss Wolfe.

You know my name, what's yours?

Eugene McBride, he said, holding out a hand. Forgive me my manners, Miss Wolfe. I should have introduced myself straightaway.

She shook his hand.

Things for you are about to get significantly more difficult and I cannot be any more clear with you. Things are going to be hard. You are going to want to quit. You will want to die. In fact, there will come a night where you contemplate taking your own life. But you must stay strong.

It sounds like it's already been decided for me.

Oh no, Miss Wolfe. You have choices and you will have to make the best of them to succeed.

Succeed at what?

Protecting the Variant.

My dream.

I'm sorry?

I have this dream that reoccurs. There's an iguana and he talks to me. Weird, I know. But he talks to me. He's been telling me the same thing for months now.

Then you know what you must do.

But how will I know who the Variant is?

How did you feel when you saw Mickey's painting?

Mesmerized at first. The spinning galaxy was intoxicating. But then I felt disjointed, a sailing ship was approaching the galaxy. It was wrong. Should have been a space ship.

Why?

Because space ships belong in space. Sailing ships belong on the ocean.

That's based on your perception though, no?

Sure.

Maybe things have changed in this world. Moved past your pre-conceived notions of what looks right or wrong. Maybe, try looking at things from a different angle. Maybe you'll see more clearly.

She thought about what he said and glanced over his shoulder back to the painting. The sails of the ship were billowing and the ship was beginning its entrance into the spiral galaxy. It was then she saw the afterburners in the tail of the ship, glowing red.

Maybe you were right all along, he said.

So I'll know.

You'll know. Trust yourself. Protect the Variant.

Then the piano went silent and the room faded to black.

From somewhere in the darkness, she heard a train whistle. She could smell burning wood in the dark and then fragrances like bleach and ammonia filled her nostrils. Lights slowly rose and she realized she was in a metallic room with a ceiling of soft lights as though someone cut off the roof and allowed the morning sun in. She was sitting on the edge of a hospital bed but she couldn't determine why. Across from her, she saw herself in a floor to ceiling mirror. Her hair fell across her brow and she looked like she'd been running through mud.

A door to her right materialized in the center of the metal wall and a woman approached her. She wore black medical scrubs complete with a black, half-face respirator, black goggles and a black surgical scrub hat. She said something to April but the woman's voice was either obscured by the respirator or she was speaking a foreign language. Or both. April couldn't tell.

Shuom wirr hulph u sruk, the nurse said nonsensically.

The nurse reached for April's arm and while April wanted to retract it immediately from her grasp, April found that she couldn't move. The nurse slipped a needle into a vein on April's left arm. A warmth filled her arm and she found herself fading into darkness again.

As she tried to keep her eyes open, the mirror across from her shimmered and suddenly she was looking through glass. A man sat in a room similar to hers. He was tied down to the bed though. His hair was disheveled and his face was red with stress. Beads of sweat rolled down his face toward his neck. He looked like he had been struggling. A nurse entered his room and he began to thrash about, fighting against his bindings. The nurse pulled a syringe and approached the man as the glass partition shimmered again and became a mirror.

Her eyes were heavy as the door opened again and two nurses wheeled a six-wheel machine into her room. She drifted off as they placed her legs in the stirrups.....

..... She awoke on the floor of the tunnel, just beneath the ladder to Franklin's. Her wrists were bound together and she could barely feel her hands.

I said get her up!

A Grey Suit lifted her up and began dragging her back down toward the jail. Her legs ached and her ribs screamed every time she took a breath. She felt like she'd been run over by a car. Her thighs ached and were discolored with purple, blue and black bruises.

Variant

Blood pooled in the crotch of her pants. Her lower back screamed in pain and she could feel each and every punch they inflicted on her when they took her. Her hair, matted and sweaty, fell in her face. She dropped her head and let her legs drag behind her. They dragged her the entire way.

CHAPTER 23

Sometime in 2108

Len sat in an uncomfortable wooden chair in a barely lit office across a nondescript table from Roosevelt Cleveland. His hands were tied beneath the chair with thick strips of graphene tape. His feet were anchored to the floor. He couldn't tell how they'd done this but it felt like he was in a pair of immobile ski boots. The cigarette he'd requested sat before him, unlit, and he had no way of picking it up.

The smoke?

Cleveland scrutinized the Camel resting before Len. There are those that still refer to those cancer sticks as smokes. So, in answer to your query, yes, it is a smoke.

Can I get it, Fuck Face?

Interesting choice of words. You're in no position to demand anything.

I gave you Cathey. Without me, you're still shooting blanks.

You know, Mr. Stipe, your supposition that you were the only one to contact us about Mr. Cathey is foolishly naïve. How many did you tell before you called us?

No one, he exhorted. Then he remembered Tony and then Keith, the bartender that he'd worked with for the last fifteen months. Awareness spread over his face and he shook his head.

Fifteen million is a lot of dough, as they used to say. I'm not sure all the calls we got were from people who know how to share.

I'll cut em all in, Len said.

I'm sure you wouldn't, Mr. Stipe. You're a vulture. A shark. A predator. You smell blood and you attack.

Who do you think you are, assessing me like that? I don't know you.

But, Mr. Stipe, I know you. I know how you came to be out here. You're nothing if not a mercenary.

You know me too well, Mr…?

My name is Roosevelt. Roosevelt Cleveland. My parents had a sense of humor. One of the greatest Presidents and one of the worst. Let's name him after each, they said.

And yet, Len said, taunting him, you're neither a great nor horrible President. You're just a lap dog for Serafino.

Cleveland stifled a laugh but smiled nonetheless. You are a brave man Mr. Stipe. Stupid. But brave. I ate my parents in a stew later in life. But that's neither here nor there.

I've heard of you Roosevelt Cleveland.

Oh good. Then we don't have to waste any more time getting to know each other. I can move straight to business.

Fuck you, Psycho, he spat.

Oh? Well, we could arrange something like that a little later. Right now, I need to know what he told you in that hangar. And I'll not stop until I've got your skin peeling from your muscle tissue while you beg me to stop.

Do whatever the hell you want. I ain't begging you for shit.

Ah, Mr. Stipe, you might. You just might. Tips of fingers and toes are sensitive. I'll take them all. And the sick part? You ready? I'll enjoy it. I may even fry them up with some baby carrots.

You might as well kill me.

Oh, Mr. Stipe. So serious. I don't want to kill you. I don't even want to eat your fingers or toes. Although, human flesh is tastier than bovine. But that's neither here nor there. I just want to know what Cathey told you all those years ago and how you ended up smack in the middle of his capture. Seems like a coincidence. And I don't believe in coincidences.

Then what? I'm working with him?

You are?

No, I mean, is that what you think?

You're going to tell me what to think, Mr. Stipe. And I'm going to decide if I believe you.

I survived the self-destruct at Carson – he began and Roosevelt folded his arms across his chest and listened intently. But before he got too involved, he grabbed the Camel from in front of Len, put it between his lips and snapped a match from nowhere, lighting it. He inhaled deeply and blew the smoke back at Len. The smoke, Mr. Stipe. The smoke. Len boiled, but continued....

.....He lay before Clara like a crumpled mass. Whatever Cathey had attached to his head had done nothing more than fry his scalp and render Lennon Stipe bald. The hair never would grow back. Never. But the memories were safe. He always felt he was mentally tough and surviving the mind wipe was just another reason why he was so tough. His muscles ached though and his back was on fire.

The trauma team put him on a stretcher and carried him from the production room to deep within the infirmary. His room was at the end of a hallway with no other rooms and no windows. The pale lights of the corridor strobed occasionally and flickered as aftershocks were felt from the explosions across the base. Given the force, Len assumed Cathey had set the units to self-destruct. They wheeled him into a darkly lit room and two male nurses moved him from the stretcher to a bed. They began attaching all types of sensors to his body. A machine in the corner hummed to life and began tracking his heart rate.

Do you know where you are, Sir?

Len thought about it for a moment. Colorado was his only response.

Where in Colorado, sir?

I don't know. I can't remember.

Do you know what building you are in?

Carson. Fort Carson. I don't know exactly where.

Your name?

He fought against the fog that threatened to derail him from pulling his name out for them. Lennon. Stipe. I hope, he said.

Cleveland slammed his hand down on the table, I don't give a rat's ass about your backstory, Mr. Stipe. I need to know what he told you as he left. We have surveillance video of the two of you talking. What did he say?

He told me he was going to mind wipe me. And something about making sure his wife survived.

Cleveland creased his brow.

That lady that was all shot up with us. On your surveillance video?

Ah yes, the missus. I wonder why he would tell you to make sure his wife survived?

I don't know. Maybe it was just something to say.

Perhaps. Let's assume, for the sake of argument, that you are correct. My next issue with you is the fact that you had distinct instructions, dare I say orders, to report to Sioux Falls when you were released from the hospital all those years ago. Help me understand why you didn't report as ordered?

Listen, I knew that might come up –

Might? You thought disobeying a direct order *might* come up when talking to the very people who gave that order? That's rich.

Ok, I know. I knew it was going to come up. I've thought about it every day since I left.

Oh good. Then you've had plenty of time to concoct the Nobel Prize of excuses. I can hardly wait.

It's not an excuse. I got released from the hospital, I reported to my new unit, I got on the L-ATV and we headed east. Then all hell broke loose.

And by all hell breaking loose you mean when you blew up the L-ATV well before you reached Sioux Falls?

I didn't blow it up. It was blown up by those Rising idiots. I had no other options. I had to hide. I had nothing with me, no ID, no weapons, no nothing.

So you just decided at that point your responsibility to us was over?

Look, it's not like that.

Then tell me what it's like.

I got captured, okay?

Okay, now we're getting somewhere. And let me tell you, Mr. Stipe, it's a tremendous story. It actually makes sense, which I find odd given your level of education. But even if you were captured, you still made no attempt to rejoin our little army. And for that, there must be punishment. I cannot allow a soldier to just go AWOL and quit. That's not how these things work.

Listen, keep half the money for yourself. I'll give you half. Just let me go with ten mil and I'll never darken your door again.

Cleveland raised an eyebrow at him and said, do you know how much half of fifteen is?

What did I say? Ten? Give me seven. Or five. You take the rest.

So bribery now? I suppose that's one way to go. Not what I would have chosen, but creative. I'm not going to accept your offer. What I am going to do, though, should serve as a lesson to those men and women who join our armed forces every day. Nurse, he shouted.

A young woman of no more than twenty entered the room. She wore yellow scrubs that covered her from head to toe and thick rubbery gloves. She carried a square steel case with her in one hand and a plastic covered package in the other. She placed the two items down on the counter, near the door. Len watched as she removed a circular rod no bigger than a pencil from each side of the box. When she completed that task and laid the rods next to the box, she then removed the top. It slid up the steel sides and she placed the top next to the rods. She carefully pulled at the elastic tab on the package and removed a foil backing from it. From inside the package, she removed a pair of polished metal tongs and then very deliberately held them above the top of the box. She took a deep breath and then removed a vial from inside the box. It contained a solution of crimson liquid. Bubbles floated at the top of the vial.

Dear, Cleveland said, I certainly appreciate you being cautious but could we hurry things along just a bit?

Sorry, Sir, she said in a muffled voice. As Len watched her, he realized that not only was her head covered with a vented hood, she also wore a gas mask underneath the hood. She withdrew a hypodermic syringe and needle wrapped in plastic from the package. She removed the plastic covering and inserted the end of the needle into the vial.

Ok, let's hold right there, Sweetie.

Cleveland stood and hit a switch on the wall and the room lit up. Len could see that the walls rose forty feet into the air and there were curtains at the top covering windows. Cleveland turned a dial and the curtains rose into the ceiling revealing the top floor of the room. Grey Suit cadets stood at the glass, looking down on Len.

Welcome, cadets. I do hope we didn't keep you too long. Mr. Stipe and I had some things to discuss before I could bring you in. As you know, we considered the issue of abandonment of duties the other day in class. Basically, what happens if you decide you don't want to work for us any longer. I do hope you recall that. Now, in Mr.

Stipe's case, he had a perfectly reasonable explanation as to why he didn't report to duty in Sioux Falls. He was, Cleveland paused and looked down at Len, what was it you said, Mr. Stipe?

Captured.

Right, he was captured. Perfectly reasonable excuse for not reporting to duty as ordered. However, and this is where I had trouble with his story. Mr. Stipe, tell the cadets when you reported for duty after your capture.

I didn't, he said in a muffled voice.

Sorry, Mr. Stipe, do speak up.

I didn't report.

Ah. You didn't report. And that's why we're here folks. If you fail to follow orders, trust me when I say, I will ensure it's the last mistake you make.

Cleveland, listen, I gave you Cathey.

You didn't give me shit, Mr. Stipe, except for yourself. Now keep your mouth shut or I'll have Miss HazMat over here sew it shut.

Cleveland, please.

Shut your miserable mouth. Nurse? Please proceed.

The nurse pulled the plunger on the syringe and filled it with the red bubbly fluid from the vial. The syringe's barrel filled up and the vial was nearly empty when the nurse withdrew the needle. She carefully placed the vial back in the box.

Cleveland, please, I'll do anything you ask.

And I asked you to please shut your mouth but you obviously can't follow that simple instruction. Nurse, sew his mouth shut.

Oh my gods Cleveland. You're insane.

How many times are we going to have this conversation? I'm not insane. I've been tested. I know exactly what I'm doing, Mr. Stipe. Now hold still.

The nurse approached Len and looked confused. Sir, she asked, how do you want me to do this?

Cleveland, so help me. He glared at Cleveland and focused all his strength on ripping the graphene tape apart, but not even a Mech could pull that tape off. Sweat pooled on his brow and trickles of it slid down his cheeks and the bridge of his nose and splattered on the table in front of him.

Struggling won't help, Mr. Stipe. Do stop.

If I get out of this, so help me –

Oh, I know, Mr. Stipe. Death and destruction. This will be over soon enough. Nurse, I'll hold the syringe and you can sew him up.

Sir, you want me to sew him up with suture?

Did I stutter?

No, Sir, it's just –

Just what, Nurse?

I don't think it will hold. And it could take quite some time to do it.

Cleveland thought about what she said for a moment. Perhaps not, he said.

He walked over to the cabinets above the countertops that lined the wall by the door. He opened several doors and finally found what he was looking for. He turned around with a surgical stapler.

Cleveland, please, please, please, by the gods' graces!

Mr. Stipe, the time for appeals is over. Boys, he shouted. Two large soldiers entered the room.

Hold his head, he can't seem to keep that mouth of his closed.

The men grabbed Len by the head and held him tight.

One of you grab his lips, I need some meat to hang these staples on.

The one nearest to Cleveland grabbed Len by the lips and fought to keep them tightly closed.

Len fought against the men but his head wouldn't cooperate. He forced bloody spit through the sliver between his lips.

You're making me enjoy this way too much, Cleveland said and thrust the stapler at Len. His first attempt went high and hit Len at the base of his nose. He jerked his head with such force that the room heard the snapping of something within his neck. He tried to scream but the soldier held Len's lips tightly.

Let me try that again, Cleveland said, hold him tight. He steadied the stapler and hit Len in the middle of his lips. He then clipped fourteen more staples across his mouth. Len fought against the pain ripping through his lips but the more he pulled, the more agony he experienced. He finally dropped his head and let the blood leak through the staples.

Sorry about that little delay, cadets. Nurse, please proceed. The nurse approached Len and stuck the needle into the side of his neck. She pushed the plunger down and the crimson fluid entered Len's body.

Now cadets. Let's watch what happens when you disobey orders.

For a few seconds nothing happened. Len sat stoically in his chair.

I should have mentioned what we've given Mr. Stipe. As you can see, we had to take serious precautions to introduce that substance into Mr. Stipe's body. You may be asking yourself, I wonder what's in that syringe? Why is the nurse all decked out in a hazardous material suit? Why isn't Cleveland similarly dressed? Well, in that syringe is the deadliest strain of the Cluster we have found to date. It can be inhaled through the air. A drop of that blood can kill a room full of people. So, the nurse took proper precautions. I don't give a fuck, so I didn't take any precautions. Bring it on, I say!

As Cleveland spoke, Len lifted his head and listened to what Cleveland was saying. He began to shake violently back and forth and Cleveland couldn't tell if he was fighting off the Cluster or just trying to escape. Len's body trembled in the seat as his mouth filled with blood. It trickled out between the staples and Len tried to roar. He fought against the staples and they finally started to rip apart. Pieces of his lip hung to each and the blood started to pour out of his mouth. He finally ripped his lips apart and blood and phlegm shot out of his mouth, onto the floor. His skin popped with blisters and turned deep red to purple. Clear liquid spilled onto the floor from the blisters.

Cleeeeeeeeeveland, he shouted. I'll kill –

Then he buckled over as the pain ripped through him like electricity. Blood poured from his eyes and nose. His ears bled pink fluid. He tried to scream but blood filled his lungs and he couldn't catch his breath. He buckled over as the blood flowed from every hole in his body. Then he began pissing blood and shitting himself. The smell was overwhelming but Cleveland stood nearby, enjoying every minute. He bent down, in front of Len and lifted his head.

You still with us?

At that moment, Len vomited blood and bile in a projectile manner. Cleveland moved out of the way at the last moment. The muck splashed his shoes and pant legs.

That was close, he said, surveying the cadets. They looked on in horror but their faces remained stoical. No one dared show the least bit of emotion. Cleveland smiled.

Finally, Len stopped shuddering. Cleveland looked up to the cadets. And that, my young soldiers, is why we follow orders. He wiped his hands on his legs and passed by the nurse.

Get this mess cleaned up, he said as he passed. His heels clicked along the tile as he made his way down the hall. He started laughing as he rounded the next corner.

Variant

CHAPTER 24

Sometime in 2093

The baby slept against her chest as she walked through an alley in St. Louis. Reports were coming in that a high value asset, as the media kept calling her, was needed for urgent questioning. They didn't dare say she escaped from the local hospital because that would imply she was being held there against her will. But she had been held there since they found out she was pregnant. She tried to escape on three separate occasions but never made it out.

The Grey Suits threatened her with various forms of discipline but for the most part she figured out that they couldn't hurt her as long as she was pregnant. She didn't understand why and they never said. But they made their threats and April did what she pleased within reason. While being a prisoner.

They'd given her internet access but she assumed they were monitoring her communications. She contacted Elizabeth once but coded the message to her. The conclusion of it said something about April finding a pair of scissors left behind by an orderly and how she was going to pry this baby out of her, no matter what. They were in her room within seconds ready to stop her from the assault. She laughed but knew she couldn't tell Elizabeth anything of any importance. Sometime around the second trimester, she stopped hearing from Elizabeth all together. That broke her heart, but not as badly as she thought it would. In the world before the Cluster, she would have been devastated, but in this ever-changing new world she found herself in, her emotions for others seemed numb and distant. She certainly missed Eli, but she didn't long for her like she once thought she would if they ever separated. Of course, that had been her sophomore year and everything seemed so vitally important. Come to find out, it didn't mean shit. Or so she told herself.

April wandered into a drug store the second day of her freedom. She walked down the aisles, baby on her back, and noticed the gaps on the shelves where products should have been and would have been before everything got so sideways. A teen boy in a red promotional vest for the store walked by and asked her if she needed anything.

Baby food, she said, looking down the empty aisle that was tagged as the baby section.

All that stuff's locked up now, don't you know? Nobody keeps any of that stuff out anymore. Where are you from?

She hesitated and said, here.

Here where, he asked and pulled a walkie talkie from his back pocket.

St. Louis, she said, although it sounded more like a question.

Uh-huh. Where in St. Louis.

She hesitated again and this time he clicked the mic button and said, 2470, Rite Aid. The speaker crackled and a voice responded, received.

What's that about, she asked.

You'll find out, he said, backing away.

What's wrong? I just need food for my baby. I can pay, she said, pulling a crumpled wad of bills from her jacket pocket.

You'd know to ask the druggist. They would've told you that when you left the hospital. Something's not right about you. Plus, where's your Code bracelet?

She maneuvered to his right at the end of the aisle. If he was going to run, he'd have to turn and she'd have the advantage. But instead of turning, he approached her quickly, suddenly he was in her face.

You're just a kid with a baby. You don't scare me.

She leaned in and said, *you're* just a kid and slammed her forearm into the boy's cheek, sending him reeling backward, against the empty shelves. She pounced on him like a jackal and crushed his windpipe with the heel of her right hand. She brought it down again as he collapsed and didn't stop until the baby started crying.

What's all this, a voice called from behind the security glass of the druggist. He opened his plexiglass door and stepped down, turning down the aisle where April had just dismantled the young clerk.

Where's the baby food, she asked, blood dripping from her lips where she bit into them while mustering the strength to beat the living shit out of the clerk.

He began to back up, immediately regretting his decision to leave the safe confines of the pharmacy. It's put away. To prevent robberies.

Well, this isn't a robbery. I just need some food for my baby. I can pay, she said again, holding the wadded bills out toward the druggist.

Whatever you say, he said and remained motionless in the aisle.

What's the problem, Doc? Take me to the food. Like now!

He turned and made his way back to the pharmacy. She was right behind him as they ascended the three stairs to the pharmacy when he turned and stuck out a weakened leg that stunned April. With the added weight of the baby, she fell backward but managed to keep her footing. He slipped behind the door and locked it immediately. She quickly gathered herself and leaped up the stairs and started pulling on the door with all the strength she had. An alarm sounded and suddenly the entire store looked like a seventies-era disco. The overhead lights strobed and at various intervals on the wall red cone lights whirled like police lights. In the corners, bright

225

white rectangular lights flashed rapidly. The doors to the store instantaneously locked and blast doors lowered. The windows went dark as the steel plating lowered, locking everyone in.

Open the doors, Doc, she said.

Or what, little girl? The authorities will be here soon. They're the only ones who can open the doors now.

She panicked. They'd take her back and she'd lose the baby. That hadn't been a threat from the Grey Suits. It was fact. She couldn't let that happen.

Throughout the store, she could hear whispers of those that hit the floor when the sirens and lights went off. She looked down several aisles and the patrons lay flat on their stomachs, hands over their heads. Like they had been through this before. She peeked down another aisle and a man in his late forties sat with his back against the aisle. He was greying at his temples but otherwise had thick, plush, black hair. He pushed it back with his hand and looked up at her as she stood at the head of the aisle. The man was dressed in weathered jeans, black motorcycle boots and a black leather jacket. His blue eyes blinked a few times and a smile spread across his oval face. He rubbed his stubbled face and laughed.

You *are* just a girl. I thought that kid was just being a pussy.

What's it to you? He's still lying back there in a heap barely breathing. I'll do the same to you or anyone that wants it.

Those Grey Suits are going to bust in here and want some. Trust me.

They won't hurt me. At least they haven't.

That's odd. Did you escape from one of their fine establishments?

Maybe, she said and bounced the baby up and down to keep her quiet.

Kid yours?

Yeah.

A little young for that sort of thing, aren't you?

I dunno. Ask the Grey Suits when they get here. They did this to me.

Ok. Well, they're going to be here in about five minutes. That kid called in a 2470 or suspicious person alert to the Greys. Those calls take about two hours for a response these days. But when the druggist goes and seals the place up, they take that more seriously. Can't have anyone getting Cluster drugs for free, now can we? So they assume someone's in here trying to steal their supply. Not sure they're going to give a damn about some baby food, but something tells me they might be interested in you.

Maybe, she said, still bouncing the baby.

You got a name, he asked.

April, you?

I'm Sullivan. Michael Sullivan. Friends call me Sully. Do you want to get out of here?

Do you know how?

Yeah, something like that. He stood up and towered over her. He had to be at least six foot four. He wasn't skinny but he wasn't fat, either. Muscular, April thought. He strolled up to the druggist and knocked on the safety glass.

I'm going to blow this place into a million fucking pieces, man. Unless you hit that other switch you have down there and open that back door.

There's no other button.

Sully pulled a large caliber handgun from behind his back and struck the glass with the barrel. I don't want to hurt you.

Bulletproof idiot.

These are Mech-piercing rounds. Your bulletproof glass won't last a second. If you make me fire it and waste this round, I'm going to blow this entire place up. No shit. Hit the switch. Let me get this girl out of here.

Civilians, a loudspeaker shouted over the scream of the alarm. Take cover immediately, we are coming in.

Too late, he said and fired the round at the glass. It shattered into thousands of pieces and the concussion of the blast sent the druggist flying backward. The safety glass fell in on itself and rained down on Sully. Sully climbed on the counter and put a foot through the opening. He held out a hand and said, c'mon April, we gotta get you out of here.

She hesitated for a second but could see the flashing blue-grey lights of the Grey Suits outside. She took his hand and climbed atop the counter. They both stepped through the opening and jumped down. Sully reached under the counter and hit the alternate switch, opening the back door. From under the counter he pulled several cans of formula. Here, he said to her and tossed her the cans of formula. She stuffed them in her backpack.

Can you carry more, he asked.

She nodded. Instead of handing her additional formula, he went to the wall and started pulling Cluster drugs down. He shoved them into a bag and then handed the bag to April. Will this fit? She rammed the bag down into her backpack and then zipped it up. She tossed the wadded bills onto the counter.

Stay close, there'll be Greys everywhere. But they won't be expecting us out the back. He took another gun from a holster inside his jacket. You know how to use this, he asked, handing her a revolver.

Aim for Greys. Pull the trigger?

Pretty much, he said. He grabbed her hand and led her to the back door.

Here goes nothing, he said and opened the door.

They were immediately surrounded by Greys shouting orders from all directions. Sully started firing to his left. Take right, he yelled at her. She looked right and started blasting Greys. Within minutes, they were down the alley and heading for a clearing on the outskirts of town.

A large truck sat idling on the side of the road. As she approached, she saw the Grey Suits' insignia on the door. She panicked for a second but figured they'd stolen the truck. Otherwise, why had he been shooting at the Greys? Sully opened the door and ushered April in. She climbed aboard and slid next to a hulking vision of a man. His meaty hands seemed to consume the steering wheel and despite the seat being pushed back to the back of the cab, he still looked like he was sitting on the dashboard. His head was as big as a beach ball, shaved or he'd lost all his hair, April could not tell which. Two small, yellow-gold eyes swam near his creased forehead. They seemed to dart in multiple directions at once, studying this new person who just climbed into his cab. He wore black fatigue pants and black combat boots, similar to Sully. He was stuffed into a leather jacket that made him look like a sausage. To April, it looked like at any moment he was going to explode through the leather.

Who's this, he shouted to Sully as he climbed in.

Why don't you ask her yerself, asshole. Be polite. We're still civilized, aren't we?

He craned his neck to the right and glared at her. Beads of sweat threatened to spill down his face onto the top of April's head.

I'm April, she said and waited for him to say something.

Your kid?

She nodded.

Aren't you a little young –

I'll fill you in, Nick, that's a bit of a story. Let's get out of here before more Greys show up. Those alarms are going nuts in there.

They drove west for more than an hour. The city turned into the suburbs and, eventually, turned into the plains. She worried they'd be stopped by Greys, but Sully assured her they had safe passage once on the open road. He explained to her that they had commandeered the truck early on in the Rising against the Greys. It had been used as a collection truck for the Greys gathering supplies and food. There were operating codes for the vehicles and although they were using dated codes, they still worked, thanks to contacts Nick still had within the government.

She desperately wanted to sleep but she couldn't force herself to do it in front of these two men. Although Sully had saved her, she certainly wasn't going to let her guard down around him or anyone else. When she felt herself nodding off, she would prick the skin at her wrist with her fingernail until nearly drawing blood.

They turned down a tree-lined dirt drive and continued down that path for another twenty minutes. Sully mentioned isolation and safety as she fought against her heavy eyelids. They finally arrived at a large white farmhouse. Two dormer windows stared down at April as she disembarked from the truck. A large porch wrapped around the length of the house. Several children played on the porch while others were running in the back. The dirt road continued around the right side of the house, leading to several row houses. April took it all in and then noticed the heat. It was nearly unbearable.

An elderly woman walked down from the house and smiled warmly at April. She looked for the woman's Code bracelet but she noticed no one out here was wearing one.

Looking for my Code? I'm well past dead, Honey. Just waiting on the good Lord to take me home. But every day I wake up alive, I'm thankful and I tell Him so. He who has health, has hope. Right? I've got plenty of hope.

This is Olivia Sullivan, April. My mother. She'll outlive us all. This large farm is hers.

It's the Sullivan's farm, she said. I'm just the current caretaker. Been in the family since well before the Great Surge and years before the heat killed most everything we tried to grow out here. Used to have a couple hundred head of cattle. Big ol cornfield. Raised some soybeans back when my daddy's daddy was a boy. Then it just got too hot. Like today. It's a whopper today. And who is this here, she asked, reaching for the baby.

April flinched and turned immediately away from the woman.

Mom, that's April's baby and we can talk about that some other time. April's been through the wringer. She might be tired.

Olivia tilted her head and said, you do look tired dear. Maybe get you and that baby a bath and then something warm to eat. Get you into some fresh clothes. Then a nice soft bed for you and –

She paused, waiting for April to tell her the baby's name.

Yes, April said. Yes, that would be nice.

Isabelle, Olivia called back toward the house. A brunette about the same age as April came through the screen door. She wore a bright blue scarf on her head and April saw that she lacked eyebrows. Despite the heat, she was wearing long sleeves and pants. Her face was haggard and she looked like she hadn't slept in a month. Her cheeks were sunken and black circles surrounded her yellow gold eyes. They were the same color as Nick's. April noticed most of the people over about eighteen all had the same inexplicably-colored eyes.

I told you to call me Luna, I'm not Isabelle anymore, the girl said, walking down the steps to April.

I'll call you what your parents named you, Olivia retorted.

They're dead. So's Isabelle.

Well, everyone else can call you Luna, I'm calling you by your given name and you can just deal with it, Honey. Now, won't you escort our guest up to Natalie's old room. Let her have whatever she can fit into up there. And show her where the bath is. I'll whip something up for lunch. She patted April on the back.

You rest, Olivia said. We'll keep your lunch warm.

Isabelle pointed to the door and followed April into the house.

Olivia turned to Sully. What in the gods' names possessed you to bring a stranger out here, Michael?

She was in the middle of my shit, ma. She was trying to get formula for the baby. I figured she wasn't from anywhere near St. Louis. Didn't even know where they kept the baby products. That's someone on the run.

Or a really good actress. She's pretty easy on the eyes.

Good lord, Ma. She's a baby. Plus, she didn't see me until she got into it with the druggist. I was trapped. I had to get out and she helped. So, here she is.

Was she Coded?

No. That's why I thought she might be safe. She handled herself pretty good in the store. She might be an asset.

She might die tomorrow, then we're stuck with that kid. What's the deal with it anyway?

I don't know. She said it was the Grey's fault. Whatever that means.

I don't like it, Michael.

What? Her or the kid?

Both, she said. Now an outsider knows where we are.

Nick knows too. He's not family.

Michael, we've known him since he was a baby. He's family.

Have Nick do some follow-up. See if there's anyone looking for a girl with a baby. Can't be too hard to tell if she's wanted or not.

Okay. I'll let him know.

Variant

CHAPTER 25

Sometime in 2108

Cleveland stood at the foot of Serafino's bed. A ceiling fan spun on the ceiling, slicing through the musty Sonoran air. At least down in the caverns, it was cooler than up top. When Cleveland arrived, it was over one hundred and thirty-five degrees. In the caves, it was a mere seventy-nine.

A monitor kept time with his heartbeat, which was much too slow. A tube cleared his throat of the blood that was pooling there. They had misidentified him as a continuing Code White nearly five years ago when his last Coding had taken place. He was, in fact, a Red, so he disregarded the pain in his lungs and the double vision he'd been experiencing for the last several months. When he started pissing blood, it was too late. The Cluster had taken over and was feasting on his organs and breaking down his muscle tissue. Now, he waited for death. And it was near.

Cleveland walked to the chair next to the bed and sat down. A nurse cracked the door ajar and Cleveland shook his head. She shut it immediately and retreated down the hall.

Funny it's you here and not me, he said to Serafino. Funny for me, not for you.

Serafino opened an eye but it was difficult to know whether he understood Cleveland or not.

That idiot Barnes is going to declare himself acting director this afternoon. The vote with Kelland could come as soon as tomorrow. We know how that's going to go. He's been sucking their dicks since they took over production of the Cluster drugs. The Rising will be pleased.

Serafino blinked several times and tried to clear his throat. Kelland is the key, he said. Control Kelland and the Greys will follow. And vice versa. He coughed violently, spewing purplish blood across his blanket. He gasped for air and reached for the oxygen mask dangling on the side of his bed. Cleveland helped him place it over his mouth and nose. He leaned back, inhaling deeply.

He's got Kelland, Cleveland said.

You've got the Greys and the Mechs, he said through the mask. The new codes for them have been transmitted to you on the secure line. Only you have them. With those codes, you control most everything. Do you have your team in place?

It's your team, but yeah, they're on board. They'll fall in line.

The kid?

Still nothing. The search coordinates led the team to a miserable patch of earth with about thirty feet of snow in a five-hundred-mile radius. Well north of the Yupik Front. We acquired a few Mars-One Humvees. They can damn near float on the snow. But the forest is so thick in there that it makes passage nearly impossible. I've got boots on the ground too, but so far it's empty.

Underground?

Cleveland thought about it for a moment. I suppose. But we've surveyed that area over and over with nothing found.

Those satellite scans don't go deep enough. They could be a hundred feet down and we'd never know.

We'll keep at it.

The girl? What have you done with her?

She's still locked up.

It's dangerous to have them both here together.

He's under control. Not going anywhere.

Serafino began to cough again and he wasn't fast enough to remove the mask before splattering it with blood and mucous. The heart monitor spiked for a moment, rapidly beeping. He tried to take a breath but Cleveland could hear the liquid in his throat. Like he was trying to breathe under water. Serafino reached for the mask while violently coughing, choking on the blood. Cleveland reached for the mask. He held the mask down with one hand and held Serafino's arms down with his other. The mask filled with blood and Serafino continued to choke. The monitor was racing. His eyes bulged in his head and vessels broke across the whites of his eyes. His face turned red, then purple. In a minute, it was over. The monitor line went flat. Cleveland kicked the plug out of the wall and walked to the door.

Nurse, he called. Come take care of this. He turned and walked down the hall. He couldn't wait to take his new toys out for a test drive. The first stop would be Kelland Corp.

Variant

CHAPTER 26

Sometime in 2093

The truck bounced over the severely washed-out dirt road. Sudden rains threatened to turn the whole countryside into a lake. It was the first moisture April had seen in months. Nick couldn't remember the last time he'd seen rain. Sully didn't care. They needed new Trendelenburg chairs for the patients they had going through chemotherapy. The few they had were wearing out and putting their people in jeopardy. So they were headed to Sioux City, where the Greys maintained a very large warehousing system collecting everything from medical devices to missiles. Its centralized location (after the heat of the south pushed many cities north) was perfect for distributions throughout the country.

April sat in the back of the crowded, six person, L-ATV. Nick, as usual, was driving and Sully sat in the front passenger seat, manning the fixed blaster. Nathan, Caleb and Piper filled in around her. On the floor, between the second row seating and the driver, sat Damian, against the blast door. His laptop was straddled across his legs, ready for action.

April didn't care for Piper and assumed the feeling was mutual. Many of the girls at the Sullivan farm seemed disconnected from April. She thought it was because of the kid. But she didn't know for sure. She didn't much care. In her mind, the baby was getting big enough now that she could move properly on her own. The protection she may have once needed seemed redundant now. She'd been with them for nearly three months and the time was coming for her to move on.

Sully had asked her to come on this raid at the last minute. She didn't like her lack of preparation. What she really didn't like was leaving the baby with Olivia at their camp outside Harrisburg.

She knew she couldn't take her into a firefight with Greys, but she wished she was closer. It was the first time she left her with anyone. Her anxiety was worse over leaving her behind than it was going into a hive of Greys.

Sully reassured her that it would be fine leaving the baby at the camp. Olivia had initially wanted to keep the child at the farm but the fight that erupted over that was solved when Sully suggested just bringing the baby with them, but leaving her with Olivia at their base camp. April was still not happy with the thought of leaving her child behind. She even considered bolting before the raid, but they needed her and she felt obligated because she had been on Sully's ass for awhile to go on some outside operations. The kid was always the sticking point.

They finally pulled onto a paved highway and for a while they were the only thing on the road. Behind them, four fully loaded L-ATVs approached, headlights flashing, light bars on top of the roofs pulsing blue then grey. They were approaching at a high rate of speed.

April turned to see them advancing and she called out to Nick. He glanced in his mirror and saw them coming. He switched the radio over to the Grey's designated frequency. He motioned for Sully to give him the correct clearance codes. Sully tapped the receiver twice and handed it to Nick.

A voice crackled over the short wave, Unit 2317, be advised, we are in pursuit, identify your current trajectory, over.

Unit 2317, Nick started and then dropped the sheet of paper with the trajectory codes on them. Sully scrambled for it and handed it to him. They were flying down the highway at speeds approaching one hundred miles an hour. Trajectory is forty-three point five four four six degrees north, ninety-six point seven three one one degrees west, he said boldy into the short wave. It was the last known Greys' coordinates for the check-in at the storage facility in Sioux Falls. These codes were known to change on an almost daily basis. But they also rotated positions. Based upon what Nick and Sully knew about the Grey's warehouse operations, today's code should have been the one they just announced.

There was a crackle and then a pause. April watched as the pursuit vehicles continued to gain on them. Roger 2317, what is your intended destination?

Nick was unprepared for this question. Each L-ATV was linked to the Greys' tracking beacon. They knew where each one of their trucks was at any time of any given day. Unless the truck had been stolen and the system hacked. Unit 2317 was just such a unit. It had gone off-grid for approximately twenty-seven minutes about a month ago. During that time, Nick and Damian, the resident hacker, re-routed the vehicle and installed dummy plans that appeared to work. No one came after them. But Damian never said they would be answering questions about intended destinations. That information should have been hard coded on the system.

Damian, what the hell, Nick asked.

Damian was already on the laptop keying in information. April watched him as he feverishly typed away.

I don't know. Tell them Detroit. That's what I entered when we took the unit over. I don't know what it is they're asking.

Sully turned, It sounds like they're asking us where we're headed after we hit the warehouse. You're sure you input Detroit?

I think. That was a month ago.

Can you change it now?

Not without them seeing that I'm doing it.

Tell 'em, Sully said to Nick.

2317, destination is Detroit, over.

There was a crackle and then silence. Unit 2317, that is a roger. We identified your unit as one and the same, Detroit final destination. Unit 2317, command ordered us to make contact with you and, with our apologies, demand that you take on a passenger to Detroit.

Nick looked to Sully who shrugged his shoulders. Tell them no way, we're all full up here at the inn.

2317, that's a negative. We're seven by six here now as it stands.

Roger 2317, we will take Lance Corporal Reeves with us. He is to report to Sonora for a briefing in a few days. Works out well.

Unfortunately, Lance Corporal Reeves was currently in a ditch somewhere outside Atlanta from where this particular Unit 2317 was stolen. His Blue Code bracelet, ID tags and index finger were back at the Sullivan farm under lock and key. The remainder of Lance Corporal Reeves was being snacked upon by wild dogs and the occasional buzzard.

Damian furiously typed away on the laptop, trying to verify if the unit gaining on them knew the whereabouts of Lance Corporal Reeves. He shook his head. He just didn't know what they did or did not know in the pursuit vehicle.

2317, that's a negative, Nick began. Lance Corporal Reeves was delivered to Hattiesburg Hospital. He was verified Code Red and deemed to be failing fast.

Nick at least sounded legit.

Damian paused on the laptop. April watched from behind as the pursuit vehicle continued toward them. They're still gaining on us, she said.

They know, Nick said.

Suddenly, there was an explosion at the hood of the vehicle and then another. High Explosive Frag, Sully shouted. The vehicle skidded to its right and was hit two more times.

Nick slumped over the wheel as the windshield exploded inward. Metal fragments burst through the glass and peppered Nick's body with fine slivers of metal. Slicing past the Kevlar armor of his vest, Nick was riddled with holes. He looked up just in time to get a large splinter of copper through this throat. As he reached for it, the vehicle careened into a ditch. When he finally pulled it free, his throat split and blood poured into the cab. He moved a hand to cover the wound. His heart beat. Barely.

Sully fared no better. Scrap iron pelted his body from all directions and a large metallic icicle drove through his right eye and impaled him to the seat of the L-ATV. The vehicle slid and ultimately rolled. April was the only one bolted in. The remaining three were tossed from the vehicle as it went end over end five times, coming to rest on the roof.

Smoke and dirt swirled about her head. She hung upside down. Voices were shouting over the short wave but there was a piercing ringing in her ears from the explosions. She fumbled with the seat belt and saw through the gaping hole that used to be the windshield an army of Mechs approaching. They were each equipped with shoulder units for the HE-Frags. Two-apiece. She couldn't get the strap out of the shoulder belt holster and instantly needed a knife. Hers was in her bag, but she didn't see it amongst the wreckage. Sully, dripping blood from the shrapnel like a tapped maple tree, had a survival knife resting against his hip. She stretched for it, but it was just out of reach.

Here, a voice said and handed a knife into the vehicle. Hurry! It was Damian. He stood outside the vehicle with rifle drawn. As the

Mechs approached, he fired. Several stood in place, but many more still advanced. He was quickly running out of Mech-piercing bullets.

She pulled the knife across the belt and it split in two. She dropped to the floor which was once the roof and scrambled out the broken window. Damian stood outside the vehicle, scanning the horizon. His right ear was trickling blood and it was obvious his nose was broken. It leaned to the left a good bit and was oozing blood. When he spoke, he spit blood.

Move, he shouted, spraying blood as he did so. They bolted from the L-ATV and headed toward a grove of trees about a half mile from the ditch. She ran past Piper and Caleb who were lying dead in distorted contortions no human body could achieve naturally. April bent down, grabbing Piper's knife from her belt and threw Piper's backpack over her shoulder. Her arms were bent behind her neck, resting beneath her. She had skidded across the rough ground for several meters and her face now resembled hamburger meat. April pulled Piper's map from her breast pocket.

The Mechs continued their advance. April and Damian scattered into the forest. April moved through the dead brush and fallen Maidenhair trees. The heat, while not as overwhelming as in the southern states, was still wreaking havoc on the landscape in the Midwest.

She bent down and tried to get a bearing on where Damian was currently hiding. Looking left and right, she couldn't find him. She thought of calling for him but the Mechs were rolling over the countryside toward her. Several Grey Suits were pulling what they could from the L-ATV. They extracted Sully and immediately covered his body with a tarp. Nick, on the other hand, was placed on a stretcher. He disappeared in the back of a Grey's L-ATV. April pondered her options. Her only thought was for her child. She had to get back to her. With everyone dead or injured, the raid was over.

The remaining Grey Suits marched behind the Mechs, waiting on them to flush April and Damian out. She pulled her compass from her pack along with the map and spread it out on the forest floor. To the East was several miles of forest. She would have enough cover to remain somewhat hidden. Then she could head south, back to Hattiesburg and her daughter.

She ran as long as she could and then she walked until she collapsed. The Mechs remained back where she and Damian entered the forest. When she broke south, she was alone. She rested for a little less than a half hour and then started again. It took her most of the next two days to reach Hattiesburg and the base camp. As she walked up, she knew they were gone. There was no sign of them. Or her child. She crumpled to the ground and wept. She let out no sound but she sobbed, silent tears coursing down her cheeks.

She didn't know how or why they were gone but there was no evidence of Mech or Grey Suits' strikes. It looked like they had just folded up camp and left. A box of baby food jars was left behind as though they weren't planning on caring for the child for long. Any trip out of here and back to the Sullivan farm would certainly need those jars of food. She placed them carefully in her backpack. As April made her way through the camp, she also found the little stuffed panda bear Abby loved. She had found it one day scouting in Sioux Falls. Once it was in Abby's possession, she couldn't sleep or nap without it. Now it lay in a puddle of mud, its once black and white fur stained brown. She picked it up and that familiar feeling of slipping into a foreign world washed over her…..

…..The forest disappeared as she clutched the bear. She once again stood on the melting blacktop of Highway 118 in Alpine, Texas. The sign for the highway loomed large and appeared too big for its slender metal pole. Brilliant white tracer lights snaked around the numbers rapidly, giving the sign a Vegas feel. She looked down the

highway and the boy with the Mechs stood before her. The Mechs'
eyes glowed blue and they seemed to stand at attention behind the
boy. He was obviously in control of them.

Who are you, she called. But her voice was faint, as though
an echo across a vast chasm.

He did not respond. Instead, he took several steps down the
highway toward her. The Mechs followed, their enormous legs
hammering the asphalt with each step. She could feel each step deep
in her bones.

She called again, with greater force, who are you? Her voice
thundered across the highway.

This time he responded, just a boy. Before she knew it, he
was next to her. She was surrounded by Mechs, but she felt safe.
Safer than she had in years.

Why are you in my dream, she asked.

I don't think this is a dream. I was in a way station. Waiting
on a train. But back there, I was much older. I don't know what this
place is.

Were you alone?

In the way station?

Yes, in the way station.

No. There were people waiting on their train.

Was there a man there, with a thin black moustache?

There was.

Did he tell you about me?

No. We talked for a while but he never mentioned a girl. He
spoke of these machines here. And of a series of caverns. I'm
supposed to find them. He said when I did, I could stop this.

Stop what?

The dying.

As they spoke, the familiar purple-bodied iguana with yellow streaks walked slowly across the highway. His bulbous eyes glanced back and forth between the two. Then he paused. He always paused.

The train is never on time here, he said. Once upon a time, it was. You could set your watch by it, but not anymore. And the routes are all muddled. Just the other day, I was trying to get to get to Poughkeepsie, but ended up in Akron.

You take the train, she asked incredulously.

I most certainly do. Faster than walking. At least for me. Do you two know your purpose?

The boy thought about it for a moment and said, I do.

And what is that, Lad?

To stop the dying, he said.

The iguana nodded its head slowly up and down like a dashboard bobble head.

And you, my dear?

I am to protect the Variant.

Again, the iguana nodded. The two purposes are not mutually exclusive. To do one, is to achieve the other.

So this boy is the Variant? The one I need to protect?

You need to protect the Variant but much stands in your way. You are quick to anoint but slow to realize that the answer is not so simple.

I keep having these dreams or visions or whatever the hell they are and everyone keeps telling me to find this Variant but no one can tell me who it is or where I'm supposed to go to find this person.

Boy, the iguana called out, you know your purpose, no?

The boy nodded his head in agreement.

But do you know how to fulfill that purpose?

The boy thought for a moment and then shook his head no.

The boy doesn't know either.

He's supposed to stop the dying, she says. What dying?

The iguana climbed atop a rock and tilted his head to the scorching sun. All of it, he said.

This is so messed up. I don't understand.

Understanding will only come when you cease to look at things so one-sidedly. I can only lead you to the answer. The answer is all around you. But you don't see. Not yet. Focus. The Children of the Infinite await.

The iguana crawled down from the rock and began his steady slow march across the scorched earth. In the distance, a train whistle blew.

It's getting close, the boy said.

Do you have a name, she asked.

I don't. At least, not one I remember.

Are you the Variant?

The what?

The Variant? The one without the sickness?

I don't know. I don't feel sick.

Me neither, but I think I'm still going to die.

We're all going to die, aren't we?

Some sooner than others.

But hasn't it always been like that?

I don't think it's supposed to be like this.

The boy looked up and waved a hand to an invisible conductor. April turned to see nothing but the flat desert landscape of Texas.

Who are you waving at, she asked.

The train. It's here. I need to go. Escaping the Yupik Front is nearly impossible this time of year. Without help. The boy put a hand on the railing of the cab and took a step up. To April, he appeared to be hovering in mid-air.

She shook her head to clear it. Where will you go?

The boy looked up into the train and then back down to April. Why, here. It'll just take me some time to get here.

April turned and surveyed the highway. Here? What's here?

The boy took another step as the conductor walked down the dusty highway. He appeared from nothing and he ushered April aside.

Ticket, Miss?

No, I don't have a ticket.

Then we'll kindly ask you to step aside. We've got a schedule to keep and right now we're way behind.

Where are you going?

South, miss. South. The Children of the Infinite await.

She backed away from the stranger who was dressed in grey slacks and a blue, long-sleeved shirt. He wore a black vest with a crest sewn into the pocket over his heart. They were yellow letters on a black oval. It read KMC. Beneath that were the words, Digging New Worlds. He tilted his cap to her and began to climb the ladder to the cab that April could not see. The boy turned before disappearing aboard and said, you know where we are, you always have. And you know who you are to protect. You just have to trust yourself. You're the only one that can do it. Just as I am the only one that can do my job. If you fail, or if I fail, the Children of the Infinite fail and all Mankind is lost. Before she could respond, he disappeared into the cab and slipped from her sight. He dissipated into nothingness.

The conductor wiped at his brow and April thought it was from sweat. But instead, he was clearing snow from his vision. She could see it clearly, swirling about him.

Getting colder, he said. Gonna be a rough ride. He took a final step before disappearing and April said, how do I know where to go?

April, he said, its right in front of you. He stepped into the ether and disappeared.

Then she heard the train whistle and felt a sudden burst of cold air. To her right, stretched out for what seemed a mile, was a sleek black train. Steam poured from beneath it and clouded her vision. Then she saw the train wasn't on wheels. It was on snow treads. They began to churn like a bulldozer and she backed away. The treads churned and churned, billowing snow toward her. She held up a hand to protect her eyes and the train sped past her, into nothing. And then it was gone.

She held the panda in her hand and stared at the spot where the train disappeared from view. All she could see was the Highway 118 sign. It was still blinking like a slot machine....

.....April awoke in a diner, clutching the panda and feeling disoriented. It was a feeling that she had lost time and, waking up where she did, she certainly missed out on something. Her stomach rumbled and she didn't recall the last time she had eaten. She surveyed the diner which appeared to have served its last meal about a decade ago. There was nothing but a storeroom. She opened the door and saw row upon row of canned goods. Taking a step in, she figured she at least wasn't going to die from starvation. Her daughter was on her mind, but she had to survive to find her. She crawled into the storeroom and pulled the door nearly shut. That night she ate four cans of tuna, a large can of cherry pie filling and washed it down with a Fanta orange. The orange drink was hot, but it was a sweetness she hadn't had in months. She slept on and off for nearly twelve hours.

She was three weeks away from meeting Cathey for the first time.

CHAPTER 27

Sometime in 2106

If I tell you something, do you promise not to get mad, April asked Cathey.

Why do you always wait until the end of a brutal day to ask me a hypothetical question you know I'm not going to answer?

Shut up, Cathey. I'm being serious.

I am too. I can't tell you I'm not going to be mad. I don't know what you're going to say.

My name is really April.

That was a long time ago, April. I sorta figured that out.

I'm a Black, a Heteroclite. Like you.

He nodded. Okay. Since we're being honest. I'm that guy that blew up that Army base and kidnapped his kid. How's that?

Yeah, I sorta figured that out way back when too.

You could have turned us in. Maybe saved your parents. The Grey Suits would have paid big money to have me back in custody. Still could.

No, I never could have done that. Not to you. You got Mattie away from them. I wasn't so lucky.

What do you mean?

When you found me, do you remember that diner?

Cathey nodded. Even after everything that had happened over the last several years, he thought that was a bright spot. And one he wouldn't trade for the world. April was like a daughter to him. He loved her as such.

I had all that baby food with me, remember?

I remember. It was the only thing that quieted him down.

You didn't think it was odd that I was carrying all that food?

251

I think I remember you telling me something about a sister. I assumed that it was for her.

No, she was dead long before that. She shook her head. Another story for another day, Cathey. No, I was carrying it for my baby. I had a girl. Not three months old when she was taken from me.

She told Cathey the whole story or as much of it as she remembered. She tried to leave nothing out which was hard because she was ashamed and afraid of what Cathey would think. Plus, she'd been lying so long about the past, it was hard to remember what was the truth or a lie. As she finished, she broke down and cried harder than she'd ever cried before. She hated showing this weakness to Cathey, but she couldn't help it. He reached for her and hugged her tightly.

I'm sorry for lying, she said through sobs.

It's okay, Honey. It's okay. He kept hugging her until she pulled away. She rubbed her eyes with her hands and then wiped the tears on the legs of her pants.

Sorry for being such a girl.

It's okay, April. Really. That's a load of shit you were carrying around with you. But, if I can ask, why are you telling me all this now? There's a million things we probably didn't tell each other in the beginning because we didn't trust each other. But that's been seven years. The past is the past.

The past is prologue Cathey. I saw that on a statue in Washington, D.C. when I was twelve. It's because of the past that I have to do what I have to do now.

And what's that, April?

My dreams. The ones that wake you up sometimes?

Yes?

I have this one that I've had since before the world went to shit. It's always been something crazy, but when I met you, I thought you and Mattie, well, Mattie, was the subject of the dream. I always thought that from the minute I met you. Then to see him grow and see his abilities. I really thought he was it.

It what?

This Variant they talk about in my dreams. In my dreams, I've been told for years that my role in this world is to protect the Variant. And I just assumed it was Mattie.

It's just a dream April. You can't –

You don't understand, these aren't just dreams. I think it's like another world, like ours but different.

April, listen to yourself.

Cathey, I know how it sounds. But now, now I can access that world without sleeping. I can will myself there.

April, please sit down. This doesn't make any sense.

Cathey, I've spoken to Mattie in that world. He's older. He's on his own. You're not around. I don't know what's happened to you, but Mattie is on his own. And I've heard for ten years now from various people and creatures in that world that I have to protect the Variant. I thought it was Mattie. But I don't know anymore. I think maybe it's my daughter I'm supposed to protect.

We only have a few more weeks until we're in Alaska. We can get the boy there safely and then you and I will head out to find her. I promise.

It's not your journey though, Cathey. Your journey is to keep Mattie safe. Get him to Alaska. Hide him from the Grey Suits. Raise him. Then, then I don't know. But I know in my heart what I have to do. I think you'd do the same for Mattie.

He nodded his head and a wave of sentimentality washed over him. He dabbed at his eye with his index finger.

I'm sorry, Cathey. I have to do this.

The boy loves you, April. He'll be devastated.

I love *him*, Cathey. And you too. You're the only family I have except for my daughter. Its why I have to find her.

I'll get the boy situated. Then I'll come. Take the satellite communicator with the access codes. When I'm on my way, I'll let you know and we can find your daughter together. We can bring her up here and then finish what we started.

April shook her head. Cathey, this isn't your deal. It's mine. I've got to do it alone. I know it sounds crazy but I've ignored my dreams for so long. It's time I started listening.

Where will you go?

Cathey –

No, I'm not asking because I'm going to follow you, I just want to know if you'll be safe.

The dreams revolve around Highway 118 in Texas. There's a town there, Alpine. My grandmother lived there until she died. I was only five or six. But I went there to visit. I don't know what it means. But I've got to go there and find out. If it means finding my daughter, I have to do this. I have to protect her.

Just for the sake of argument, what if it is Mattie you're supposed to be protecting?

Why didn't the dreams stop when I found him? They keep telling me to protect the Variant. I thought it was him for the longest time. I wanted it to be him. I never wanted to be apart from him. But the dreams keep coming. Urging me onward.

So you think your daughter is, he paused, thinking of the right words, like Mattie?

I know. I know how it sounds.

The men that did this to you –

Yes, Cathey. I know.

They were just marching around with a Heteroclite? Waiting to find another Heteroclite so they could mate them? That makes no sense. And then the likelihood that your child would be like Mattie.

Look Cathey, I know how it sounds. But you weren't there the night she was born. A lot of the shit you talked about with Mattie, happened with me. Listen, I never told you this, hell, I didn't believe it myself, but lately I've started to remember things. Before the Greys got me in Mount Enterprise. I told you that I blamed them for the child, but I didn't tell you the truth because I didn't understand what happened. I still don't. But I know the day they grabbed me, something happened to me before I was in their custody. I was in a tunnel and there was a whole other world in this tunnel. A passageway. I was in a speakeasy and then I was in a room made of metal. Stop looking at me like that, Cathey.

Cathey shook his head. I've had dreams too, April. But what you're saying is –

I know how it sounds. I've ignored it as long as I can. Mattie's there in that world. And I know that I didn't run into you in that diner by mistake. It's all connected. I just don't know how. I need to find my daughter and figure it out.

If we don't make it to Alaska –

Then that's on you, Cathey. I'm sorry but I have to do this. Don't make it any harder than it already is.

Okay, okay, okay. I'm sorry.

She walked away from him and stood at the stove. The difference in temperatures here in Canada compared to the States was remarkable, she thought. The weather fronts passing south were drenching the Canadian Rockies. Snow had returned for the first time in years. She looked out the window and figured now was the best time to leave. She didn't know how long the snow would last or if it would get worse. There were still passable highways and she could be in Texas in a week or two.

What do I tell him?

The truth, Cathey. Try the truth. Tell him everything.

Will you talk to him?

She nodded her head and went to the room where he was sleeping.

She woke him from a dream and he wiped a tear from his eye. The low lights of the living room filtered into the darkness of his room.

Hey kiddo, she said.

He turned away from her, pulling the bedspread up over him. It's cold, he said.

You're not cold.

I know. I just don't want to talk to you, he said. I'm tired.

I know that's probably a lie too.

So, what if it is?

Why don't you want to talk to me?

Because I know what you're going to say.

What am I going to say?

That you're leaving.

How do you know? Were you listening at the door?

No. The man from the way station told me. He told me to be brave. He said my time with you was over for the time being. I have to let you go, he said.

Did he tell you why?

He told me we all have jobs to do.

Has he told you what your job is?

He says lots of things.

Such as?

I have to save the dying. But I don't want you to leave.

256

I know, Honey, but I have to. The man in your dream, what does he look like? Does he have a funny moustache?

Yes. Like the old movie people. He wears funny clothes too. Puffy Suits. With black arm bands over his arms.

He talks to me in my dreams, too.

You talked to him?

I did. In the way station, she said.

I've been there. There's a giant picture of a galaxy. With a pirate ship.

She smiled. I've seen that same picture. It helped me see what I was missing all these years. I've got a job to do too. Just like you. I have to protect someone.

But it's not me?

I don't think so. I think you're doing just fine on your own. And you've got your dad.

He's sick, you know?

She shook her head. No, what do you mean?

I walked into the shed the other day and he was on the ground, grabbing at his side. I ran to him and helped him to his feet, but he slid down again. Said his legs were weak. He overdid it, he said. But I could feel the heat coming from his side. It's his kidneys or something. I researched it the best I could, but I think he's got the Cluster finally.

She grabbed him by the hand. That was the last piece of my dream. Here, take my hand. I've got to show you something....

Variant

CHAPTER 28

They stood in the shed with the poster print spread out over Cathey's work station. It's the same one from the way station, right? Or, at least it looks like that one.

Mattie nodded his head. Yeah, that's the one from my dream.

Mine too, April said.

So what do we do with it?

Something told me to grab it when your dad and I were out about two weeks ago. I saw it in a store, behind a plastic sleeve and I got chills. So I ripped it out.

Did you leave money for it, the boy asked.

You know me too well Matthew Cathey. Of course I did.

Yeah, that's annoying.

Well, when everything gets back to normal, we'll be the good guys. We didn't take what we didn't need.

It's never getting back to normal, Mattie said.

Mattie, please.

You're leaving. What am I supposed to think?

That's why I brought you out here. When you mentioned your dad being sick, I remembered the painting.

I think that's more like a bad copy of the painting we've seen in the way station.

Well, I'm hoping it still works.

Works how?

Do you see it spinning, or is that just me?

I see it. Spinning like a clock.

Yeah, that's what I see too. I saw it spinning in the store. Can you take my hand?

He reached out, grabbed her hand and interlocked his fingers with hers. She was warm and everything was okay. With her right hand, she reached out and suddenly the shed whizzed past them and they were thrown down a black tube. Just as suddenly as it started, it stopped and they stood in the tunnel entranceway to the speakeasy. They opened the door and it was empty save for a lone table. A candle burned in a jar giving off a faint light. The piano was quiet. The bar was empty.

I don't really understand how it all works. But I think the painting is some sort of transportation device.

That's as good an explanation as any, the man said. He stood in the darkness and approached them. They recognized Eugene McBride, the man with the pencil-thin moustache.

Glad you found the print, Eugene said. Getting to you in the dreams was getting harder by the day. This one, he said, pointing to Mattie, fights us daily. We can barely hold him down here to get him any information. Mickey suggested the painting. He does love that painting. You're here now to show him?

She nodded her head.

Did you tell him?

Tell me what? I'm standing right here.

Well, Mattie my boy, just as things are a bit slower down here for you toppers, once you go spinning the Here Gather the Stars painting, time can get a little squirrely.

What, Mattie asked.

Eh, squirrely, you know, uh, you toppers, hard to communicate with sometimes, squirrely means weird, okay? What she can show you might be off your time line a bit.

He's trying to say I can show you the future. Or the past. Or both. Sometimes at the same time. That's a little messed up.

That's a lot messed up, the boy said.

McBride continued, Mattie, I've got to warn you before you endeavor to step through that wall, things have a way of working themselves out, in a cosmic sense. You are a very special boy and an exceedingly important adult. The Grey Suits will not hesitate to collect you no matter where or *when* you are. Do you understand?

Not really.

April looked at the boy. He means, they want you. They won't stop trying to get you whether you're here or up top.

Up top?

The real world. They call us toppers because we're not from around down there.

So tell 'em the rules, Miss Wolfe.

The rules. If you travel down here and by down here I mean Interzone, it's a name I saw in a book one time and it seems to fit. I don't know what McBride calls it because we've never talked about it. She paused and looked at McBride.

I've heard it called Interzone myself, he said, continue.

If you travel down to Interzone by yourself, you must leave by yourself. Snatching people from here and bringing them up top can have disastrous consequences.

Like what, Mattie asked.

April paused, thinking what to say.

May I, McBride asked.

April nodded.

Mattie, McBride began, we strive for a certain bit of balance between your world and ours. If someone is from my world and doing their thing down here or that someone is from your world and enjoying themselves in my world, it's best to let them be. Unless they decide to go up top. They have to make that decision. And even then, they have to find their own passage out of Interzone into your world. You can't just grab them and take them with you through whatever passage you've created, no matter the emergency or threat. If you arrive in Interzone alone, you must exit Interzone alone. Got it?

Mattie nodded.

Continue Miss Wolfe, McBride said.

Okay, April continued, so like he said, if you come down here alone, you have to leave alone. Similar rules follow if you arrive down here with someone else. Then you both have to leave together. If one stays behind, crazy shit can happen to both people. No matter where they are from. Understand?

Mattie nodded again.

Finally, to enter Interzone together, we have to both concentrate on our entry point or, in this case, the painting. That's our common portal. I think it has to be the same every time. But I don't know. Our course is already plotted. But we have to choose the correct place and time.

Okay. How do we do that?

I was just there. I'll take you. Usually, you just have to think about a person or a place. Concentrate on them. For now, just think about your dad. They spun the galaxy painting one quarter turn. Are you thinking about him?

I am, Mattie said. If you end up some place you don't want to be, it takes a minute or two to figure that out sometimes, you must return to the painting or print or however you got here and think hard on where you just were. And sometimes that's hard to do down here. Really hard. Otherwise, she paused, remembering the few times she'd ended up back in their clutches, otherwise, it's bad Mattie. Really awful.

She turned the painting again a quarter turn. Ready, she asked.

Ready, he said. She turned the painting a final time, one quarter turn and suddenly the bar was gone and they stood on the threshold of a hospital room......

CHAPTER 29

Sometime in 2108

…..Cathey lay in the bed, heart monitor beeping at forty beats a minute. The tube intubating him twisted down his throat. He had fought them when they tried to get him air. In the end, he was too weak to argue. An IV fluid of narcotic painkillers dripped into a line that snaked into his hand and kept him sedentary. They decided against any Cluster drugs because one, he had killed over a thousand people when he escaped last time and two, they were running dangerously low on supplies after the Rising attacked last week. Instead, they chose to keep him sedated.

She was handcuffed to the chair next to his bed. Her gaunt face was shadowed by the lone light in the room. It felt like death and she wondered why. They were supposed to be the survivors. At least when this all started. Now they were dying. She reached for his hand and was stopped by the cuffs. All she could do was lay her head next to his hand. Even in his stupor, he felt her near him. He lifted his hand and placed it on her head.

The room spun a quarter turn. While noticeable, neither Clara nor Cathey registered the spin in their current conditions. In a minute, the room spun another quarter turn.

The white board on the far wall changed from a board keeping tabs on Cathey's vitals to a painting of a girl holding a watering can when the room turned the first time. Then, on the next turn, it changed again, this time to a spinning galaxy with a pirate ship.

The room spun again a quarter turn and the wall and painting disappeared. April and Mattie stood at the threshold.

He had never seen his mother in anything but pictures. In her current state, she appeared to be dying. Her eyes wilted and her hair hung limply about her head. He could see areas where she had lost

263

her hair. He approached her slowly, not wanting to jar her. She lifted her head and wept as the boy stood before her. He noticed it almost immediately. The color of her eyes was a sickly yellow. The color of pirated Cluster drugs.

April bent down and somehow released the woman's cuffs. The woman reached for her son and hugged him tightly. He put his mouth to her head in order to kiss her and he noticed she had no scent. As though she didn't exist. He would have the same feeling again some time later at Summer Cabin. When he crossed a similar clone's path.

The woman clutched Mattie and he forced himself to feel something but there was nothing. As she did so, she reached an arm out to April.

Thank you, she said. April only nodded, wiping her own tears.

You know each other, Mattie asked April.

It's complicated. I've only met her in my dreams but I feel like I know her.

So, is this real?

April thought about it and glanced at Clara. I think it can be.

April, I don't think – he started but April put a finger to Mattie's lips and he stopped talking. She concentrated on him and his face and held her finger on his lips. She projected her thoughts to him.

I had to be sure, she said in his mind.

He looked startled to hear her in his head, but her lips hadn't moved.

April, he thought.

It's not her, is it? Not your mom?

No. My dad said they cloned her. I don't know how many there were but this one isn't my mom. What's going on? Where are we?

See, I don't know. I don't think it's a where as much as a when. I know how to find them. I have seen them several times. It's always at this very moment. When your father touches her head. Something happens and that painting in the way station becomes so much more. It's like a bridge between time. But in my dreams, when I've seen this scene, I knew I had to get you here to confirm my suspicions.

When is this?

It's later, Mattie. Much later. You'll know. We'll see each other again here, I know it.

How? How will I know?

It's taken me a long time to figure it out. No one can tell you. You have to figure it out for yourself. But I had to bring you here. So I could see for myself.

To see if she was really my mom?

For one. Yes. I needed to know who that woman was. For me, with you and I down here, it's like confirming what it is I am to do. You have to promise me that no matter what happens, you don't go jumping trains or running down tunnels trying to find me. Do you understand that?

I think so.

I also need you to see what it is you need to do.

To save the dying?

Yes, Mattie, yes. To save the dying. The Children of the Infinite await.

But how?

I don't know, sweet boy. That's your burden in all this. To figure that out.

He walked around the bed to his father.

Dad, he said out loud. His father struggled to open his eyes but willed himself to do so. He looked up at Mattie and thought he was an angel for a moment.

Son, he said.

Can you hear me?

Yes, I can.

He gripped his father's hand and felt the liquid heat flowing through his veins. Mattie looked up at the IV and placed his other hand on the bag.

It's warm, the boy said.

Feels good, his father replied.

Mattie let go of his father's hand and pulled the needle out of the vein. It spurted blood and April immediately went to cover it with gauze. Mattie let the liquid from the IV drip into his palm and then he dipped his tongue into it.

He didn't know what he was doing. He simply reacted by instinct. When he tasted the solution, a thousand voices screamed in his head. His vision went red and then faded to black and he struggled to remain standing. He fought off the desire to lay down and then steadied himself. The voices quieted down and then disappeared. Cathey blinked several times before asking, what is it?

Mattie shook his head, I don't know. Poison I think. It tastes like a thousand deaths. Voices called out to me. It was a warning. I don't think I can save you.

He turned to the clone of his mother and said, either of you.

I think they're trying to kill you, Mattie said to his father.

Then they would, Cathey said. They're waiting for you, Son. They still need you. They're running out of Cluster drugs. And if they run out drugs, they lose power. George Richmond tried to tell me that at the Lighthouse. The Grey Suits maintain power over the people so long as they give the people something. If you rob a man of everything, that man will no longer be in your power. He said that all the time, in various ways, but I never understood what he meant. If they run out of drugs, they run out of power.

No, Dad, Mattie said, in a voice suddenly much older and wiser than fourteen. Suddenly he was a young man and April saw him for the young man in her dreams. The one that commanded the Mechs with his mind.

It's not if they run out of drugs. It's if they find a cure. If they use my blood, maybe that's the cure. And it's the cure they fear. The cure takes their power because then they'll have nothing left to give the people. And the people will stop dying. And the Grey Suits will crumble.

How do you know this?

A dream or another time. I don't know. Maybe another world. But I know it as sure as I am standing here. I've got to stop the dying and the Grey Suits.

That's why I took you to Alaska. To keep you from them. For your protection.

But don't you see, Father? I wasn't meant to be hidden. Protecting me has only delayed my ability to fulfill my purpose. April has a job. She's to protect the Variant.

But you need protecting!

Not anymore. You have to let her go. And I have to save the dying.

How will you do that?

We can start with these, April said and pulled several vials from her backpack. It's the best I could do, synthesizing his blood. It'll keep you well so long as you use it. I don't know its long term effects. I haven't had enough time to study it. But for now, it'll keep you alive. The remaining vials are for a doctor you'll run into. McBride didn't tell me more than that.

Dad, the Mechs. They keep showing up in my dreams. They are the key. If I can control them, I can control the military.

We can't control them from Summer Cabin.

But they are still controlled by a central unit, right?

That central unit was destroyed when I blew the Aerospace Defense Command to shit.

Yet, the Mechs are still operational. We've seen them. Do you think they'd suddenly switch their operational systems to include multiple command posts for the Mechs? Or wouldn't it make more sense that they just moved it after the last time?

Okay, Cathey said. Maybe they just moved it. But we don't know where and we don't have the fire power to go on a wild goose chase at various Grey Suit bases looking for it.

Maybe they don't have to, the Clara clone said. Maybe it's right here. It's been here the whole time. And the idiots brought you right to it.

What are you talking about, Cathey asked.

Here, this base. They hid everything in a mountain last time. That didn't work out. But they still believe they've got to be underground due to the heat. We're in a base that's basically a series of caverns in the Sonoran desert. Underground. Centralized. I've been here since the beginning. A high value asset like me could only be housed at their most secure base. Where else would they hide the Mech command?

A door opened beyond the threshold. A doctor dropped the chart and stood in awe, staring into a giant swirling galaxy on the other side of the door. He could hear voices but the whole of the room appeared to be taken up by the galaxy.

As the doctor approached the gaping hole, the Clara clone approached Mattie and suddenly shoved him through the gloom of the painting. Go now boy, she said. He fell through the darkness of the universe and landed back in a gloomy room. On the other side, a flickering blackness was left. The painting spun several times on the wall. But now there was no swirling galaxy. Just a picture of one. It was missing a pirate ship too. And April was nowhere to be found.

He rubbed the back of his head and felt the floor beneath him. He looked about for the picture of the galaxy but could see nothing in front of him or behind him. Suddenly the floor illuminated and Mattie could see three tall figures standing in front of him. The lighted floor extended several hundred yards in every direction. Mattie felt as though they stood in the middle of the room and he lay before them. He could see no walls. Just darkness on the horizon and upwards.

They each wore a suit of a similar style save for the color. There was one dressed in white, with hair and eyes to match. His shoes were as white as his tie which matched the color of the vest and shirt he wore. Even his belt was white. He stood on the far left, next to a man dressed in red who stood next to a man dressed in all black. The three of them matched. Their hair was the color of their suits. Their eyes the color of their shoes. They appeared to be different men but Mattie couldn't be sure. The only thing not colored on them was their skin. While they had pinkish skin, they also carried small reddish blue blisters about their necks that rose from the collars of their suits and threatened to crawl up their cheeks. The Man in Red separated himself from the group and approached Mattie.

He took ten steps, his shoes click-clacking like a tap dancer across the well-lit floor. He held a blistered hand out toward Mattie.

I'm fine right where I am, Mattie said. He scooted his body away from the man.

The Man in Red folded his arms across his chest.

I know, he said out loud. Mattie looked at the other two, confused.

You know what, Mattie asked.

The Man in Red said nothing.

Did he tell you about us Mattie, the Man in Black asked from where he stood.

Who?

McBride. He was the one that sent you down here, wasn't he?

He didn't send me. I was in a room and then I was shoved out of the room. How do you know my name?

Irrelevant, the Man in Red shouted in a voice much too loud for the surroundings. The ending echoed across the vast space, Vant Vant Vant Vant Vant Vant, until it faded.

So you didn't come on your own volition, the Man in Black asked.

No, Mattie said, confused.

You lack the ability to travel between the worlds don't you?

I don't understand any of this, to tell you the truth.

Perfect. We are the Distorters. We seek passage to your world. We must find our fourth.

Mattie, April's voice called from somewhere deep within the darkness that surrounded them.

Ignore her, the Man in Black said.

Mattie, she called again but her voice sounded like an echo, from a million miles away.

April, Mattie called and suddenly the Man in Red grabbed the boy with his mind and lifted him into the air. Mattie realized the man never touched him with his hands. He simply willed him up and now Mattie floated before him.

We told you to ignore her, he said. The three men turned toward the sounds of footsteps approaching and suddenly Mattie was on a rectangular, wooden frame. His ankles were tied to a roller on the bottom of the table that pointed downward. His wrists were chained to another roller, above his head. A creature stood next to Mattie holding a steel ratchet. His elongated head was purple colored and stretched a few feet in the air and ended in a tip. His chin hung several feet down, nearly reaching his legs. A clump of thick black whiskers sprouted at the top of his head and dangled to one side. He had a large protruding beak in the center of his face. It was orange and was littered with red blisters that oozed a pink puss. His stubby body was portly and looked like it would topple his skinny legs. Two large oval eyes sat widely apart from the nose on the side of the creature's head. The yellowish eyes focused on Mattie and he bent to sniff at the boy.

Fear, it said, tastes so good. He opened the slit beneath his beak exposing four rows of razor sharp metallic teeth. A thick blackish tongue unfurled from the creature's throat and lapped the sweat from Mattie's face. The tongue was as rough as sandpaper but as moist as river moss. He curled the tongue around the boy's neck and hummed softly as he squeezed Mattie's neck, cutting off his air.

Mattie, April called again, this time she sounded closer.

The creature's tongue whipped back into his mouth and he put a crooked, clawed finger to his beak, shhh.

Phobos, someone shouted. He immediately pulled at the steel ratchet a few times and Mattie felt the joints in his arms pulled upward and the joints in his legs pulled down. Excruciating pain exploded through his body.

Mattie, April called and suddenly she burst through the small wooden door where Mattie was tied up.

Phobos, be gone, she said and held a hand, palm open toward the creature. Mattie briefly saw bluish electricity gather in her palm and then spin out like a spider's web toward the creature. The webbing surrounded it, lighting it up with neon blues. Before it winked out of existence, he saw the galaxy swirling in the ceiling. He reached for April and for a moment they catapulted through the darkness together. Mattie tried to scream that something was wrong. We've broken their rules, April replied. The two voices melted together in the darkness. Somewhere along the way, his fingers slipped and April slid somewhere else.

CHAPTER 30

Sometime in 2108

He awoke from the dream as he always did, reaching for her in the darkness but always waking in his bunk at Summer Cabin. This time, every joint in his body ached. He'd never been through a dream like that and yet it was fading faster than normal. Somewhere, in the distance, a proximity alert was beeping. He couldn't believe he slept through it. He slowly gathered a shirt, flung it on and pulled hiking pants over his thermals.

The control panels were embedded on an island in the galley. Sixteen screens monitored every acre of the facility. The US military built this facility in the nineteen fifties as a nuclear arsenal and it was wired as such. Mattie and his dad had replaced most of the wiring, updating it over the years. He now watched as multiple cameras showed Mechs moving in. How they got through the trees, he didn't know, but these new Arctic Mechs didn't walk on stilted legs. These Mechs rolled atop the snow like snow cats. He counted thirty of them, approaching from all sides. They were each equipped with .950s and HE-Frag devices. They were coming for war.

A group of four A-Rexs stood nearly on top of the buried blast doors. Their drills whirled and began to tear through the ice and compacted snow, spewing ice and crystals into the air. He'd never seen bits like these. They were making short work of the snow. It would be minutes before they were into the soil. Then he'd have to see how well they did with the doors. By then, though, they'd know someone was down here.

How had they found him?

He ran a diagnostic on the Cabin but nothing in the operating systems came back as faulty or breached. Then he saw it on the monitor at the furthest reaches of the property, smoke coming from

one of the vents. Those vents allowed air to circulate at the lowest
levels of the cabin to prevent dangerous moisture from building up.
The vent that was smoking allowed the bathrooms on the bottom floor
to release their moisture. The bottom floor. Where she was currently
located.

Immediately, he took five deep breaths. To clear his mind and
remind himself of his father's words. Just like always. Begin to pack.
Think only of those things you will need to live a few days. Your
weapons. Your knife. Your pack. Your fire. Jerky. Your flesh coat.
Sunglasses. Always sunglasses because the white of the snow could
blind you, he would say in his calm, reassuring voice.

Mattie crossed into the ready room and picked up his pack. It
was already loaded with Levin and jerky. A small compressible
sleeping bag now rested at the bottom of the pack. He also made a
small ultra-light tent that he'd tested at thirty below and fifty-mile-
per-hour winds. It was a solid effort and would keep him alive for a
few days. The knife rested in the scabbard that was sewn into the
pack. He took the flesh coat off the hook and pulled his arms through
it. His father had finally come around to just calling it for what it
was: a flesh coat. Parka and jacket never fit as a name because his
father described the coat as the flesh of a bear, when Mattie was
younger. He called it simply flesh coat and the name stuck. He
pulled the interior layer together and zipped it to his chin. Then he
pulled the wide swaths of bear flesh together and buttoned them up to
his neck. He flipped the collar up and buttoned that portion, covering
his mouth.

He took the stairs down to the bunks on the bottom floor.
From here, he could access the solar skis he and his father parked in
the converted grain storeroom. Two years into his ownership, Cathey
discovered the storeroom with a tunnel that had rails leading outside.
He assumed they brought in grain by rail for the long winters. Which

would make sense, given the distance between the cavern opening where this tunnel led and the weight of the grain they would need to survive a winter out here.

Mattie made his way down the stairs and stopped at her door. He punched in the code and swung the door open. She lay on the bed, her legs dangling off and her left arm flung over the side, dripping blood from her wrist. A large pool of it was snaking its way down toward the door like a demented river. It was nearly black. Her face was purple and the skin of her neck was like rubber as he felt for a pulse. He waited a moment, thinking she was dead and then a faint tremor in her vein rippled across his fingertip. It was shallow, but she was still alive. He looked around for what she used to slice her wrist but couldn't see anything. The smoke was seeping through the bathroom door. He had to get her out of here.

He went to the door and touched it feeling the molten heat from the fire. He couldn't begin to comprehend how she had started it. Turning, he went to the closet to pull out her coat, pants and winter boots. The closet was empty.

The items you're looking for are fueling that fire in there, a voice called out to him.

Mattie turned and faced several large men in ski masks in the doorway.

She was always crafty that one, the lead man said, pointing to the woman who claimed she was Mattie's mother. But not as smart as your mother. There's a difference, you know.

The man stepped into the room and he bent to clear the doorway jamb. He was a massive human being standing nearly six foot eight or nine. His chest and arms rippled with unnaturally large muscles that threatened to split the fabric making up their black uniforms. The men he faced appeared to be the same men that attacked them at the trapper's cabin.

Who are you? How did you get in here?

It took us a while. But she figured it out. Once she was healthy enough to move around. Found the tunnel system. Contacted us. Right under your nose. That must be disappointing.

Grey Suits, Mattie said.

The man shook his head. We're the ones they send when the Greys can't do it. Nice to meet you.

I've got to warn you, I'm sure you know this, but this isn't my first encounter with your group. I killed three of you back a few years ago. You guys don't look much tougher.

We're designed not to fail.

I'm sure your friends were too.

You need to come with us. They took a few more steps into the room and Mattie stood his ground.

Listen, fellas, I'm sure you guys think you're bad asses. And I'm sure in most situations, you are. I mean, my dad was tough and you nearly killed him. But I'm not like my dad. Or anyone you've run across. You've got about ten seconds to turn around, take your little army tanks with you and get the hell off my property.

They moved with the speed of gazelles. The four men were instantly on Mattie, ripping his arms in opposite directions and pulling his legs until it felt like his groin would snap in two.

Despite the pressure they were applying, Mattie closed his eyes and summoned every ounce of strength he had. He planted each of his legs on the ground and pulled his arms toward himself. His attackers kept pulling, but suddenly they were being pulled toward each other. Mattie then brought his arms together smashing two of the soldiers together, dropping each of them. The men on his legs backed away but assumed attack positions.

Last chance fellas, he said and swung at the man closest to him. His swing missed wide as the man dodged the punch. In return, he pounded the side of Mattie's head with a left hook that sent the boy careening toward the wall. He bit his cheek as the flesh of his jaw collided with his teeth. His jaw exploded and blood poured from the fracture. Despite the gash, the pain was minimal. The soldiers backed away, thinking they had him, but Mattie attacked. He swung fiercely for the one that struck him. Mattie's blow immediately sent the soldier reeling toward the wall. His head ricocheted off the wall, cracking the plaster. The man slumped down the wall. The others continued backing away but Mattie didn't retreat. He struck the slumping man again, this time cracking his forehead. Blood poured from the wound but Mattie kept at him until he finally crushed the man's skull. He pulled up, blood and bone and brain dripping from his fist, yellowish fluid mixed with blood across his face.

The other men quickly activated their hyperstealth units. The crackle echoed across the room and the men disappeared. Mattie held his ground, thinking they would attack immediately but he heard them crackling down the hallway. They were retreating.

Mattie ran for the main level control room. He bent beneath the desks housing the CPUs and pulled out a pair of Illumination Goggles. He switched them on, flooding his vision with neon blue. Then he killed the power to the entire Cabin. Lights went dead. Air circulating systems ground to a halt. Doors swooshed locked, shutting off access to all but a small fraction of the Cabin. He waited for a moment, allowing his eyes to acclimate to the blue field of vision. Touching the side of his goggles, he activated the heat tracker, an enhancement to the Illumination Goggles his father added.

The range for the heat tracker was a quarter mile. Up and down the Summer Cabin was a quarter mile each way. The goggles showed five cloaked individuals in the main living quarters, now cut off by the closed blast doors. Four more cloaked soldiers were scattered down below. Each in various locked down rooms. He didn't know if he could survive nine of them. One was bad as his jaw could attest. He was strong, but he didn't think he could fight them all off. He was still human, after all. He rubbed at his jaw where it had been ripped open. Although it was sore, he could feel it healing.

He had two choices as he saw it. Fight them all, one by one, which might not be a real option, or set the Cabin for self-destruct. He still had the Mechs outside to contend with and he figured the explosion to Summer Cabin might take some of them down as well. He transferred central control to the tablet and ran out of the control room. There was only one blast door between him and the grain storage. It took him less than five minutes to power the control panel back up and enter the code for his exit. He set the self-destruct codes in place as well. He had five minutes to get as far away from Summer Cabin as he could.

Mattie ran down the hallway to the storage and the smoke was thick. He could feel it getting hotter as well, despite the draft pouring in from the bitter cold outside. The Illumination Goggles cut through the smoke and as he inhaled, he realized the smoke was merely just an irritant.

He came to the door of her room, flames were pouring out now and spitting thick plumes of smoke. He glanced in to see if there was any chance to save the woman. The bed was aflame now. In the goggles, a white flickering blaze roared across the bed. He couldn't see her. He touched the side of the Goggles for signs of life, but the heat from the fire masked any human pulses. Mattie backed out of the room and made his way down the tunnel, to the grain storage room.

The room was vast. Capable of storing over two hundred thousand pounds of grain, roughly enough to last ten people ten years in the silo. Mattie didn't know how long it had been since grain had been stored there. Probably decades. Now, it was just a big garage.

A really big garage capable of storing every known Mech on the planet. Or close to it.

A fleet of solar skis sat lined up. He went to a panel on the wall and opened it, pulling out an apparatus with a curved metal hose surrounding a thick plastic hose. At the end was something that looked like a spout. He placed it in the ski and pulled the trigger on the side of the hose. In a few seconds, a metallic sound clacked together connecting two internal pipes and then rapidly clicked in succession. The dial on the ski went from E to F in less than a minute. He'd only need gas if the solar panels failed to recharge. At this point, he didn't know how reliable either method would be for him.

He released the trigger on the hose and it shot back into the wall. He held the red trigger on the ski and pushed the oval power button on the panel of the ski between his legs. As he pushed the button, the ski tried to turnover. He took his finger off the trigger and tried again. This time it made a sound like WHIR-WHIR-WHIR, but failed to start. He tried one more time and the WHIR morphed into a steady rumble. He spun the accelerator back and the tracks locked into place and he took off down the long tunnel.

Somewhere inside the Summer Cabin, a control panel blinked to life and the doors suddenly opened. The super soldiers moved quietly through the Cabin. Once together on the main control floor, they spread out, looking for the boy.

The ski bounced over the gravel of the tunnel floor. Light flooded in where the super soldiers made their entry into the compound. The ski strained against the elevation gain which Mattie assumed to be about eight thousand feet. It was roughly about eight miles down the tunnel, so the machine struggled against the gravity. Plus, it had been awhile since he had taken a solar ski out. With the Mechs in the area, it hadn't been safe.

Snow started to filter into the tunnel and the temperature dropped considerably. As he approached the cave and the exit, the snow increased and as it did so, his vision decreased as well. He pulled the Illumination Goggles down and pulled hard on the accelerator.

As he approached the exit, he slowed the solar ski and reached into his backpack, pulling out his sunglasses. Swapping the goggles for the glasses, he clicked the right side of them and a grid appeared in his vision, giving him the distance to the cave exit. He gunned the snow machine and made his way to the outside.

Once free of the cave, he shot out into the snow in an explosion of snow and gravel. Trees popped up on his sensor and he turned left and then right to avoid a few. Then his vision field flooded and he pulled the sunglasses down. What he thought were trees, were actually Mechs. He was surrounded.

CHAPTER 31

Time unknown, perhaps 1860s, Interzone

Dr. Emanuel Walsh scanned the unfamiliar faces around him. While he wore his white lab coat and held his tablet to his chest, the men seated near him looked like something out of an Old West photo. Dusty boots and pants with revolvers on their hips surrounded him. Most of the men wore hats of varying degrees of cowboy. Tall ones, shorter ones and the occasional bowler. Most of the men in the saloon continued their routines, playing cards or discussing the troubles they were having with the free grazers.

Schomacker plucked at the keys on his newly-minted piano. The men seemed pleased with the sound but would not have been able to tell you why. Two women sat outside the saloon, waiting on the train and their husbands to finish their drinks. One of the women, a girl of only twenty, glanced at her father's pocket watch.

How much longer, the other woman, about thirty or so asked. It's 2:40. So a half-hour.

One of the men, a tall, slender sinewy man, approached the doctor. He carried two Smith & Wesson Schofield Model 3 revolvers in leather holsters that were tied with rawhide just above his knee. His boots jangled with each step as his spurs connected with the hard wood of the saloon's flooring. He wore a unique hat with clean lines and a tear drop crown. It's pulled low across his brow and when he tilted his head to speak, one could only see one of his eyes. A pencil-thin moustache crawls across his upper lip. His teeth are too white for the time.

He wore a bone-white leather jacket with Royal Army Pay Corps buttons. Each one included a lion over a crown over a scroll which read "Fide et Fiducia." Roughly translated, it meant "By fidelity and confidence" or "Trust and be trusted."

You waitin' on the train, Doc?

Dr. Walsh stumbled backward until he connected with a poker table, spilling whiskeys and knocking over stacks of chips.

Hey, asshole, one of the men said, standing and putting his hands on the butts of his revolvers.

Take a seat J.B., the man with the pencil-thin moustache said, putting his hands on the butts of both his revolvers.

Alright Sheriff, J.B. said, sitting back down and immediately restacking his chips. The other men at the table did the same. There was some discussion as to how much each man had before the disturbance but the sheriff redirected the doctor from the table. He led him to an adjacent table and whistled for the barkeep. As they sat, an elderly man put a bottle of whiskey on the table and two small glasses.

The sheriff pulled the cork from the bottle and poured two drinks.

So, you waitin' on the train, the sheriff asked again. He picked up his glass and clinked it to the one in front of the doctor's and said cheers, downing the brownish liquid in one swallow.

The doctor sat transfixed. It was as though he couldn't move. He tried, but the signals in his brain weren't connecting with his body.

Take your drink, Doc. It'll calm your nerves.

Dr. Walsh reached out and put a shaking hand on the glass. He brought the glass to his lips and could smell the alcohol long before he took his sip.

The drink warmed his throat but threatened to leap back up. He coughed a few times and the sheriff refilled both their glasses.

Only thing good about that first drink, is the one that follows.

The doctor stared at the man before him, still in shock.

So the train question seems to be a bit much for you, the sheriff began.

I'm not here for the train, Walsh said.

Very good. Now we're off and running, Dr. Walsh.

How do you know my name?

That tag there on your coat says Walsh. I put two and two together.

He glanced down at his lapel where his name tag hung and then back up to the man in the wide-brimmed hat. Okay, sheriff. He hung his head, feeling tired and confused.

I'm not really a sheriff. Ol' J.B. calls everyone sheriff who has a pistol on his hip. I'm more like the Facilitator. Make sure everyone's where they're supposed to be. Real name's Eugene McBride.

I don't even know how I got here, Mr. McBride. I was working one minute and then the next I walked through those swinging doors. None of this makes any sense.

It rarely does, Doc. It rarely does. It might if you were waiting on the train.

Where does this train go?

All over. We got one heading out to the Arizona Territory in a bit. Where you headed?

I'm not even sure where this is, the doctor said, scanning the saloon again. Or when.

This little hamlet is Mount Enterprise, Texas. An unusual, even idiosyncratic community. A safe town, but strange nonetheless. I don't have the time, nor the inclination, to educate you on the full history of our little piece of the universe.

I don't even know how I got here. This looks like the Old West. Like a frontier town.

You make several valid points. This is indeed the West. It could be considered the frontier. And not even I know how you got here. That would be a you problem. Like I said, I'm just here to facilitate matters. Get you to where you need to be. What's the last thing you remember? Before you walked in here?

I made a note to check Cathey's oxygen levels. Also follow up on the blood test. I grabbed my tablet and walked down to his room. I opened the door and there was nothing but the darkness of space staring back at me. I could see stars, galaxies. The emptiness pulled me toward it and as I stepped through the doorway, I found myself moving through those bat-wing doors and into this saloon. The hospital just disappeared. I must be having a grand mal seizure or the Cluster has killed me. I'm dead, that's it. This is my bizarrely accurate Old West purgatory.

No, no, Doctor. You're right where you need to be. Of that I'm certain.

How can you be so sure?

Like I said, I'm the Facilitator.

Yeah, you said. Getting people where they need to be.

Good then. You understand.

No, I just listened to what you said ten times. I don't understand anything.

Open your mind, Doctor. Free yourself of those earthly constraints.

I thought you said I wasn't dead.

I did, indeed. Being dead and freeing yourself of your earthly constraints are two different things.

But if I'm not on Earth, then I'm dead, the doctor said.

Are you? Those are the constraints I was talking about.

The doctor took a deep breath. He focused on the brim of McBride's hat.

I can't save Cathey or his wife. I can't save anyone. I took an oath and now I just keep people alive long enough to serve their purposes.

They?

The Grey Suits. They're poisoning him. Her too, the doctor said.

Who are we talking about, Doc?

James Cathey and Clara, his wife. They're my only two patients now.

Well now, we are getting somewhere, aren't we? And why are you participating in this poisoning?

My kids. My wife. My brother. My whole family. They need the Cluster drugs. They're all too sick to work to afford it. The insurance ran out long ago. So I work for the Grey Suits and they provide them with their top-of-the-line care.

Have they gotten any better, Doc? With this top of the line care, as you say?

No, but they're not dead.

Is that living, Doc?

No. Not really. But a cure is beyond medicine right now.

Indeed it is. But did you know, from this sleepy little town, more than half of the Heteroclites descended?

How is that possible? We looked all over the world for the Heteroclites. On a planet of nine billion, we found fifteen. And you're saying seven or eight came from this town?

The number is seven, and, yes. In one form or fashion, seven of the world's Heteroclites came from this DNA pool. Odd, isn't it?

The doctor nodded his head. The odds of that are –

McBride held up a finger, silencing the doctor. Odds are an earthly constraint. I'm not talking odds, Doc. I'm just telling you. The cure you seek springs from this small town.

But how? I don't have any equipment. No computer. Nothing.

You aren't listening. You're giving me constraints. Earthly constraints. Those rules don't apply down here.

They'll kill me, if I restart the work on the cure.

So sure of this, are you?

They've killed others before. They don't want a cure.

Do you see J.B. over there? The gunslinger that you bumped into?

The doctor nodded.

He has cancer. Just normal cancer. Not that twisted sickness you call the Cluster. His is the kind that lurks in the shadows and kills you when you're unawares. He knows there's something wrong with him, he's just not sure what. Came here to go out on his own terms. He'll draw on somebody and that'll be that. He'll leave this world doing what he loves.

What the hell does that have to do with me?

Why'd you become a doctor?

I saw what the Cluster was doing to people. I wanted to help.

Are you helping now?

The doctor shook his head no. McBride nodded and said, could you be doing more?

I just don't see how. I wish I could.

Stop wishing. Do.

They'll kill me.

That cancer prowling around J.B.'s lungs is going to kill him. He hasn't let that stop him. Look at him over there. Drinking, smoking, playing cards.

That's just because he doesn't know.

He doesn't know the name bronchogenic carcinoma but he knows sometimes at night or in the morning when he wakes, he spits up large globules of black-red blood clots. He feels it in his lungs when he does. So he knows. It's just how he chooses to react to it.

He's been a gunfighter his whole life. It's all he knows. That and drinking, smoking, playing cards and spending some of that dough on a whore. So he does those things. But what really drives him, what gets him up in the morning, is being a gunslinger. So he works on that one the most.

You said that would kill him too.

It will. But that one won't hurt. He's slower than he once was when he was a kid. His eyesight isn't what it once was a younger man. The tremble in his right hand isn't noticeable yet. But when it is, they'll come for him. The younger guys. Wanting to make a name for themselves. That's how it works out here.

So even though it's going to kill me, I should find that cure?

You keep saying cure like it's something to be discovered. You just have to know where to look.

You're not going to tell me?

I already have, McBride said and as he did so a commotion broke out at the poker table. Multiple voices shouted about chips and cheating. Cards and whiskey flew toward the doctor as the table was turned over. McBride squirted out of the way as three of the men drew on J.B. The doctor backed away, toward the door. Somewhere a train whistle blew. Time drew to a crawl. Cards floated in mid-air, droplets of whiskey hung suspended above the men. The doctor saw the bullets burst from the three barrels before J.B. could even draw. As J.B. pulled his Colt, one of the bullets ripped through his throat. J.B. smiled as it sliced through his aortic artery. Another bullet shattered his teeth as he smiled. It blew the back of his head out. The last thing he thought as the third and final bullet pierced his heart, was something about health and hope. He'd lost both.

Dr. Walsh pulled himself through the saloon, fighting against the denseness of time within in it. He willed his legs to move. To get him out of the saloon before anything else happened. He felt the bullet hit his lower back just as he pushed through the batwing doors.

McBride stood in the saloon, his Smith & Wesson smoking. He had fired at the three men standing in the doorway but the bullet reacted unexpectedly as it collided with the passage back to the real world. It twisted in an odd trajectory. McBride didn't know if he hit his targets or not. Just before the portal closed, as the doctor was sliding through, McBride bent down and picked up a Colt from the saloon's dusty floor and tossed it in after him.

Dr. Walsh landed with a thud on the floor of Cathey's hospital room. Had he been lying in the bed, he may have been hit by the time (or galaxy)-traveling bullet. Instead, it grazed Walsh and punctured the wall above Cathey's bed. The sound of a bullet being fired was silenced as soon as the portal in the wall closed. The three soldiers guarding Cathey's room were at the door in seconds though, blasters drawn.

Walsh picked up the Colt that was lying underneath him and he stood slowly. Turning, he aimed the pistol at the men.

Doctor, what is this, one of them asked.

I need to get this man out of here. He's being poisoned. I've got work to do, you see. And I just need to get out of here.

You know we can't do that. Drop the pistol, Doctor.

I can't do that.

That little gun is no match for these blasters. One shot from you and we'll have you on the ground in seconds.

I guess we'll see. He pulled the trigger on the one soldier he had in his sights and the bullet flew from the barrel like a beam of light. Faster than any bullet should travel on earth. He pulled the trigger five more times, hitting each man in the throat and chest twice before the gun even made a sound that was audible to the soldiers.

They were dead before they could react. All three dropped in the doorway.

Where'd you get that gun, Cathey asked, feeling better as the blood that April delivered flowed through him. Mattie's blood.

Walsh simply looked at it and then slid it into his coat pocket. This place is going to fill up with soldiers when they figure out those three are dead. We've got a few minutes to get out of here.

You'll need these, Cathy said, handing the doctor the vials of Mattie's blood.

Variant

CHAPTER 32

Sometime in 2108

The effects of Mattie's blood on Cathey was almost instantaneous. The tenacious pain in Cathey's stomach that signaled the onslaught of exocrine pancreatic cancer was gone. His skin, yellowish and itchy from the buildup of bilirubin, was returning to its normal hue. And he was famished after a month of not eating. He trailed behind the Clara clone, April, and Walsh but he was walking again and he was feeling like his old self. Almost. He still didn't understand how April got to the base again, but her dismissive response told him not to ask again.

They were proceeding down a hallway none of them had ever been down. To trust what Dr. Walsh was telling them as they ran behind him was foolish in Cathey's eyes. But with April suddenly appearing from utter nothingness, it didn't seem so farfetched. He was the only one offering to help them escape the Grey Suits. They didn't understand when he told them he was free of his earthly constraints. Cathey thought the good doctor had either suffered a head injury of some sort or even started sampling from the narcotic cabinets. His behavior was completely contrary to what he was accustomed to with the doctor. Where before he was distant and cold, now he was engaged and truly wanted to see the trio escape. Cathey just didn't understand where it was coming from.

April jumped when he mentioned McBride's name and all but forced Cathey to come along. I know him, she shouted. If McBride came to Dr. Walsh, then Dr. Walsh is like us. He wants to help. I think we can trust him.

But he's the one that's kept us here. Against our will –

I don't have time to explain every detail, Cathey. Maybe later. But now, we have to move. It might be our only chance.

It is our only chance, Dr. Walsh said. They're going to kill us for sure if they figure out the link.

What link, Clara asked.

Your link to the town I was in. Mount Enterprise, Texas. Aren't you all from there?

I'm not from Texas, Cathey began, I'm from Oakland. But I remember something about a great-great relative being from a strange sounding place in Texas. It could have been Mount Enterprise.

I lived in Texas when I was little, Clara said and paused, in Mount Enterprise. She looked to Cathey.

I had no idea, he said.

Right, Dr. Walsh said, I think you're all either from there or you're a descendant of someone from there. I think.

April stopped right where she was when she heard what the doctor said. She said, wait, wait, wait. Hold your damn horses for just a minute. I *am* from Mount Enterprise. What does that have to do with any of this, April asked.

It's connected somehow. I don't know exactly how though. But McBride –

McBride is – Cathey held the *is* in the air for a second too long as he tried to figure out how he fit into the story.

He's the guy from the bar, Walsh said.

In the Old West, Cathey asked, confused.

From Prohibition, April said.

Well, in my vision, or whatever the hell it was, he was a gunfighter in the Old West. But it's the same guy, it sounds like, Dr. Walsh said.

Then the Clara clone remembered an implanted dream. The one they tried to extract from her. The one she hid from them.

In mine, he worked in the hotel lobby bar. Oh my gods. I remember it. I was so sick with, Clara paused and looked at April, Mattie you call him?

April nodded her head, go ahead, you were sick with Mattie.....

.....Clara lay in the bed and Cathey hovered over her like a nervous mother. He dabbed her forehead with a luke-warm rag. She asked him for more ice chips and when he was finally out of the room, she exhaled a bit and tried to relax herself. Her only view was of the ceiling. To try to forget the raging pain in her stomach, she focused on the patterns in the ceiling's paint. She bounced from swirl to swirl but found nothing to take her mind off the excruciating pain.

Then, just as she was going to shut her eyes and try to rest, she saw it. In the middle of her vision field. Camouflaged in the cream-colored ceiling was a swirl that seemed to spin amongst the swirls. It was hypnotic. She reached for it but it was too high. And then she longed for it. She wished to be in the soothing spin of that swirl. Then it changed. It looked more like a galaxy and less like a paint swirl. It spun like a hurricane and she grew tired.

When she awoke she startled herself. She was in a vast hotel lobby, seated in the middle seat of a three-seat-leather-connected system. Scanning the lobby, she found no one around that saw her dozing. And then, there he was, behind the bar, wiping a spot that needed no further work and humming something she couldn't quite place, though she thought she knew the song.

She hummed along and then whispered, heroes, forever and ever. And then she lost the tune. She stared at him with his jet black hair, the color of crude oil, swept to the right in a rigid part that split his head a quarter of the way up his scalp. He worked tirelessly on the spot and as a result she couldn't see his eyes. And she wanted to.

Walking over to him, he lifted his head. He looked as he always did. A slim, angular face with a nose that seemed just a little too thin. His hair pasted into place with a product of the time. His dark-colored eyes were not what she was expecting. The shamrock scar on his right hand was also unexpected. He smiled warmly as she approached.

Good evening, Miss, he said as he placed a napkin down in front of her. Something to drink for you tonight?

She felt sluggish and disoriented. Where had she come from? Where was she going? She couldn't remember. A faint pain in her stomach struggled to remind her but passed without success.

A drink sounded good and she nodded her head. She already felt drunk, but pulled up a seat just the same. The bartender smiled and waited for her order. His face was aglow from the light coming from the counter of the bar. It gave off an eerie yellowish glow that seemed unnatural.

Quiet tonight, she said.

Is it, he asked, scanning the lobby behind her. She turned and faced an empty lobby.

Seems like it. I'm sorry to say.

It's early yet. He began working on the spot again and she could see the light below him suddenly glow a little brighter. You're thinking of something sweet, he said to her, looking up and wiping his hands with the towel.

She thought about it and agreed. That sounds nice. He turned and grabbed a bottle from a shelf behind him. There were four, six meter shelves hanging across a mirrored backdrop. The shelves were lit from below with dusty yellow lighting. It looked as if the entire place needed a good wiping down.

He turned from the shelves and had a drink in hand. While odd, she didn't even question it. She took the drink and took a sip.

Nice, yes? He stood back and admired his concoction.

It's sweet, that's for sure, she said.

Hides the liquor better. No need to suffer while you cut the edge off the day.

She stopped herself mid-sip as he spoke. What's that you said?

Sorry, Miss?

What was that you just said?

No need to suffer?

Yes, what was it?

No need to suffer while you cut the edge off the day. He took a small step back and watched her reaction.

That's the strangest thing. My father used to say that. Cutting the edge off the day. He'd say it every day when he got home. I remember being no more than six or seven and wondering why he was always having to cut edges off his day. I gave him a pair of my mother's sewing shears one year for Christmas, and we all had a good laugh about it. That's probably the last time we all laughed like that. He died shortly thereafter.

Your father a businessman, if you don't mind me asking?

No, it's fine. He was a police officer.

The Cluster take him?

No, he was killed on duty. My mother always said it was a tragic accident. I was too young to know either way. We moved right after that to Boston. Moved in with my aunt. She took a sip of the green-colored drink. It warmed her throat and centered her. She still felt lost, but at least she was warm.

Where was it you moved from?

Oh, you wouldn't know it. It was the middle of nowhere.

You traveling for business or pleasure?

I can't for the life of me remember. Maybe it's this drink!
She laughed. Am I dreaming?

I guess that depends, Miss.

Oh, sorry, my name is Clara. Clara Strong.

Pleased to meet you Ms. Strong.

Please, call me Clara. Do you have a name?

Eugene McBride, he said as he tilted his head and shook her
hand.

Well, Mr. McBride, let's be friends. So you said it depends.
What does whether I'm dreaming depend on?

Then a darkness washed over him, clouding his features. It's a
more serious question than you realize, Clara. Down here things
aren't what they are up top.

Up top?

You're from up top, he said, pointing to the escalator that led
up into the rafters of the hotel. The real world. Down here, time's
slowed to a crawl.

What do you mean?

Did you take that escalator down to the lobby?

She thought about it for a moment. I can't recall. I just don't
remember. My god, I'm losing my mind!

Not necessarily. Have you ever been in this hotel before?
And think carefully, Clara. Take a moment.

She looked around but nothing about the space seemed
familiar.

I'm sorry. I just don't know where I am or why I'm here.

The bartender picked up a glass and began wiping it. He
twisted the towel down into the bottom and then snapped it back up.
Leaning in, he said to her, that's too bad. A lot of people pass
through here. Some to grab a drink before boarding their train,
headed home. Some just to drink before passing out for the night in

the hotel. Only to do the same thing again tomorrow. Still others, others are here but headed elsewhere. Sometimes those people carry a darkness within them.

Clara pulled back from him and regarded him with suspicion. She wondered what the hell he was talking about.

You don't know it, Clara and I hate to be the bearer of bad news, but you're just such a person.

What are you talking about? Darkness? I'm not sure I like your tone. I don't even know you.

But you see, Clara, I know you. I know that little town you fled when you were just a girl is Mount Enterprise, Texas.

How in the world could you guess that?

I know your father died as a result of a drug deal gone bad.

My father never dealt with anything illegal.

I'm not talking illegal drugs. I'm talking black-market Cluster drugs. In the infancy of the Cluster, he couldn't afford the drugs they were offering in Dallas and Houston. So he was stealing them from deadbeats that were selling them on the black market.

You're not making any sense. He wasn't sick. And he'd never steal from anyone. He was a good and honorable man.

Your mother was sick. Remember her yellow eyes?

Clara remembered. At night, she'd peek in on her mother and she'd know right away if her mother was awake because her mother's eyes glowed a haunting amber-yellow in the darkness. She nodded her head.

The black-market Cluster drugs would do that to people. Turn their eyes yellow and their piss the color of cola. Sometimes, if it didn't kill them, it might keep them alive for a month or two longer. How long were you in Boston before she died?

I don't know. Maybe a month. I'm very uncomfortable. I'm not talking to you anymore. I want to get out of here. She stood, ready to bolt across the lobby.

Where will you go? You don't even know what this place is, you said so yourself.

I don't know why I told you any of that. She looked at him and saw her mother in the reflection. Her father would have done anything for her. He loved her more than life.

You needed to remember. Down here, it's all we have. But you are here for another reason. It has less to do with you than it does with your son.

My son, she asked, I don't have a son.

You will. That pain you've been feeling in your stomach? Up top, it's a baby boy. And he's itching to come out. He's going to cause you a lot of pain. And then you're going to want to do the same to him. But it won't be your fault. Everything you do will be to try to save your husband and yourself. Your father did the same. It's in your DNA.

She struggled to comprehend what he was telling her. Her hand slipped from the edge of the bar and she took several steps back.

To save yourself, you will betray the Variant. No one but you will know. Not James. Not your peers. No one. But you will have the choice. Save yourself or save your son.

Listen, she said, approaching the bar and leaning in closer to McBride. I don't know who you are. I don't know where this is. I don't know what the hell a Variant is. The only thing I'm sure of is that if I had a child, I'd do anything to protect him or her.

I believe you, Clara. I really do. But when you're lying in that bed, blood pouring out of every orifice of your body, and you are struggling to survive, remember what you've told me. You see, everyone down here has a job to do. I'm the Facilitator. I make sure everyone's where they're supposed to be in the end. You, unfortunately, are the Betrayer. And right now, you will betray the Variant.

I am a Heteroclite. My husband is a Heteroclite. I've studied six others for a total of eight of the fifteen Heteroclites we've found.

Yes, Clara, he said, continue.

There is nothing known as a Variant. You're either a Heteroclite or not. So I don't know what you're talking about.

But don't you? Hasn't your research hinted at it?

What? True immunity? From all cancer?

Precisely.

I mean…, she started and then felt a flush of warmth across her face, acknowledgement that she had toyed with the idea of discovering someone completely immune. But it had been only hypothetical. Yes, I've thought about it, but it could take hundreds of years for a mutation like that to take hold.

Is your mutation, the one the Heteroclites carry, true immunity?

No. It just delays the inevitable.

What about the others you've studied?

The same. We may live twenty years longer. But probably no more than that.

Then you seek the Variant.

But you said I would betray the Variant.

You will. But I told you when the time comes, you will have a choice. There is still a choice to betray the Variant or not. You will always have that option.

What do I do?

You must decide for yourself. But I see the darkness in you. I don't know if you can make the choice to save the Variant.

Then what will happen?

I know a great many things, but even I do not know what will happen if you betray the Variant. Maybe all this, he points with outstretched arms, goes away. Maybe the up top all goes away. I don't know. But my job, as the Facilitator, is to see to it that everyone knows their purpose. Then it's out of my hands.

You say everyone, are there others?

Oh, most definitely, there are others.

She scanned the hotel lobby again. Just not today?

Everyone finds their path here at different times. They come here with their own baggage. You see what your mind allows you to see and you understand what your mind allows you to understand.

Will they all betray the Variant?

He grimaced and patted her hand that was gripping the bar too tightly.

No, Clara. They won't. They are the protectors of the Variant. Just as there is darkness, there is light.

Good and evil, she said.

That is your problem Clara. Things for you are black and white. Distinctions between good and evil are perceptual, not real. What I am suggesting is something more complimentary, rather than opposing. The day does not fight the night. It simply rests when the night works. The darkness does not fight the light. It slumbers as the sun shines. It is an invisible whole. You are necessary. To complete the whole.

But if I succeed and betray the Variant? What then?

As I said, I do not know the answer to that question.

I'm a good person McBride. I swear to you.

It's not a matter of being good, Clara. I pass no judgement upon you if you betray the Variant, but there are forces at work that will try to stop you.

I refuse to participate, then. I'll simply leave this place and I'll just refuse.

As I said, the choice is yours. McBride turned to put a bottle back on the shelves. Clara turned her back to him and saw the lobby suddenly fill with people. She could hear their chatter begin with a whisper and then fill the lobby with laughter and indistinct voices. It got progressively louder until it was almost overwhelming.

When she turned to ask McBride another question, he was gone and the bar was full of conference goers and symposium attendees. A young man with a hipster moustache and wide-brimmed glasses laughed as the older woman at the bar said something particularly funny. Or maybe he was just working for his tip. He looked out toward Clara and winked.

A young African man approached her, Dr. Akintola stamped on his name badge. He held out a hand to her.

Dr. Cathey, it is an honor to finally meet you. The din of the lobby threatened to drown him out. His accent gave her trouble and she realized her ears felt as though they were full of fluid.

I know you're busy, Doctor, he said, but I just had to ask about the research you were doing on the new young female patient you mentioned. It sounds truly remarkable. You said her results –

She grabbed his arm and pulled him toward her. Her lips inches from his right ear. She said to him, too loudly for the given proximity of her voice to his ear, but so that he could hear it over the din of the conference goers, they are everywhere watching me. They are listening. Do not ask me about it again. The statistical error is much more significant than ten percent.

Dr. Akintola tried to pull away but she held him closer. Her hot breath on his cheek. The Coding, as you suspected, is wrong. It's being manipulated by the government to keep people thinking they're sick. Even when they aren't. She let go of him and he withdrew from her grasp.

He smiled wanly at her and surveyed the lobby. Anyone could be with the Grey Suits. They most likely attended the conference. He looked down at her and asked, what should we do?

Well, she said, backing away from him slightly and assuming a more professional posture toward him. She knew they were being monitored. She smiled and said, we just keep on with our research and hope for better results. I do have this file for you summarizing my results. I hope you find it useful.

The file was in a microchip on a period at the end of a sentence which did indeed summarize her false results utilizing an old protocol in studying the Cluster. The Grey Suits didn't have the time to auto-scan every file that left the facility in Sonora for something as small as a chip. The microchip she imbedded in the report contained the last eighteen months of work she completed on the Cluster. Due to a statistically infinitesimal error that was applied over a substantial number of individuals (that is, those who were not currently affected by the Cluster in the general population of the planet Earth) a relevant, non-negligible, number of subjects who were incorrectly classified as having terminal Codes within the Cluster was produced. These false positives made up nearly ten percent of the Earth's population and currently, they were being poisoned by Kelland's Cluster drugs. But to admit that now would be devastating both politically and financially.

The shiny, black bio-plastic folder bound the report. On the cover was the KMC logo in yellow with the medical division's motto, Restoring Worlds in red. The medical division's motto was no less self-assured than the mining division's Digging New Worlds. She put it in his hands and wished him well, He who has health…, she said and waited for the new traditional finish.

Has hope, he said and kissed her on both cheeks. As he
passed her left cheek, he said, thank you. I'll wait to hear from you.

He backed away from her and disappeared into the crowd.
She hoped he made it.

Variant

CHAPTER 33

Sometime in 2018

…..Clara, he shouted again for the sixth or seventh time. He shook her by the shoulders and then she was back.

If I try to leave now, she said to the three people dragging her down the empty hall of the hospital, I lose my ability to study these diseases properly. I lose my laboratory.

It's the Grey Suits' lab, Clara, April said. We'll find you a new lab. Where you can really do the work necessary to find a cure.

She shook her head. I'm doing the work I need to do, under their noses, with their equipment and their money. I've been giving them false results for years now. They trust me. None of you in the Rising can get the access I can. I fear all of you, once you leave here, will simply die. Either by their hand or your own. The Cluster drugs on the outside aren't as powerful as they are here.

So what are you saying, Clara, Cathey asked, that you're staying with them?

I'm not staying with them Jimmy. I'm just staying behind. It's been my fate to stay behind. I just never told you. Everyone's talked about their own visions or dreams. Well, I've had my own. Since before I met you Jimmy. When they brought me in here and declared my DNA different from practically everyone else's. I knew my path wouldn't be your path and it broke my heart to keep that from you. But I'm darkness in our child's life Jimmy. April, you don't know. You get to protect the Variant, whoever that is. Jimmy, you too. Dr. Walsh, you have a path with them as well. The three of you and Mattie. You can all save this world. I can't.

Clara, you're not making any sense. Of course you can. You're Mattie's mother. My wife. He needs you. I need you. We can get out of here and start trying to find a cure. A real cure. Not just this temporary solution they're selling.

Jimmy, you've got to stop. All of you. I can't. Not because I
don't want to run out there into the world with you and save it.
Because I do. I can't because I'm really very sick. Mattie's blood
has helped but it will kill him to save me. I've gotten a very virulent
strain of the Cluster. It's in my lungs, my brain, my stomach. It's
aggressive and it's consuming every part of my body. Eating me
alive. I'd need blood intravenously for weeks, maybe months.

And my visions weren't all blissful and cheery. They were
dark. This guy everyone's talking about in such glowing terms,
McBride? I saw him too, but he told me I would betray the Variant.
And I couldn't do that. Not for a second. So I stayed back. I made
them trust me. If I walk out that door now, I'm their enemy and as
soon as I hook myself up to my son, I'm his as well. And yours.

Clara, isn't it something else entirely, asked April.

What do you mean, Clara asked.

You're not her.

Not her? What's that mean?

You're not Clara Cathey.

Run my DNA, code my blood. You'll see. This is a
ridiculous waste of time.

April, what are you saying, Cathey asked.

It's not her, Cathey! Not the real her. Mattie saw it.

Mattie? Mattie was here?

In a manner of speaking, yes, I brought him here. In a dream.
In McBride's world, the Interzone. I brought him here to confirm my
suspicions that she wasn't who you wanted her to be.

Clara, he asked, reaching for her.

She's wrong Jimmy. I don't know what she's talking about.

How'd you get here, after you escaped?

We don't have time for this Cathey, April said. You've got to
trust me. I've spent the better part of two years making sure I'm

306

right. You questioning me about something you just learned isn't going to help us get out of here.

That's why you don't want to go with us, Cathey said to her.

She turned to him and pleaded with him with her eyes. He noticed the yellow peeking out from behind her blue contacts. Cathey approached her, as if to kiss her and he inhaled deeply.

Fucking butterscotch, he said. Something's going on, April. You're right, she's not Clara. Her eyes are all wrong. And she smells like a clone.

No, you're both wrong. I have to stay to work on the cure. I'm so close. They brought a child to us, years ago. She had not been Coded. I coded her and coded her again. And then I pulled Mattie's blood again and coded it. The two were similar in nature, but I ran out of samples of Mattie's blood before I could conclusively study his versus hers. She's very similar. Her blood's kept me alive. But my Cluster continues to change, to adapt. It's not working anymore.

So you just had her blood? What happened to the girl?

No, she's still with us. She had no family. I'm not proud of what we've done with her, but she's saved a lot of people.

April's heart sank. When did she come to you?

The Clara clone thought about it. It had been near the time of Mattie's birth, she remembered. Maybe a few months after. But it couldn't have been more than a year. Or maybe it had.

She looked at April and saw the desperation on her face. What is it, April?

Just…when did she come?

It was before 2094. I know that. Mattie was born in 2093. They could be the same age. I don't know.

The feeling in April's throat, the lump that grew as the Clara clone spoke, threatened to choke her. Clara, what happened to her?

The Clara clone began to speak but the evac alarm sounded and a calm female voice came over the loudspeaker as the siren wailed, be advised, we have a breach, intrusion protocols are in place. Lock down and await further instructions. Defense Readiness Condition level two. All soldiers report to Command Center. Warning, Mechs are armed. Anyone traveling underground or base side, without proper identification, is subject to seizure and/or termination. This is not a drill. Repeat, this is not a drill.

You've got to go, all of you, the Clara clone shouted to them. The blaring of the alarm threatened to drown her out. She shouted for them to run.

The girl, April bawled, where is she?

In the nexus, the center of the facility, the lowest cavern. You've got to go, though. They are coming.

April turned to Walsh and Cathey. It was Cathey she hated to leave again. She implored him with her eyes and it got him every time.

I know, he said. Go. We'll figure stuff out up top.

No, the Clara clone screamed, you all have to leave. They'll kill us all if we're found together.

Cathey, April screeched. He grabbed the Clara clone by the arm and said, let her go. That might be her daughter.

What? The Clara clone pleaded with him but he let her go.

I don't know which one you are, but you don't limp, so you're not number 2. Whoever you are, just let her go. She's been looking for her daughter for fifteen years. She thought for years that she was dead. And she thinks the girl might be this Variant strain, like Mattie. Immune.

April slid her backpack off her back. She handed it to Dr. Walsh. Take this, she said. There's enough vials of Mattie's blood to

308

jump-start your research for a cure. Mattie's job was to save the dying. I'm hoping this blood will do just that.

Dr. Walsh nodded at her and said, thank you.

I've got to go Cathey, she said.

I know, Cathey said. April turned quickly and sprinted down the hallway, running for the Nexus. She knew if she didn't immediately turn and run, she'd never leave.

The girl is so much more than just immune. There's not a name for what the girl is or what she means to this facility. But Jim, there's no way in hell April's going to get her out of here without a fight.

There's still time for you, he said.

I ran out of time a long time ago, the clone said.

Walsh typed in his code and placed his thumb on the security panel. It blinked red once and then returned to solid red.

Security protocols, Walsh, she said. She pulled a black card reader from her pocket and waved it across the panel. Now enter your credentials. The red blinked once and then glowed green. The door unlocked and Walsh pushed through.

Here, she said and threw the card reader to Cathey. You guys are going to need this to get out.

Cathey turned his back on her for the last time. He bolted through the door and found Walsh waiting at a dead-end, with doors to the left and to the right.

I know the right leads us back up into the interior of the facility, what Clara, or the clone, was talking about as the Nexus. To the left, should get us out of here. What are we going to do?

We aren't going to do anything. You've got a job to do, you said. Work on this cure without interference from the Greys. And you've got a family to protect. I'd say you head left. I'll head right. Maybe I'll be lucky enough to run into April and get her and that girl out of here. Maybe I'll just take out enough of them to make this whole ordeal worth it. I've still got unfinished business with them.

Here's to your health, Cathey.

Yours too, Doc. Health and hope. Good luck!

The doctor swiped the black card across the panel and then tossed it back to Cathey. He disappeared around the bend as Cathey sprinted toward the Nexus.

CHAPTER 34

Sometime in 2108

Mattie stood among the Mechs. The ARexs stopped their digging and now stood defiantly silent. Hex Bots stood guard at the perimeter of Summer Cabin. The Mechs were armed, dual-wielding their blasters and loading frags into their HE-Frag devices on their shoulders. He lost count how many there were before him. Their blue vision sensors now pulsed red. They were in war mode and he didn't know if he could survive more than one or two high explosive frag hits. At least twenty Mechs stood directly in front of him. He held up his hands and waited for the end to come.

There was a crackle of static over a radio that suddenly switched on. It sounded as though it was being amplified through a loud speaker.

Mech Unit 1138, this is Sotillo, do you read, over?

Mattie waited for the voice to repeat. He recognized the name Sotillo from one of his father's favorite books. The voice repeated the call signs. Mattie knew it was his father.

Dad, he shouted, can you hear me?

Mattie, dear gods, yes, I can hear you. Are you okay?

I just got the crap beat out of me by some super soldiers, but now they're locked in Summer Cabin. It's set to self-destruct. I'm surrounded by a fleet of fully armed Mechs and some of their friends, but other than that, I'm great.

You were just here, Mattie. With April. How –

There's so much to tell you, Dad. Once we're through this, we'll all sit down and try to make sense of it. Suffice it to say, while we missed several years with April, she didn't miss any time with you. I don't really understand it myself, but hopefully in time it will make sense.

The clone pushed you through the spinning galaxy painting.

Yeah, back to the night April left.

We seek passage to your world.

She gave us your blood.

To save you. And to save the dying.

She said that.

But, Dad, there's so much to do.

I've got quite a situation here myself.

Where's here? What's happening?

It's a long story. I'm in Texas.

Texas? The caverns?

Yeah.

So that's where we went that night. Are they still running the Mechs from there?

You read my mind, Son. We're about to find out. Hang on.

The line went dead for a minute. Mattie lowered his hands and the Mechs, each one, took a step forward and a piercing whine filled the air as the HE-Frags armed themselves.

Dad?

The shoulder systems of the HE-Frags adjusted their angles, pointing down, toward Mattie.

Dad?!

Suddenly, the radio crackled and the vision sensors to each and every Mech shut off. Even the Hex Bots and A Rexs shut down.

Son, you've got about an hour. Then this system is going to revert back to its protocols.

How can I access them? I thought you said that was the flaw? No one could access the system but for the centralized computer system.

I've set the CRM sensors to receive. Once you have access to the CRM, you can communicate with them. Input the proper RSA code and you can control the Mechs from anywhere. Otherwise, the system will block any transmissions other than those preceded by the set code. It was my out. The only way I could save my creations. It's the recall code they could never find. It would take them years to find it now. It's seven hundred and sixty eight bits long. RSA-768.

The code, based on semi-prime numerology, required the code breaker to come up with a natural number that is the product of two prime numbers. His father's code had two hundred and thirty-two decimal digits. It would take a 2.2 GHz AMD Opteron-based computer over two thousand years of computing to come to the correct answer. Mattie had solved several similar equations during his Lessons, but it had taken him years, not minutes.

Remember that, Cathey continued. RSA-768. With it, Mattie, you control the Mech army. If you don't find it or get it entered in time, the machines go off-line. You lose whatever power these machines can provide you. I've got to go, Son.

Dad, I don't think I have time.

You'll be fine, Son. Just breathe. The information you need is right in the notes.

I can't get back in there before Summer Cabin self-destructs.

He thought for a moment and purposely slowed himself down. I've given you the information you need Mattie. Use it.

He ran a hand through his matted hair. The boy didn't have enough time to factor the correct numbers. Without the notes, even Cathey would be at a loss as to the correct numbers.

Dad, what do I do? I can't –

April is here, Mattie. I've got to go try and find her. Soldiers are coming. Your Lessons. Don't forget your Lessons. The power of the pen is mightier than the sword.

The communicator went dead. Mattie walked between the behemoth Mechs, looking up at them, marveling at their size and the ingenuity it took to create and design them. He stood among them for a moment and thought, with them, they could end all this. Together. Save the dying.

He pulled his tablet out, the screen shone to life and Mattie studied the swirling galaxy that stared back at him. He concentrated, just like she told him, on his desired course. He had to have those numbers. So he thought of his father working. But he had no idea where that would have been. Colorado? Before he was born? Was it possible to go that far back?

Remember Mattie, as April told him, focus on the galaxy. Let it pull you in. Person and place. Don't force yourself to enter.

What would happen if I do?

Awful things, Mattie. Remember, they can get you here or there.

CHAPTER 35

Mattie continued to focus on the swirling galaxy. It lulled him into a trance. He thought of his father, Colorado, the Mechs, the numbers. They swirled together and he felt himself enter, dissolving into the darkness…..

…..He felt himself awaken but he stood in a cold darkness. Neither the cold nor the darkness bothered him, but he knew it wasn't a place people visited regularly. It smelled of earth and rot like someone had just excavated a fresh grave and the maggots weren't done with the decomposing flesh. He could feel the vastness of the space he was in but he dared not move for fear he stood on the edge of a mountain and any false step could lead to his sudden death.

Then he saw two lights, bobbing toward him like warning beacons on a boat being tossed about at sea. He wanted to slide into the darkness, but he still couldn't tell where he was or where it might be safe to step. So instead he froze.

The two men approached and stopped in front of him. They said something to him but he didn't understand the dialect. It might have been German. Or Russian. In any event, he didn't understand them. Their faces were obscured by the bright lights shining from their helmets. As Mattie glanced to his left and right, he could see he was in some sort of tunnel.

He took a step back and felt hands behind him, grabbing his arms. He jumped instinctively and assumed a fighting position, striking out at the man who tried to grab him.

Whoa, whoa, whoa there, Mattie my boy. Guess they should've warned me about you in the dark.

Mach das Licht aus, the man said and suddenly the lights went out as the men obeyed the order to dim their lights. As eyes adjusted,

Mattie could see the man with the pencil-thin moustache standing before him. This time he wore an old miner's hat with a carbide lamp. McBride angled the light up and suddenly the tunnel was clearly visible.

They asked if those machines were yours.

Mattie looked down the tunnel but didn't see anything.

I don't see anything.

Big monstrous things, cutting right through that rock that's taken us nearly six months to clear. Your machines did it in seconds. Cut clear through to the Pass. I think we're finally through. You saved us thousands. Four years and twenty-eight men's lives lost but the tunnel is finally cut through this bitch of a mountain.

Well, you're welcome, I guess. I didn't mean to bring anything with me.

Yet, you did. Brought 'em from up top down here. That's a special power. Not one I've seen too many times before.

How long have you been – Mattie paused, searching for the right word. Down here, he asked with much hesitation.

Down here is as good a way to explain it as any. And to tell the truth, like I told you before, time down here is screwy. I might've been down here a year or maybe a thousand. Scary, but I don't know. And Mattie, you don't mind that I call you Mattie, do you?

No, it's fine.

I'm only asking because your father seems to have so much difficulty with it.

It just reminded him of the past. When we lost April, I don't think he wanted to think about her.

But, you know he did. Every day.

He didn't let it show. That's not his way.

He will sacrifice himself to save her, if it comes to that, Mattie.

I'm sure we all would.

She is in trouble, Mattie. I can't get to her. Sometimes, in your world, the deeper you go, the further away from here you are. It's been a challenge trying to get to her.

Can I help her?

You may have that chance. But Mattie, just like in all things, there will be choices. Those choices either define the individual or the individual defines those choices. Do you understand?

I think so. I have to make the right choice. Not the wrong one. To save the dying.

Sometimes, right or wrong isn't easy to distinguish. It's muddy. Down here, they go together. And it's a hard and fast rule, where there is darkness, there is light.

Good and evil, the boy said.

It's the hardest concept I have to convince you toppers of. Distinctions between good and evil are perceptual, not real. The things I suggest are more complimentary, rather than opposing. The day does not fight the night. It simply rests when the night works. The darkness does not fight the light. It slumbers as the sun shines. It is an invisible whole. You are necessary. To complete the whole.

Then what do I do?

You have to remember Mattie, why are you here?

To save the dying.

No, Mattie. That's your purpose. Just as your mother and father and even April have their purposes –

We're not all trying to save the dying?

Mattie, would you be surprised if I told you there are those in your group that are fighting for a cross-purpose?

He thought about it for a moment but couldn't imagine his mother or father or even April not being committed to saving the dying. He shook his head no.

Then you still have much to learn. Things I cannot teach you by simply explaining them away. No matter who you face, remember, your purpose is to save the dying. Don't allow your purpose to become sullied by anyone who claims to know what your purpose is. That is vital to your survival. And to the completion of your purpose. Now, do you remember why you are down here this time?

He thought hard. No matter how clear his thought process was going into this place, once here, it was always a challenge to remember what brought him here in the first place.

The Mechs?

The Mechs, okay, good. What about the Mechs, Mattie?

I need something. Numbers.

What sort of numbers?

Mattie concentrated hard. What did he need? They're special numbers. For – he trailed off. He couldn't remember. He just knew they had to do with numbers.

Let me give you a hint, to help with your thinking when you're coming down here. I know it gets murky crossing over. That's why I rarely do it. Last time, whoa, well, that's another story for a different day. You must concentrate –

A code, Mattie shouted. A code, that's what I'm here for!

Excellent work Mattie. Okay. A code. For your father?

Not for my father, not really. It's from my father. Something he created.

Walk with me boy. McBride adjusted the carbide lamp and they walked for a bit down the gravel path that several men were leveling for the new tracks soon to be laid. They continued for some time down the tunnel and Mattie noticed doors, inset into the tunnel wall. As though they had been there long before this tunnel had been dug. It looked like they just so happened to uncover the door while they were digging the tunnel.

These doors, in the tunnel wall, Mattie started. McBride stopped walking and turned his attention to Mattie. The bright carbide lamp shone directly in Mattie's eyes. He held up a hand and McBride adjusted the angle.

Sorry about that my boy. Now what is it you're asking me?

The doors we are passing. Where do they go?

Doors, you say?

Yeah, doors. With knobs and everything.

McBride looked confused. There's just one door down here and it's a good ways down.

No, we've passed a few. That I counted.

McBride crossed his brow and pulled out a handkerchief. Despite the chill in the tunnel, he wiped perspiration from his brow.

Show me, he said and proceeded to follow Mattie a short distance up the tunnel. They came to a small door, no more than three feet high. If Mattie was to go through this door, he'd have to crawl.

See, a door, the boy said, pointing with his outstretched arm.

He swallowed hard. He continued to sweat despite the chill and Mattie thought he was losing his color. Down here you should only see doors directly related to you.

Do you see it?

McBride remained silent.

Mattie walked back from where they came and stopped at another, taller door. Another one, he said. Twenty-eight, Mattie said pointing to the numbers on the cross of the door. McBride stared at the space where Mattie said he saw a door. McBride shivered but wiped more sweat from his brow. He saw nothing but earth.

Where do these doors lead?

McBride thought back to when he walked up top and had the power to lie. He wished he could lie to the boy now. But he knew he could not. He was making himself sick and he couldn't keep it up.

I don't know, Mattie.

What do you mean? Aren't you in control down here?

I'm just the Facilitator. I've told you that I'm only here to make sure people get to where they're going. The problem is, I don't see the doors. The universe is showing you things I'm not even aware of. And that scares the hell out of me Mattie.

These doors. What are they? Like portals? Passageways?

Of sorts.

And if I go in this one?

Like I said Mattie, I can't see it. I don't know where it will take you. Or when.

You're not the least bit curious what lies behind a door you cannot see?

Curious? No Mattie. Down here, curious will kill you. Your path lies ahead. I know that for certain. These doors you see? They are another's path. Why you can see them is beyond me.

How can you be sure if you've never had this happen before?

Because you seek a code and I know of a code breaker just down the tunnel. In these doors you claim to see, I don't know what lies on the other side.

I want to go through. I want to see what's on the other side of these doors.

Mattie, these are the choices I was talking about. You came down here for a reason and that reason was to get a code. I can take you to the code breaker.

Mattie reached out and turned the knob to Twenty-Eight Centennial Court. As he opened the door, he saw a brightly lit room approximately twenty feet by twenty feet. In the center of the space was a steel table. Four oversized halogen lights hung from the ceiling and sprayed the room with brilliant white light. A disheveled man sat at the table, mumbling to himself. Mattie could see his leg was shackled to the table.

The man looked up with big insect-like eyes. Drool trickled from his mouth and splattered on the table below. His nose was sharp and blistered. His eyes, yellowed and deranged. The man licked his lips and Mattie saw that he was missing most of his teeth except two on the upper right side. His gray hair, fibrous and matted to his scalp, belied his youthful age. They called him crazy, but he was anything but that.

You, the man said, raising his head and staring at Mattie.

Do I know you, Mattie asked.

I seen you. Once before. Crossing over Millers Creek. You and that girl. And those machines. You was with those machines.

He spoke succinctly and with force. His hands were active and he pointed at Mattie while he spoke.

You the reason I got shut up in this place.

What is this place?

Bridle Veil Falls, but I'm sure you already knew that. Else why would you be here? Don't you have someone else to haunt?

Mattie didn't know what or where he was talking about but it sounded ominous.

I told 'em I seen you. Leaving that spot where the little girl died. I found her there, after you left with your machines. I told 'em. But they didn't believe me. Now, here you are again. Why you here? Got another body for me to find?

You don't look like you're going anywhere, Mister.

You'd be surprised. I'm pretty good at escaping. They just pretty good at finding. Seems like all the doors lead right back here. So, I asked you a question, why you here?

Just curious, Mattie said.

About?

Where that door would lead.

So you just walked through it, like you had permission.

There wasn't anyone stopping me.

I see. I can tell the type person you are. Take whatever you want. Consequences be damned.

I just walked through a door.

A door that wasn't yours to walk through, he screamed, spit spraying and collecting at the corners of his mouth. This ain't your time!

Mattie backed up, toward the door he had come through and then suddenly he felt it give way and two men walked in, barely missing him.

They were dressed in an unfamiliar fashion. Light blue cotton pants, white shoes, light blue tops. They carried no weapons but based on their size, they didn't appear to need them.

Oh good, fucking Distorters. You see how big they are? They're not even real.

Mr. Jeffires, who are you speaking to?

That fucking kid right there. He's standing next to you! If you reach out, you could grab him! But you won't. You're trying to drive me mad so you'll tell me there's no one there.

Mattie stepped back on instinct but the men made no move toward him.

Mr. Jeffires, you're not doing yourself any favors talking about people who aren't in this room. But it's not going to get you out of the trouble you're in.

It ain't trouble boys. Just a bother. He had it coming.

You ripped your cellmate's ear off and swallowed it, Mr. Jeffires. That's serious business in here.

It wasn't even that good, he retorted. Weak he was. I can't tolerate that. I won't.

Doctors think you're looking for a section thirty-eight.

Ah, you boys and your codes. Section Thirty-Eight. I suppose you're referring to Ling's Behavioral Analysis? Insanity? No thanks. I'm totally sane. I just don't suffer fools easily. You see Boy? What I'm dealing with? Incompetence on the highest level.

Mattie looked to the men who were concentrating on Jeffires.

They don't see you Boy. But they're going to see me. Crazy thing about those doors, when you open one, sometimes the universe has to correct itself. I shoulda got away the last time I saw you, but it just wasn't the right time. Now, here you are again. This time, he motioned with his hands, free of their shackles, this time I'll find you. Crazy or not. I'll fucking find you and feed you to creatures in the darkest pits of hell. After I'm done with you –

The two behemoths leaped at Jeffires to subdue him. He was much faster though and pinned the first one to the ground. Despite his wiry appearance, the man was preternaturally strong. This is fun boy, he shouted. Do come join me. Blood spewed as Jeffires dissected the men.

Mattie had only seconds to grab the door knob and flee back to the tunnel. He turned the knob and stepped into the darkness, expecting to see the tunnel and McBride. Instead, he now stood on a narrow mountain path, thousands of feet in the air. Snow blanketed the path and howled in his ears. Here, the cold was painful and he was not immune. The snow and ice pelted his exposed skin. It burned and sizzled as though he were being splattered with hot grease.

They would love nothing more than to have you down here exploring, McBride said, standing just down the path. He sat beneath a rock outcropping, warming himself by a fire. Come, he said.

Mattie sat next to him and held out his exposed arms to the warmth of the fire. You're free to make decisions. I can't stop you.

But those decisions have consequences. Sometimes those consequences aren't felt for years. Decades. But there will be consequences.

I just wanted to see what was behind that door.

Did you find it? What you were looking for?

I don't know what I found.

I can tell you this as well, sometimes the doors don't just take us back to where we came from. Depending on where you end up, that could be bad. Like a blizzard bad.

I'm so cold. I'm never cold.

The up top rules don't always apply down here, Mattie. Sometimes, you're not special down here. Sometimes, you're just a boy.

I want to go back. I'll listen better. I'll –

Mattie reached out for the fire again but before he could finish his sentence or warm himself up, he suddenly found himself back in the tunnel. Still standing in front of the closed door to Twenty-Eight, Centennial Court.

Well, McBride asked, walking several paces ahead, are you coming? The code breaker is just this way.

They stopped in the vast chasm of the tunnel and faced an austere-looking door, wedged into the rock with no street number. It was painted a drab olive-green. There was a brightly splendid brass eye hole cut remarkably high into the door. In the middle of the door were the words C-Block 17.

C-Block? Mattie asked.

The code breaker is currently incarcerated for several deviant behavioral issues. To keep him occupied, he gardens and sometimes he works on RSA codes. And Mattie, this isn't like most doors down here or most prisons. I can't come, so I won't be there to help you if the need arises. Don't get too involved. Just get the code and then get out.

Mattie nodded as he reached out to turn the knob. And Mattie, McBride called, you're looking for Kogh Gleason. Father Kogh Gleason.

He turned the knob and the door opened to reveal a long metal corridor. The floor, walls and ceilings were polished steel. Each step he took echoed like a ricocheting bullet. At the end of the hall, a man sat behind a desk. Sitting on the desk was a banker's lamp with a green shade. It illuminated the way. He walked up to the man who had his face buried in a book. Mattie could see only the title, *Invisible Monsters*.

May I help you, the cherub faced slightly overweight man asked as he put the book down. Mattie could see a sign in sheet. The last entry was from 1987.

I –uh –I need to see the prisoner?

Do you?

I do. The code breaker?

I'm not familiar with that nomenclature. Do you mean Father Gleason?

Mattie nodded his head. Yes, that's right. Father Gleason. I'm sorry.

It's okay. He's just beyond these double doors here. Keep in mind why you're here. Don't allow him to interact with you too long. He does have a way of sidetracking people.

Okay, Mattie said.

The guard stood up and took out an ancient set of keys. He pulled a rusty skeleton key out from the collection. A horned head was carved into the crown of the key. A red ruby eye stared back at him.

Be as quick as possible. This isn't any place you want to be any longer than you have to be. I will lock the doors behind you. You will notice the light here peeking through the fence. Knock once on the fence, then, when you hear the key enter the lock, knock three times.

Do you need to pat me down or something? Make sure I'm not taking any contraband in to him?

The man laughed. No, not necessary. There's nothing you could bring to him he doesn't already have. Plus, there's nothing you could bring him that would help him escape. There's no escape from the prison he's in.

Mattie was confused but nodded anyway and pushed his way into Father Gleason's cell.

CHAPTER 36

Time unknown, Interzone

It was an overcast day. Mattie looked up to the sky but couldn't tell the time for the clouds. He glanced at his watch but it was dead. Behind him was a fence. No door. But when he cocked his head to the right, he could see the light from the hallway seeping through a small crack between two grayish slats of wood.

Knock once…wait for the click…then knock three times

A small city unfurled before him. Quaint homes lined a quiet street. Lawns were mown. Sprinklers sputtered in the distance. The smell of charcoal was in the air. This was unlike any prison he'd ever seen before. A man, not far from the fence Mattie stood next to, worked in his white undershorts and an equally white tank top. He hummed a song and clipped away at his bougainvillea.

Mattie approached the man and startled him when he tapped him on the back.

He dropped his pruning shears and held his hands up. He turned slowly and saw Mattie.

Where'd you escape from?

Nowhere.

You look like you escaped from somewhere. How'd you get in here?

I was granted access. I've come for the codes.

Oh. I see. Straight to the point. Here I am standing in my underwear and I've got an unannounced guest.

Father Gleason put his hands down and Mattie saw before him a simple man with thick, black glasses on a stub of a nose. His brown eyes were amplified by the lenses he wore. He had salt and pepper gray hair, shorn tight to the sides and tops of his head. He wasn't tall but neither was he short. Five foot seven or eight perhaps. His belly stretched the tank top, threatening to poke through. He hadn't missed many meals, Mattie thought. Despite being in his boxers, he wore bright green dress socks and shiny brown penny loafers.

He saw Mattie staring.

I didn't expect company today. I usually have the run of this place. They don't allow me many visitors. I have deviant behavioral issues. Several they say. I can't think of one, but they say –

Listen, I'm not here to visit or make friends. I've come for the codes.

Yes, yes. You did mention that. I understand. Did that fat one come with you?

Mattie stared at the man and looked confused.

He's that insufferable man that works the front desk. A most detestable creature, in my opinion, but they don't ask me. He sent my own mother away when she tried to visit.

I don't care, Mattie said, trying to keep his distance from the man.

Oh, of course not. It wasn't my mother anyway. She was crushed by a car when I was just a speck of a boy. Tragic, really.

Gleason, Mattie shouted.

Yes, of course. Now, where are my manners? Won't you come in and have some lemonade, I think it's lemonade today, could be a red fruity beverage, I can't keep up. Please allow me to get dressed and then we'll see about those codes.

He turned to walk up the steps to the front door. Mattie grabbed his arm and forcibly turned him back around.

Listen Gleason. I don't care what the hell you're wearing. I don't have time for you to find your manners, your pants or anything else. I want the codes and I want them now.

Father Gleason backed up a few steps. Well, aren't you direct? Suit yourself. I'll fetch them from the office. Are you coming in?

No! Get the codes!

Oh, suit yourself, but be warned. Here, there be dragons. He turned and proceeded up the steps, pausing as he reached for the screen door.

Wait, Gleason, what the hell does that mean? There are dragons here?

Oh, no dear boy, he said, turning and coming down the steps once again. He stood close to Mattie. Close enough to grab him if he wanted to. Mattie could smell the stench of decaying meat on his breath. He looked down the street, focusing on something Mattie couldn't see. He pointed faintly and continued, not actual dragons. Just a turn of a phrase. In medieval times, the cartographers would place dragons, sea serpents and other mythological creatures in uncharted areas of maps to warn of dangerous or unexplored territories. So, if you're warning somebody of danger, you can say, here there be dragons. I've got the most wonderful example of one such map, straight from the Vatican and produced all the way back in 1430. It's called the Borgia Map. But, I digress. You need those codes. I shall endeavor to provide them to you.

In the distance, a howl or maybe a scream rippled across the landscape. Gleason's door slammed as he stepped into the house. A shrieking cry echoed down the town block and Mattie changed his mind about waiting. He hurriedly scaled the stairs and stepped into Gleason's home.

The first thing he noticed was the smell. Citrus boiling on a stove with cloves and cinnamon. It reminded him of a Christmas he spent at the Lighthouse.

When he thought of the Lighthouse, he was reminded why he was here. For the codes. He was about to call out to Gleason when he stepped out of the kitchen with two steaming cups of whatever smelled so good.

Here, do have a tea. I'm not certain of the origin of the fruit but it mimics the orange fairly well. Don't know how they get it to grow down here, but it's divine all the same. He handed a cup and saucer to Mattie. He took a sip and the warmth went from his throat to his feet.

Now, that map, the Borgia Map, is right here on the wall.

Mattie looked to the wall and swore when he walked in, it had been bare. He glanced at the piece and it was indeed magnificent. Intricate and detailed. The hours it must have taken the man who produced this piece, he said absently.

What's this in the upper quadrant here, Mattie asked. There was an ancient text written over an elaborately drawn dragon.

That's Latin. It means, here there are even men who have large four foot horns, and there are even serpents so large they could eat an oxen whole.

Was it true?

No, dear boy. Just a warning. To keep people away. Here there be dragons.

So, a lie?

Do take some more of that tea.

I don't want more tea. I want those codes. You were just screwing with me out there? Warning me so I'd come in here and drink tea with you?

No, no, no. Although I am pleased you decided to come in and have tea, I was merely warning you of dangers out there. This isn't the sort of place one comes to go exploring. Even though I can, I keep to myself right here, near the house. I've seen awful things out there. If you wish, you can wait on the porch or the lawn or wherever you're comfortable.

It's fine. Just get the codes.

If you don't mind, and I know you said you didn't care, but I would feel better if you permitted me to get dressed. As I said out there, I wasn't expecting company today.

Fine, get dressed. Just don't take too long.

I'll only be a minute, Gleason said. Do enjoy your tea and feel free to have a look around.

The home was simple and dated. In the entryway, where Mattie stood, was a short walkway to the living room and kitchen. To his left was a sitting area with a mustard yellow woven Apel sofa and two white and grey polka-dotted Tyley chairs. A white shag rug stretched across the floor and was held in place by a wood and chrome nesting table. Accent tables sat on either end of the sofa and contorted lamps rested on top. The room was dimly lit until Mattie stepped down into the sitting area. He had not noticed that it was sunken and he nearly fell over himself before he caught his balance. The lamps on the tables came on as he passed them. He took a seat on the sofa. Taking another sip of the tea, he suddenly found himself empty of thought and free of any burden. The more tea he drank, the more the feeling increased.

To his right sat a novel of short stories on the end table. *Dark Carnival.* He wanted to pick it up and read the dust jacket, but his arms were like lead. He couldn't move.

Somewhere in the house, he heard the wailing of a child. And then the crack of a tree limb. The sitting room grew hot and he noticed the walls now were filled with what could only be described as graffiti. In front of him, on a large wall between two darkened windows, as if the sun suddenly stopped shining, was scribbled:

331

Variant

Cry like a child,
Wasted my time with those children might be
My burden to keep,
Accept my bloody curse
In this garden prison
My view of them reaches from fence to wall,
I have no words for my actions,
Just watching them devour one another as they fall.

The handwriting dripped as though it was made from hot wax. As Mattie stared at it, he realized it had been written in blood. He tried to stand but his legs felt cemented to the floor. Like someone had bolted him in place. The ceiling was full of glowing texts that shone in the darkness in a neon yellow script:

I want to see people
I want to see life
Never take me home
Because it's no longer mine

Behind him, scrawled in blood but with pieces of fingernail that scrawled the text into the sheetrock left behind:

I began to cry
The joke was on me
No longer can I
Conceal rage with tears,
Nothing but alone
With no safety
There is no reason
They've left the room

Isolation equals madness.

Be as quick as possible. This isn't any place you want to be any longer than you have to be.

He heard the voice like an apparition whispering to him in his dreams. Finally, he forced himself to move. He stood and immediately doubled over from the stench. The citrus smell failed to mask the scent of death and decay hovering in the air like a fog. He fought through it and stumbled into the kitchen.

There, he saw bright orange carnival lights jammed into the beige wallpaper. Tiny blue water buckets danced across the wallpaper.

EQUIPMENT NOT
NOR AUTOMATIC
I'M NOT DOGMATIC
DON'T GIVE ME MORE ORDERS
FOR PEOPLE LIKE ME
THERE IS NO ORDER

The lights dimmed further and he crashed into the kitchen table, knocking jack-o-lanterns to the floor. As he kicked them, he realized in horror that they weren't jack-o-lanterns. Instead, they were the hollowed out heads of children burning a devilish orange through their little mouths. He tried to scramble away but slipped in the blood and brains of the children's heads that had been sitting in a pile on the table. Now he crawled through the leftover mess, skidding atop the blood. Scratched into the wood floor was more insane scrawl, blood filled the crevices of the letters that seemed to be lit from within:

THIS WORLD IS A LIE, ALL IS ALLOWED
THIS WORLD IS A LIE, ALL IS ALLOWED

THIS WORLD IS A LIE, ALL IS ALLOWED
THIS WORLD IS A LIE, ALL IS ALLOWED
THIS WORLD IS A LIE, ALL IS ALLOWED

He continued to try to escape but couldn't get his footing in the blood. A maniacal laugh lumbered through the house and as Mattie clawed his way back to the front door, he was face-to-face with Father Gleason and a ghoulishly-tall, slender figure. Mattie immediately scrambled backward and got his footing once he hit the carpet of the living room. He bolted to the back of the house and found a narrow stairway leading up to the second floor. He fumbled for lights and found them, but it made matters worse. Red, hyperkinetic lighting rained down on him and from somewhere deep within the house, intense bass began pounding with screeching guitars. Someone screamed in rhythm with the bass but making sense of the shouting was impossible. With each pulsing strobe and beat of the bass, Mattie tried to ascend the stairs. He felt rain pouring down on him as he made it closer to the top. In the red haze, Mattie couldn't see that it was blood falling from the ceiling and soaking him.

Gleason, close enough to touch Mattie, reached for him just as he made it to the top. He missed the boy by inches. Mattie turned to his left, his heart breaking in his chest, blood dripping from his soaked hair and unable to think through the spiked tea and thumping bass that threatened to splinter his eardrums. He turned a knob and slammed the door behind him. The room flashed with the same red strobe and Mattie could see two figures in the corner. One, a young female dressed in eerie white that might only appear in black and white movies, sat at a table eating. She held up a human leg, teeth marks littering the calf down to the ankle. She paused and flashed

Mattie a red devilish grin. Her teeth were stained with the blood of the leg and she laughed viciously.

Join me, she said, he won't let you leave.

Mattie felt something tugging at his pant leg and jumped when he looked down to see another child, a boy, trying to pull himself up Mattie's pant leg. The boy had no legs, only bloody stumps. His strength was immense as he pulled toward Mattie's waist.

Sissy says I taste better than she's ever had. You're next.

Mattie swiped at the child like he was trying to drive away an annoying fly. But the child snapped at him, biting his finger and taking the tip of his ring finger with him. Mattie turned full circle on the child and reared back with his right hand and hit the child in the head with all the force he had. He crushed the boy's skull between his eyes and blood poured from his eyes, nose and mouth. Yet, the boy didn't let go. Mattie hit him again and again until finally the child relented and slithered away in a pool of blood.

The female child screamed. The boy wailed in pain. The red lights pounded with the bass. The door swung open and Mattie had no time to think. A window across the way was his only escape. He dashed for it and exploded on the other side.

HAHAHAHAHAHA! LOL BITCH! The ghoulishly-skinny man howled with laughter and roared as he spoke.

Father Gleason stood behind him, arms folded across his chest.

Excellent work, Gleason. You found him. The little twat thinks he's safe down here. Well, you aren't safe as long as Roosevelt Cleveland is alive, he shouted, looking down from the window.

Mattie couldn't remember where he was or what was happening. Spine-chilling howls echoed across the yard.

Cleveland shouted, I know about you. I know you're nothing down here. And to think, you don't even realize that it was you that gave me my exit from that inhuman prison they were keeping me in. I guess I should be thankful but I don't have time to be courteous. You have my Mechs, he said. He jumped from the window and stood above Mattie. He placed a boot on the boy's neck and pressed, I want them back.

Mattie tried to scissor kick Cleveland but his legs didn't cooperate and they barely moved. He wondered if he was paralyzed from the fall. Cleveland stepped harder on the boy's neck.

Suddenly, from high above him, cutting through the darkness like a bullet, a creature swooped in and knocked Cleveland over with two large talons. He rolled several times, away from Mattie, as the creature landed and approached. It stood over nine feet tall with large bird-like wings. It was the color of variegated dragons and had twin horns on either side of its human-like head. The creature had no eyes, but despite this obvious defect, it was remarkably accurate on the attack. Additional talons tipped the wings and the creature slapped them at Cleveland, trying to force him from the yard. Cleveland rolled with each swipe and finally he started to glow an eerie neon green. He stood before the creature and began to block the creature's attacks.

The creature bellowed, you are not virtuous. The boy shall be defended.

Cleveland, glowing green, laughed. This is my world, Fei. You have no power over me.

You are powerless without the others.

Not true, Cleveland said and placed his hands together as though he were praying. He placed his connected hands to the bridge of his nose and shouted, moonlight flux, chaos rage, laws of rupture take this creature to its cage.

Oh. Well, consider yourself lucky you didn't have to witness that. Or share any stew with him. I've heard it's usually quite good until you find out where he sources his meat from.

Mattie shook his head in disgust.

Will there be anything else Mattie?

I don't think so.

And yet, you're still here. Was there something else you needed Mattie, my boy?

Mattie thought about it for a moment. He had another thought on his mind. Perhaps that's why he didn't just wake up on the other side.

Can I use it to travel, Mattie asked.

To what are you referring?

The tunnels. Can I use them to travel?

The answer is yes. But it depends on the person. I know some people that can use them like a subway system. Others? Not so much. It's just pop in, get what you need and then back to the real world. Someone, though, who has adapted himself or herself to the unpredictability of the tunnels could travel through to places quite a distance apart. In minutes. If not seconds.

How do I know if I can use them for travel?

You've just got to try. Mattie, McBride started, choose your path carefully. These are dark times. Both up top and down here.

I can be the light.

Indeed you can. But there must be balance. Destruction of the dark would lead to destruction of the light because the light would get no rest. No slumber. Do you know why we keep Father Gleason down here?

Mattie shook his head no.

If we were to destroy him, something darker and more powerful would take his place. It's how it's always been.

I don't understand how you can allow that beast to remain alive.

Mattie, that's an argument for another day. Please just remember to choose carefully. You are an awfully powerful young man. What you think of as your limitations are just powers you haven't discovered yet. Do not assume you can make everything right. Temper your power with that knowledge. Your job –

Is to save the dying. I know.

Don't assume you know who or what the dying are either.

All the people with the Cluster, he shouted. But he felt himself fading. Mattie didn't understand. He willed himself to hang on to the image of McBride and for a moment he could see McBride clearly but then he was gone. The darkness washed over Mattie and then he stood in the hanger. Staring at the spinning galaxy on his tablet.

The words echoed in his ears, *don't assume you know who or what the dying are*…he suddenly felt lost like no other time in his life. The wailing of the self-destruct alarm brought him out of his haze. The timer on the tablet was at four twenty-eight. He logged into the CRM and input the access code 114. The screen blinked for a few seconds and was replaced by a black screen with yellow letters. It read, for further access, the proper RSA factorization code must be input. Please choose from the following RSA Factors

There was a list that read as follows:

100, 110, 120, 129, 130, 140, 150, 155, 160, 170, 180, 190, 200, 210, 220, 230, 232, 240, 250, 260, 270, 280, 290, 300, 309, 310, 320, 330, 576, 640, 704, 768, 896, 1024, 1536, 2048.

Mattie chose RSA-768 and waited for the code screen to pop up. The screen did nothing. The cursor blinked in the space reserved for RSA-768. Now it was blank. But it wasn't offering a space to input any code. Either the code Gleason had given him was wrong or his father had hidden the code in the wrong RSA factorization or had factored it incorrectly.

The self-destruct siren for Summer Cabin continued to wail in the distance. The countdown clock on the tablet read 2:23. The place was going to detonate and Mattie didn't have time to get very far away. He fired up the solar ski again and hoped the Mechs remained silent.

He was several meters beyond them when the explosions started. He had to find a way to communicate with them.

Variant

CHAPTER 37

Sometime in 2108

Roosevelt Cleveland stood in the foyer of the newly christened Kelland Corporation. A large KMC logo floated in the center of the tile and took up most of the foyer. Cleveland noted small changes in the motto. Instead of Digging New Worlds, now the motto was simply Transforming Worlds. The KMC logo remained largely unchanged but where the KMC letters of the past had been solid yellow on a white background in the black oval, now the stems of the K and M were black with the remaining portion of the letter in yellow and the curved portion of the C was now black as well, with the top and bottom of the letter in yellow. Small, subtle changes, but changes nonetheless. And no one had cleared any of that with Serafino or Cleveland would have heard about it. Cleveland could see Barnes was already making his play for control of KMC.

Kelland Mining Corporation still took up the most space in the building, including the top two floors, but Kelland Medical Corporation now had three floors. Right in the middle. Cleveland was here for it all. They just didn't know it yet.

The receptionist, Meghan, tapped her head set and placed a caller on hold. She was stunning in her beauty. Tall and slightly undernourished but that seemed to be the norm for people these days. She had long auburn hair that reached to the middle of her back. Green eyes rested peacefully on either side of a slender nose that had a small diamond stud embedded in her left nostril. She smiled warmly at the man who approached, dazzling him with her white teeth and red lips.

Cleveland smiled back at her, but in a creepy, child-molester way and she wished they would come and take him from her space. She went so far as to button the top button on her amethyst-colored silk shirt rather than leaving herself modestly exposed to those who usually made visits here. Her confidence left her while he stood next to the desk and she wished he would take a seat.

Sir, she said, needing to clear her throat, please have a seat.

He smiled wildly and said, what and miss all this? He pointed at her and touched her shoulder.

Sir, she said, trying to sound firm, you're making me uncomfortable.

Am I?

You are.

Do you know who I am?

No sir. I'm sorry.

What's your name, gorgeous little girl?

Sir, please. That's not appropriate.

Your name's not appropriate? Oh…that intrigues me.

No, Sir, that's not what I meant. I mean, you can't call me gorgeous little girl and touch my shoulder. That's inappropriate.

Is it?

Yes, Sir. Please stop.

Cleveland leaned in, over the shallow credenza of the steel and wooden desk. He examined her face and said, you sit here flaunting your body, flirting with whoever might come in -

Meghan let him go just long enough. She put her hand under her desk where the .40 caliber blaster rested just underneath. It would take her less than two seconds to put a bullet through his two insect-like eyes. Her fingers clutched the weapon.

I'm just saying, the things I could do to you, he said and smiled his sinister smile at her. She smelled dead fish and decay emanating from his mouth, inches from her lips.

Get one inch closer and I'll split that shit-eating grin off your disgusting face, she said through clenched teeth. Cleveland backed up a few feet and assessed the situation. He heard her cock a weapon beneath the desk. He smiled again.

Roosevelt Cleveland, a voice from behind the two of them shouted, trying to break up whatever was about to happen.

Cleveland stepped away from the desk and held a hand out for Nathan Barnes. Nathan, he said with a wry smile, so good to see you.

Meghan didn't move. She was firmly convinced that if the creepy dude made a move, she was going to kill him graveyard dead. She maintained her grip on the .40.

As they shook hands, Barnes steered Cleveland away from the desk. She's a beauty, Cleveland, but deadly. One of the few elite women Grey Suit soldiers we have. Can't be too safe with security these days.

She's a Grey, Cleveland asked.

That's right, Meghan said. Hoorah!

Meghan, now, Mr. Cleveland is our guest. Let's show some respect.

Run the feed back, Barnes. With audio. Then come back here and tell me to show some respect.

Ok. Well, we'll be in my office. Carry on Meghan.

As they walked past her, Cleveland let himself follow her gaze just a bit too long. She'd finally had enough and ripped the gun from the holster, centering a red laser sight in the center of Cleveland's mouth. He turned his attention immediately back to Barnes.

So she's one of those genetically-altered Greys?

She is. We've got to have protection out here Cleveland. People are desperate these days, but I can't afford to have one of those bulked-up genetically-modified meatheads sitting up here. It would destroy the illusion that everything's great. With her, at least, it looks like an office building.

I'm sure she'd be pissed if you said it only looks like an office building because there's a woman at the front desk.

Probably. Promise me you won't tell her I said that.

Our little secret Barnes. I understand. But wow, that girl is something else.

I know! Could you imagine?

Oh, I did. I think that's what got me in trouble.

They walked down a long hall chatting and found their way to Barnes' office. It was two stories tall and comprised of floor to ceiling windows. He had a vast library on the second level with comfortable early Twenty-First century chairs made from bovine hide. There was one hundred and twenty-five-year old scotch in the sifter and even older, perfectly preserved cigars from Cuba, handrolled and cryo-chambered until today. He led Cleveland up the spiral staircase to his personal space. A painting greeted the two men as they reached the summit of the stairs. It was of a young girl in a blue dress with a watering can. Cleveland mentioned that he knew the painting but couldn't place the artist's name or the name of the print.

Oh, it's no print, Mr. Cleveland. This is the actual original painting. It's entitled *A Girl with a Watering Can*, an impressionist painting by Renoir from 1876. He painted it in Monet's famous garden at Argenteuil. This painting is of Mademoiselle Leclere in her blue dress holding a watering can.

 I suppose it's worth some money then?

Barnes laughed. Yes, yes Cleveland, it's worth a considerable fortune. I paid well over two hundred and fifty million for it.

Dollars, Cleveland asked.

Indeed, Barnes replied.

You must be paying yourself really well then, Cleveland said as he looked over the painting and marveled that anyone would pay that much money for paint on a canvas in a frame.

It was just after we discovered the diamond preserves on Saturn. The bonus that year was quite substantial. Had you been working with us then, you would have been handsomely rewarded as well, but that was some time before Serafino hired you.

Before I beheaded the man whose job you took, Cleveland thought.

The two men found their way to the leather chairs. Cleveland ran his hands over the supple leather.

That's one hundred percent genuine leather.

Cleveland nodded his approval, it's magnificent. Truly. How long has leather been banned?

Since the mid-2030s. Back then, they thought raising cattle was the cause of global warming. Little did they know, he said and laughed.

How did you come across these?

Oh, we've got a warehouse full of banned products. We'll have to get you some for your office.

My office?

Please, have a seat and let's enjoy our cigars and scotch before we talk business. The men sunk down into their respective chairs. Barnes leaned over and poured two glasses of scotch. He handed one to Cleveland along with a cigar. Barnes clipped the end of his cigar and pulled a high-powered lighter from a small brown box on the table before them. He focused on lighting his cigar and, once lit, handed the lighter to Cleveland.

Cleveland lit his cigar, sinking down further into his chair. He blew a large plume of smoke out over his head. Quite the set up you have here Barnes.

Only the best. Once we merged the mining and medical operations here at KMC, we really spared no expense.

Well Barnes, that's obvious.

You don't approve?

Cleveland took a deep drag on his cigar and let out another large plume. No, it's not my place to approve or disapprove of anything you do here. Just an observation. I noticed you tweaked the logo and motto though.

We felt a bit of an overhaul was in order. After we took over production of the Cluster drugs and established Kelland Medical, along with the expansion of our mining operations to Saturn, we just felt a change would be smart business. We're not just miners anymore. We're so much more. But, again, it was just small changes. Nothing serious.

No. But changes nonetheless. Cleveland took one more large drag on the cigar and then stubbed it out in his glass of scotch. He hadn't taken a sip.

Mr. Cleveland, that's several thousand dollars worth of sin you just ruined.

Yes, well. I'm more of a bourbon man. Can we talk business now? And somewhere more suitable for two professionals to discuss important matters? Not your little grotto up here.

Barnes said nothing. He was still seething over the waste of the cigar and scotch. He saw thirty-five hundred dollars floating in the crystal glass now sitting on the coffee table. He ushered Cleveland down the stairs to his desk.

Much better, Cleveland said, taking his seat behind the desk.

Really Cleveland? That's my desk.

Is it now? Doesn't it belong to the Company?

Well, yes, but it's my office. My desk.

Have a seat Barnes, Cleveland said, pointing to one of the two chairs sitting across from him. You use *we* quite a bit I noticed.

Barnes, clearly uncomfortable sitting across from Cleveland at his own desk, said, well, the Board and I. That's what I mean by *we*. We work pretty well together.

So those minor changes? Those were your idea?

They came to me and suggested the changes. I authorized them and now here we are.

That's outstanding. I'm so glad to hear that you take the recommendations of the Board seriously. They are integral to the company's success.

I agree. Why are you so interested in our little venture now? You've not shown such interest in the past.

Things have changed Barnes. I'm sure you know that. Since Serafino died –

That was tragic, Barnes interjected.

Yes, please allow me to finish, Cleveland locked stares with Barnes and wouldn't let him look away. Since Serafino died, we have assumed control of nearly every local police force or we've had them removed and replaced with our soldiers. Thus, we have an extensive network of our people out in the field. Pretty firmly entrenched, if I do say so myself.

You've done excellent work Cleveland. Serafino trusted you, he named you Special Projects Director after all and I know you have the full support of the Board and the entire Kelland Corporation. Quelling insurrection keeps us all safer and the two of us in business.

Sure, sure. But, you see, and please don't take this the wrong way, I'm not really concerned about keeping you in business. And by you, I don't mean Kelland, I mean you, Nathan Barnes. You're not my concern. Not anymore.

I don't know where this is coming from, Cleveland. I've been nothing but accommodating to you. I supported the decision to elevate you after Serafino's death.

Did you have any other choice?

You're not exactly a career military official Cleveland. A lot of good men got overlooked.

They all have their fiefdoms out there. They were all rewarded handsomely. I haven't heard one of them complain.

All due respect, you don't allow for much in the way of complaints.

That's effective leadership Barnes. I prefer compliance to complaints. Things run much more smoothly that way.

That's not always possible or feasible.

For you, maybe. I don't have many problems with it. And that brings me to the nature of my visit today. I've come to seek your compliance with a few new directives from the Board.

What the hell are you talking about? The Board would come directly to me if there was anything they needed to discuss. Why would they contact you?

You see, Barnes, we feel that your service to this company would be best served in a different capacity, Cleveland said, flashing a sinister grin.

You're insane Cleveland, you know that?

There is more than one medical doctor that would agree with you on that one. But that's neither here nor there right now. I'm here now to inform you that from this point forward, you report to me.

This is lunacy.

Perhaps, but I purchased the Board's shares of the corporation and then convinced the Kelland family that it was in their best interest to divest themselves of their portion as well. In a show of good faith, I allowed them to maintain a minimal seven percent stake in the company and one voting member on the Board. I control the remaining eleven spots and ninety-three percent of the corporation.

There's no way this happened. You've completely lost your mind. This company is worth trillions. Not ten years ago, you were living in a padded cell. You don't have any money. You couldn't afford to buy that drink you just ruined.

Sometimes, in negotiations, it's not all about the money Barnes. For you maybe. I've listened to you drone on and on about the price of this piece of art or this piece of furniture or this bloody glass of liquor. For me, it's more about the relationships. The Board understands my vision. The Kelland family appreciates my desire to see this company grow to even greater heights than it has over the last twenty years. Once Kelland Manufacturing begins production on the new upgraded Mechs and their various incarnations, the company will be worth twice what it's worth right now.

But the military, you and your henchmen, you manufacture the Mechs. For free!

You have a different understanding of the word free than I do. It's become cost prohibitive for the military to continue to manufacture these units. We need the men and women who are spending time in warehouses and production facilities building these units and their weapons back out in the field. With Kelland Manufacturing on board, we can triple production on the units. Not to mention Kelland Weaponry and Arms. A one-stop shop for all the military needs of this country.

Why in the world would you need to triple production of Mechs?

The Rising, Barnes. It's a real threat. We have to stay ahead of it lest we let the masses run roughshod over us. And I for one will not let that happen on my watch.

There's no way the Board allowed this. No way they turned over a trillion dollar corporation to a psychopath.

Uh, uh, uh, I'm more closely aligned with the diagnostic criteria for sociopaths.

I'm contacting Charles right now. This is madness.

Was he the short, pudgy one, with the gray goatee and a total lack of hair on his head?

Barnes nodded.

Yeah, that's too bad. He, Charles, didn't quite make it through our initial meeting.

You killed him?

He had choices. He chose poorly. But the new guy I've got in his place. Sharp as a tack. Trust me on this one. Sharp as a tack. We'll get you all introduced soon.

Did you kill them all? The entire Board.

Oh, heavens no. Like I said about our military leadership, you give them something to do and they're happier than a Voaklind in Martian pyroclastic slurry.

Barnes looked at him, confused.

Oh, you didn't get that? How about happier than a pig in shit?

Barnes stood and made his way over to his desk. He swiped his thumb over a small fingernail-sized button and a computer screen rose from the desk. A keyboard glowed into existence on the desk and he punched in the necessary coordinates to call up Gladys Smolders. The communicator buzzed once and then went dead.

You calling someone else, Barnes?

Gladys Smolders. No way you talked her into this disaster.

You seem to think I sat down and spoke to them like I'm speaking to you. Please understand, this was a hostile takeover. I didn't have time to debate with them.

Barnes punched in another number and waited. Once again, the communicator buzzed once and then went dead.

You won't reach any of them.

I thought you said you didn't kill them.

I didn't. But you're not going to reach them, all the same.

What did you do with them?

I knew you weren't going to quit until you saw how the sausage was being made. Cleveland approached Barnes and Barnes backed away. He watched as Cleveland typed in a series of commands and then Barnes could see a camera. Cleveland shifted the camera angle down and then illuminated the scene with bright white halogen lights.

There they are. Look at them, team-building.

The ten remaining Board members sat huddled together in the center of a large industrial building. Four small, glowing fires burned faintly in the four corners of the room. Four conference tables, each eighteen feet long, sat near each fire. Round yellow boxes with black raised dials sat in the middle of each table.

What is this Cleveland?

Choices, Barnes. Choices. You see, we're working on trust. I need the Board to trust me. If they can't trust me, we can't be successful. Right now, we're working on cause and effect. As long as they stay in the middle of that warehouse, nothing happens to them. Unfortunately, that warehouse is near the Yupik Front, so it's pretty damn cold in that building, especially at night. Temps drop to nearly thirty below. As you can see, no one dressed for the weather, so they are slowly freezing to death.

You're a monster.

No, now, they have plenty of opportunities to keep warm. They just have to trust me. I've given them a code, because who doesn't like codes and puzzles to figure out. It's the sequence that will light the four fires and keep them nice and toasty through the night. Simple really. I couldn't make it too hard because, you know, I want them to trust me. I even told them how to make it back to the center of the room without being killed.

What do you mean?

Ah, yes. Let's see. Let me just move that camera this way, Cleveland maneuvered the camera to the left of the group. There, in the center of the wall, Cleveland focused the camera on a caged opening. As he increased the zoom, Barnes could see two wooly creatures sleeping behind their closed caged door. The zoom stopped and Barnes creased his brow in disbelief. The wooly creature had the snout of a pig with short stubby pig-like hooves. It had triangular ears that popped up through its fur and red, beady eyes. Giant, black whiskers protruded from the snout. The creatures looked to weigh about four hundred pounds each. Long, sinewy tails with bristly, little black hairs, curled around each creature. Barnes was aghast.

What the hell are those? They aren't Voaklinds, are they? They can't survive here.

Oh, those? Well, technically, they are the first Voaklinds born on Earth and in captivity. Obviously, they're native to Saturn's moon Enceladus, but with some modifications, we've grown quite the little herd right here on little 'ol Earth. And man, they are fucking vicious. They got after Charlie. He wasn't too fast. If you look close in there, you can see his shirt and pants. Tore his ass up the first day. That's when they agreed to sell. Made me an offer I couldn't refuse.

You won't get away with this, Barnes said through gritted teeth.

Well, you see, I will. And here's why, you're going to help me or you're going to be replaced. Each one of those Board members has a choice. They have several, actually. To keep nice and toasty, they hit those black buttons on the tables by the fireplaces in order and viola! Fireplaces roar to life and keep the warehouse at a nice temperate eighty degrees. But, alas, only for four hours. Then the codes reset and they have to figure it out all over again to light the fireplaces.

But here's where it gets fun. This is my favorite part. If they go out there and enter the code in the wrong order, the door to that cage there opens and the Voaklinds get released. And man, let me tell you, they are hungry. It's been a few days since 'ol Charles went out there and mucked things up for himself.

You sadistic bastard.

See, there you go again, name-calling. Not very becoming for the assistant to the CEO of a major corporation. And to call your boss such names. I'm not sure I can tolerate such insubordination.

Why don't the Voaklinds just eat everyone while they're out of their cages.

They can't. You see that center circle line drawn around them?

Barnes nodded.

Cleveland pointed out the circle and continued, it's electrified and connected to the collars on the creatures. If one of them gets close to the circle, zzzzzzzzz, they get zapped with about fifty thousand volts of electricity.

Which leads me to their other choice, the Board can stay in the center and nothing happens. No Voaklinds. No one gets eaten. They can huddle together and try and keep warm. That's the easiest thing to do, but unfortunately for them, I'm pumping air from the outside back into the warehouse and the temperatures continue to drop. For the first few days after Chuck got eaten, they just sat huddled together and that worked okay. But it's probably nearly ten to fifteen below in there now. They're going to have to do something soon or they'll all die. Then, it's interviews and resumes and work I don't want to do to replace them all. Such is the life of an executive, I guess.

I won't be a party to this. I can't. I'm a successful business-man. I've built this company into what it is today.

And what is this company Barnes? Pirates looting planets for their resources. Poisoning people who can't pay the exorbitant prices you extract for your shitty drugs. Then you sit up here in your tower and drown yourself in extravagant liquor sipped from centuries-old crystal in barbaric chairs beneath looted art work.

I want you out of here now!

Are you ordering me out of my own office?

Meghan! Meghan!

Oh, I'm sure she's been restrained by my men. Cleveland stood as four armed Grey Suits ushered Meghan in. Barnes turned to see his only bodyguard bound and gagged. She was bound with her hands behind her back in a pair of electro shock cuffs and a facial restraint. As she struggled against the bindings, warning alarms sounded.

I'd stop struggling Meghan, those electro shock cuffs give off a wallop of an electrical charge if you keep struggling. Those two small plastic pieces you're biting on will also jar your pretty white teeth right out of your head. I'd relax.

Meghan tried to shout through the restraint. All she managed to do was ooze spit down her chin. The warning alarm stopped and suddenly Meghan's body went into a violent spasm as electricity flowed through her mouth, to her jaw and down her neck. She dropped to the floor and continued to shudder.

I told you that was nothing to mess with, Cleveland said as he squatted down and caressed her cheek. She glanced up at him through one eye and swept her legs around, taking Cleveland's legs out from under him.

He landed on his back and instantly popped back up and straddled her torso.

Get her legs, you useless pricks! He grabbed her neck with his hands and she fought against his grip. The Greys struggled to restrain her legs as she kicked against their advance. The alarms sounded again but she fought against him anyway. He pressed her body on top of her arms. In the struggle, he heard snaps and cracks which made him back off a bit. Electricity surged through her, but before Cleveland knew it, she was somehow free of the cuffs. She brought both arms out from under herself and drove both her elbows and forearms into the sides of his face. He was stunned for a moment and she scrambled to her feet. Cleveland retreated, but not before Meghan kicked him with a roundhouse to the jaw. He dropped to the ground, blood pouring from his mouth. He spit a glob of blood out and slowly got to his feet.

You're dead, he said to her.

I was dead the second I walked in here. Nothing you or these goons do to me will change that. She held up her wrist and showed off her red bracelet.

So, come and get some, she said, holding up both fists and assuming her fighting position.

Who hired a Red Code? Oh wait, Barnes? What were you thinking?

Barnes said nothing. Then a shot rang out and Meghan dropped. A single shot, to the back of her head, blew out the front taking with it her eyes, nose and mouth.

Who the hell? Cleveland looked into the hallway and saw a unit of Grey Suits all holding blasters, aimed at the group in Barnes' office.

Who fired that shot, Cleveland demanded. He walked to the group and looked at each one of the genetically-altered soldiers before him. Who? They stood silent, eyes focused ahead, ignoring him.

I'm telling you right now, if someone doesn't speak up –

You said she was dead, Sir, a monotone voice from one of the men said. She was a direct threat to your safety. Those are all part of the protocols you established.

He thought back to the protocols but couldn't recall them verbatim. He'd been half kidding when he implemented them but figured they needed some guidance when it came to pulling the trigger. He remembered something about direct threats to his safety.

Well done in that case, men. I was simply trying to isolate who to congratulate for following the protocols I put in place. He waited, hoping one of them would speak up, so he could terminate his service in front of the others. At no time did he want that girl killed. He had so many things he wanted to do to her. She was no threat, he thought. Especially now.

What should we do with her, one asked.

He thought about it for a moment but couldn't realistically keep her body. He said simply, get her out of here.

And this one, another said, his beefy hands on the tiny arms of Barnes.

Cleveland walked up to him and looked at him like he was trying to look through his eyes. See what was going on behind the curtain.

Barnes turned his head and Cleveland promptly struck him to get his head back up, facing him.

I didn't tell you to turn your head.

Fuck you psycho.

We've already spent more than enough time on my mental condition. You look at me when I'm addressing you.

I'm not your fool, Cleveland. Just get it over with. I'm not going to cooperate with you.

I don't understand why. I've offered you a job. Hell, it's the same job you have now. I'll double your salary even. Think of all the useless shit you can buy then? Maybe a couple more Renoir paintings. Maybe a bear skin rug to match the décor up in your little tree house. Besides, I don't know anything about looting planets or making Cluster drugs. That's all you. All I know is running these grunts around.

Barnes tried to shake the two soldiers holding him back, but they kept him corralled.

You have people locked up with, literally, man-eating creatures. These are serious-minded individuals trying to do the right thing for this company.

Like poisoning people. Right?

I don't even know what you're talking about. Ravings of a madman. These people don't deserve to be terrified and murdered.

I'm sorry you disagree with my teambuilding program. I thought I was on to something. So you think I should just let them go?

Yes! Yes, I think you should let them go.

Cleveland turned his attention to the keyboard on the desk and typed in a few commands. The camera came into view on the seventy-inch screen on the wall behind Barnes' desk.

Thank the heavens you and the Board didn't spare any expense on this office. Look at that picture up there. Magnificent. Now, let's see. Let them go. He typed in a few commands and a large door started to rise on the opposite side of the building from the creatures.

Cleveland continued typing and the room was filled with the sounds of moaning and wailing. You people are free to go, he shouted at the screen and motioned with his emaciated arms.

The Board members didn't move but a few of them glanced up at the ceiling where the camera was mounted.

There you go Barnes. Door's open. They're free to go.

Everyone in the room watched the Board members. It was clear they heard the announcement. Slowly, each one stood up. Their voices were indecipherable on the video as they moved about the circle.

Dennie O'Hurley made the first move to the door. He took a few steps out of the circle.

Oh look, Cleveland exclaimed, who is that? He sprinted up to the large screen and craned his neck to get a better view. Is that Dennie O'Hurley? I had a feeling about him. He's a no nonsense guy. Told me so when I met him. I hadn't noticed that limp before. Odd. But if anyone's getting away, it's him.

O'Hurley took a few steps outside the circle and suddenly a rusty scraping racket could be heard.

Cleveland shook his head and dropped it dramatically. He spit another wad of blood out and then looked back up at the screen. The others in the room watched as the caged door rose and the two Voaklinds realized someone was moving. Their ears popped to attention as their mouths opened wide. Despite the cold, they panted like dogs from the Mississippi Delta in summertime. They took in deep wide gulps of air and their extraordinarily long whiskers danced in the frigid air. The long serrated incisors of the creatures were gleaming even in the relative darkness of the cage. The male Voaklind stepped out and an audible gasp could be heard from the Board members. O'Hurley turned at the sound and saw the cage door open.

362

He looked up at the camera and screamed, damn you Cleveland! You promised us!

Cleveland shook his head. He hit the red communicate button on the speaker, I promised you nothing, he said. Now quit complaining and run. You know those things are fast.

O'Hurley gave one last glance behind him and considered just returning to the circle. But he felt he had a chance. He was only forty. Still slightly athletic, if not a dedicated gym rat. Unfortunately, the Yellow Code bracelet he wore gave him more confidence than he should have had in dealing with the Voaklinds. The cancer in his intestines was progressing rapidly. Had he been diligent with his follow-up appointments, he would know he should have started treatment months ago. Instead, he figured he had time, but the clock was ticking. Exertion was probably the worst thing he could do.

He started running and had nearly a hundred meters to go before hitting the door. After only ten meters, he slowed. The pain in his stomach roared to life and his entire lower body was on fire.

The Voaklinds didn't start fast. They passed by the others in the circle and gave them a quick once-over and even darted a snout over the line only to be snapped out of it by the massive jolt of electricity from their neck harnesses. They turned their attention to the doubled-over man. They sensed his vulnerability and gave chase, grunting and snorting as they ran. Snot burst from their noses in mini-explosions with each exerted step. The yellow-white muck dripped from their snouts covering their chests and forelegs with a slimy yellow film. Their small legs and hoofed feet bounced on the cement floor of the warehouse. With each bounce, the creatures' bellies threatened to drag on the floor but somehow they remained upright and moved with deceptive speed. As they galloped for O'Hurley, they gained speed like a bowling ball rolling downhill.

O'Hurley saw the Voaklinds begin to sprint and he felt the surge of adrenaline course through his body as a result. He sprinted in his business slacks and white button-down. The air was frigid and getting oxygen became increasingly more difficult. With twenty meters to go, the Voaklinds closed in.

C'mon, he screamed. I've got them!

The others hesitated, unsure if the nasty creatures would continue after him once he left the warehouse. He approached the door and ran as fast as he could to the right. Spurred on by Dr. Baillo who was making his way to the door, the others gathered their courage and walked from the safety of the circle toward the open door. Only Don Neimand, a twenty-something tech guru, stayed behind in the circle. He waved them off as they pled for him to come with them. As they shuffled toward the door, he sat in the center of the circle with his legs pulled up close to his chest.

O'Hurley, now out of camera range, made it nearly twenty meters out the door before the Voaklinds closed in. The larger male gave ground to the female who nipped right at O'Hurley's ankle, bringing him down in a cloud of ice and snow. The male was right behind and immediately sank his jagged incisors into O'Hurley's neck.

The man screamed for just a second more before the male Voaklind tore out his vocal chords and feasted on them. The creature thrashed about and eventually separated O'Hurley's head from his torso. Blood sprayed out of his neck cavity and washed over the creatures, freezing instantly in the creatures' bristly hairs. They devoured the body in a matter of minutes and were pulling at bones when the others stepped tepidly out into the cold.

The Yupik Front raged. They had no idea where they were stranded and certainly knew nothing of the Yupik Front. None of them had ever seen snow or experienced freezing temperatures. The cold swirled about them and the wind howled. Visibility was less than a foot. In the blowing snow and white-out conditions, they couldn't see or hear the Voaklinds but the creatures smelled the humans on the air as soon as they made it out of the warehouse. Their fear was palpable and made them smell like gravy.

Somewhat satiated from O'Hurley, they moved slowly toward the group. The group stayed together until Marissa Lecter, a legacy Board member who took her father's place when he died of the Cluster, shouted that they should split up.

The others leaned in but shook their heads, unable to hear her due to the howling winds.

I said, she shouted once more to the nestled group, we need to split up. They nodded in agreement.

Where will we go, T.D. Williams, an owner of the world's largest casino (also inherited), shouted.

Just run, Marissa shouted.

The others began to disperse into the snowy wasteland.

So, there you have it Barnes. Your Board, except for Donnie there, is out.

They're out in a freaking blizzard that never stops with no idea where they are, where they're going, or even any viable means of survival. They're in business clothes, not arctic wear. They're either going to freeze to death or end up eaten by those beasts. Or both!

You do see the challenge in every situation don't you? That must be what makes you such a valuable leader to the Company. I do wonder what made Donnie stay put? Any ideas?

He's the only one with an ounce of intelligence. Why would you go running out into that storm?

I agree with you Barnes. See, this is easy. Mr. Neimand, Cleveland said to the screen. Donnie looked up at the camera. Can you hear me, Mr. Neimand.

Yeah, I hear you.

Just a quick question from HQ, what made you stay put?

What kind of question is that?

We were just wondering.

You can't see a meter in front of you out there. I don't know where out there is, geographically speaking. I have on jeans and a hoodie. My feet are already freezing. I wouldn't survive more than ten minutes out there without one of those things attacking me. I guess, in a nutshell, I didn't feel like dying today. I'm a White Code, he said, holding up his bracelet, I've got some years left in me. The others? Hell, they're probably better off out there.

Very good Mr. Neimand, Cleveland said. He went to the keyboard and typed in a few codes. Within seconds, the fireplaces flickered on. Soon, they were blazing. The door to the outside began to shut as well. When it was nearly closed, two figures slid underneath the door. It was Olive Ferguson and Marissa Lecter. Cleveland noted their re-entry. Congratulations, Ladies. You three are safe. You'll be the founding Board members for our new venture when it's launched. The fires out there will soon have that place nice and toasty. There's a compartment in the back of the caged room filled with supplies. There's no code, no shenanigans. Just rotate the dial one full turn and it'll open for you. I'm sending someone to get you. It'll give you time to reacquaint yourselves with one another. A real teambuilding experience. Shouldn't be long.

The others, Olive asked, looking up at the camera but shielding her eyes.

The others have been reassigned. Needn't worry about them.

A shrill cry could be heard near the warehouse. Then another. The camera rotated toward the disturbance. Suddenly, Roy Beck, the principal shareholder for the country's largest genetically-modified food supplier, appeared outside, grasping onto the bars on the window by the cage. He screamed nonsense and then was silent. They watched in stunned silence as the Voaklind jumped onto his back and chomped off a large section of his scalp. From the right side, the other fiend jumped onto the man's shoulder, tearing the arm away. He collapsed and the Voaklinds feasted. Again.

Olive looked back up at the camera as it redirected itself to the center of the room.

Like I said, I'll send someone to get you.

Olive started, But –

Cleveland shut the communication down and the screen went black.

So, are you going to take some guys with you and get our Board back?

Barnes blinked a few times, his arms still held by the two soldiers. Are you kidding? You lack a GOFO, my friend.

A GOFO? I do like acronyms.

A grasp of the fucking obvious.

I see. Clever. I didn't even see that one coming. Cleveland walked up to the soldier on the right side of Barnes. He withdrew the soldier's service revolver and put it in Barnes' mouth. Let's see you grasp this. Cleveland pulled the trigger and splattered Barnes' brain, tongue and teeth across the neck and chin of the other soldier.

You two get this mess cleaned up and then take the rest of those idiots with you and get my Board back here as soon as you can. He dropped the gun on the ground, withdrew a handkerchief and wiped his hands with it. When he got to the door of Barnes' office, the phone out front was buzzing. He dropped the handkerchief to the ground.

And get me someone to answer these damn calls!

Variant

CHAPTER 38

Sometime in 2108

Mattie stopped the solar ski several meters away from Summer Cabin. He had to find out if his dad had left any other codes or hints or help to get access to the Mechs. He swiped through screens on the tablet to get to the picture of the galaxy. It spun slowly and he thought of where he needed to be. He had to find his father. But thoughts of April rippled on the outskirts of his mind. He forced himself to think of his father and not April. It was his father he had to find. She would come later. His father…April…..

…..When his eyes cooperated, he found himself sitting on the solar ski and staring at the tablet. Within a few seconds, the cold was replaced by a blistering heat that pounded down on him. No longer was his vision clouded by bleached-out snow landscapes. Now, the scorched earth of the desert lay before him. His solar ski sat just off a highway.

He was immediately overheated due to the flesh coat and layers of clothing he was wearing. Stripping down to shorts and a tank top, he ripped the lining out of the flesh coat that kept him dry and put it on. His father often told him about the burning skin that took place after the Great Surge and in the Interzone, he wasn't taking any chances. Many people contracted fierce cases of the Cluster with skin lesions that ate the hosts' bodies from the outside. Once inside the bone, those Clusters spread like wild fire. As he slipped the jacket on, he felt the earth shake from a great explosion. That was followed by two more detonations. Each one, worse than the last.

Summer Cabin, he thought.

He surveyed the landscape he found himself in and was disappointed to see neither a tunnel nor a train to aide him in his escape plans. Having no idea where he was, or where his father was, he stuffed the excess clothes into the solar ski and took out his grandfather's spyglass. He withdrew it from the wooden box it rested in. Despite all the advancements since the era this scope was made in, his grandfather would say it was still the best way to see if someone or something was coming to get you. He extended the scope and scanned the horizon. As he scanned, he came across a block in his vision and backed away from the lens to see a figure standing before him.

April, he shouted.

Easy, she said.

How'd you get here?

I hope the same as you.

I've got to get to my dad. But when I was thinking about him and concentrating, you kept popping up in my mind.

Aw, sweet kid, she reached out and hugged him. He backed away a bit after she let him go. There wasn't the warmth there that he usually felt when they embraced. Her scent was different, muted.

What's wrong, Kid?

I don't know. That's weird. It felt like I was hugging nothing. You don't smell like you or feel like you. I can't explain it.

Yeah, I know. I've been seeing you in dreams of mine for years, but that's the first time I've ever tried to hug you. And you're right, it doesn't feel the same.

It's not real?

I don't know. When we both concentrated on your dad and we found him, that was real. I stayed behind, remember?

Are you still there? With him?

Things got serious, Mattie. I'm still here. Where we saw your dad. But he left. I thought to get back home to you.

I don't understand. So you were able to stay? What we saw was real?

Very real Mattie. So real I'm still there looking for my daughter. She may still be alive.

You have a daughter? I thought you just had a sister.

Your father, you know your father, he didn't want to get into the hows and whys of me having a kid. He's old-fashioned. But yeah, when you two ran into me, I had recently lost my daughter. She was taken from me.

And you didn't know if she was alive?

Right. I still don't.

Then what are you doing here?

You called me. I heard you in my dreams like a beacon. The next thing I know, I'm here.

But this isn't real?

I don't know Mattie. I don't understand it any better than you do. It's usually underground or at a train station.

Right. I see tunnels and stuff.

I've seen this time before. Usually, I see it when whoever runs Interzone needs me to see something. This highway is somewhere between Alpine and Sonora, Texas. I followed it to the caverns of Sonora and found my way to that base. That's where I think they have my daughter. And if you turn around very slowly, this might explain why you're here.

He did as she said and turned around slowly. He looked behind him and saw the expansive landscape of West Texas.

I see miles and miles of miles and miles. Nothing stands out. What is it?

You're kidding right?

No, what?

I can see about a hundred of those robots you guys call Mechs. And there's the big bulky cargo carrier ones, too. Hexes. And then big drilling machine looking ones. I forgot what you guys called those. There are little Mechs, too. Ones I've never seen before.

Mattie turned again, hoping to see what she was talking about but he continued to see nothing. April, I don't see anything.

I don't get it. I'm going to wake up or suddenly come to and all I'll be able to do is think about you, Mattie. I wish I could help.

So you can see them but I can't. You're here and they're here. I'm here, but I can't see what you're seeing.

April surveyed the Mechs standing behind Mattie. You can't see what I'm seeing because I'm seeing something that hasn't happened to you yet. That happens to me a lot in my dreams.

You can see the future?

I think so. At least here. And I know you can too. I've seen it.

Yeah, but that's in the real world, not the Interzone. I don't think I have the same powers in the Interzone that I do in the real world. It's weird.

That's odd. So we gotta figure out why I'm seeing these Mechs all lined up behind you and you're not seeing anything.

I can see you.

Right. And I can see them. So, I'm here to act as your link between the two?

Maybe.

Tell me again what you were looking for when you started thinking on the galaxy picture.

My dad. I needed to talk to him. It was about the Mechs.

What about them?

He embedded a Cargo Radio Maintenance (CRM) failsafe in them.

A what?

It's like a code that turns the Mechs off until you enter the correct code to communicate with them. Then there's this viral program hidden deep within the software design of the Mechs' memory. Activating the CRM and then executing a series of commands would place the Mechs in the control of whoever had access to the failsafe codes. Any attempt to recall the Mechs from that point forward would result in a total block of all transmissions other than those preceded by the CRM code. The CRM code allows the holder of the codes to operate the units via radio frequency or computer. My dad believed that if the Mechs needed to be recalled, computers might have failed or the grid operating the computers might have been compromised. Radio frequency operation was central to recalling them. The code my dad imbedded was CRM-114. That's fairly simple. The difficulty arose once the CRM was set to receive transmissions. The only way to recall the Mechs at that point would be to enter a lengthy RSA code.

RSA code?

It's a factorization code of some sort.

And I take it you can't just figure that out in your super smart brain?

No, he said and laughed. It would take some computers over two thousand computer years to figure them out. At this point, if we don't have it, we will lose the Mechs.

Okay, so where'd he store the code?

He had that code in his notes but the Summer Cabin was overrun by Greys and I had no choice but to blow it up. Notes and all.

I think I felt those explosions when I got down here, she said.

Mattie nodded and continued, so I went down to see McBride, in the Interzone and asked him about a code breaker. He sent me to one and I got a code.

Sissy says I taste better than she's ever had. You're next.

The child's words echoed across the vast desert landscape and froze April where she stood. They were haunting in their pronouncement and ominous in their meaning.

Tell me you heard that, she said.

I did, Mattie said.

Why does that shit sound so creepy?

Because it was.

What's it from?

I've never heard it, Mattie said, unable to recall the horror he witnessed in the Interzone.

She looked back over her shoulder to make sure no sinister kid was about to attack her. Once she could see the horizon was clear, she said, okay. So, you got the code and then what?

I came back and entered the code like my dad said to and nothing. It didn't work. But then the Mechs turned on and now I'm sitting amongst them, back up top, with no way to turn them off and no way to stop them from destroying me. I don't know how many direct hits I can take from them.

Are you sure about this code?

I mean, pretty sure. He was clear when he told me where to find it and what it was.

How'd he tell you this?

Over the comm with the Mechs.

On an open comm?

Well, yeah, I guess so.

Is your father that stupid?

Mattie shook his head.

So there's every likelihood he created something just for you, right?

I guess so, but, he would have said something.

Maybe he did. Besides finding the code, did he mention anything else?

Just to remember my Lessons. But he always says that. You know him.

Nothing more specific?

Mattie thought about it. He said something about the pen being mightier than the sword.

And he remembered. That warm fFll day when they swatted at mosquitos the size of hummingbirds. His father had said governments rise and fall with the swipe of a pen. Even with technology, man still felt the need to put ideas into writing and have them signed. It made them more official. More permanent. Despite the ephemeral nature of parchment made from trees subject to decay with markings derived from oils that faded over time. Mattie never understood how civilizations had functioned before technology but as his father explained the power of the pen concept to him, he realized that technology failed daily, replaced by older, truer forms of communication.

Mattie looked down at his forearm. A tattoo his father had given him when he was only eight stared back at him. It was written in improvised black ink made from soot and shampoo. Cathey had gotten the tattoo two millimeters down into the boy's skin despite the provincial pen and needle he used to mark the boy. At the time, Mattie didn't know why his father insisted on tattooing him. But now, as he sat on the side of a highway in the Texas desert, he thought he might. He read the tattoo, Fide et Fiducia. He stared up at April and she hung her arm down. She, too, had the same type of improvised black ink tattoo. Although hers had been given to her in a barn by Elizabeth using her father's dubious tattoo gun.

She turned hers over and he read it aloud, Trust and Be Trusted.

Suddenly, the Mechs came to life and Mattie could see them. When he repeated the words, Fide et Fiducia, Trust and Be Trusted, they shut themselves off. When he repeated the phrase again, they roared back to life.

Voice control, he said. He gave me voice control. But we had to disconnect them from the centralized computer control first. The codes Cleveland entered simply disconnected them. It's the voice control that operates them now. He left the channel open. Do you know what this means April?

From the looks of things, it's good. Turn around and see, you control all that.

Mattie turned and saw the extensive army of Mechs he now controlled.

He commanded them to arm themselves and he heard thousands of clicks as they responded to his orders.

The tattoos. That's what I needed. April nodded. Then they both turned when they heard a sinister cackle seemingly reverberate all around them at once.

A voice screamed, I ain't equipment, I ain't automatic, there is no order. Mattie could hear the evil in that voice. For some reason, he thought, or knew, that it was coming for him.

You must leave now, April. I don't want you to, but you must.

Why, what is it?

Something is coming. Something evil. You've got to get back to my dad. To your daughter. Protect them.

Mattie, just come with me.

We can't. You said it yourself. I came down here alone. So did you. We both have to leave separately. I think that's why it feels so weird. We're not really down here together. I mean, we are. But we didn't come together. There's something weird if we don't come down here together. Just go. I don't think you have much time.

Okay. But Mattie, you're down here all alone. Be careful. Remember they can get you down here just as easily as up there.

Yeah, I know. Please, go April. I'll see you soon.

She walked up and gave him a flaccid hug. He wished he could smell her and kiss her cheek but everything felt so off.

In the distance, they heard what sounded like a thousand horses beating the earth with their hoofs. They sounded as though they were traveling at breakneck speeds. She backed away from him and blew him a kiss. She said, always, and, as she did, she disappeared on the air like a wind-blown dandelion. He made a wish and closed his eyes as the thunder grew from the west.

Always, he whispered.

ALL ARE DAMNED, a voice boomed in the distance. I HEAR THEM WEEP. Suddenly, Mattie could feel the earth shake and in the distance there was a great reddish-brown cloud coming toward him. The Mechs stood behind him. He ordered them to arm themselves and waited for the hellish voice, pulled by the thousand horses, to arrive. He reached for his pistol and found it missing as was his pack. Everything had been left behind. The horses thundered closer. He did not panic, but he had nothing with which to defend himself.

In a spray of rock and gravel, the horses finally came to a halt. The cloud blew toward him and suddenly he was surrounded. He could barely see right before him and it was five minutes before the sky cleared. From somewhere within the gloom, a fist grabbed him by the throat and pinned him to the ground. The force was exquisite and he pinched and pulled and punched at the figure that held him down but he lost consciousness before he could fight back. Before he knew it, he had a hood thrown over his head and electro shock cuffs binding his hands behind his back. They shocked him with something else every time they touched his sides. He passed out from the force.

CHAPTER 39

Now, 2108

Swarms of soldiers streamed into the hallways leading to the nexus. They thundered down the pearl-colored tile in search of a ghost no one had seen in fifteen years. Many of the soldiers wondered if it was just another one of Cleveland's tests but after so many of his previous tests had ended in actual deaths, they dared not voice those concerns to any officers. Instead, they marched and followed their orders, searching for the man whose face now intermittently flashed across their blast shields. They were on high alert and ready to shoot anything that moved.

That face belonged to Cathey and he stood at the threshold of a lab buried deep within the caverns of the base at Sonora. He leveled two blasters at the clone. The two women, in turn, had blasters leveled at each other.

What do we do Cathey, April asked, eyes focused on Clara, gun aimed steadily at her head.

Drop your gun Clara, he said hoarsely.

Cathey, look in there, she motioned with her head to the right, look how screwed up it is. She's floating in a tank. All hooked up to machines. Draining her blood like vampires. Even if I can get her out of here, her muscles are atrophied and she'll probably drop dead.

Jimmy, Clara began, she's wrong. Wrong. Wrong. Wrong. This child was donated to us. Given to us in the interest of science. And that's the purpose she's been serving.

It's my *child,* you monster, April roared, not a fucking donation!

Jimmy, you don't understand. You've been gone a long time. This isn't what you're thinking. The family bestowed this child on us and we in turn helped them with their treatments.

She wasn't their child to give! Cathey, seriously, tell her if she opens her mouth again, I'm going to leave it gaping open.

You don't intimidate me, Clara said. I've been through more than you could ever know. I did, in fact, lose my son.

Cathey shook his head and said, that's just a residual memory we implanted in you. You never had a child.

I had a son. But he died. You don't know anything at all about me. All of the clones lost their children.

The Grey Suits were impregnating the clones?

They tried, she said. It was, for lack of a better word, a colossal failure. Most of the clones died right along with the children.

Did any of the children survive?

I can't discuss that.

You can't discuss it, April screamed. What does that mean?

I'm not at liberty to discuss the success or failure of our clone reproduction program.

Oh my gods, April said, dropping her blaster to her side. I'm seriously going to kill her.

Let April in there. That child isn't yours. Not anymore, Cathey said.

They turned when they heard footsteps enter the lab. Glistening black shoes tap-danced into the room. A seamless pair of grey slacks hung perfectly from his hips and he wore a white shirt with a purple tie clasped at the neck. His long stringy hair was swept back across his head, looking as though it had recently been dipped in motor oil. He smiled widely, his chipped teeth a reminder of the devastation he left in his wake.

I do hope I'm interrupting, Cleveland said and clapped his hands together. Several genetically-modified soldiers stood behind him, blasters aimed at each figure in the room. A hooded figure squirmed between two of the men. They each whipped out a laser prod and stuck the figure near its head and jolted it quiet. The figure's legs went limp and the men let the figure drop to the floor with a thud.

It's so nice to see families reunited. When Cleveland said this, Cathey immediately turned to the hooded figure lying on the ground.

You noticed, Mr. Cathey? That bound and hooded figure there, your son, is apparently knee deep in this Rising nonsense.

I just talked to him. He's –

Right, right. I don't have time to go through all the nuances of how I got from point A to point B. Let's just say, I yanked his ass out of Alaska and brought him here posthaste. Had to skirt that idiot McBride along the way. He's always so particular about his rules. In the meantime, I got your boy connected to this Rising group stealing supplies of Cluster drugs. The public has no love lost for him, I can tell you that. Coupled with the story about you being a mass murderer, you two won't make it ten feet on the outside. I'll tell you this though, lesson learned, it's the last time I send a clone out to do a human's job. That's for sure.

The good news is that the good people of this country realize this Rising for what it is: terrorism. Domestic terrorism. You see, those people out there, the ones doing the living and the dying and more dying, the ones who are dependent on these drugs we make, they see those attacks on us as attacks on them. This Rising isn't about toppling a corrupt government, not to the noobs out there, no. They see people choosing not to conform. Choosing not to wear their Code bracelets. Choosing to send society into chaos and anarchy. These are people who want the world back to the way it was before the Cluster. These are people too stupid to realize that it will never be the same ever again. But as long as they're on my side, helping Kelland suppress this Rising, then they're my kinda people. They have hope that they'll live longer, more fulfilling lives with these Cluster drugs.

When you attack our bases and destroy our supplies, especially of Cluster drugs, they see that as an attack on their hope. And right now, it's all they have. So you're the enemy. For that, I thank you. I mean, really, why fight? We're all on the same side. With that being said, do drop those weapons. Pointing those things at each other can only lead to bad outcomes down here for us all.

Now!

He shouted and the walls trembled and flakes of dirt and sand dislodged from the earthen tunnel. They each lowered their weapons and placed them on the ground.

Good. Good. I do hate to get off on the wrong foot. Speaking of families, before I was sidetracked by that Rising drivel, I often dreamed of getting my own family back together again, but due to circumstances beyond my control, that might be a tad bit difficult. I say the circumstances were beyond my control. They were totally in my control until I chewed that old sonofabitch's throat out when he came after me again. After all my protestations, he still came at me and I ended his sorry excuse for a life.

Cleveland paused. He blinked several times and appeared disoriented. Where was I? Certainly not discussing my family life with the likes of you. You people have the corner of the market on dysfunctional family relationships. Now let me see if I can connect the dots. James Cathey, I don't *know* you, but I know of you, he said, wagging a finger toward the man. Very impressive. Fifteen years you've eluded us, but you just couldn't let this one go could you?

He walked up behind Clara and grabbed her throat and pulled her close to him. With his other hand he pulled her hair back and exposed her neck line. He bent as though to kiss it. She is a good clone wouldn't you agree, Cathey?

There were better.

But you blew the rest up. I can honestly say this is the last of 'em. I do often wonder where you sent her? The real one.

Since we're being honest, I can tell you I don't know.

Oh good. Honesty is so much fun. Cleveland nodded toward one of the soldiers standing next to Cathey. The soldier leg-whipped Cathey, sending him to the floor in a crash. Then, the soldier put a boot on his neck and Cathey felt the air slipping from him.

Now, now, now, Mr. Cathey. Or is it Lieutenant Colonel? I do get confused. I'm going to just go with Cathey, how's that? Let him breathe, you brute, Cleveland said to the soldier standing atop Cathey. He shifted his weight off the boot and let Cathey take a breath.

Now, let's try that again. Where is the real Clara Strong?

Cathey lay on the ground, silent.

Cathey? He peered around the clone and studied the body before him. I do hope you didn't kill him with that enormous, meaty leg of yours. Check him for a pulse.

Both the clone and April watched as the soldier took the pulse.

No boss, he said. He's alive.

Well, good. We were just getting started here. That would have ruined all the fun. Give him a quick kick to the ribs just to rouse him.

The soldier reared back and kicked Cathey in the ribs with his full force. Cathey made a muted oof sound and then rolled onto his back. He spat a wad of blood out of his mouth onto the floor next to him.

I'll assume you can hear me now, Cathey.

Fuck – he gurgled the rest of what he was trying to say and more blood poured from his mouth. I can hear you.

Communication! The cornerstone to any good relationship. Good. Good. Now. We were talking about the location of the real

Clara Strong. The one you left behind fifteen years ago. I know you know where she is. Or did. I figured you'd go looking for her sooner than you did. But I guess you had the kid to raise. Couldn't have been easy.

I don't know why any of you doubt who I am, the clone said.

He kept her close to him and with his exceedingly long tongue, licked her neck to her ear as she struggled in his grasp which just made him more satisfied with himself.

Oh, you don't know why. We had to keep you around. You two were so similar. I do believe you are one of our top scientists. Clone or not.

She hissed at him as she responded, you don't know anything about me. We were working on a cure.

Were we? I know we've enjoyed your work with that young lady floating in that tank in there. She's been a real marvel. I don't think any of the more seasoned executives would still be alive without what that child has given us.

Let me go, she said.

I don't want to, Cleveland purred. She swiped at him with her leg but he managed to avoid her kicks.

Do stop kicking my dear or you'll end up with no legs. Try me. I'm serious. I don't think killing a clone has near the legal repercussions of killing a real human. But, then again, I don't care. He held her tightly against his body and she could feel him controlling her, as he had strength that belied his wiry frame. He stood her up, knees locked and placed his left leg in front of her. With his right, he snapped her knee backward and she let out a shrill cry.

Be still, he said through clenched teeth. He could smell her fear and her sweat and he wanted to taste more of her but he had work to do. So much work to do.

He kicked her in the back, sending her flailing into the wall. She hit it with such force that she collapsed right beneath it, smearing a bloody forehead wound all the way down.

Useless clone, Cleveland said.

Next, he reached for April and she knew what was coming. She caught his grasp and spun him around, sliding his right arm up his back to the point of breaking. She forced it higher and he thrashed about for her with his left arm. He went to his knees and she kicked him with a round house kick in the head. He flew toward Cathey and the soldiers started toward her.

No! Cleveland shouted. She's mine! You want to fight little girl? He bolted toward her and was so fast, she was caught off guard. He slammed a fist into the temple above her right eye and her vision was immediately cloudy with blood. Stunned, she backed away but found nothing but a chair and stumbled over it. He pounced on her and grabbed the sides of her head and began smashing her against the earthen floor. She could feel her skull compressing against the ground. Soon, it would crack. Cleveland pulled her head back again, ready to deliver the death blow, but then someone was above him, ripping him from the floor and away from April.

The figure threw Cleveland across the room and was on him before Cleveland could take a breath. Cleveland held up a hand and was saying truce over and over.

Mattie backed away from him. His hands were still bound together with the ADRs, but he'd found the strength to dislocate his shoulders and bring them around to the front of his body. He bent near his father and found a weak pulse.

Father, he said. Cathey turned his head toward the boy. He nodded his head, which was cracked in the center, and tried to speak but nothing came out.

Mattie said to him, don't talk. We've got to get you out of here. All of us out of here.

Cleveland inched himself up and surveyed the area. The super soldiers were in a heap, six of them, dead at the hands of this boy.

You don't disappoint, Son, Cleveland said to Mattie.

I'm not your son.

Well, of course not, Cleveland said and laughed through bloody coughs. We just haven't been properly introduced. I'm Roosevelt Cleveland. He held out a bloody hand.

I don't shake the hands of the enemy.

Oh now, you do sound like your father, he coughed again and smiled at the same time. Okay, Mr. Cathey, I'll save the handshake for a more appropriate time and place.

Cleveland wiped the watered down blood from his lips. I don't know where everything went so wrong. The enemy? The enemy of my enemy is my friend. Have you heard that?

No, Mattie said bluntly.

Well, we have a common enemy for sure. At least, we did. It wasn't the Grey Suits that wanted you and your family tested, it was Kelland.

The mining company?

Oh, they have their fingers in quite a few pies Mr. Cathey. Once they took over production of the Cluster drugs, you were a threat.

Threat?

The synthetization of your blood, Mr. Cathey, could lead to a cure. At least according to the scientists we had studying the remaining vials of your DNA. When Kelland learned that our scientists were so close to a cure, you became the most wanted man on the planet. They need you dead, see? With you gone, there's no one else around that's immune. No immunity, no threat. They can

386

keep the people sick and pumped full of their Cluster drugs. They make their money, increase their power and stop the drugs when the people can't pay. Perfect system.

Mattie shook his head. If they want me dead, then why are you here? Why did they send the clone?

I own Kelland Corporation now. In all its derivations. I'm trying to right the ship, so to speak. So, I control the military industrial complex and the only pharmaceutical industry that matters - the Cluster drugs. I thought I'd make you an offer.

No.

You haven't even heard it.

I'm not agreeing to do anything with you, Mattie said. The clone made all sorts of offers.

She was in no position to offer anything, Mr. Cathey.

The answer is no.

But we could synthesize your blood and continue doing the same with the girl in the tank. Work on that cure. Save yourself, your mom, your dad. Whoever you want. April too. I'd give you riches beyond your wildest dreams.

Mattie glanced over at April who had still not moved.

What do you know about April?

Oh plenty, Mr. Cathey. I didn't mention that we've grown quite, how shall I say…close?

Mattie lunged toward Cleveland. Before he could make it to the strange lanky man, Cleveland slid two pin-point blasters down the sleeves of his shirt, into his outstretched hands.

Uh, uh, uh. I'm no dummy Mr. Cathey. I came prepared. Did you?

These PPBs carry Mech piercing rounds. The ones your dad was so fond of. Now, why don't you have a seat on that chair over there, Mr. Cathey. He motioned Mattie to the chair near April.

My name is Mattie. He spoke the words through clenched teeth and took two deliberate steps toward Cleveland.

Ok, Mattie. Now we're getting to know one another. Don't come any closer. You're close enough right there.

You're not prepared, Mattie said. He took another step. One more and he'd be close enough to grab Cleveland.

I warned you, Cleveland said and fired multiple rounds at Mattie.

Mattie stood firm and took the hits. He had no idea if they'd pierce his skin or not. They sped through the air, ripping through his clothing and finding his chest and neck. Each one crushed into the boy's skin, folding in on itself like an accordion as it collided with him. Cleveland fired until the PPBs were empty. He stood looking at the boy that was now a man.

What the fuck, he said, looking at the guns.

It's my skin, he said, taking off his shirt. He pulled the flattened bullets from his chest and dropped each one to the floor. Twenty-two rounds dropped to the concrete floor, pinging each time. It's my skin. You were woefully unprepared. Didn't the clone tell you about me? The Variant X?

Mattie stepped forward and grabbed Cleveland by the throat. He lifted him into the air.

She had very limited quantities of your DNA. That's why we needed you back here. At least initially. Then we found April.

What was so special about April?

She never told you, he asked and again laughed his sinister cackle. She is a Heteroclite. The last female one we knew of besides your mother. When we found her in Mount Enterprise, we ran tests on her. They confirmed our suspicions. Then she was pregnant. It was only later that we learned she was pregnant with another special child. These people here didn't understand but I did. She was pregnant by someone from my world.

Your world, Mattie asked, not sure of what Cleveland was suggesting.

It's all connected, Mattie. At least now. Of course, April, like your father, couldn't sit still long enough for us to all sit down and talk. We could've worked everything out.

Is that her child in there?

Cleveland looked into the stasis chamber. He nodded.

What is she? Like me?

Oh, Mattie. You have no idea. They had a name for her when we first Coded her. Like you, they called her a Variant X. A variant of the Heteroclites. When we studied the code, it wasn't just that we didn't know how long she would live. She wasn't just different. She wasn't just a variation. She was completely irregular. No cancer genes. Complete immunity. And she's kept us all alive.

So you keep her alive just to save yourselves?

Precisely. Now, if you put me down, we can talk about your surrender.

My surrender?

You won't make it out of here, Mattie. Between the soldiers and the mobs, you don't stand much of a chance.

I'm walking out of here with my family. And the girl. How do we get out of here?

He smiled, while gasping for air. If you kill me, you'll never know.

Mattie forced him higher, squeezing tighter. I'm not going to kill you. How do we get out of here?

Cleveland wheezed as the air flow to his lungs was cut off. Mattie, I'll tell you, just let me down.

Tell me, Mattie screamed, his anger fueling his grip. Small bones in Cleveland's neck popped against the pressure. His eyes filled with blood.

Nexus, Cleveland said.

Nexus? What about the nexus? Isn't that where we are?

Train station deeper, he whispered. Train…he muttered and then he passed out from the pain.

He threw Cleveland against the far wall. The frail skeletal man crumpled against it. He slid down and came to rest with his head on the concrete. Blood poured from his mouth and ears.

Mattie went back to his father's side and felt for a pulse but this time he found nothing.

Father, he shouted. Dad! Dad! Mattie shook him but the man who'd brought him this far had breathed his last breath. James Cathey was dead. He bent his forehead to his father's and said simply, always. He closed his eyes to gather himself. Then he rose.

Mattie staggered over to where Cleveland was resting, meaning to kill him.

Mattie, April called. Mattie turned to see April standing. Blood trickled from the back of her head and she was unsteady on her feet, but she stood strong for Mattie. Don't do it, she said. If you do it that way, it's just revenge. Then you're no better than them.

My father is dead.

She limped over to him and fell into his arms. He held her tightly. He put his head on top of hers with his mouth and nose on the top of her skull. As he held her, he wept and inhaled deeply. She smelled of spices that he could never place but she smelled like April. You're real, he said to her through tears.

She nodded, crying. Yeah. This time I'm real. I'm sorry about your dad. I loved him so.

A tear rolled down Mattie's cheek and he held her for a moment longer and then said, I know. He loved you too. He came here for you. Not her. I think he knew the whole time that she wasn't real. He just had to save you. The damned fool. They glanced over to the spot where the Clara clone had lain and she was gone.

Abigail, April said, breaking away from Mattie. She started down the hall, limping on a severely sprained right ankle. Mattie followed. They reached the stasis chamber but were blocked from entering because the clone stood in the doorway, dripping wet.

This is as far as you two are going, she said, shouldering a naked female figure, also dripping wet. The figure was pale in color and had no hair. Her bald head was smooth and round. Milky white eyes sat vacantly about her slender nose. Multiple, black, plastic tubes hung from her body. Three on her left side, three on her right, just beneath her arms. Two others hung from her back at either shoulder blade. There was another in the center of her back and then two more at each hip. Now that she was disconnected, she was bleeding from each port.

April stepped into the doorway and immediately recoiled, shocked by an electric blue force field that jolted into being when she tried to enter.

You won't get her. You can't. I won't allow it.

If they're going to kill Mattie, they'll just kill her too, April said.

No, see, they can't. The Cluster drugs don't work. They know that. She's the only thing keeping us alive. If we start dying, the people will see that we've failed them. The hope we provide is just an illusion. They need her. I need her. Without her blood, I'll die tonight.

That's my daughter, April said, pleading. I just came to get her. I mean you no harm. But if you fail to let me take her, I assure you, you will die tonight.

But don't you see, this is bigger than you or me? I can save people. I can save the world. The dying.

Mattie approached the force field and stuck a hand into it. It sparked around him as thousands of volts of electrical current entered his body. It hummed, and, in its humming, sounded human. He couldn't make out what the current was saying. He didn't know if he was supposed to, anyway. He withdrew his hand. He didn't know if he would survive entry.

This isn't your job, he said, locking eyes with the Clara clone. That's not your job. Saving the dying.

It's all bullshit, she said as she backed away from the doorway. I won't betray anyone.

These aren't your memories. They're my mother's. Let the girl go, Mattie said.

They are mine, she said and a second electric-blue force field snaked down from the ceiling and blocked Mattie in. April stood on one side, the clone on the other. But I know you are a threat and now I've neutralized that threat.

Mattie stepped into the force field on the clone's side and the electricity coursed through him and whipped him back into his space. His hair singed, smoke boiled from his scalp and his fingernails turned black. Voices cried out to him.

Sissy says I taste better than she's ever had. You're next.

Can you hear that, Mattie shouted but the jolting electricity drowned him out.

Ugh…we're losing him. How much of that shit did you give him?

392

Mattie looked back at April. Her face was clouded by the electricity in his eyes.

Mattie, don't let her get away, April called from the other side but too quietly to be heard. She sounded like she was screaming underwater.

Mattie turned and said, I can't get through, but April couldn't hear him. She could feel him though. The current was strong. Look, he shouted, holding up his blackened nails. She heard the voices from her dreams, save the Variant. When she listened closely now, the electricity hummed and it sounded like it was saying Variant.

Variant, it whirred again. April stepped into the current without thinking. She stood next to Mattie and the sound of the buzzing electricity was overwhelming. Her hair didn't burn, though. Nor did her nails. She took Mattie's hands and placed them on either side of her face.

The worlds they stood between teemed with electricity, vibrations, pulsations and whirrs of static. When she clutched him, he could hear it too.

Variant.

She stood on her tiptoes and kissed his cheek. She found his ear and said, save the dying. Then she stepped through to the other side of the force field.

The clone backed away, still clutching the dripping wet female body. You can't, she screamed. This is the only pure blood we've found. This child. She belongs to us.

The face of evil is always the face of total need. You need her. Her blood is your drug.

I'm not evil. I'm trying to save the dying.

Didn't you hear him? That's not your fucking job.

April squared herself in front of the clone. The clone blinked and April noticed that her eyes were now solidly yellow, but that

393

would be impossible if they had a cure. If the girl she carried on her shoulder were like Mattie. But she couldn't think on such things. The only thought she had was to protect the Variant.

Give me back my daughter, you bitch, she howled. With the force of the words, she hurled herself at the clone, knocking her down and dislodging the body from her grasp. The girl's body dropped to the ground. She continued bleeding from the ports.

The whirr of the electricity was strong but then April heard something else, something out of place. A train whistle. And it was coming toward her.

She scrambled on top of the clone and beat her with both her fists. The clone's face was soon just a bloodied pile of meat. Mattie watched through the blue haze as April killed the clone. He tried to shout that he heard a train but even he couldn't hear his own voice over the drone of the electricity. The electrical waves fluctuated and grew even brighter blue. The snaking currents of power doubled their force. April continued to beat the clone. The blood was purple on her hands and he wanted to stop her but the force field was much too strong now.

She turned to see Mattie burning in the electrical field. Without thinking, she grabbed her daughter and drove her through the electrical field. The three of them stood in the current.

Take her, she implored. Her voice was laced with static and sounded like a cell phone losing service.

Where, Mattie asked, holding his hands out as she put the girl in his arms. She was so light that he pulled her to his body with little resistance. The plastic tubing snaked about like a live wire still flowing with electricity.

Wherever it is you're going. That train. Take her with you. Save the dying, Mattie.

In the static, all he heard was, you go…train…her with you. The last thing she said boomed across the electrical field and nearly deafened him. SAVE THE DYING!!!

Mattie's back was pressed against the electrical field. It burned and he smelled his flesh cooking. He yelled, you're coming too April!

She looked into his eyes, willing herself to move and protect them. But out of the corner of her eye, she saw Cathey move. The train whistle blew before them. When Mattie looked up, the train streamed by him. April, no, he screamed. The conductor reached down, grabbed him by the collar and brought Mattie and the girl on board. April disappeared in the field of blue, crawling toward Cathey.

The force field suddenly winked out of existence and the train whistle silenced. The clone lay butchered on the floor. Cathey shuddered and April went to him.

Cathey, she called.

Love, it's an emotion I'll never understand. Cleveland stood before her, pouring blood from his head, eyes, mouth and nose. He wobbled on his feet. Those are just electrical pulses in his dead body, but you left certain safety to check on him, knowing he was dead.

No. That's where you're wrong. I came back to protect the Variant. That was my job.

And you failed, Cleveland said, laughing.

She's gone away from here, April said.

But she's headed right where I want them. Right to Interzone. These people are all just cogs. I'll finally have the control I've been seeking, and you'll be dead.

He pulled the revolver from his hip and began firing aimlessly at her. Blood poured from his eyes clouding his vision. His skeletal arm flopped in the air and he pulled the trigger again, hitting April in the shoulder. The bullet tore through her breast and she let out a howl.

Oh good. I really can't see you, bitch, but I can smell you. Direct hit!

April scurried to the wall and reached for the blaster Clara had dropped. She pulled it into her hand and turned to fire at Cleveland. As she did, another bullet ripped through her throat. Blood exploded from the exit wound and sprayed high into the room, hitting the ceiling.

She lay bleeding out. Cleveland staggered in like a drunk beggar looking for handouts and tripped over April's body. He crashed to the floor. In his stupor, he grabbed at whatever he could find. Finding a leg, he began to climb it and was soon on top of April. He found her hair and wrapped his hand and forearm in it. He brought it up, ready to smash it into the earthen ground when a bullet tore through the center of his forehead.

The clone fired again and again, aimlessly. The first two bullets found their mark. He scrambled on the ground for a minute or two like someone had lit his hair on fire, then he calmed and went slack. The clone fired again and again but she was empty. Then she collapsed.

As they all lay dying, a siren began to wail. Cleveland smiled. The auto failsafe. No one was getting out of there alive. No one moved. They couldn't. He thought of that swimming hole in Jackson. The one his aunt had in her back yard. In the days he was still allowed to play with his cousins.

April put a hand to her throat to stop the bleeding. For some reason, she thought of a tree on the side of a highway in Mississippi. In the distance was a train station that had an old wooden sign that had just been painted. It read, Welcome to Centerville.

In an instant, the explosions started and then the sucking of the air coalesced into the nexus of the caverns and exploded in a giant mushroom cloud over Texas. The Sonoran base ignited in multiple flashes of yellow white and then silence. The boom was heard two thousand miles away. It shook the foundation of houses nearly that far too.

Variant

CHAPTER 40

Unknown time, Interzone

The bullet train zipped through time, a sleek pod screaming down a vacuum-sealed tube. It floated frictionless above its rails using magnetic levitation. Its speed approached eight hundred miles an hour. Mattie had the girl on the floor of the train screaming for a doctor. None of the patrons seemed to notice them. He scanned their faces and they returned vacant stares.

McBride, he shouted. McBride!!!

Through the rear door, a whoosh slid a door aside and McBride strode down the aisle. He wore a conductor's cap but the remaining portion of his outfit was like nothing Mattie had ever seen. Light powder-blue pants creased down to a cuff resting above white patent leather boots. They shone so brightly one could see one's reflection in them. The pants were held up with white suspenders over an equally light powder-blue shirt. A darker blue jacket hung about his shoulders and a silver badge hanging on his left breast pocket announced he was indeed the conductor.

Mattie, he said, how'd you get here?

We need a doctor, McBride, she's bleeding out.

Is there a doctor aboard, McBride called out. The train passengers looked forward, ignoring the desperation in McBride's voice. Give me a minute Mattie. He walked to the front of the cabin and pulled a microphone from the wall. He called out, is there a doctor on this train. If so, please report to cabin forty-two. Cabin forty-two.

Mattie held the girl in his arms and he could feel the life slipping away from her. He rocked her and willed her to live. He began to shout, live, live, live! From the back of the car, a whoosh sounded and a man walked toward Mattie. Sir, I'm a doctor, he said and locked eyes with Mattie.

You're Cathey's boy, he said.

Yes, I'm Matthew Cathey. Can you save her?

I'm Doctor Samuel Walsh. I have no idea how I got here.

Doc, can you save her, Mattie shouted.

He felt for a pulse and shook his head. She doesn't need a doctor, Son, she needs an undertaker.

No, Mattie shouted. We've got to do something.

There's nothing I can do. Apart from removing those tubes from her body.

Mattie immediately started to rip the plastic tubing from her torso. As he did, he tore flesh and opened wounds. She gasped as he pulled them from her. The meat of her ribs, connected to the interior portion of the tubing, ripped out, spilling more blood.

Pull, he screamed at Walsh.

They pulled all ten tubes from her body and she lay prone on the floor. Her pulse slipped away. The blood stopped. She simply had no more to spill.

Mattie, McBride said, putting a hand on the boy's shoulder.

No, Mattie shouted. Noooooooooo!

The girl began to gasp and Mattie instinctively bit his wrist and held it to her lips.

She can't ingest it Son, the doctor said. Let it drain into her rib cage. He held his wrist over her ribs and the blood flowed between them.

Suddenly, the gaping wounds where the tubing had been started to crackle. As if on cue, the wounds began to heal, sealing themselves up. She took several deep breaths and in time, her pulse steadied. The train continued to scream along.

You both did well, McBride said, sitting on a plush leather seat in front of Mattie. The train continued to scream down the tracks. The seats vibrated ever so slightly from the speed. Mattie held the girl in his arms. He held her tight, fearing she would die if he let her go.

I did what I could. She is a fighter, Mattie said, pointing his head down to the girl.

No, I don't mean her. I meant you and April. You saved your dad, for as long as you could, and you saved her. She was dying, Mattie. But April. Whoa. April's the one, though. She did exactly what she was supposed to do. She protected the Variant.

Her daughter, Mattie said.

That's what she couldn't get right, Mattie. She couldn't get her mind around the fact that you could both be her responsibility. You're both Variant. They may call you Variant X and her something else, but you're both special people. Unlike anything the Interzone or your world has ever seen. And she saved you both. You may never know what she sacrificed to get you both out of there.

Is she –

Your stop's coming up Mattie, McBride said. He stood and reached to pull Mattie up. Mattie fought against his pull. The next thing he knew, he was tossing in his sleep. Dreaming of the bullet train.

Variant

CHAPTER 41

Six months later, 2109.

Mattie pulled at the barb wire and felt it trying to dig into his skin but he forced the wire around the fence post. He wasn't really worried about anything penetrating his skin anymore. Nothing could. He surveyed the fields and wondered how anything would grow when the frigid temps came, but he trusted that the high tunnel he'd constructed would keep the crops warm to at least eighty degrees throughout the winter. Hopefully, some of what he planted would grow and the fence would keep out anything he didn't want in.

Two dogs, Hudson and Hoke, lay on their sides, soaking up the mid-day sun. He shook his head. He wished he could sleep like they did, but sleep was tough to come by these days.

He heard the footsteps approach before they got too close. He moved with the speed of a gazelle to the blaster leaning against the fence post. He pulled it to his shoulder and stood behind the largest tree he could find nearest the high tunnel. As he waited, he closed his eyes. He inhaled deeply and tried to locate the smell. It was something new he was trying. The footsteps grew closer and he silenced himself, then they passed. Mattie leveled the blaster at the creature as it made its way toward the high tunnel. He fired two shots and hit the flank of the animal, piercing its lung.

As he approached, he realized it was one of those bizarre creatures he'd seen in the woods not too long ago. The beast looked like a pig with the face of a rat. Nasty creature, but the meat was quality lean pork. He grabbed it by its hind legs and dragged it to his house.

Several Mechs stood guard and, as he approached, they lowered their weapons. Sir Matthew, they each said, in unison. He waved a hand at them.

Sir Matthew? C'mon. What did we talk about fellas?

Our apologies, Sir, they said together.

Gut this thing and quarter it for me. Let me know when you're done, he said. The Mechs moved together and had it drawn before he had his boots off.

He heard the chime going off faintly but he really wanted to put the creature on for a stew. A Tekkaman stood sentry in the kitchen and he touched its head, bringing it out of sleep. Four purple lights winked on.

The unit was the smallest Mech he had toyed with creating since coming back to Summer Cabin. Its head was the size of a lime with a smooth panel just above the eyes for touch controls. Two antennae sprouted out from the head at forty-five degree angles. If the Tekkaman was in sleep mode, it didn't mind having its panel touched. When it was awake though, it hated it. It would snap at Mattie and thrash his rather sharp arms toward him as well. It was a work in progress. The unit housed the smallest CPU Mattie had ever designed as well. The body unit was the size of both his palms placed next to each other. It had two offset visual panels on the front and rear of its head. Attached to the body were two legs that bent like in two like a biped but could also make wide turns left and right at the joint joining the two metallic pieces. At the bottom of the legs were V-shaped bases that kept the unit upright. This particular unit, TK-4, was a sleek, polished steel version of his new Tekkaman line. It could cook like a five-star chef, but it could also kill like a silent assassin.

Sir, it asked.

Stew. Potatoes. Onions. That meat in the hangar. I'd like to eat in a few hours. Maybe three hundred fifty degrees.

I would say four hundred and fifty sir, if you want to eat soon, the Tekkaman said.

You're the boss, Mattie said to him.

Sir, as you wish. It went outside and brought the meat in. Then, he heard the Tekkaman dicing vegetables as he opened the chiming message. It blinked orange on the tab list. He clicked on it and noticed it was a live feed, meaning someone was trying to contact him on the closed circuit. No one knew about the closed circuit, at least not anyone that he'd contacted recently. He thought about it for a moment, considering the pros and cons of accepting the message, and then he hit receive.

There was static and then a clean line. He heard nothing. But he dared not say anything. He didn't breathe even though they couldn't hear him until he hit the send button on the machine.

I don't know how this thing works. Is there someone there?

Mattie said nothing.

We were cut off. On the way to Rhys Creek – there was a pause and he could hear the female voice ask if Rhys was correct. She never stopped the feed and then she came back on and said, yes, on the way to Rhys Creek. Cut off.

He knew Rhys Creek. Knew it well. But whoever was contacting him on the closed circuit would also know the protocol and wouldn't just be sending messages out into the ether for all to hear.

Are you there, she asked again. Okay, she said, sorry. Um, this is THX-1138.

He sat in stunned silence. It was her code. April's.

THX-1138, she said again. Mattie sat quiet in the study. Goosebumps chased up and down his arms. The hair on his neck stood up at attention. He looked up at the galaxy print April had left and thought of her.

Best to be safe, he thought. Even though he hadn't heard from anyone in six months.

THX-1138, the voice called again. They'd talked about the codes. He grabbed the mic and thought about his response. If he responded, anyone on the channel would know he was out there. If he didn't, he could go on doing what he was doing. But it could be April.

The damn dream haunted him every night. Not just a few nights anymore. Now it was nightly. Save the dying. He couldn't get his mind to shut it off.

He hit the open comm button and said, THX-1138, this is KDK 12, over. He waited and he waited. But then the line went dead. He hit the open comm button several times, but nothing. He turned the dial on the radio but couldn't find the voice again.

Several nights later, as he was preparing for bed, he heard the trill of the alarm again and he walked downstairs to hear the same female voice, THX-1138. She repeated it twice. He replied, THX-1138, this is KDK 12, over.

Receiving you KDK 12, the voice said. Please identify the position of the Dippers.

He thought about it for a moment. The position of the Dippers was the Lighthouse SOS. Position of the dippers had originally been called out by NASA when the first terra-formers landed on Mars. If it was anyone associated with the Lighthouse, they'd understand what he was about to say. If it wasn't. Well, if it wasn't, he had problems.

He hit the open comm channel, that's not my sky, over. The same thing the first terra-formers said all those years ago when they'd been so confused about where they landed on that first mission.

There was a brief pause followed by a female voice, Matthew? Is that you?

His heart leaped in his chest. Someone knew he was out there.

He swallowed hard, trusting the dreams, yes, it's me, he said.

Another brief pause, my name is Elizabeth. Elizabeth Garza. I'm from Mount Enterprise, Texas. I know your April. She gave me this information to contact you.

What happened last time, Mattie asked, impatiently.

I had to terminate the connection. Things are a mess out here, Matthew.

What do you mean?

The Rising is failing. The Greys have painted us as terrorists, hell bent on destroying the country by destroying the Cluster drugs. It's been pretty effective. Without leadership, we've had mass defections. No one trusts anyone anymore. The Greys just keep taking, cutting us off. We don't have anywhere to turn really, so we retreated.

April? Is she with you?

Matthew, I don't know if any of this is going to make sense. She's in some place called Interzone.

How do you know about Interzone?

It's where she found me. It has to do, I think, with Mount Enterprise. But she's trapped there. She said I had to find you because the fate of the Children of the Infinite was at stake. I don't know what that even means, but she made me write it down.

He listened as she spoke but he didn't believe what she was saying. He cut the mic off and sat in silence.

She made me write it down too and bring it with me. In case you didn't listen to Eli.

Mattie turned and a striking figure stood in the doorway of the study. She had hair the color of fire whose tips were golden blonde. Her eyes were the color of the greenest freshest cut fields he could remember seeing. She carried a sword with her that glowed the cerulean color of a proton blade, sheathed in a scabbard that clung to her back. Her clothing was black and she wore black leather boots that rode up high on her legs. She looked as dangerous as she was beautiful. And she looked just like April, but she also looked like the beautiful girl he held in his arms that night on the bullet train.

I know you, he half asked, half said.

I'm Abigail. You rescued me. And then I don't know what happened. But my mother sent me to find you. She's in trouble. And she said you're the only one that can save her. She gave me this, she said, and approached Mattie. She held her hand out and placed the item in Mattie's hand.

He looked down and saw that it was a purple-bodied iguana with yellow streaks like lightning bolts coursing down its torso. Except this time, it was made from rubber.

He studied it in his hand. And then it moved slightly. His bulbous eyes scanned the terrain and then stopped on Mattie.

She needs you, he said. Mattie stood and locked eyes with Abby. He reached for her hand with his free hand. The rubber iguana climbed up his arm and came to rest on his shoulder.

When he touched her skin he experienced that familiar spinning feeling he had when he and April would enter Interzone. He saw them standing on a platform in a red-dirt desert. Her white dress was stained with the red from the sand and his fedora was pulled tightly down over his brow.

A sheriff approached and pulled a pocket watch from his vest. The three-ten is late. Again.

McBride, Mattie said and smiled as recognition spread across his face.

I'm glad you two have finally met officially.

My mom, Abby asked hopefully.

She's here too. She's just, he paused and glanced down at his time piece again, she's not well.

What's wrong with her? Father Gleason?

McBride shook his head and said, I wish it was as simple as Gleason. But this is so much more.

So much more what, she asked.

Complicated. When you two escaped the base explosion by getting on the train –

I didn't escape, McBride. I was taken. I would have stayed and –

Yes, Mattie, that's why you were taken. It's why you were protected. We knew you would stay. That was a poor choice of words but nonetheless, when you were taken, it inadvertently disrupted the lines between our worlds. There are holes everywhere now. Portals open to anyone. These disruptions have put us all at risk. Creatures from Interzone have entered your world Mattie, putting everyone there in jeopardy. And vice versa, people from your world have found themselves in Interzone and put us all in danger down here. Especially the Children of the Infinite. And the dying. Your work isn't done, Mattie. You must save the dying.

Then why am I standing here in Interzone talking to you?

Because Cleveland and Freemont have the dying collected in Peaksville.

Freemont? Peaksville?

Anthony Freemont. I suppose you could say he's Cleveland's right hand now. He is truly the face of evil. Peaksville is an Interzone territory. It's radioactive. Dangerous. And the problem for you will be staying in Interzone. It's not easy.

How do I do it?

Keep her with you, he said, pointing at Abby. She's the link between the two worlds.

She creased her brow and said, how am I the link?

Because you are the child of both worlds. Your father. Your mother has never mentioned him?

Never, she said flatly. I don't think she knows who he is.

Down here, we know. His name is Derek Gill. And he too is of both worlds, yours and Interzone.

.....Suddenly, Mattie sensed himself spinning with Abby still holding his hand. As the spinning stopped, they sat on a red beach with waves that crashed at their feet. Three young children, similar in every respect, frolicked in the foam. Abby cautioned them not to get too deep. They giggled and splashed the rose colored water at each other.

McBride, they both asked, looking for him in the spray of the waves crashing before them. The ruddy water lapped at their feet.....

.....Then they were back, standing on the train platform. They both stared at McBride.

Holes. I'm sorry. It's going to happen. Until the dying are saved. And Cleveland and his henchmen are destroyed. But beware the Distorters. They seek to claim their inheritance in your world, Mattie.

Their inheritance, Mattie asked.

Long ago they were promised things. But I cannot go into that now, McBride replied. They cannot be allowed to succeed under any circumstances though.

What was that back there, she asked. The beginning? The end?

Yes, it is both the beginning and the end.

Who were those children?

They are the Children of the Infinite. They await both of you, and so much more, McBride said.

They turned in unison as a shrieking train whistle blew in the distance. From the horizon, they could see a large moon rising, its colors morphed from red to purple to pink.

McBride looked down at his pocket watch. Nineteen minutes late. It's getting worse. When he looked up from the watch, Mattie and Abby were gone.

About the Author

Patrick Pearce spends most of his time traveling through Interzone, riding the rails. While many of his works are available there, including The One-Eyed King and the Locksmith, this is his first published work for our world. He lives, as many suspect, in an old trapper's cabin in the woods on a mountain-side somewhere between Alaska and Colorado. His wife, two kids and a dog named Sioux reside there too. They hope the snow never melts. He can be reached at patrickpearce.com and on Facebook.

Variant